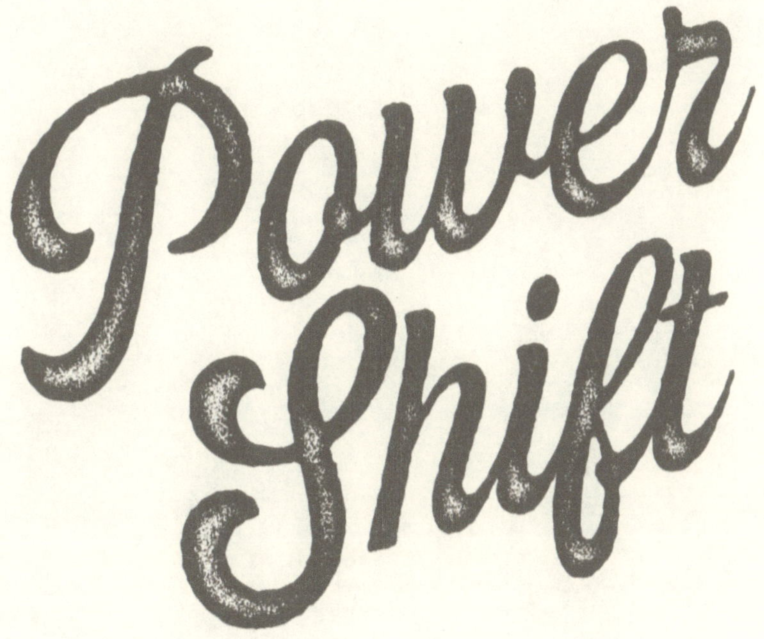

HARBOUR OF HOPE BOOK 1

HANNAH COWAN

Also By Hannah

Snowbell Ridge

Snow Harm, No Foul

Till Cupid Do Us part

What Is An Omegaverse?

If you're new to omegaverse, I have you covered! Omegaverse (also known as A/B/O) is an alternate reality where characters exist within a biological hierarchy. **Alphas, betas, and omegas** each have their own traits, instincts, and roles in society. Every person in an omegaverse falls into one of these three designations.

Alphas are physically bigger and stronger than every other designation. They're dominant, possessive, and territorial. Naturally born leaders, they are typically at the top of every pack totem pole. Every alpha gives off a unique pheromone or scent that is meant to attract omegas.

Alphas tend to form packs with other designations. Alphas are biologically compelled to find a partner based on scent. They **purr** to soothe omegas in distress, **growl** when threatened, and can use what's called a **bark** to deliver a command when angry. Sometimes, they can go into a **rut** when around an omega in heat, becoming frenzied and feral with the need to . . . well, fuck.

There is a thick bulge at the base of a male alphas penis known as a **knot** that expands when they're aroused, and grows to its full size during an orgasm. This is meant to lock an alpha in his partner and trap their cum to increase the chance of pregnancy. Female alphas have locks inside of their vaginas that perform a similar locking maneuver on their partners. An alphas cum can provide nourishment during an omegas heat when food is not consumed. It can also help soothe an omega during intense heat spikes.

Betas are the most like everyday humans. While they still have a draw to be part of a pack and carry their own scent, both are weaker than alphas and omegas. They are smaller in size, do not experience heats or ruts, and do not have knots.

Not every omegaverse includes betas with pheromones. In this one, they have them. Their scents are much more muted than an alpha or omega. They can not bond with another beta.

Omegas are much smaller and softer than both alphas and betas. They are naturally submissive and can be easily startled or overwhelmed. Omegas are built to handle the demands of an entire pack, and are always the centre of a pack bond. Without an omega, a pack can never experience a pack bond.

Their biology draws alphas in with their unique **pheromone** (scent). This scent is strongest for both alphas and omegas, and grows stronger at times of **arousal**, or **distress**. When an omega is aroused, they start to **perfume**. This is meant to signal their desire to nearby alphas. It's a straight shot of their specific scent.

Alphas and omegas can have intense physical and emotional responses to each other's scents. This is called scent-sensitivity. When alphas and omegas are referred to as scent-sensitive, it means that they're **scent matches**, or rather, **mates**. Yes, the fated kind. Once an omega or alpha meets their scent match, it's near impossible to be away from them. Prolonged separation can cause an omega extreme distress and pain and make an alpha a growly bastard.

If a scent-matched pair rejects one another, they could experience what's known in this omegaverse as **rejection sickness.**

Omegas experience **heat cycles**. While in heat, an omega becomes obsessed with finding a compatible alpha, or alphas, nesting, then breeding. Heats can be physically painful unless the Omega is knotted by their alpha(s). They enter a state of delirium and produce a substance called **slick**, a natural lubricant that eases the chafing that comes with getting railed for a week straight Before falling into a full heat, omegas can experience spikes (heat spikes). Over the course of said week, they grow very hot to the touch, and often will refuse to eat, AKA the reason behind the nutritious alpha cum.

During heat, this is also when a pack may choose to bond. Each alpha will **bite** their omega to create a mating mark.

Depending on the world, the omega may bite them back. In this omegaverse, the omega's bite isn't required to complete the bond. To alphas or omegas outside of a pack, a bite mark symbolizes that they are not on the market and to keep on moving. They are **claimed**.

Nesting is something omegas do to feel secure. This includes during heat and pregnancy. It involves creating a secure, safe space full of soft materials like blankets and pillows that smell like their packs' scents. The nest is where an omega will want to spend their heat.

Omegas can take **suppressants** to lower their hormone levels. This can make their heats more tolerable for those who do not have an alpha to help ease their pain. Over time, suppressants can become less effective, and even dangerous.

When an alpha finds an omega they want for their pack, they can **court** them. This is when they pull out all the stops to convince her/him to join their pack. This usually involves the entire pack.

RAYTON RIPTIDE
Important Names

LANDON MONTGOMERY	CENTRE #29
RONAN MONTGOMERY	DEFENSEMAN #5
JASPER MONTGOMERY	RIGHT WING #17
DASH MONTGOMERY	GOALIE #99
RASMUS EKLUND	DEFENSEMAN #7

Playlist

The Summoning — Sleep Token	6:36
Monster — Imagine Dragons	4:09
Long As You Let Me — Mitchell Tenpenny	3:44
Heart With Your Name On It — New Medicine	2:53
Blood Sport — Sleep Token ★	4:07
Kiss Me — Ed Sheeran	4:41
Stuck In My Head — Sleep Theory ★	3:17
Without Me — Dayseeker	3:44
Turning Page — Sleeping At Last	4:16
Everything in My Mind — Nevertel ★	3:43
Roses — Awaken I Am	3:13

# Briar

"Push it, omegas! Asses up and loose. Let me see those hips sway!"

I grunt and push back, struggling with my slick palms to keep a good hold on the stationary bike handles. Salty liquid drips down my forehead and into my eyes and mouth as I gasp in the hot air around me. It's like I'm drowning on my own sweat. It's only a matter of time before I start gargling.

My ears ring from the volume of the music blasting in the airless room, and I'm pretty positive that I could collapse at any given moment. Continuing to pump my legs isn't really a reality at this point. They might very well just fall off.

"That's it! Only thirty seconds longer. Keep your backs straight and pump!"

Thirty. Seconds.

Will I even make it ten? This class was a giant, massive mistake. I'll be stuck at home for the next three weeks recovering now.

"Twenty seconds!

My lips are crusty, and the taste in my mouth is repulsive. There's iron coating my throat regardless of how often I swallow.

The constant sawing of air into my lungs has most likely stripped layers of flesh off, resulting in said iron.

"Ten seconds!"

Oh, fuck. I'm soaked. I've never been wetter in my entire life, and that's saying something. Is there a puddle beneath me?

My left hand slips from its handle, and my right arm wobbles as I tilt slightly, off balance. The world darkens as I try to regain my hold and stabilize myself before I fall onto the wet floor.

"And time! You can slow to a cooldown."

I don't just slow to a cooldown. My legs stop pushing entirely as I collapse against the front of the bike. Any minute now, I'm sure I'll pass out. At the rate my heart is pounding and my lungs are screaming for a break, I'm absolutely destroyed.

"They should call an ambulance for me. I've got mere seconds left," I wheeze.

"It's . . . not . . . *that* bad."

I don't have the strength to turn to give my best friend the look I want to be giving, so I don't bother. Instead, I keep my arms slung over the front of the bike and continue to gasp for breath like a fish tossed out of a fishbowl.

"You're . . . dead to me," I dig.

"You'll feel good . . . tomorrow."

I doubt that.

I've successfully been turning down the offers to join her at her spin class for months. If it weren't for her nasty breakup last week, I'd have done it again. I couldn't leave her on her own tonight, with how devastated she's been. If I did, she probably would have spent another night at a club being reckless in an attempt to mask her hurt with a different alpha's scent than the ones belonging to her dickwad ex and his pack of discount losers.

Clover has never been one to like using her scent-blocking perfume—claiming she hates the way it sticks to her skin—and while I agree with her, it's just not safe to go completely without it. Ever since I found her doing exactly what I worried she would last weekend, I don't trust that she won't try it again, this time opting out of calling me midway through the night.

Not using scent blockers or at least a dampener in a situation like that isn't something an omega should be doing often, especially when we're out somewhere like a club and loose with alcohol. One second of wavering control is all it would take to risk turning a crowd of drunken alphas into beasts with one thing on their brain—finding whichever omega it is that's spraying out their scent and rutting them into tomorrow.

It's certainly not fair, but it's the reality of living as an omega. The odds of anything happening like that are low but not impossible. To most people, it wouldn't be a concern. But to someone like me, the type of woman who has a habit of thinking too much and worrying even more, anything is a possibility.

I prefer doing things that I already know how to and going places I know well. It makes everything simpler.

Clover and I both have strong scents. We have since we were teenagers. While hers is more of a decadent variation than my overall sweet one, we've both been drawing far too much attention to ourselves since we realized how easy it was to make a hormonal alpha growl at a simple walk-by. I never forget to wash my body with a scent-blocking wash or spritz myself before leaving my place.

"Hello? Earth to Briar," she says, pushing my head up with a palm to my forehead. Her microbladed eyebrow is lifted as I peel open my eyes and meet her gaze. "You're not actually supposed to die from a spin class."

"Not dead. Just . . . dead."

"Did you do the cooldown?"

"No."

"You'll feel even worse tomorrow, then," she says, helping me into a proper sitting position.

"I'm already going to feel like death. What's a little more pain?"

"How are you going to explain your limping to Greg?"

"I'll say that I was helping a friend in need and got a little carried away."

She twists her mouth. "I'm not in need."

"Don't even try it, Clove. You're one bad decision away from me locking you up in my closet for the foreseeable future."

Her puffed exhale fans my face. "You only say that because you've gone too long without dick, Briar. And your closet is so small I'd have to become a contortionist to fit inside of it."

"What does dick have to do with you losing your mind?"

"Everything. It has *everything* to do with it."

Yeah, I should have thought that question through.

I've never been with a pack before. Not the way Clover has. Every alpha I've dated in the past shared my dream of finding one, but we just . . . never could. They were either too busy to make it —and me—a priority, or there just wasn't anyone around who fit what we wanted whenever we got the nerve to start the search.

My heart has always ached for my scent-matched pack. My mates. With every failed attempt to find them, my hope has dwindled.

With Greg, I've come as close as I ever have before. If dinner goes well Friday night, I might actually have a chance of meeting his packmates and finding the closest to a scent-matched pack as I fear I'll ever have.

"I've been doing pretty alright on my own, haven't I?" I ask a bit too self-consciously.

The other omegas in the class have already started filtering out of the room, leaving scuffing sneakers and light chatting in their wake. I'm in desperate need of a shower, but I would prefer to go once the locker room isn't so busy. The less judgmental omegas in one place, the better.

Clover leans against the handle of my bike, her perfectly smooth, pale skin glistening with sweat in an almost pretty way. Like instead of sweat, she's dripping liquid diamonds.

"You've never done a bad job of taking care of yourself, Bee. Alphas are more work than they're worth sometimes. Betas are where it's at, I'm pretty sure. Do you have their box checked on those fancy apps of yours?"

"You're pretty sure? That's not a real boost of confidence."

"They can't be worse than knotting, growling alphas who pitch fits every time you don't let them gnaw on your neck like a bone."

I choke on a laugh, carefully swinging my leg off the bike. When I wobble, I lean against Clover and wince at the burn already growing in my hamstrings.

"You should put that on a T-shirt."

"You know what? I just might."

With Clover supporting nearly all my weight, we finally head for the door. We're the last ones out, and I release a sigh of relief.

"So, tell me about Greg's pack. You've kept all the juicy details close to your chest, haven't you? I feel like I know nothing," she says when I flop down on the bench in the empty locker room and stretch my leg with a groan.

The pain has travelled from my hips all the way down to the tips of my toes, and as I stretch, it only gets worse. In a really twisted way, it almost feels good. *Almost.*

"Well, there isn't really anything to share yet. There's only three of them, including Greg, and they work for the same bank he does. He speaks really highly of them."

"Well, obviously. They're his packmates. He isn't going to shit-talk them right before you meet them. Pack loyalty is insane. They choose each other first every single time."

Clover tosses me the gym bag I brought with me and then strips out of her sweaty shirt, exchanging it for a tight tank top. Her bitterness is understandable after her experience with her last pack.

I force myself to walk to the mirrors above the long marble countertop and use half a tube of deodorant beneath my arms. She's already watching me in the mirror when I look at her.

"They're thirty-six, like him, and have known each other for the past five years," I add.

Her nose scrunches. "Thirty-six? Have they ever had an omega before? Five years isn't that long."

"Don't say thirty-six like that. They're still pretty young. We'll be there before we know it."

"Twenty-five, Briar. You're twenty-five. They're over ten years older. And you didn't answer me. Have they ever had an omega before?"

I set my deodorant down and brace my hands on the countertop, leaning closer to the mirror. My pale blue eyes are dull today. I'd love to say that it's more noticeable due to the pink in my cheeks, but it would be a lie.

Truth is, I'm still tired from my last heat. Not just the lack of sleep but the lack of intimacy. I'm tired of being alone and having to spend a week locked up in a room with an alpha who's paid to please me or, like my most recent heat, alone with a thrusting dildo. I want something real.

My heat only made that yearning inside of me worse. I've never been so bone tired after one before. It was like I gave more than I had in me and got nothing in return for the last time.

"No, they haven't had an omega. Greg is nice, Clove," I mutter.

"Yeah, I'm sure he is." She finishes getting changed. "Get dressed, Bee. We're going to get some ice cream. No more alpha talk."

I blink away from my reflection and at hers instead. "Isn't that the worst thing to do after a workout?"

"Why else did you think we worked out if not so we had room to scarf down bad food?"

Ice cream sounds really good right now. Anything frozen does.

"Alright. Give me five minutes."

"You have three," she barters, kissing the top of my head and wrapping an arm around me in a quick hug.

I sigh, fighting my first instinct to nuzzle into her. I'm too close to reaching touch starvation status, which is only yet another reason why I need Friday night to go well with Greg. In a perfect world, he'd bring me home to meet his pack, and I'd get to spend the night snuggled up in bed with all of them.

That could be moving too fast, but in my mind, it's the perfect pace. I've known Greg for a few weeks now, and if his pack is as great as I'm hoping they are, there won't be any need to go slow. I'm ready for this. Ready to be a pack omega.

With a new pep in my step, I change out of my damp clothes and follow Clover out of the studio, more excited than ever for Friday night.

2

Jasper

I'VE ALWAYS LOVED HOCKEY.

I don't love the violence the way Ronan does or constantly strive to prove I'm better than my father was like Landon. Unlike my pack brothers, I enjoy the way hockey makes me feel free.

With every push of my feet, I feel like if I could just go a *bit* faster, I'd be able to fly. The stick in my hands feels weightless, and the fans chanting our team's name in the stands disappear completely.

I'm not the fastest player in the NHL because I just really love the burn in my lungs or the constant risk of injuring myself. I'm the fastest player because I want to do something incredible.

That's who I am. The guy who doesn't settle for anything less than the best. There isn't one person out there who knows me who isn't familiar with that quirk.

The boards get closer and closer as I hesitate to slow my speed. I'm heading for them too quickly, but the uneasiness brewing beneath my skin is distracting. I was hoping practice would have helped dissolve it, but it's almost worse now than the last couple of days.

The sweat dripping down my neck and beneath my jersey is like liquid fire. My lungs constrict, trapping my breath inside as I turn my feet and force myself to stop with only an inch between my body and the boards, snow flying.

"You're going to break your ankles stopping like that," Landon bites out, mouthguard hanging out of his mouth. He narrowly avoids plowing into me, a slight tick in his jaw the only sign of his frustration.

"And you'll break a tooth biting on that thing like a chew toy," I return with a shove against his shoulder.

"Is this the part where I lick your face?"

"I'd prefer if you didn't."

"If you break your body against the boards, you're going to be out for a long while."

"I knew what I was doing," I say with a half-smile.

"If you say so."

Landon might be my pack leader, but that doesn't mean he needs to be right about absolutely everything. And even if he tried, we wouldn't let it slide for long. Naming any one of us as leader wasn't a choice we made easily or even wanted to do in the first place.

Society requires things to be a certain way, though. And honestly, without some sort of leader, we probably would have collapsed already. Landon as pack leader was an easy choice for us to make when it came to choosing someone years ago.

Not only is he the biggest in size of all of us, but his alpha pheromones can be so intense that they're borderline nauseating. I've only heard his bark once in my entire life, and it was years ago when we were only teenagers.

Standing about three inches taller than me with his skates on, Landon frowns around his mouthguard and wiggles it around. The cleanly shaven expanse of his jaw strains as he gnaws down on the guard and pops it back into his mouth. Without another word, he knocks the blade of his stick to the backs of my thighs and takes off.

Ronan eyes us curiously, his hulking shoulders snapping

straight as he lingers by the other defenseman. His dark, piercing brown eyes ask the question he's too far away to speak.

Are you all good?

I give him a gloved thumbs-up and skate around the net, avoiding looking at Dash where he lingers, pretending to wait for the next puck to block. The final member of our pack and the team's goalie is always a bit too eagle-eyed. Maybe that has to do with his gentler beta nature. Being surrounded by three alphas every single day does that to a person. He's been the one holding us together for years, but surely, I can't be the only one feeling the cracks starting to grow.

I feel more on edge today than I have in a long time. My quick pace on the ice isn't exactly the safest, so I can't blame them for the lectures I'm about to hear at home.

It's like I can feel something brewing in the air. A glinting tip of a freshly sharpened knife poised above us. Every day, it drops another inch, contact inevitable.

Our coach blows his whistle, and I sweep up a puck from along the boards, toying with it as I skate toward him and the other players who've beaten me back. Ronan keeps his distance from the rest of the team, hovering a few feet away. I settle at his side and tuck the puck between my skates.

The speech Coach gives us is the same as always. We've got a pregame skate tomorrow morning before we play at home in the evening. Don't stay out late and show up hungover. Don't be giant knotheads, honestly.

It's easy enough for most of us—the majority who take the sport seriously.

"You nearly smashed into the boards," Ronan grunts quietly enough for just me to hear.

"But I didn't."

"You're not a risk taker."

"Maybe I'm changing."

He flexes his hold on his giant stick and tugs off his helmet before shaking his head and stretching his neck. Without his helmet on, the onyx-black hair he keeps neatly buzzed is exposed alongside the diamond stud in his ear that he refuses to take out. With how often he's begun fighting during games, I have very visceral nightmares of him having it torn out.

My packmate is as stubborn as he is broody. There's no way to convince him to do anything he doesn't want to. Not even Landon can command him to do much unless he wanted to piss us all off with his bark.

"Something's up with you," he says.

"Dash swapped my decaf out with his espresso this morning."

He stares at me for a beat longer, not giving away a single thought before turning to Coach. It's the Ronan special.

"Right."

"I didn't swap anything," Dash puts in, heaving a breath beside us.

The only beta in our group narrows his eyes as he inspects me, seeing everything. I huff a sigh and focus on the only member of our pack who hasn't joined our little huddle.

Landon stands by Coach, absorbing every word he's saying. Many people assume his concentration is coldness, but I know better. All three of us do.

Minutes later, we're dismissed and stepping into the locker room. I crinkle my nose at all the different pheromones brewing in the hot, sweaty room. The scent blockers blowing through the air ducts are pretty useless in situations like this. We're too sweaty for anything to be masked well.

"Reeks in here," Ronan mutters, shucking his clothes off at lightning speed.

I laugh. "You say that every time we're in the locker room."

Dash grins. "It's not too bad. I'm just fine."

"Lucky you." Ronan's glare is sharp as he pulls on his sweatpants and zips his bag.

With a glance around the room, the only member of my family I don't see is Landon. It's not surprising. He's the most scent sensitive of any alpha I've ever met.

"What are we having for dinner tonight?" Dash asks, rubbing at his stomach.

Ronan shrugs a loose shirt on and stares blankly at him. "It's only two."

"And? I'm still hungry."

"You're always hungry."

"I'll make something," I volunteer.

Dash shoves his gear into his cubby. "Nuh-uh. It's Landon's turn to cook."

"You're not that hungry, then," Ronan says.

I chuckle and change into my clean clothes before zipping my bag and tossing it over my shoulder. The other three do the same thing, and I say goodbye to a few of the other players on my way out.

Landon is waiting for us in the hallway, his phone in one hand and bag in the other. When he notices he's not alone anymore, he looks over, exhaustion dulling his eyes, turning the blue a shade darker. His hair is shoved back and out of his face the usual way, but it's longer than ever, curling at the middle of his neck.

"Ready to go?"

"Yep. And Dash says it's your turn to cook tonight," I say.

We fall into a line, blocking the hallway as we make our way to the players-only parking garage.

"Why me?" Landon asks.

"The dinner chart," Dash sings.

Landon huffs. "Whose idea was that?"

We're all terrible cooks. Cooking classes haven't helped, either. It's quite pathetic.

"Mine. If we're ever going to convince an omega to join our pack—" I start before Landon cuts me off with a low, warning growl.

"We're not taking an omega."

I stiffen, straining with the effort it takes to check my words before I say them. Ronan shifts subtly toward me, feeling the shift in my energy.

Landon rolls his neck, adding, "We're not having that conversation now."

"Now or ever?" I snap.

His silence is answer enough. He knows better than anyone else how desperately I crave an omega. I'm off balance, and that feeling grows worse every day that I go without one. What happened today on the ice is a result of how odd I feel. Like I'm not right.

There's a piece of me missing, and the hole in its place is doubling in size at a rate that worries me. What happens if when I do find our omega, the hole is too big for her to fit? I'll be incomplete forever. Our pack won't be able to endure that.

"Not never, Jasper. Just not here," Dash says, covering for Landon.

Ronan's words are gruff, tense. "We can't keep pushing it off."

We all know that, including Landon. Ronan has never said he wants to find an omega, but even he isn't as against it as Landon is. And our beta is more excited than our pack alpha is. That's just . . . wrong.

Too frustrated, I don't say another word about it. Not in the garage or the SUV or on the drive home. And once we step inside the pack house, I'm beelining it into the gym, claiming the treadmill for the fifth night in a row.

The yearning in my chest is impossible to stifle, but at least when my lungs are on fire, I don't feel it as badly. For now . . . that will have to be enough.

3

Dash

ANOTHER PUCK SAILS INTO MY PADS BEFORE I SHAKE myself out of the net and pass it off to the ref. My pixelated team celebrates on the flat screen in front of me with slaps to the back of my player's helmet as the commentators praise the easy save.

My palms sweat around the controller. I grip it tighter, leaning forward on the couch. I've been playing this game for hours while the rest of the pack does their own thing. It's the norm for us as of late.

I pass my thumbs over the controller and signal to the refs that I'm ready to continue. The other players on my team are made up of random online users like me. Some are good, but the majority of them aren't ready for the level I like to play on. I'm not sure if that's more embarrassing for them for still trying or for me because I've spent so much time getting this good.

My mom loves to say that I play video games so often she's shocked my brain hasn't leaked out of my ears. Somehow, she's still the most loving beta out there. Her sass is a love language that I've become a pro at distinguishing from real annoyance.

"I could have called for a review on that save," one of the opposing members says, his voice a nasally drawl in my ears leaking from my headset.

I have no idea who he is behind the username he chose, but he sounds like a sore loser.

"Why didn't you, then?" I ask, tracking the tiny puck on the screen as it moves between players.

"Not worth it."

I huff a laugh. "Yeah, okay."

"You got something to say?" he snips, sending his player plowing in my direction.

He can't see my smirk, but I make sure he can hear it in my voice. "Nah. Not worth it."

In the span of half a second, he's got his player winding back for a slap shot in front of my net. His breathing grows in volume, so loud I can hear it clearly through my clunky over-ears as I track the movements of his player.

I'm ready when he lets the puck fly. One jab of my finger on the controller has it in my goalie's glove.

"Fuck off, man!"

"There's no shame in turning on aim assist," I coo, stretching my legs out in front of me.

The couch in my bedroom is extreme and big enough for the entire pack to sit on, which they never do. I'd hoped that by having the space, I'd be able to convince them all to take a night off and hang out, but nights like that have been far and few between, especially recently.

If we're not all at practice, Landon is at the rink putting in extra time, and Ronan's in the gym working himself to death. Jasper likes to pretend he's not as affected by our withering pack relationship by spending his spare time pruning the massive green bush he keeps in his room. I'm pretty sure it's not supposed to be an inside plant, but I'm not going to be the one who tells him that.

"Aim assist is for pussies!" the guy hisses.

"Has anyone ever told you that using pussy in a derogatory way is incredibly sexist?"

"Oh, fuck all the way off."

"Therapy is always an option, sweetie. Losing in a video game shouldn't affect you so deeply."

"Coming from the guy that probably lives in his mom's basement."

"Not even close."

"Whatever! I'm blocking you. You're not good enough to play with me."

"See ya, Breadlover69," I sing.

With a roll of my eyes, I cross my ankles before exiting out of the game and pulling my headphones to drape around my neck. It's too easy to get a rise out of some people, especially guys like that.

The bright light from the flat screen burns into my retinas, drawing a sigh from deep in my chest. I set the controller on my stomach and rest my head back against the couch.

The hard pulse of music coming from the room beneath mine grows in volume, the lyrics becoming clearer and clearer. It's impossible not to smile when you know that the hard-as-granite Ronan has an unhealthy obsession with New Medicine and Sleep Token. The song he chose to start his workout with is one of the harder songs in his playlist, but it isn't anything close to what Landon forces us to listen to when he joins us in the gym.

I've already worked out today, but hey, I'm bored. After getting changed into some loose shorts and a tee, I head to the basement and join the big bad alpha in the gym.

His grunts are audible over the music as I stroll to where his phone lies on the bench press and turn the wireless speakers down a bit.

"You're going to blow your eardrums one of these days," I tell him.

Dark eyes pierce into my light blue ones from across the gym. Ronan keeps his expression blank, emotions completely at his control. The sweat already beading on his forehead and across the wide, muscled expanse of his chest is a sign of just how hard he's pushing himself.

Both of his hands are wrapped around the bar above him. He doesn't let my presence take away from his concentration. Calm and steady, he pulls himself up until his bent knees hover above the black mats and his chin touches the bar.

I step up onto the treadmill and watch him while choosing the options I want for tonight. I'll be dead for practice tomorrow if I do too much. The only reason Ronan and Landon can push themselves as hard as they do and not face repercussions is because they're alphas. They wouldn't have such luck if they were betas like me.

"Is there a reason why you're spending another night in the gym?" I ask.

The treadmill kicks into gear beneath my feet, and I start walking. Without spending any time stretching, a fast walk is all I'm planning on doing.

Ronan grunts low and continues his pull-ups. The pace he's keeping is a bit concerning. Every confident rise of his body has his biceps bulging so fiercely the veins threaten to pop right out of his skin.

His jaw is tight enough to crack in two. "Can't sleep."

"What's keeping you up?"

Instead of answering, he drops to his feet and abandons the bar, thumping his way over to the weight bench. His silence isn't surprising in the slightest, but it is a bit frustrating. Especially when all I want is to help.

"I can't help if I don't know what's wrong," I add.

He busies himself with overloading the weight bar, giving me his back. The black ink on his shoulder matches the ink on mine. It's a reassuring sight with how tense we've all been recently.

"I never asked for your help, Dash," he bites out.

Now lying on the bench, he spreads his legs and presses his heels firmly to the mats. There's at least two hundred and fifty pounds on that bar already, and without a spotter, he's risking crushing his entire upper half.

"Christ, Ro. We're pack, in case you forgot. Ask me to spot

you next time," I scold before turning off the treadmill and jogging toward him. "You're no good to anyone, including the team, if you've got a shattered trachea."

Stepping up behind him, I hover my hands beneath the bar with every rise and fall, tracking the movements. Fifteen reps later and he doesn't show any sign of stopping.

"Talk to me, Ronan."

"It's too quiet," he forces out.

"Too quiet in what way?"

His eyes glue themselves to the ceiling. "Nobody talks."

"You've never talked much."

"There are four of us."

I tap the bar when he lowers it again, this time watching as his arms shake on the push up. "I know. When was the last time everyone was home all at once?"

"Landon prefers to be anywhere but here."

"He's under a lot of pressure."

His scoff is deep and full of resentment that I've known has been inside of him, growing and growing with every passing day.

"We all are. But you and me? We're here."

I nod, understanding where he's coming from. "Do you think calling a pack meeting would help? Maybe we could bring it up—"

"No. I'm not planning any fucking meeting. If Landon and Jasper don't want to be here, then they can keep pissing off," he snaps, slamming the bar into its holder.

When he shoves into a sitting position, I round the bench, standing in front of him. My chest caves in at the frustration burning in his eyes.

"We both know why Jasper's been avoiding us. He's started locking his bedroom door," I murmur.

"If he's wanting to avoid Landon, he doesn't need to bother locking himself away."

"I think it's easier for him to just . . . be where we're not. If you're feeling the emptiness this badly, I don't want to imagine how fiercely he's feeling it. You know how he is, Ro."

"Landon doesn't get to make a decision that important on his own," he grunts, swiping a hand over his sweaty forehead.

Turning, he sits on the edge of the bench and slouches over his knees. I take a seat beside him and kick off my sneakers, hating how restricting they are.

"He's the pack leader. You know how it works. We might not have to let him make all the decisions, but if he doesn't want an omega, bringing one into the fold will only make things worse between us."

"We don't know that."

"Don't we? Do you think forcing his hand will do us any good? Yeah, Jasper might be happy. So will you and me. But that fracture you're feeling is only going to grow deeper if we push Landon too far," I explain.

We might not share a pack bond yet, but that doesn't mean we haven't unofficially bonded in every other possible way. The only thing we're missing is an omega and the mental bond we'd be able to share if we were to mark her as ours.

Pack bonds don't work alpha to alpha. They're created the moment a pack alpha marks an omega, and then with every bite that follows, the bond spreads between each member. If you never find an omega, you never have a pack bond. Simple as that.

Jasper believes all our problems will cease to exist the moment we awaken that bond, and while I do believe it would be life-changing, I also worry that at the rate we're going, the gap will be too wide to close with anything. Even an omega of our own.

Ronan abruptly stands and stares down at me, blank-faced but not closed off. Not completely. The pain in his eyes has me pushing off the bench and crowding him, rubbing my arm against his.

His deep coffee scent overshadows the sweet notes of caramel that sometimes appear when he's happy. Tonight, he's all broody alpha, and it has me wanting to offer as much comfort as I can.

It's not me he needs, though. Somewhere out there is a soft-as-cotton omega wanting everything that we have to offer.

I can only hope that we find her sooner than later.

"We'll figure it all out, Ro," I swear.

His silence is answer enough.

Don't make promises you can't keep.

4

Briar

WHOSE IDEA WAS IT FOR ME TO WEAR THIS DRESS? OR these shoes? I'm one wrong move away from tripping over myself and breaking my neck. That, or I'll rip my dress right in half after one too many breadsticks.

Seeing Greg's expression when he picked me up made it the tiniest bit worth the risks, though. The subtle spicy shift in his warm citrus scent was a confidence booster for sure. Even if he refused to keep it in the air for long.

Ever the gentleman, he was quick to usher me into his sleek sports car and drive us to the high-class restaurant without so much as a hand on my leg.

"How was work this week?" he asks, swirling the expensive red wine he's chosen for tonight around in his glass.

I cross my ankles beneath the table and smile. "It was busy. I was there for the delivery of the sweetest little girl last night. She had bright green eyes, and I don't think they'll change throughout the next few months like most do. They were just *so* vibrant. And her mom was a superhero. She squeezed my hand so hard that I thought she was going to snap it in half. There's something incredible about a woman's body, Greg. To be able to create life the way we can is out of this world," I ramble, my passion for what I do throbbing with its own heartbeat inside of me.

Greg's mouth lifts in a slight smile, but it feels placating, forced. It has me slowly crawling back into myself before I freak him out, even as my stomach pangs. I've come too close to risk losing my future pack now, even I have to trap a whine from escaping at his dismissal.

"That's nice, Briar. Have you ever considered going to medical school? So you can deliver children for real?"

"No, I don't want to be a doctor. Providing support and encouragement for women during childbirth is what I truly want to do."

He takes a long sip of his wine as I reach for my once abandoned water, suddenly parched.

Setting his glass down after a moment, Greg leans his forearms on the edge of the table and gives me that pitiful smile again. I hide my hurt with a swallow.

Sure, this alpha isn't exactly the type of guy I gravitate toward, and he certainly isn't my scent match, but he's willing to give me what I want more than all else. I only have to make it through tonight, and then I'll get to meet his pack. Maybe one of them will see my passions and be proud of them. Or if I'm lucky, all of them will. Greg can always learn to appreciate what I do. We'll have the time for that.

It helps that he's handsome. A bit too clean-cut with his perfectly swooped hair and expensive watches, but his eyes are a nice shade of brown that glows with knowledge and experience. There are many things he can teach me, and I could be up for the challenge.

Right?

I give my head a subtle shake to clear that question and set my water down. He clears his throat and folds his hands on the table.

"Well, if you're not planning on going to school, maybe you would consider quitting."

I pause, blinking twice. "Quitting?"

"Your job. It's nothing serious, which means you wouldn't have anything to lose if we asked you to quit and stay home," he explains.

"You want me to quit my job?"

His frustration leaks from him in the form of a huff. "Yes, Briar. If we were to take you as our pack omega, there would be no need for you to work. Especially if your job was simply a hobby."

"My career isn't a hobby, Greg. I like what I do. It's important. A good chunk of my clients don't have support systems in place that could be there with them during childbirth. That's what I am to them. I stand at their side and help them through the gruelling hours they spend in endless pain."

"But you're not a doctor. They could find someone else quickly. If you were our omega, you could be your own doula."

Shock zaps through me. I grip my knee beneath the table.

There are so many ifs in these statements, and each one sounds more and more like a threat. *Agree, or I'll leave right now, taking your chance at having what you want with me.*

"I thought these types of conversations would happen once I've met your packmates. You know, after we've all gotten to know each other a bit," I ramble, fear burning the edges of my scent despite the de-scenting perfume I doused myself in before Greg picked me up.

He takes a sniff of it and twists his features in subtle disgust. I gulp, but my throat is so dry there's nothing to swallow. There's a restlessness in my bones, a sign that something's not right.

"I need to use the washroom," I whisper, jerking to my feet.

My hands are ice-cold as I push away from the table and search for the washroom sign. It's too far away. For an outrageously expensive restaurant, it's busy enough that with every step I take, I hear the sharp intakes of breath from those at the tables I pass.

Instead of a warm lemon shortbread, I'm spraying charred

cookies everywhere. With every gasp or judging guffaw, it grows in intensity.

The bathroom is so close. If I just keep my eyes up, I can't see anyone—

There's another burning smell over here. It's not anything like mine, though. This scent is supposed to be this way. There's an intense cinnamon addition to it, and . . . is that vanilla? The combination is unique, and I breathe it in, something about it settling me.

I press a palm to my throat and sway, a low whine escaping me before I have a chance to shove it back down. There's an overwhelming longing sensation causing my chest to quake as if it's about to cave in. My feet move on their own, forcing me to chase the origin of my new favourite scent.

It's second nature to ignore everyone now. Without the putrid burning of my fear cutting through my blockers, I blend in, becoming invisible.

Turning past the last of the booth-style tables, I recognize this area as the same one we passed on our way to our more secluded section. The windows out here make it brighter, illuminating my path.

The vanilla in the scent becomes more prominent, overtaking the burn of the cinnamon the further I walk in this direction, confirming that I've gone the right way.

I can't be that far now—

My heel catches on the carpet.

I don't have time to gasp before I'm tumbling forward, my arms flailing helplessly. There's no chance for me to catch myself. Preparing to smash my face on the floor, I cover it with my arms and hold my breath.

It's not the floor I make contact with, though. It's a person.

The nauseating scent of tomato sauce and parmesan cheese slips up my nose, stealing my focus from the smell I was chasing as I grunt at the impact, my elbows jabbing against something hard and sharp. Several things fall to the floor before I notice the sliminess on my skin. I wince at the burn in my forearms and slowly lower my hands, exposing the sight in front of me.

I didn't think it could get any worse than tripping over nothing in the middle of a high-class, busy restaurant. That should have been the most mortifying thing to ever happen to me. Surely, only someone with a lifetime's worth of terrible karma would not just trip but also face-plant into the most beautiful man they've ever seen and spill his food all over them both.

From the pasta crawling down the front of the gorgeous stranger's button-up and smears of red sauce that have been sprayed up his throat, beneath the collar of his shirt, and down his sleeves . . . I'm very wrong.

Splatters of meaty sauce have flung onto his flexing jaw and down the strong, aristocratic swoop of his nose as the nostrils flare. My heart tumbles behind my rib cage when I notice it clumping in his black hair. The shiny curls at the back of his neck are accented with specks of cheese and whatever meat was in the sauce.

Mortified, I sprint into motion. With shaking hands, I start sweeping the pasta from his shirt.

"I'm so—I'm so sorry. I don't know what happened. It's . . . not as bad as it looks. I'll clean you—clean your clothes. Just give me a second," I ramble, only half aware of the words escaping my mouth.

Oh, I'm panicking now. With every passing second, I grow more aware of the people staring at me. Their eyes have nothing on the flames burning through the skin of my face from the glare coming from the man I'm pawing at.

With every swipe of my hand across his chest, he grows stiffer, and I think he's holding his breath. I jerk back, my scent scorched. Too many things hit me at once.

He's an alpha, and I stink.

He's an alpha, and I've just spilled his dinner all over him and the entrance of the restaurant. The fact I haven't been tossed across the place by a protective, angry omega or his packmates is a miracle.

My throat is constricted so tight I can hardly get a breath in as I search for something to use to clean him that's better than my red hands. I'm filthy, and with noodles hanging between my fingers and wrapped around my elbows, I'm doing more harm than good.

The first thing I see is a white tablecloth. I reach for it, yanking hard. The clatter of glass dishware hitting the ground and shattering only makes everything worse. Tears prickle my eyes, but I keep moving, bringing the fabric to the skin of his neck and swiping away the sauce. My stomach falls between my legs when a firm grip circles my wrist, stilling me.

The alpha's touch sears me. I crane my head back and lift my eyes, two crystal blue ones waiting. One second ticks by, then another and another. The air thins, my throat relaxing enough for it to slip through. I inhale greedily, filling my lungs with vanilla and cinnamon.

Vanilla and cinnamon . . .

A whimper escapes as I wobble, finding myself leaning against the strong body of the delicious-smelling alpha with my chin to his chest. The one I was searching the place for, just needing another whiff. Needing to know who smelled so *freaking* amazing.

My scent spikes, an ache spearing between my legs. The large, strong fingers still clutching my wrist somehow intensify the pulse of arousal between my legs.

I'm wearing two pairs of panties today, but not because I was expecting this. I thought . . . I thought just in case I had this reaction to Greg's pack, I'd be better safe than sorry.

This is not Greg's pack. This is a stranger. His scent isn't like any of the ones I've smelled on him before.

To make matters worse, this male isn't showing any sign of liking the way I smell. For some reason, that makes the burn in my eyes intensify. A tear clings to my lashes as I squeeze them shut, wanting to let my emotions out but refusing.

Scent blocker or not, if I'm having this type of reaction to him, shouldn't he be able to smell me even a little? Is that what this is, or is my scent just *that* charred? The dominance he's projecting is almost smothering. It's stronger than I've ever felt around another alpha before. There's no reason an alpha that strong can't smell a regular omega.

That both intensifies my interest and worries me.

"Back off." The deep rasp of his voice is thick with demand, stroking the line of becoming a bark.

"What?" I whisper, positive I heard him wrong.

He uses his hold on my wrist to push me away from him before releasing it like the thought of touching me any longer is repulsive. The move sends shock waves of pain through my system to the point I stagger back a step.

"Stay away from me," he spits.

My eyebrows knit together as I wrap an arm around my middle, not caring that I'm smearing pasta sauce all over my dress.

This stranger looks worse than I do. I've ruined his clothes and covered him in his dinner. It's no wonder he doesn't want anything to do with me.

"Ma'am, we have to ask that you leave now," an unfamiliar voice says.

I don't look away from the alpha in front of me. "I'm sorry. I should have been more careful. If this is because I wiped your neck—I should have asked if you were mated first."

Shame chokes me. Shame and jealousy at the potential that this man has a mate and I was just touching all over him. *He could have an omega.*

Something ferocious snaps in my chest. I bite back a possessive growl and drop my hands, fists clenched.

The alpha shakes his head only once, top lip curling. He retreats, finally taking the time to look down at his clothes. His eyes are like twin balls of blue fire as he huffs and shakes his hands out, sending pasta flying.

Someone places a hand on my back. I flinch, a startled noise slipping free. The cinnamon scent darkens, taking on a deeper, smoky edge.

"What is going on here?" Greg asks.

The loose snarl that appears doesn't sound anything like him. It's too . . . rough.

He keeps a hand on my back but then drops it in a flash. When I catch him lifting it to inspect the mess on his palm, I fear my cheeks will melt off at the heat in them.

"Are you together, sir?" the same voice who told me to leave asks.

It's a hostess. A different one from when we arrived.

"Yes," Greg says exasperatedly. "What did she do?"

I straighten at that question. The alpha across from me hasn't looked away yet despite his obvious hatred. My omega preens beneath the attention, trotting in a proud circle even as I scold myself, trying to force myself closer to Greg. I almost wretch when his citrus scent washes over me. It's suddenly so . . . *wrong*.

I don't want it close to me, and I surely don't want it on my clothes or skin. I'd rather smell the parmesan in the pasta than citrus right now.

Acting on pure instinct, I lean away from him and take a generous step in the other direction. Greg frowns, a vein in his forehead thumping.

"What are you doing?" he asks, lowering his voice.

What *am* I doing? Nothing makes sense. I'm never this sensitive, yet every moment that passes without this mysterious, gorgeous alpha touching me, I'm flirting with an emotional breakdown.

My instincts are more prominent than they've ever been, my omega on edge and trying to tell me something that I'm too frazzled to understand.

Instead of searching for the meaning behind my actions, I

look to the alpha in front of me, searching for clarity. His stare is narrowed, his chest rising and falling rapidly. I've been around big men before, but this one is intimidating even without his wide shoulders, intense dominance, and the thick pheromones that seem to be getting stronger—

Greg reaches for me again, this time grabbing my bicep and tugging me into his side. The mystery alpha snarls at where Greg's fingers make contact. He lunches forward a step before stopping, forcing himself to stay rooted in place.

My lips part, every inch of my body wanting to leap across the space between us and ask why he's reacting this way. God, I want to be close to him. Maybe I just need one more sniff of his vanilla and cinnamon scent. Right from his throat this time.

Not missing anything, the alpha grinds his teeth together and shudders, spaghetti-coated fingers curling at his sides. Excitement claws at me. Maybe he can smell me after all.

In one forceful movement, he spins on his heels and stalks out of the restaurant. The door spits a forceful wind at me as he rushes outside. I don't move an inch.

He'll come back. He has to.

Only no, he doesn't.

When Greg tugs at me again, muttering something to the hostess about our bill, I fight him. With a pull, I'm shaking him off and chasing after the alpha. Panic threatens to send me into a spiral as I stand on the street and search for him.

Tears fill my eyes, and with my attention focused on finding the man, I don't blink them away. They spill down my cheeks as I stand on the street, more devastated than I've ever been.

5

Landon

No fucking chance in hell.

My molars are dust, and there's a heavy, spiked boulder rolling around in my stomach. I've never been this on edge. Not. Once.

That sharp twist of lemon twirled around a warm, buttery shortbread cookie lingers in my nose and on my clothes, maybe even soaking into my skin. I gasp at the fresh air, but it doesn't help. The omega's scent won't fuck off.

I'm jostled around by people shoving past me on the sidewalk before I duck into an alley and brace my hand on a brick wall, my chest heaving. I focus on the bite of the jagged edges against my palm and pull a shuddered breath in between my clenched teeth.

Cinnamon flares in the dark alley as my scent spikes again. The smokiness of it is no match for the citrus that I can almost taste on my tongue or the pasta still all over my front. I'm drowsy, swaying on unsteady legs as I flare my nostrils and inhale another hit of it.

My knot pulses in my slacks, cum wetting my briefs. *Fuck*. I need to go back there and—

No. I'm going the fuck home.

Grip unforgiving, I turn my back to the street and palm my cock. A soul-deep groan flies up my throat at the relief I feel, even from just one squeeze. The world swims in my vision, the alley closing in around me as I fight to keep my feet glued to the filthy gravel.

I rip my fingers through my hair and cringe at the clumps in it. That fucking omega did far more than mess with my cock. She's responsible for the current filthy state of my clothes too.

My cell vibrates in my pocket. I ignore it, knowing it's most likely Dash. He tried to come with me tonight, and if I wasn't in need of some time alone, I'd have let him. Now, I'm grateful for my desire for loneliness.

If he'd been here, that omega would have been with us right now. I wouldn't have been able to escape alone.

The soft-hearted beta is too similar to Jasper for his own good. Both of them want an omega to fill a gap in our pack that I've become fan-fucking-tastic at ignoring.

Releasing my groin, I thump my head back against the side of the brick wall and pull my phone free. There are two missed calls, but only one came from Dash. The second name isn't one I expected.

Ronan's cold baritone is instant when I call him back.

"Get lost?"

"No."

Fuck, I sound as messed up as I feel. There's not a snowball's chance in hell that he won't notice. Ronan doesn't care much for words and instead prefers to read too much into other people's. Even when we were kids, Jasper always spent more time speaking on Ronan's behalf than he did his own. We've hardly ever been able to hide a damn thing from him.

"What happened?"

"There was a mix-up."

"At the restaurant?"

"Yeah. I'll figure something else out."

A weighted pause. "Did you get pulled over again, Lan?"

"That was weeks ago. I didn't know the taillight was busted."

"You were speeding."

I roll out my shoulders and squint at the bright street ahead of me. "The highway should have been marked as a hundred, not eighty. Who drives eighty on a major highway, Ronan? We both know the cop only pulled me over to be a dick."

He releases a long exhale. "How long is this going to take?"

"Tell Dash that we're ordering in next time."

"Yeah, he heard. So?"

"So, I'll be a while. I've got to find replacement food."

"Just come home!" Dash shouts from somewhere close to Ronan. "I've already opened my bag of emergency chips!"

"He doesn't have emergency chips," I mutter.

Ronan grunts. "Tell him that."

"I'll find something else and bring it home."

"We'll order something," he argues, falling in line with Dash and most likely Jasper.

I grit my aching teeth and peel a clump of pasta from my shirt before tossing it across the alley. "I'll take care of it. My mess, my fix."

"Too late! I'm putting in an order for donairs," Dash sings.

I can already hear Coach's chastising for not sticking to our meal plans. If Dash had it his way, he'd survive off all-dressed chips, ice cream, and Sour Patch Kids.

"Fine. I'll be home in twenty," I grouse, my jaw ticking with frustration.

"Bye," Ronan says before hanging up, not waiting for a reply.

I step out of the alley and thank fucking god that the rush of people has died down. It's easy to cross the sidewalk to the curb where I've parked the giant mammoth of an SUV Jasper forced us to buy last year. *The safety features are the best of the best*, he said. Because we take *so* many road trips outside of a plane.

The doors beep when I unlock them and hover at the driver's side, staring down at my red-splattered chest. It's too easy to strip out of my shirt and leave it on the street. Without it on my body, only two smells linger. The pasta is gone, but the lemon . . . that's still far too fucking obvious. It's like it's been rubbed so deep into my skin that I'm going to be bleeding it soon.

At least I'd be rid of it that way.

Yanking on the door handle, I ignore a surprised squeak from the sidewalk before sliding inside, away from the public eye. I hide behind the tinted windows and start up the engine.

I'm still filthy—even without the soiled shirt—and I'm already dreading the moment Jasper sees the stained seats. I've never hated white leather so much before.

Or my own skin.

I roll down both sets of windows to try and air out the scent of that omega. Still rock hard and fighting a battle within myself to go back to that restaurant, I speed off down the street, praying that by the time I get home, the only thing I'll be able to smell is my pack.

MONTGOMERY
PACK

Nope.

Even out of the SUV, all I can smell is lemon shortbread. I'm pretty sure my face is blue from the lack of blood and oxygen in my upper half, considering it's all in my fucking dick.

I got halfway home before I had to pull over on the highway and jack off. An orgasm only made everything worse. Not only did I come enough to have to use a damn near entire pack of tissues to clean myself up, but now it just reeks like jizz *and* that cursed omega in there. Not to mention my hyper-inflated cock that's so far beyond normal I'm seriously considering calling the team doctor for advice on how to get it soft.

A bleach bath sounds incredible. That or burying my nose in one of Ronan's tuna salad containers.

"Are you Dash Montgomery?"

I stall on the long, three-car-wide driveway. Bare-chested and with a very short fuse, I turn around and snatch the bag of food hanging from the hand of the teenager staring at me. His eyes bulge as he stands frozen, mouth gaped.

"No," I mutter gruffly. "But this is my food. Thanks."

"Yeah—yeah, sure. You're welcome," he rambles, still not moving.

I stare at him blankly. "You can go."

"You're Landon Montgomery," he whispers.

It's the worst outcome for a terrible fucking day.

Dash knows better than to use our last name when he orders anything, let alone to our house. This delivery boy is one minute away from whipping his phone out and recording me on the driveway.

It's not like we live in some guarded castle, but we don't exactly livestream on our front lawn with our address for all to see. Privacy is important to me. I had too little of it growing up.

I really can't do this today. I'm one blown fuse from drop kicking this kid into the neighbour's yard.

"I don't know what you're talking about," I bite out, leaving him there in a rush to get inside.

His footsteps pound on the cement as he chases me. "That's the Montgomery pack tattoo! It's right . . . here!"

The finger that jabs into my left shoulder blade flips that last fuse. My lip curls as I pivot on my back foot and swipe in the direction of the guy. Instead of a shirt, my fingers clutch air, and I glare at where Ronan now stands, clutching the delivery boy a few feet away.

"Don't," he chastises me while giving the kid a rough shake.

I don't bother hiding how pissed off I am. Each word is spat from behind my teeth. "Don't. What?"

The delivery boy continues to stare at me in awe despite being seconds away from tasting the rocks on my driveway. It makes me uneasy, but it's not the first time I've experienced this, and it sure as shit won't be the last.

Ronan might look worse off than I do with his shoulders approaching his ears and eyes narrowed. Even wearing a ripped tank top and a pair of loose sweatpants, he's the more intimidating one. He's the guy who constantly finds himself in my current situation. I have a gut feeling he's going to use this strange occurrence against me someday.

I may be an asshole, but it's very rare I get violent. Today is a rarity in every single possible way.

A stiff wind pushes past us, forcing the lemon scent from my skin and into the air. I hold my breath, refusing to take any more of it into my lungs as my cock throbs to the point of pain once again. Bitter cinnamon swirls when my scent spikes, and I lurch back from Ronan and the random fuckface who's still on my goddamn driveway.

There's a shift around us, a telltale sign that something's about to go to hell only a second before Ronan's snarl tears through the yard.

"What is that?" he snaps, stalking across the distance between us. Without a shirt to help disguise the smell, there's no chance of me avoiding this.

Ronan's the only one of the guys who's nearly my height, standing an inch shorter than my six four. He's also the only one who I know with absolute certainty would and could kick my ass if he knew the truth behind the secondary scent that won't leave my skin. Jasper would take a more emotional route, which may even be worse.

Ronan's nose twitches as he paws at my shoulder and sniffs me. The brown of his eyes gets swallowed up in a sea of black when he gets a good lungful of the omega. A flush builds up the middle of his neck and behind his ears as his entire body quakes.

"What. Is. That?" he repeats, wilder this time. "Who?"

Panic flares low in my gut. The lie escapes before I've thought it through.

"I don't know. Maybe it was someone at the restaurant."

Ronan cocks his head and watches me, a threat creeping into his pupil-blown eyes. "You're lying."

"I was a little preoccupied having our dinner dumped all over me to be paying attention to smells, Ronan."

He lifts his gaze to my hair, as if only just realizing the messy state of it. "Someone threw it at you?"

"You could say that."

"Why?"

"I don't fucking know. For fun? An accident? I didn't linger long enough to ask."

No, I only stayed long enough for the omega to fuck with my head and threaten my pack's trust in me.

"What's going on out here? Are you inviting the delivery guy to stay for donairs? I'm afraid I only ordered enough for us," Dash says, strolling toward us at a leisurely pace. He tilts his head, focused on my bare chest. "Where's your shirt?"

Jasper bypasses us, too concerned with the stranger lingering to pay attention to what's going on with us. He takes the delivery guy by the arm and swiftly guides him down the driveway.

"Thanks, Jas!" With a loopy grin, Dash leans back on a heel and inspects me. "So, seriously, where's your shirt? And did you stop to take a bath in my rigatoni? Is that why we had to change dinner plans?"

"Don't you smell it?" Ronan asks him, still leaning into me, chest heaving. There's more focus in his gaze now, like the omega's scent has weakened in the outside air.

Dash sniffs. "The only thing I smell is Landon."

"Try harder," Ronan demands.

"Try harder to smell what, Ro? I'm a cinnamon fan, but it's like someone's burning a candle and has left it on so long it's melted all the way through. Wanna chill a bit?" Dash asks me, crinkling his nose slightly.

I've hit my limit. Without saying another word, I leave them on the driveway. If, somehow, Jasper gets a whiff of the omega when he returns, I won't have a chance to disappear like this again. Not without getting the fifth degree from him.

Lying to Ronan is bad enough. But Jasper? Especially about an omega?

Fuck. All he's wanted since the moment I met him when we were ten was an omega of his own. The facts of the meeting won't matter. He'll assume she's something she isn't and that it was more than just a terrible mess. Our pack is already weak enough without adding yet another crack in our foundation. The mess from earlier isn't important. I don't want anyone getting the idea that it could be.

"Wait up, Lan! I'm sorry about the comments about your scent. I've just never smelled it like that before. Are you okay?" Dash asks, rushing up behind me. "Did I upset you?"

When he gets to my side, he subconsciously rubs his arm against mine. I release a tight exhale and hand him the bag of food. He takes it eagerly, continuing to glance at me.

"You didn't upset me. I just had a shitty evening. Need to shower, and then I'll be good."

"You sure?"

"Yeah. I've got pasta in my hair."

A light chuckle. "Yeah, I see that."

"Thanks for checking in, D."

"That's what pack is for. I'll get the food dished up for us for when you're done de-pasta-ing."

"Alright," I mumble, exhausted.

I swing the front door open and let the familiar, comforting smell of my pack soothe me. Every step inside helps, and once I'm in my room, I'm out of my pants and in the ensuite shower, the hot water cranked.

My wrist is sore by the time I step out, and while the lemon shortbread scent may have swirled down the drain, I stay rock solid for the rest of the night.

And the following days.

6

Briar

I wish I was in the position in my life where I could hide away under the covers and mourn for days. I've already licked my wounds more than I should have, and I knew it was only a matter of time before Clover came to pull me out of my nest by the hair.

Well, what I call my nest but she considers a pile of clothes and flat pillows with lumps of feathers built in the corner of my bedroom.

"It stinks in here," she declares, hovering at the entrance of my hideaway.

"No it doesn't."

"I almost expected to find you dead. You know, since you haven't responded to any of my messages or calls in five days."

"Well, I'm not."

My voice is scratchy and sore, dull. It exposes the emotions roiling around in my head. The same ones I've been drowning in the last few days as I hid from the world.

I got lucky to not be called into work at all. Clover knows as well as I do that regardless of what I'm struggling with, the one thing I'll never do is turn my back on another omega in need. What we do is too important to let my focus sway. Even if I'm suffering what feels like a heartbreak but without the broken relationship to go along with it.

Clover drops to a crouch in front of the entrance of my pathetic attempt at a fort and surveys me and my surroundings. I push back against the wall away from her when a vicious protectiveness springs to life inside of me. It's not so much in defense of this place, but just . . . myself.

Tears burn my eyes as I bury my face in my hands and curl tight around my knees. This is far from the first time I've cried over what happened in the restaurant last week, but I wish it were. I wish I hadn't shed a single tear over the embarrassment I felt or the mortification at the realization that the only alpha who has ever had that much of an effect on me ran at our first meeting.

I've tried to reassure myself that the situation was just really bad and that it had nothing to do with who I am as an omega. That only made me cry even harder because I knew I was lying to myself. It had everything to do with me, and that's the worst part of it all.

Clover sighs softly, and I lift my head enough to watch her reach a cautious hand into the nest, offering it for me to take.

"Please don't bite my hand off, sweetie. I kind of need it for work," she murmurs.

The immediate change in her tone startles me enough for my spiky energy to smooth a bit. Without crawling out completely, I scoot forward on my butt and take her hand. Her warm brown sugar scent welcomes me closer before wrapping all the way around my body.

"I'm not a birthing omega," I mumble.

"I know."

"So you don't need to use your ultra-special soothing powers on me."

She rolls her eyes and tugs me closer, forcing me out of my cocoon. "You make me sound cooler than I am."

"That's because I wish I could do what you can."

"You do just fine without any 'ultra-special soothing powers,'" she says, using air quotes with her free hand.

It's rare but not unheard of for an omega to have a scent that's able to soothe those in distress. Clover is just the only one I know who has that ability.

We don't quite understand why some scents were crafted a bit more special than the rest of them.

"Tell me what happened, Bri," she encourages, bundling me up beneath her arm.

"Promise you won't laugh?"

"It's that bad?"

I dig my elbow into her side. "Just promise me."

"Fine. I promise I won't laugh."

"It's over with Greg."

She takes a few moments to reply. "Why would I laugh at that? I'm sorry. What happened?"

"That's not the part I was worried about. It gets worse."

"Alright . . ."

I groan, slipping out from beneath her arm to sit across from her instead. Her curious gaze lacks judgment, at least.

"I don't know what I was even doing with Greg in the first place. He's a terrible alpha, Clover. Literally the worst. You should have heard what he said about working," I rant, some of my self-pity transforming into anger.

"Let me guess. Did he say that because you're a beautiful omega, you shouldn't work once you've mated his pack? Staying home to take care of the kids is so demure and oh-so mindful, right? Fucking puke."

"That's exactly it, actually. I told him that I liked my job, and he said, 'Well, it's not like you went to medical school and have that much to lose by giving it up.'"

Clover gasps, her entire expression hardening to stone. "What a lard-for-brains, misogynistic asshole. As if your job is any less amazing because you didn't spend a million years in medical school."

"I know. And I've never wanted your job. My heart has always yearned to give comfort to those in need of it. Getting elbow-deep in a cervix isn't my personal calling. It's yours."

"I'm glad you're done with him. But keep going. Don't leave anything out."

I divert my eyes, unable to look at her as I say, "Alright. After he told me that he didn't imagine me working once I was in their pack, I left to go to the bathroom. I got close to it when I smelled something."

"Something . . . bad? Because you were about to go into the bathroom?"

I crinkle my nose. "No, it wasn't like that. The smell wasn't bad. It was amazing. God, amazing isn't even the right word. He smelled like a dream. Like I'd tripped on my way to the bathroom and woke up in a custom-made paradise. I all but ran after the scent, and the next thing I knew, I was ruining everything," I ramble, emotion clogging my throat at the reminder of everything that happened.

I'm still so out of whack. With every mention of my mystery alpha, somehow, I continue to get worse. More out of control. Something happened to me that day, something that I can't help but be fearful of.

"He?" Clover asks, her tone softening once again. "He as in an alpha? One other than Greg?"

My heart clunks around in my chest. "Yeah, an alpha. Not Greg. This one was—I don't know how to explain it exactly. I felt dainty in front of him, like he could have crunched me beneath his foot if he wanted to. I've never met an alpha that big before. Not just in height but strength and energy. His dominant vibes were smothering, and he spoke all of ten words to me."

"And he smelled incredible?"

"Better than anything I've ever smelled before. I could have bottled it up and kept it with me all the time."

"I'm still not hearing the embarrassing part, Briar."

"Which part should I start with? The whole tracking his smell through a restaurant like a dog part or the smashing into him and causing his dinner to go all over the both of us part? I also can *never* forget about when I started pawing at him to try and clean him up before ripping a tablecloth off a table full of more food and dishes and using it to wipe the spaghetti sauce off his face."

Clover winces, her lips pressing together. I rub my temples and nod.

"I've never been more mortified. He stood frozen and let me make everything worse before telling me to go away."

"He told you to go away?" she asks, brows knitted. "That's it?"

"That's it. Then he ran out."

"Could you tell that he thought you smelled even half as good as you thought he did? Did he have any claiming marks? Was there a pack somewhere nearby?"

I feel my throat growing tighter with every question.

"No. If anything, I think he thought my scent was disgusting. There weren't any marks from what I saw, but I wasn't really paying attention. The only thing I wanted was to go back a few minutes and not plow him down while actively fighting the urge to jump onto him."

"I'm sorry, Briar. I know how badly you want a pack."

"For a second, I thought—" I cut myself off, shaking my head.

"You thought you'd found your scent match," Clover finishes for me.

"Maybe."

Despite the distance I've put between us, she invades my space and pulls me into a hug. My breath catches in my chest at the comfort, needing it more than I thought I would.

"Don't lock yourself up and hide because of one shitty alpha. Or, well, two, I guess. Maybe he had walked by someone on his way to the restaurant and gotten their scent on his clothes," she suggests.

I nuzzle my cheek into the crook of her shoulder. "I wish I had been more conscious of what was happening. It was like my brain switched off and my omega instincts were the only things controlling me."

"And you're sure he didn't react to you at all?"

"Unless disgust counts, no."

"Well, you deserve a better alpha than one who would leave you standing all alone in a restaurant anyway."

"And preferably one with a pack," I add weakly. "I couldn't smell anyone else on him in the time we were close."

"Exactly. We don't settle for the bare minimum here, Briar."

"Never."

"But in all seriousness, I do want that for you. The whole pack life," she says with a steady hand stroking my back.

"Even after what you just went through?"

"Especially after what I just went through. My time in a pack may have gone up in flames like a dry field in the summer, but it was great while it lasted. There's nothing quite like it, babe. And you of all people deserve a life like that."

"Thank you," I whisper.

"You're welcome. But I'm not going to let you sit here and wallow for much longer. We've got three meetings this week, including one with a new omega."

I lean back, glancing at her as my curiosity sparks. "Who is she?"

"Sadie Clark. Her brother called me yesterday asking if we had any availability."

"What day is the meeting?"

"Wednesday. This one might get intense."

"Is she on the run?"

Clover eases out of the outskirts of my nest and stands. With the new information, I'm eager to follow suit.

"As far as I know, there's a restraining order in effect for the two members of her old pack. The pup is theirs, and her brother was adamant that Sadie wants neither of the alphas anywhere near them during the birth."

And this is exactly why Harbour of Hope is so important to me.

The OB/GYN clinic Clover and I opened last year is accepting of all omegas in and around Rayton, British Columbia, but with an emphasis on those who may need extra support and are fleeing dangerous situations. We contract security for situations where it's required and offer support and medical help to those who have nowhere else to turn.

It's a project I hold close to my heart and isn't one I plan on giving up anytime soon.

"I'll be there," I swear.

Clover grins. "I figured you would be."

"Do you want to stay for dinner? We could order something."

"How about you come to my place so I can make you a real meal. You look like you could use it, and I'm betting your fridge is empty."

"I'm not sure if I should be offended or not," I say, tucking my chin to stare down at my outfit.

Yeah . . . it's a bit rough. Maybe I do stink.

Reading my mind, Clover gives me a gentle nudge toward my open bedroom door. "Go shower. I'll be here when you're done."

My legs are weak when I wobble my way out of the room. I offer my best friend an appreciative smile before ducking through the doorway.

"Thank you, Clover."

She waves me off, mouth tipped at the corner. "Thank me by returning to the land of the living."

"Done deal."

Starting tonight, I'm going to go back to how my life was before I ran into that alpha. It should be easy enough.

Right?

7

Ronan

The minute I step out of the car, I'm locking the doors. Twice.

The neighbourhood my mother continues to live in has never been safe. It's a cesspool of crime and danger that, if I had it my way, wouldn't exist at all anymore.

Having a stubborn-as-a-mule beta for a mother makes things far too complicated than they need to be. Too similar to an alpha, she's hard-headed and protective. There are few things that scare her because she considers herself a force to be reckoned with.

I've spent hours trying to convince her that playing hero isn't all it's shaped up to be. The world can be a cutthroat place, and we have to be hard enough around the edges to withstand each of the blows it swings at us. We can't allow pride to put us in dangerous positions like the ones she inserts herself into every day that she continues to live in this rundown building. It's where she raised me and now my younger sister and can't seem to leave behind.

After searching the area for anything out of the ordinary, I walk into the entrance of the building and use the panel on the wall to buzz up to Mom's apartment.

It's impossible not to notice every single crack in the windows and lifted corner of cheap linoleum on the floor as I wait for her to answer. Everywhere I look, I find something else that makes my skin crawl with unease. The place is beyond saving. If I thought it would work and that I wouldn't risk ruining my relationship with my mother, I'd petition for it to be bulldozed.

"Ronan?" my little sister says into the intercom.

"Yeah. Let me up."

"A please would be nice one in a while," she sasses before the door unlocks with a loud buzz.

I slip into the building and pull the door shut behind me, making sure the lock reengages before heading past the lone basement apartment and up to the second floor. The stairs creak beneath my weight, and I consider for a minute that they'll cave in, leaving me buried in the rubble of this rodent-infested junkyard. It's enough to have me taking them two at a time.

At least the owner of the place has the common sense to continue fixing the failing ventilation system. Like the new law states, all living locations with occupants of both beta and omega designation, including ones like this that wouldn't pass any form of code inspection, are required to blow de-scenter through the vents. It's a safety measure that I appreciate as an alpha with an omega sister.

The giant array of fake flowers looped around a Styrofoam wreath and hung on the apartment door makes it hard to mistake which one is theirs. It's a new addition that must have been added between last Sunday and today because I'm here every single weekend and sure as fuck wouldn't have forgotten something that ugly.

Dropping a hand to the door handle, I give it a test wiggle and scowl when it turns completely.

"Why is the door unlocked?" I snap as I throw open the door and stomp inside the cramped apartment.

The door snags on the entry mat, causing the flimsy material to curl beneath it. A collection of sneakers and high heels go tumbling when the corner of the door hits the shoe rack. I stumble over a lip in the floor and into the apartment, my shoulder colliding with the wall.

"That's karma for coming into my house and barking at me, Ronan," Mom chastises, appearing around the corner.

She's still in her fluffy pink robe and flannel pyjamas, but that doesn't change how intimidating she appears. I've wondered a few times if maybe she was born to be an alpha instead of a beta with her intimidating energy.

"I didn't bark."

She huffs, scurrying past me to kick the door shut. "You may as well have. And in a house with an omega? Shame on you."

"Are you done?"

Standing a handful of inches below my chin, she pulls me forward with the strength of a three-hundred-pound man.

"Yes, actually, I am. Move away from the door and have some breakfast. I made that disgusting oatmeal you love so much."

Only once I've locked the door myself do I follow her through the cramped hallway. The scent of fresh bread and blueberry jam is intense today, but I keep my complaints to myself.

I only mentioned enjoying oatmeal once in the last few years. Mom has a habit of remembering all that shit, though. Thinks it makes her a better mom.

Ciara is already slouched over the square, four-person table in the small nook in the kitchen with an array of schoolbooks splayed in front of her. Her glasses slip down her face, and her mouth twists in concentration as her hand moves lightning quick over her notebook.

"Breakfast, Ciara," Mom says, slipping into the L-shaped kitchen. She uses a long-handled metal spoon to mix the contents of the pot on the stove. "And I don't want to hear any complaints today. I added lemon zest exactly like Ronan suggested."

"It's literal slop, Mom," Ciara says with a sigh.

I step up behind her chair and read the words she's writing in her notebook. The letters are big and bubbly, far from what my chicken scratch looks like.

"History of music therapy?" I ask.

Ciara continues to write. "It's good to know you can still read. I worry with how often you get your ass cooked on the ice."

"You're funny."

"I know."

"Breakfast," Mom chides, banging the spoon against the edge of the pot. "Now."

Leaving Ciara, I move to help Mom. I make note of the loose hinge on the cupboard door as I grab three bowls and set them on the counter. Mom steals the first one and fills it to the brim before handing it to me.

"Go sit," she orders, shoving the bowl into my chest.

Taking it, I hiss at the heat against my palms and sit beside Ciara. She glares up at me from over the rim of her glasses when my knee bumps the table leg.

"Stop that," she says.

"Stop what?"

"Moving the table."

"Was an accident."

With a pointed huff, she returns to her work. I watch closely as I scrape my spoon along the edge of the bowl, making that toe-curling noise we all hate.

Her teal-blue eyes are as sharp as knives when they lift from her papers and pin me. "Do that again and I'll shove that spoon up your—"

"Ciara," Mom warns, clucking her tongue.

A steaming bowl of oatmeal clunks on the table in front of my sister, making her shut up quicker than the order from our mom. Her face pales slightly as she stares at it.

Mom takes the seat across from me and scoops some oatmeal onto her spoon. "Your brother is too old for you to be bullying him."

"I'm not bullying him," Ciara argues.

I take a bite of the oatmeal and swallow instantly. "You are."

"Don't try and put the blame on me. I'm only eighteen. My brain hasn't finished growing yet."

"Pretty sure that's only true for guys."

She flashes me her middle finger. "That would explain why you're still stupid."

"Ciara," Mom scolds, sounding far more tired than the first few times.

My sister drops her finger and waves at me. "Fine. You're not stupid."

"That's better. We have more important things to talk about than this," Mom says, meeting my gaze.

Her brown eyes are the same shade as mine, but instead of swirling gold flecks, she has green ones. And right now, there's no mistaking the anger in them.

"What's wrong?" I ask, sitting forward in my seat.

"Do you want to tell me why when I went to pay the bill for Ciara's first semester's tuition, I was told it had already been taken care of?"

"Because I paid it last week."

The muscles in her face tighten. "Why?"

"You're not paying for her education. If you're going to keep living here, then I'm going to pay the tuition."

"No. You'll be coming with me to the bank after breakfast so I can transfer you the money you paid."

I take a bite of my oatmeal, not slouching beneath her anger. "That's not happening."

"Yes, it is."

"No, Mom, it isn't. I don't need the money. I have too fucking much of it as it is."

"Does it matter who pays as long as it isn't me?" Ciara asks, cutting in.

Mom pushes my sister's bowl closer to her. "I'm the parent. Yes, it matters."

"But why?"

"It's my responsibility to take care of you. Your brother doesn't need to do that," Mom snips.

"Considering you won't let me buy you a house and continue to live in this hellhole, I think you're already sticking it to me, Mom. If you change your mind and let me buy you a place of your own in a safer neighbourhood, I'll accept the money back for the tuition."

Her cheeks flame as she sucks in a sharp breath. "Have you brought this up to your packmates, Ronan? You have a family of your own now to look out for. Stop babying your sister and I."

"There is no family other than you two. Landon is making sure of that," I bite out, the words acid.

Some of Mom's ire dulls. "Don't say that. Things aren't that bad."

The silence now draping over us is too heavy. I take the bowl of oatmeal and stand, carrying it to the sink. Instead of dumping it, I stand in front of the window and scarf down the rest of the sticky substance, wanting out of here quickly.

Our mornings together aren't usually so tense. I use my visits to this place as not just an excuse to break away from the stifling emptiness of the pack house but because I worry about my family. The guys understand who I am on a fundamental level and have never tried to change me. The same goes for my sister and parents, whenever my dad is ever home, that is. If I'm not up for being at the pack house, this is where I come.

Today, though? I'd rather sit beside Landon while he scowls about something than here while my mother tries to dig for information on why my pack is falling apart at the seams. She's never understood pack life or why I chose it, so getting into this now will only bring up topics that I'm not up for explaining right now.

"I'm going to head out," I say once I've finished eating.

The white bowl with hand-painted blue flowers goes in the sink before I spin and head for the front door. A heavy, dramatic sigh sounds from the kitchen table.

"Don't leave already. Come sit," Mom says.

I stall, coming up with a lie too easily. "Jasper needs my help with something."

"You're lying. I'm sorry I pried."

"You don't have to apologize. There's just nothing to talk about."

"Have you tried listening to music when you get upset, Ro?" Ciara asks, not looking up from her papers.

"I listen to it in the gym."

She shifts in her seat and finally peels her gaze from the table and to me. It's not judgmental, just curious. Even a bit sympathetic, which is rare with her.

"You should try it outside of the gym too. It could help."

"What kind—"

A clunking noise from the ceiling has me pausing.

"Oh, what now? I bet Jake from upstairs fell again. I'll go check on him," Mom says, already pushing away from the table.

"You're not going anywhere," I mutter, staring up at the vents that have gone completely silent. "The ventilation system isn't on a timer, right?"

Mom shakes her head. "Not as far as I know."

The confirmation isn't needed when the blueberry scent in the apartment plumes. I flash a worried look at my sister before focusing on Mom's waiting stare.

"Stay here. I'm going to call the owner of the building. Lock the door behind me," I demand sharply.

As much as my mom loves to argue with me, she doesn't this time. An omega's home is their safe place. That's the reason behind the new legislation for de-scenter in buildings like this. Without it, there's a greater risk of visiting alphas making their interest in an omega known in a space where they're supposed to be protected.

Of course, it isn't foolproof. The de-scenter they're required to use isn't strong enough to completely cover an omegas scent somewhere they've already made their own. The main point is to help provide a sense of protection and comfort to the omega population when many fear that they'll be unsafe in a building open to other designations.

The hallway is empty and silent as Mom locks the door behind me. A mix of scents has grown exponentially since I arrived. Beta and omega scents are muddled together, nearly turning my stomach.

I hover at the stairs and call the owner of the building, having his number saved from the last time this happened only three months ago. The line rings and rings until I'm sent to voicemail. After I've called another three times, I leave a message.

"The ventilation system is out again in your Howard building. You have half an hour to get it fixed."

There's an imprint of my phone in my palm when I hang up and attempt to rein myself in. My protective instincts are intense, especially with my family.

"Yes, Clover, I'm on my way. The vent system is down, so I was on the phone with Larry . . . Yeah, again. At least he's on his way. I was surprised at how accommodating he was, but I think that's only because I'm still a new tenant . . . Okay, that's rude. Two months is still new . . . Yeah, yeah. I'll be there in fifteen."

I lean over the first few stairs as I listen. The soft, delicate voice drifts toward me on a breeze. A breeze that smells like freshly squeezed lemons drizzled over cookies hot from the oven. It's almost . . . familiar.

The sound of a door closing and locking drives a stake of panic between my ribs. I jump toward the windows at the end of the hall and grip the frame in a tight fist as I search for the owner of that delicious scent and twinkling voice that I want purring my name.

Fuck.

The woman strutting down the sidewalk is almost out of view. I lean against the window, my shaking chest bumping the glass as if maybe that would bring me closer to her. Only a sliver of her is visible to me. A thick thigh, rounded ass, and an ample, curved waist that leads to a dainty shoulder and—

She turns down the street, out of view.

Disbelief rocks me. My cock is painfully hard, straining behind the zipper of my jeans. The force of the pulse in my knot makes me groan in pain as I push off the glass and hover, staring at where the woman just was.

That tart shortbread cookie scent still lingers, even as the sweetness of my caramel threatens to drown it out. My hand slides down the railing, slick with sweat, as I stumble down the stairs, chasing her scent.

It leads past the second floor and down to the first. There's something other than my mind controlling me right now. An intense pulling sensation deep in my chest that continues to guide me to the front of the building.

I gasp for breath, subtly pawing at where my heart is racing. Every inhale pulls more of her into my lungs, painting them in her scent.

For the second time today, I hear the clunking noise that was inside my mom's apartment. A thick, suffocating sense of dread threatens to knock my knees out from beneath me. I whip my head around, breathing in quicker as cool air starts blowing on my skin.

I stagger closer to the front of the building and search for my omega's scent. It's too hard to accept that it's . . . gone.

"Hey. Would you mind spreading the word that the vents are fixed? Lucky I was already here when they kicked off."

My lip quivers as I hold myself back from snarling at the man who's just stepped out of the maintenance room. Backing up, I force myself against the wall furthest from him instead of attacking him.

Red tints his appearance. Instincts I never knew existed overwhelm me, and with every second I linger, the weaker I get to the one that demands I dispose of the man intruding on my omega's territory.

My omega.

Yeah, she's mine. The faceless woman with that enthralling, exquisite scent is mine. And I need to find her.

With a curl of my lip, I slip out of the apartment building. The fresh air doesn't curb my desire. I'm on edge, a ticking time bomb. Every second I stand alone, the worse I get. So, I run.

I run until I can't anymore.

8

Briar

THE DAYS PASS QUICKLY ONCE I'VE GOTTEN MYSELF back together enough to live like normal. Busy with back-to-back baby deliveries and then home visits, it's been hard to find the time to wallow in self-pity.

I save that for once I've gotten home and start drinking fruity wine from the bottle in a hot bubble bath. My stock of bath bombs and fancy lotion bars is quickly depleting at the rate I'm going, and I'm still not over what happened.

The initial burn has died a bit. Now, I'm left with that biting sensation in my gut that has me constantly second-guessing myself. It's like something's wrong, but I'm unable to pinpoint what. All I know is that I'm just . . . off.

"Okay, she should be here any minute," Clover announces, peeking through the small gap left in the office doorway.

"She's not going to appear any quicker with you spying."

"Hush. I don't want her to hear us gossiping."

I hide a laugh in my hand. "Alright."

"We have everything ready, right?" She whips around, abandoning the door in her panic. "The pamphlets and information packets? I emailed you the forms, right? Are they printed?"

"Slow down. We've done this a million times by now. I

printed the forms and went through the folder this morning to check if we missed anything. Which we didn't. This meeting isn't any different than any of the others we've done."

She nods, hands falling to grip her hips as she sucks in a deep breath. "I know. It's just that she's in trouble, and that makes it feel different."

"I know. But we handled it last time we were in this sort of situation."

It just hasn't been for a few months. We haven't needed to hire security to hang around outside of the building since the last runaway omega sought us out. Asking for another few bodies to help was a bit nerve-racking, but it didn't change our willingness to help Sadie. If anything, it only made us more serious about what we were about to do.

"I'm being dramatic," Clover relents, shoulders slumping.

"No, you're being cautious. That's not a bad thing. Especially not today. We'll listen to Sadie's story and go from there, okay?"

Her eyes meet mine as her lips tug into a soft smile. "Yeah, okay."

"Come sit beside me and try to relax so you don't scare her away when she gets here," I urge, patting the empty chair beside me.

"You don't think she'll have trouble where to go without one of us waiting at the door?"

"No. Alicia knows to bring the patients to this room herself when they arrive."

Clover swallows and rushes toward me before plunking down on the chair. She smooths the top of her pencil skirt and wiggles her shoulders in her white coat, drawing my attention to the Dr. Clover stitched in hot pink thread on the left breast.

"Maybe my heat is coming soon," she grumbles, fanning herself.

"Are you serious? You shouldn't be here, then—"

"I'm fine right now. I'm just blaming my anxiety on hormones. Ignore me."

I lean close, my brow twitching. "Are you sure?"

That does remind me that mine should be coming in a couple of weeks. I'll have to phone the heat clinic as soon as I can to reserve yet another room.

"I'm sure. Not that I'd have let a heat affect this meeting, anyway. This is too important to postpone."

"For an OB, you're the worst when it comes to your own health," I scold.

"Don't you even start. Have you already forgotten how I found you Saturday?"

"As if you'd let me."

"Exactly."

I shake my head, leaning back in the plush leather chair. We didn't spare any expenses when it came to the furniture in this clinic, including the elaborate glass table in front of us and the comfortable chairs we're sitting on. It's not like we spend a lot of time in meetings, but for the few hours a week we are here, comfort wasn't something we were willing to compromise on.

Omegas are the most sensitive and picky of all designations, and I say that with pride instead of judgment. I love being comfortable and can get irritable quickly if I'm not. Clover and I go into every meeting with a new patient knowing that they're most likely in the same boat as us.

"How are you doing, Bri? Feeling any better yet?" Clover asks.

I force myself to smile wider than I could naturally. "I'm getting there. Work helps."

"And you haven't seen that guy again?"

"No, and I'm not about to go back to that restaurant to see if he'll show up. He's gone, Clo."

She rests a hand over the one I have palm down on the table, leaving fingerprints on the glass. "What about Greg? Have you heard from him since?"

"I blocked his number the other night."

"Atta girl. He wasn't worth a second thought."

He hadn't reached out to me since I left the restaurant that night. I took that more of an answer than I would have an outright *it's over* text. Keeping his number open was only encouraging a tiny spring of hope I needed to crush.

I don't want Greg, and once I saw the huge, yummy-smelling alpha, it became clear that I was only with him for the pack I'd dreamed of having. It's pathetic that I even entertained the idea and, honestly, makes me feel like a terrible person. A user.

"I know," I say on an exhale. "I'm back at the starting line now."

"Maybe not. You could be taking a break halfway through the race instead."

"No false hope, Clover. I'm too tired for it."

"All you need is one moment, sweetie. One heated look or sniff of someone delicious."

"Honestly, at this point, it feels like too much work than it's worth. Scent matching is what fairy tales are made of, but I guess I just wasn't expecting it to be so impossible to find mine," I say, a bit embarrassed to admit that. "My mom met her pack when she was young and didn't struggle with any of this."

Clover rubs my hand. "They tell us it's rare for a reason. Your mom's situation was one in a million."

"This is all her fault. If she hadn't found my dad's, I wouldn't have grown up wanting to find what she had so badly," I grumble.

"But if she hadn't, you also wouldn't have had the life you did growing up. You'll find your pack, Briar. I know you will."

There's a soft knock on the door that steals our attention. The wide, almost scared hazel eyes staring at me through the crack in the doorway have me lurching forward in my seat.

"Sadie?" Clover asks, jumping up to greet the omega.

"That's me," Sadie whispers timidly.

I shove my issues to the back of my mind at the first whiff of her charred scent. My best friend slowly opens the door and welcomes Sadie into the meeting room. It takes her a few moments to step inside.

"It's nice to meet you, Sadie. I'm Briar," I introduce myself, keeping my tone light.

"And I'm Dr. Clover Jones, but you can call me Clover or Dr. Clover, whichever you prefer."

Sadie swaps her stare between both of us, nodding several times. The arm that folds across her swollen belly has my heart tugging.

She's small, shorter and far thinner than I am. The round belly she's sporting looks like it could tip her over at any moment. Her clothes are baggy, at least two sizes too big, as they droop over her delicate frame. That doesn't stop her bump from making itself known.

"You can take a seat anywhere you'd like. I'll go get you something to drink. Do you like tea?" I ask, already out of my seat.

She watches me move, only speaking once I've gone still. "I like tea."

"Great. Clover will get you situated while I'm grabbing that."

My best friend smiles at Sadie and keeps a few inches away as she finds a seat at the table and sits. I don't think too much into her choice to sit on the furthest end from where Clover and I will be for the meeting.

Sadie's scent isn't as burnt as it was. I know that's all Clover's doing before even picking up on the subtle spike of brown sugar. She's calming her without having to risk speaking too much or crowding her.

I slip past them and out of the room. The staff room is across the hall and fitted with a full kitchen, including the fancy coffee machine Clover found on a massive discount a few months back. There's a tower of cute mugs beside it, and I snag one with red and pink hearts before selecting the hot water option on the machine.

A couple of minutes later, I have a steaming mug of hot water in my hand with a bobbing tea bag inside. Joining the two women in the meeting room, I offer Sadie a gentle tilt of my lips and set the mug on the table.

"Thank you," she says.

"Of course. I've never been one for tea, but Clover loves it. I hope ginger is okay. It's usually a favourite among our soon-to-be moms."

Her brown eyes warm. "I love ginger."

Satisfied with that, I take my seat and wait for Clover to take the lead with our usual introduction. She doesn't leave me waiting.

"I know you might be feeling a bit overwhelmed right now, and we want you to know that if that's the case, we completely understand. And if you feel like you need a break at any time during this meeting, please let us know. There isn't anything too complicated to go over, but we're not dealing with a simple topic or situation right now."

"Okay," Sadie whispers.

"Firstly, I want to ensure you that you're well protected here. There will be constant security on the premises while you're here. In addition, we work very closely with the authorities when it comes to these circumstances."

"By circumstances, you mean my alphas?" She tucks a chunk of black hair behind her ear and huffs. "They're not my alphas anymore. I'm just . . . not used to saying otherwise yet."

I want to go to her and wrap her in a hug. Suddenly, my problems aren't all that dire anymore.

"We know. Either way, while you're here, you don't have to worry about them. And for while you're not at the clinic, I understand you have a restraining order?"

"I do," she confirms, shifting uncomfortably.

"Perfect. We'll move to the birth-related discussion now if that's alright?" I ask.

Sadie takes a sip of the tea and keeps the mug held close to her chest as she meets my eyes. "That's alright."

"Do you have any preferences? A birthing plan ready? If not, we're more than happy to help you create one. They're kind of my specialty," I say.

Clover dives a hand beneath the table and reaches for the one I have on my thigh. She squeezes my fingers in thanks and appreciation. I grip hers just as tight.

We've been here together so many times, but somehow, every time gets better. With every omega we help, our confidence grows. The desire to strive for more is an overwhelming feeling, and I've grown addicted to it.

Giving Sadie the experience she deserves during such a beautiful, life-changing moment is what keeps me going. And I know that even if all I had at the end of the day was the work we do here, I'd be happy.

9

Jasper

THE TASTE OF IRON FILLS MY MOUTH AS I SPIN PAST A defenseman and tuck the puck back between my skates to where I know Landon waits. In a blink, I'm slammed up against the boards, the air forcefully expelled from my lungs before I'm slipping free of the hold.

Ronan's there before I make it far, plowing straight through the player who just knocked me around, leaving him crumpled on the ice. He hangs around the guy splayed on the ice, taunting him with words I can't hear over the raging *Ro-nan, Ro-nan* chants in tonight's crowd. It's electric in here for a regular Thursday night, and it isn't helping calm the players. Fists pound the fibreglass, and signs are pushed flush against it to try and grab my attention, but I keep it on Ronan, worry burning a hole in my gut.

The ref blows his whistle, ending the play. I spare a glance down at the player, slowly pushing myself down the ice before Ronan's being shoved toward me. He bounces off my chest, his helmet narrowly avoiding clunking me in the face.

A couple of players on the other team are snapping at him for the admittedly questionable hit, but he doesn't say a word in protest. Just like the past few days, he's silent, half in his own world. The only emotion he seems to show is anger.

Hawthorne, the opposing team's captain, comes skating over at the same time the ref joins us. Landon fits himself beside Ronan and clutches him by the shoulder, the C on his jersey impossible to miss with its bright blue colour.

"It'll be interference," the linesman warns us.

I flick off my right glove and thumb away the bead of sweat on my nose. "Is that necessary?"

"It's a weak call," Landon snaps, jabbing a finger toward the other team's bench. "Nothing when Orlovsky slew-footed me earlier, but you're going to call this?"

The ref skating off doesn't care what Landon has to say. My pack leader has been biting off chunks of him all game, and he knows damn well that he's one more snarky comment from earning an unsportsmanlike penalty.

Hawthorne rolls his eyes at Landon. "The difference is intent. You know anything about that, Montgomery?"

Landon bares his teeth. "Want to find out? My intent will be crystal fucking clear in a few seconds."

I slip between them and focus on the linesman, grateful for the A on my jersey. "Two minutes for Ronan. We're all good here."

Ronan isn't one for arguments on a good day, but this week, I think the idea of getting into it on the ice with the ref would send him into a spiral. He's already heading to the box without another word to anyone.

With my ungloved hand, I tug at the back of Landon's jersey and haul him away from everyone. He snaps his eyes toward me and scowls, a flash of betrayal there and gone.

His voice is tight. "You know I'm right."

"It doesn't matter if you are or not. We need you focused on the game, Lan. Not starting pointless arguments."

"Ronan was right to knock that fucker on his ass. Are you okay?"

I nod and slip my glove back on as he gives me a quick up-and-down inspection. There's nothing out of place. I *am* fine.

"I've been hit far worse than that."

"Are we all good?" Dash asks, joining us on his side of the centreline.

Standing a few inches taller than he does off the ice, our goalie watches us closely. From his net, he misses a lot of what we deal with, and I know that annoys him. The debriefs we have after every game have gotten longer in length this season.

I offer a half-smile and tap Landon behind the knees with my stick. "Yeah, we're good."

There's no pretending Landon isn't pissed beyond belief as we set up for a faceoff by our net, now down a man. Our penalty kill isn't anything to write home about, and I zone in, knowing that we're one wrong move away from losing our single-goal lead.

Landon wins the next faceoff. He flicks the puck back to where one of our other two best defensemen, Marleau, waits. I avoid the shoulder coming my way and take off after Marleau when he starts down the ice. He's blocked near the centreline, narrowly avoiding keeping the puck before passing it back to me. The defenseman guarding me tries to swipe it, but I'm there too quickly, hiding it behind the blade of my stick.

I know pulling off the play I want is a long shot. Landon's close, skating faster than he has in a long while. The two defensemen on the other team are on my ass, and one manages to jab his stick between my legs far enough to tap the puck before I adjust my hold and shift it further in front of me. Their goalie is hovering in front of the net, his knees bent as he stalks me.

The player at my back is gliding at pace with me, but I know if I go any faster, I'll lose Landon. I won't get the shot off myself. The goalie is too focused, skating back into the net and stretching out, waiting for my next move.

I see Landon from the corner of my eye, catching the way he taps his stick to the ice twice. The moment the player behind me makes another move for the puck, I shove my shoulder into his chest and send it flying across to Landon.

It should be a perfect tape-to-tape pass. The fans cheer in

preparation for the inevitable Landon Montgomery snapshot. I keep moving, attempting to shake off the defenseman clinging to me. He's heavy on my body, weighing me down as I shove at him, alarm building in my chest as Landon slows, stare vacant.

I notice Orlovsky barrelling toward Landon too late to warn him. The player behind me touches the puck while continuing to hold me, killing the play, and Landon slows his glides in preparation for the whistle. He's completely unaware of the defenseman skating full throttle toward him.

A whistle blows nearby, and the guy hanging off me lets go immediately. *Too late.*

The ref's call doesn't stop the other player. In a blink, he's lifting off his skates and jamming his right knee into Landon's. My packmate goes flying onto his back, sliding down the ice toward the net as he clutches his knee. A frigid breeze trickles down my spine.

The ref comes around me with his hand still hanging in the air to signal a holding call. I'm already moving. Ronan's voice carries from the box, his outrage threatening to crack the ice in half.

Another whistle blows three times. Landon groans, rolling onto his belly and then lifting himself onto his hands and knees. The position settles some of my nerves. If his knee was destroyed, he'd be staying on his back.

I drop to a crouch and look at his face. The sight of him trapping a growl between clenched teeth is startlingly reassuring.

"Medic?" I ask.

"No fucking medic. Not for me."

"Don't. Not today. You're not in your head."

A linesman stands above us and says, "Do we need a medic here?"

Dash smacks his stick against the ice by his net, too far to say anything without getting in trouble. I didn't notice Orlovsky being guided off the ice, but there's no sign of him now. It's a good thing he's gone before Landon got back on his feet.

"Montgomery folded! A blind man could see that was embellished," Hawthorne guffaws, skating close enough to draw another linesman.

I check myself before he's laid out on the ice beside Landon. My pack leader pushes to his feet. His hiss has me clutching at his arm, helping him up. The venom in his stare is terrifying, and when he focuses on Hawthorne, there's a break in the opposing captain's tough façade.

They're both alphas, but he's no match for Landon. Very few alphas are, and it's the reason he's discouraged from fighting in the league.

I wish I'd seen this intense focus in his eyes minutes ago. Instead, there was only a ghostly absence that still has me in knots. It's too similar to the way he's been acting for days now, like he's only half himself.

Something has happened, and I need to figure out what.

"Everyone needs to take a step back. We're all good here," I say, playing peacekeeper.

The linesman tips his chin in agreement and makes a show of separating Landon and Hawthorne.

Hawthorne scoffs, turning his nose up at us. "This is bullshit."

"Tell your players to aim a bit higher next time," Landon goads him with a wicked smirk.

"Don't make me put you in the box too, Montgomery," the ref warns from where he's skating to make the penalty announcements.

I take Landon by the arm and help him skate to the bench, unbothered by the scoffs and muttered complaints coming from the other team. If Ronan hadn't already been on the bench, things would have been very different just now, and not a single person on that team would be so open with their unhappiness.

Landon steps onto the bench, and the team medic forces him to get checked out in the dressing room. I catch Dash's stare from across the ice and nod despite not knowing all the answers yet. We need him on his game, not worrying about Landon.

The fans shout their approval when the ref calls the two penalties, and I glance behind the bench, searching for my missing packmate.

He doesn't appear for the rest of the period, and the moment the team steps into the dressing room during the last intermission, it only takes one look at him to know that I was right earlier.

There is something wrong with him.

10

Ronan

SOMEONE IS GOING TO CALL THE COPS ON ME AT THIS rate.

"Hello, Officer. There's been a strange man parked outside of this apartment building for the last three days. Yeah, he's a fucking weirdo and won't stop lurking on the street," I say to myself while leaning my forearms on my bike.

I'm in the exact same spot I have been every evening, still hulked over my bike with my helmet perched in my lap. It would have been smarter to use the SUV for my stalking, but Landon's had it at a shop getting detailed for the last two weeks. At this point, it better come back with black leather instead of white and that new car smell I fucking love.

My phone vibrates in the pocket of my jacket, and I ignore it again. I dipped out of the arena and onto my bike before the others could catch up to me, so I know it's Dash calling. The mother hen can't stand when he doesn't know everyone's whereabouts.

Somehow, I've kept my evening plans to myself. If any of my packmates knew what I was doing, they'd be hauling me back home by the scruff. Landon would try to lock my bike up just to keep me from trying to find the omega again.

He's the reason I haven't said anything to anyone about what happened the first time I scented her last week.

And possibly before that.

Fuck no.

I've convinced myself that my gut feeling is wrong. That I hadn't smelled her before, especially not on my fucking pack alpha. Landon's a dick most of the time, but he'd never betray us like that. To hide an omega from us would be the worst thing he's ever done.

I remember scenting something fruity and tart on him the night he came home covered in dinner, but there was so much going on it could have belonged to anyone. It doesn't mean shit that I reacted to the scent then. Nothing made sense that night.

The trauma Landon carries from his childhood has kept him firmly against the idea of welcoming an omega into our pack. It used to be easy to ignore that when we knew we had decades ahead of us to open him up to the possibility, but we're already one down with no hope in sight.

Going behind his back tonight feels wrong, but what other choice do I have? I need to find this omega on my own so he doesn't have a chance to intervene. I'm not risking losing out on her. Not even my loyalty to Landon matters more to me than she does. I didn't need to so much as to see her face to make that decision, and that's terrifying.

My phone buzzes again when I spread my legs wider around the leather seat and plant my heels on the concrete. Most of the apartments facing out on the street have lights shining through their windows, but that doesn't help me at all. I know nearly all of the residents by name from my time visiting my family, and not a single one of them is my omega.

Hidden between the two buildings across the street, I blow out a pitiful breath and grab my phone. The number of missed calls would be concerning if they weren't all from Dash. His text messages are what have me sitting straighter, the back of my neck prickling.

Why aren't you sharing your location with us?

Are you cheating on us with another pack?

ANSWER ME RONAN.

Fine. I'm coming to look for you then.

The last text was sent fifteen minutes ago before he called me twice more. It's only a ten-minute drive from the pack house to—

Bright headlights fan out over the street as a sleek black car crawls to a stop in front of the entrance to the alley I'm trying to blend into. I squeeze my handlebars and scowl at the man who hops out of the driver's side and rounds the hood.

"Why are you hiding in the alley? You look like an absolute creep," Dash shouts.

"I don't need a babysitter."

"You sure? Because from where I'm standing, you're about an hour away from having the cops called on you."

"I'd be gone by then."

"What are you even doing? Are you here to see your mom?"

He tucks his hands into the pockets of his jeans and strolls toward me. The teal Rayton Riptides hoodie he's wearing has a giant bleach stain on the pocket, and his light-wash jeans are ripped at the thighs and knees in very Dash fashion. He's always brightly coloured, while I make sure all of my clothes are dark or neutral.

I clear my throat and release the handlebars, stretching my fingers to work out the stiffness in them. Maybe it would be easier to start the bike and drive off past him. By the time he got into the car to follow me, I'd be long gone.

My feet stay planted on the road. "I was just leaving."

"Liar," he says, calling me out.

"I wanted to take a ride. Get some fresh air."

"And you had to do that alone? I'd have joined you after practice."

"Wanted to take the bike."

"Right."

"You can go. I'll be home soon."

He jostles a shoulder. "Nah. I'll chill with you for a bit. It's a nice night."

"Dash," I grumble.

"Yes, Ronan? Are you sure there isn't another reason why you're here in this alley instead of at home with your pack? I know for a fact that Coach picked on you more than usual today. Is that why you needed space?"

He was harder on me because I was sloppy. I have been for days, nearly costing us our last game because I couldn't focus on anything other than the memory of the omega.

Fuck, that game was a disaster.

Trapping a groan inside, I stare past Dash at the apartment building, pleading with I don't even know what for her to appear out of thin air.

"I already told you there wasn't a reason I was here," I mutter.

He turns to the apartment, his head tipping one way, then the other. "Who's inside, Ro?"

"How am I supposed to know that?"

"You're here every weekend visiting your family. Don't tell me you haven't been paying attention to everyone who lives there. You're the most protective alpha I've ever met."

Something tells me that he's looked in my room and found the list of tenants I keep in my desk. He calls it protectiveness; I call it doing my due diligence. What if a criminal was living in the same building as my mother and sister? That wouldn't be acceptable.

"I don't know everyone," I say, not having to lie this time.

If I did, I'd have a name or apartment number for my omega. It seems the list of tenants I have is outdated. I've scanned it a thousand times since I saw the omega here, and not one of the names on it spoke to me the way I know hers would have.

Instead, I only have the lingering image of her walking away and the memory of her smell that's had me spending more time in the shower than anyone should. Wrinkled skin and aching balls are my new normal.

Dash hums, leaning against my thigh. He kicks a leg out and crosses his ankles, staring down at me with a sly smile.

"Are you waiting for someone by chance? Is that why you're being so shady? Now that I think about it, I haven't seen you in the gym the past few nights."

The sound of tires crunching over the rock-sprinkled road distracts him before I'm forced to answer. With a lifted brow, he eyes the gleaming blue car that pulls up in front of the apartment building.

I lurch forward on my seat, causing the bike to rock with the sudden adjustment of my weight. There's a sense of rightness stroking my chest, calling my heart forward to pound at my rib cage.

Her voice is a gentle twinkle in my ears. I toe my kickstand down and stumble off the bike, drawn to the sound.

"See you tomorrow, Clove. Love you."

Suddenly, it doesn't matter that Dash is here. I shove past him, our shoulders knocking as he grunts at the impact.

Painted in the beams of dull streetlights, my omega spreads her perfect, apple-red lips into a delicate grin and waves at the woman behind the wheel. She's perfect, all beautiful, gentle features and a curved figure that my fingers burn to explore. It was a tease only seeing her from the back the first time I laid eyes on her, but also a blessing.

I'd have never survived these days without her had I seen her like this.

I gasp a tight breath and move closer, stepping out from between the buildings. She's so close, yet too far for me to catch a hint of her warm lemon scent.

My alpha drives me toward her at the same moment the car that dropped her off disappears down the street. She spins on her heels and starts up the sidewalk, walking away from me again.

Only I'm not leaving here without getting a chance to get close to her this time.

With a brief look for oncoming traffic, I jog across the street, my feet smacking the concrete in time with the raging pulse in my ears. The omega is only a few steps from the door when Dash calls after me.

"What are you doing, Ronan?"

I don't look back at him, but the omega does.

With a fearful squeak, she lunges for the door handle and whips her head back. Blue eyes so pale they're nearly grey flare wide when they connect with mine. I freeze with a foot on the curb, my thighs pinching tight from the effort it's taking not to plow her down.

With only a few yards between us, I can make out more of her features. Like the small dip in the centre of her chin and freckles flecked over her nose and forehead. She has a stud in the side of her nose with a diamond that sparkles even in the low light and starry sky.

The T-shirt dress she's wearing beneath a denim jacket reaches just above her knees and, even with its boxy shape, doesn't swallow all her curves. They're not as obvious as they were the other day, but I've memorized the image of them in my mind so often over the last week that I don't need another look. The only thing I need is . . . I don't know.

Everything feels like the most appropriate answer.

She doesn't run from me. I doubt I look all that warm and inviting, yet she hasn't spun around and run inside.

Cautious of every move I make and the potential repercussions of each one, I step forward with my right foot and wait for a reaction. The omega's fingers readjust their grip on the purse strap hanging from her shoulder.

"Do you live here?" she asks, her voice an enchanting song that I want to hear again and again.

It's hard to breathe, let alone speak. I open my mouth, but nothing comes out of it. My tongue lies limp, the useless fucker.

The omega pulls a short breath in between her lips. "Or . . . are you visiting someone?"

"My family lives here," I croak, lifting a weak arm toward the building behind her.

"Oh. Are they expecting you? We're not supposed to let strangers in."

Smart girl. Pride clangs in my chest. My omega can take care of herself. Now she won't have to. Not anymore.

"I was leaving."

The corner of her mouth twitches, a spark of humour appearing in her expression before she forces it back. "Then why were you running back?"

Smart, gorgeous, and clever. How lucky am I?

I take two steps forward, unable to help myself. The omega watches me, on edge but not appearing fearful anymore. Maybe she feels the same curiosity that I do. And fuck, if I'm lucky, the same draw.

"Consider me interested."

"In what?"

I swallow a possessive growl, keeping my lips flat.

"You."

She sways forward at the claim in the word. So do I.

A light breeze curls around my ear, carrying my scent toward her as it grows stronger with our closeness. I'm helpless to the spike. All I want to know is if she likes it. And me. If she doesn't . . .

"Me," she echoes.

The grass is smooshed flat beneath my shoes as I continue to eat at the space between us. She buries her teeth into her plump bottom lip and brings her head back to keep our eyes locked the closer I get. Releasing her purse strap, she drops her hand, letting it hang limp.

"I'm Ronan," I force out.

Her lashes flutter. When I breathe in, a low rumble explodes in my chest. Grey-blue eyes fill with black as her pupils swallow the colour, a soft noise escaping her. The sound of her distress flays me open.

She shivers, every inch of her body quaking. "Ronan."

"Your name," I groan, my clothes growing so tight to my body that I lift a hand to paw desperately at my shirt, wanting it off. "Tell me your name."

Oh, *fuck*. Lemon shortbread fills the air in thick puffs, creating a cloud of her perfume around us. Yeah, she's my omega alright.

My fucking omega.

I don't have to be the one to go to her. Once I've closed my eyes, trying to rein myself back in, I feel her come toward me. I snap my eyes open and focus every ounce of my attention on her.

The pink tint on her skin is a beckoning, but the tiny pink tongue darting across her lips is a warning. If I kiss her right now —when we're both in this daze—I'll never get another shot at capturing this moment. Once and done.

"Please, Petal. Your name."

She steals all the air between us in a sharp inhale. "I like Petal better."

"You can have both," I declare.

"Briar."

My cock throbs, cum making my briefs sticky as I swallow past the dryness in my throat and nod. "Briar."

She puffs out a breath, a whine following. My entire body reacts to that sound. I feel like I can't breathe as I reach a hand out, holding it in the air. The heat from her cheek crosses the space between her skin and my palm in a silent plea for me to shift it just an inch.

Leaning forward, she brings her nose to my chest and inhales deeply, nuzzling her cheek into my hand. The immediate sizzle where we touch encourages me to take a better hold of her, palming her cheek with a sturdiness I wish I felt in my legs.

Briar shuts her eyes. The immediate trust she's gifting to me cranks the dial on my protectiveness. We're out in the open right here, and I know we're not alone.

There's so much to be discussed. Does she know what's happening, or is her omega driving her right now? Is she in control of herself at all?

A cold rush drips down the back of my neck.

"Ronan?"

The male voice flips a switch inside of me. Driven by pure animal instinct, I use my hold on Briar to pull her against my chest and snarl at my packmate, warning him to back off.

He gawks at me, jaw unhinged. There's a rattling in my chest as I stare him down, my arms bracketing the omega in my arms.

Mine.

I blink, my packmate's face slowly registering. He's not a danger. He's pack. A beta.

"Alright, Ro. I'm not going to take her from you," Dash murmurs, slowly lifting his hands into the air. "You can trust me."

I nod stiffly, bringing my nose to Briar's hair and sucking her scent into my lungs.

"Who is she, Ronan? You can tell me that, yeah?"

"Mine," I grit out between my clenched teeth.

She releases another noise, this time higher in pitch. It causes my knot to swell wider, nearly painful in size.

"Briar."

It's muffled in my shirt. I stroke the back of her head, trying to remind myself that Dash is pack.

Realization dawns on me at the same moment he slides toward us. His hiss of breath isn't as startling as the tensing of Briar's body against mine. She pulls herself out of my grip enough to blink up at Dash, wonder lighting her eyes.

"Are you . . . You too?" she whispers.

Two words and she's confirmed what I knew from the moment I saw her. We're scent matched.

All three of us.

Which means that the odds are . . . Jasper and Landon too.
Fuck.

11

Briar

I'm in a dream. That's the only plausible explanation for what's happening, and even that isn't believable.

The alpha holding me hostage in his arms is my scent match. I'm sure of it.

His rich caramel scent is layered with the hint of coffee, slightly bitter, as if I made the mistake of ordering it black instead of with milk. I've inhaled it over and over, trying to search through it for the hint of someone else. Another omega, mostly.

My heart pinches at the possibility that he's not mine for the taking. Or that, similarly to the alpha from the restaurant, he won't want me once this scent spike dies down.

I furrow my brows and rub my cheek against his palm, breathing in the thick, rich caramel that might as well be running in glistening ribbons down his neck.

The collar of his leather jacket is flipped, creating a boundary between his throat and where I ache to bring my nose. He holds me firmly with a sense of sureness that I pray I'm not making up in my head.

"Ronan?"

Suddenly, I'm plastered to the alpha's firm chest. The shift has me able to press up on my tiptoes and sneak closer to his throat.

I'm still too far to rub against his scent gland, but even just this is better. His scent is stronger here, like a beacon for both me and my omega that makes me glad I always wear scent-cancelling panties. The burst of slick that escapes when that sweet scent swells would have soaked through regular ones.

Ronan grows completely still against me as his chest rattles with a growl, and he snarls at the owner of the new voice.

"Alright, Ro. I'm not going to take her from you," the man says. "You can trust me."

With a stiff nod, Ronan leans close, bringing his nose to my hair, and pulls in a long inhale of my scent. I preen at his interest, my worry that he'll retreat starting to dim.

"Who is she, Ronan? You can tell me that, right?"

"Mine," he declares, almost ferally.

I can't help it. It's not about the ownership of the claim but the pride with which he says it that draws a needy noise up my throat. It brushes his chest as I rub against his shirt and try to keep my eyes from rolling back.

"Briar," I whisper.

Ronan palms the back of my head and strokes my hair, a rough exhale blowing through it. My stomach flips over and over again as another scent drifts toward us.

I tense, sorting through the caramel to find a sweet bite of peanut butter and chocolate weaving around it. I shiver at the combination, in awe of how perfectly the scents complement one another.

Pack. They're pack.

Jolted at that realization, I pull out of Ronan's arms and blink up at the man who's just joined us.

He's so . . . vibrant. And as I let my gaze wander, I realize how much smaller he is than Ronan. Not in a bad way, just different. He's still far taller than me and without a doubt could hold his own with the bigger man. It's more of a subtle difference. A slimmer build, less prominent bone structure, and compared to his packmate, he has a much better hold on his instincts. Even his scent is softer and a bit hard to separate from Ronan's.

He's a beta.

Instead of coming to me the way Ronan did, he hesitates, blue eyes wide and thoughts busy. His wavy blond hair droops down over his forehead, and he makes no move to push it back.

"Are you . . . You too?" I whisper.

He swallows, curiosity blooming across his face. The bottoms of his sneakers scuff the sidewalk when he comes forward, opening and closing his hands where they hang by his thighs like he wants to reach for me but can't.

Ronan lingers close, not touching me again without permission. Now that I've stepped out of his arms, his energy has shifted, becoming sharper. My first instinct is to soothe him, so I take a chance and lean against his body, hoping he doesn't shrug me off now that we're not alone. He sighs, relieved, and strokes a hand up my back, fingers splayed as if to touch as much of me as possible.

It's absolutely crazy to be this at ease with a stranger so soon. So why does his touch feel so incredible? I don't want him to *ever* stop touching me. Maybe that makes me a fool. Nothing changes the fact that I've been searching for this connection my entire life.

We might have only just met, but there's no mistaking who we are to each other. Fated, scent matched, they're the same thing in my eyes. We were meant to find each other, and this beta might be meant for me too.

An echo of a pull is there, but it's not as strong as the one I feel with Ronan. Like maybe there's something blocking it. I'm positive the blockage isn't coming from my end. He sure smells like he could be mine. With a clearer mind now that my nose isn't an inch from Ronan's throat, I'm able to think through my actions a bit more.

"I'm Dash," the beta says, sounding a bit airy. "And you're Briar."

I roll my lips, trying to avoid smiling so quickly. "Hi, Dash."

"You're an omega," he blurts out.

Ronan might still be stiff, but the noise he releases almost sounds like a rough laugh. "Fuck's sake, Dash."

"Have you never seen one before?" I ask with a tilt of my head.

Dash's eyes bulge. "I have. But you—you're not like the rest of them."

I blush, my cheeks on fire. Focusing on his peachy lips, I take a step in his direction. The loss of Ronan's touch is almost painful. Like the first splash of cold water on a fresh burn. Every bone in my body aches with the distance between us.

Chest tight to the point of discomfort, I stand in front of Dash and slowly bring my eyes up to snag on the ones already watching me. There's a connection between us. A mutual desire like the one I feel with Ronan. He may be a beta, but that hasn't changed anything other than a slight stifling of his scent.

Up this close, I can smell it better. It calls to me. There's a rightness here, a confirmation that he's supposed to be someone to me, even if he's not exactly a scent match.

"How do you know that already?" I ask.

He glances at Ronan briefly. "For one, I've never seen Ro react like that to anyone before."

"Like that?" I repeat.

"I thought I was going to have to call the rest of the pack to come help me get him off of you."

Ronan all but lunges back to my side, planting himself in a position that semi-blocks Dash's view of me. The rumble in his chest is a low warning, more animal than man.

"Yeah, you're one of a kind, Briar," Dash says with a crooked grin.

"What's wrong with you?" Ronan snaps at him.

"You mean, other than being incredibly confused by all of this?"

A small nip of rejection follows his question.

Does he not feel anything toward me right now? Not even

when we're this close? Being only a few inches from this beta feels good. It's right. Maybe I'm wrong...

I hide my emotions behind a light smile. Ronan's body heat keeps me warm as the night breeze cools. The urge to fall back into his arms is overwhelming. I don't know anything about this man, and it doesn't matter.

He's safe. I know he's mine, and I've always trusted my instincts. Well, always until Dash. When it comes to this beta, I'm unsure.

"You two are pack, right?" I ask.

"Yeah, Petal."

Ronan curls a thick, strong arm around my back and palms my hip possessively. I shudder at the display, his touch sizzling through my dress.

In the blink of an eye, I'm perfuming again, this time too weak to the pull to keep from rolling into my alpha's arms. We can talk later, maybe when we're alone and I've had time to sit with all of this. For now, I slide my hands beneath his jacket and over his waist, exploring the expanse of his back. My lemon scent is intense, drowning all three of us.

"Briar," Ronan rasps.

Humming, I roll my forehead along his sternum and rub against his front, marking him. He flattens his hand to my lower back and tugs me in, forcing us flat together.

It's an intimate hold. One reserved for lovers.

That's what we are now, isn't it? Or could be?

I know Dash is still here watching. It doesn't bother me. His closeness doesn't freak me out—another sign that there's more to the story here.

Ronan lowers his mouth to my temple, his lips parting on my searing skin. Arousal shifts through me, drooping low in my belly as more slick fills my panties. If I don't leave soon, wearing them at all will have been pointless. I'll be dripping down my thighs.

Knowing that there's a clock ticking down faster than I'd

hoped, I make a move I've wanted to do from the first time I scented Ronan.

I move cautiously, shyly, and push forward on my toes in search of his throat. His scent gland is my destination, even though it's still covered by that damn collar.

A frustrated huff escapes my parted lips, followed by his low groan.

"Yeah, you want to mark me, Petal?" he asks, voice gravelled. He tugs the collar of his jacket aside. "I'm all yours."

"Ronan," Dash warns.

I curl my fingers into Ronan's back and finally bring my nose where I've needed it to be. Knuckles trace the shape of my cheek as I nuzzle against his throat, coaxing more caramel into the air while transferring my scent onto his skin.

It won't last forever, but I'm more than interested in repeating this process multiple times a day for the foreseeable future.

His strength has me in disbelief as he holds me, letting me rub against his neck. Before pulling back, I drift my mouth across the hot skin and freeze, one flick of my tongue away from tasting him.

"Do it," he commands.

I sigh happily, my eyes closing as I glide my tongue up the strong column of his throat. The mix of our scents clouds the air, making it sticky. I'm enthralled with the way it makes me feel like I'm weightless. Like there's nothing but this and us right here.

My teeth scrape at his throat as I teeter, strong fingers holding the back of my head to keep me in place. Ronan hisses a curse and bares his neck further, muscles straining as he opens himself up to me. I could bite him like this. Claim him properly already with more than just my scent—

"Enough," Dash shouts, his voice like a smack upside the head.

I jolt back, mortified. Knowing both men are staring at me, I lift a hand to my mouth and try to clear my head. Distance from Ronan doesn't help. It only makes everything worse.

Swallowing to trap a whine, I tuck my hair behind my ears and take another large step backward toward the building behind us.

My voice is a whisper in the wind. "I'm sorry."

"We just don't need any claiming right now. Clearly, there are things that need to be talked about. Our pack needs to hear about this before anything else happens," Dash says, risking moving between Ronan and me.

I latch onto the mention of their pack. "There are more of you?"

"Two more," Ronan grunts, reaching for me. When I shake my head and fold my arms to ensure I don't do the same thing, he pins Dash beneath a death glare. "I'm not leaving her here alone."

"You've only just met. It's a scent match, right? That's what this is?" Dash asks.

It sounds flippant. Like he doesn't really care about what's just happened, yet something in my gut tells me that's not the whole story. That there's more to this beta than I've seen so far.

"She's my omega," Ronan growls, inching toward his packmate.

"I believe you. But it's too soon. Landon needs to hear about this before we do anything else."

"Landon doesn't have shit to say about this."

Dash's mouth drops just enough to betray his surprise. "You know that isn't how it works, Ro."

"He can't take her from me."

My heart pangs, and a beat later, I'm back in his arms despite Dash's warning. I need to touch him, even if that looks bad to his packmate. In a few minutes, I'll be going inside alone. Even if that makes me want to hurl all over the grass.

Pressing a hand to Ronan's vibrating chest, I tip my head back to meet his dark eyes. "Nobody is taking me from you. But he's right. If there are more of you . . . then you need to speak with them, and we have to meet. This is still new. A scent match is rare and incredible, but it's not a done deal."

"Not a done deal?" he asks, confused.

I giggle. "No. Not by a long shot."

"What does that mean?"

"It means you have to court her, Ronan. Like any other omega. But there's no chance we'll be able to do that without Landon and Jasper," Dash answers for me.

Landon and Jasper. I memorize their names, already picturing what they might look like and how they smell. If both Ronan and Dash have sweet scents, maybe the other two are darker, spicy.

Blinking, I mentally chastise myself. I'm too far ahead. It's obvious whoever Landon is, he isn't interested in an omega.

I've already struck out with Dash, and if I don't recognize the other two as scent matches, I don't know what will happen. Thinking about it now will only make it that much harder to let Ronan leave.

We need time apart. All of us. Without it, we'll never think about anything properly. I've already lost all sense once, and I can't afford to do it again.

At least not until I know what in the world I'm going to do.

12

Dash

RONAN LINGERS IN THE ALLEY, HIS BIKE RUMBLING AND helmet on, but doesn't make a move to hit the road. I watch him from the driver's seat of my car, shaking my head at his stubbornness.

He didn't want to leave the omega—*Briar*. I don't blame him. Leaving her felt wrong for me too. But I also know that we can't do anything else without speaking to Jasper and Landon.

The sweet girl with the pale blue eyes, round cheeks, and a tiny diamond in her nose that glittered in the starlight stole my breath at first glance. And once I regained it, all I could smell was the hint of a comforting lemon sugar scent that stroked a part of me that I'd forgotten existed. It kicked my heartbeat into overdrive, but compared to Ronan's reaction to her, mine wasn't anything special.

She's clearly his omega. If she were mine, wouldn't I have been all over her too? Historically, time and place have never really mattered much when it comes to scent matches. The pull between us should have been strong enough to shift the entire world beneath my feet. She should be my centre of gravity now, but I'm still anchored to the ground.

Good god, when we get to the house, one sniff of Ronan and

Landon's going to lose his shit. If she truly is supposed to be our pack omega, Jasper will try to get as much information from us as he can.

Our pack is already fracturing, but if this truly goes how I'm expecting it to, there very well might not be anything left of us by the end of the night.

My fingers feel weighed down as I roll down the passenger window and lean over the centre console. "Go home, Ro!"

His face is hidden behind his matte-black helmet, but I know he's staring at me when he keeps his head tilted in my direction and kicks the bike into gear. Clouds of dirt puff up behind him when he spins into the street, the loud purr of his bike drowning out the rest of the noises in the neighbourhood.

I shift the car into gear and follow him, not wanting to risk losing him in case he tries to come back here instead. From what I saw earlier, it wouldn't surprise me one bit if he snuck into the building and found out where Briar lived before standing guard outside of her apartment door all night.

To my surprise, he doesn't try to lose me the entire way home. I keep my distance to not crowd him when he pulls into the driveway behind Landon's missing SUV. The garage door doesn't open for us. I realize why the moment I come to a stop behind his bike.

Ronan doesn't plan on wasting time pulling in around the other vehicles in the garage. Barely waiting for his engine to stop running, he kicks his stand down and hops off the bike, leaving it on the driveway. The black helmet is off in a flash before he's slamming it onto his seat and storming up to the front door.

I park my car and scramble out the door, running after him.

"Hey, calm down, Ro. Maybe tonight isn't the right time to talk to him about this," I suggest.

He ignores me.

"Landon isn't ever going to change his mind on an omega if you come in this hot. Think on it first. Maybe she's not—"

My packmate stops so suddenly I nearly plow face-first into

his back. When he whips around to look at me, his snarl makes me glad I didn't make contact.

"Time won't change who she is. Not to me and not to you."

"She's not my scent match, Ronan."

"You're not stupid. Don't act like it."

I clear my throat to hide a wince. "She's not. I'd have been able to tell."

"Maybe you couldn't tell because the only person you could think about was Landon," he spits before leaving me there.

I don't make it three steps after him when the front door opens and Jasper steps outside. There's a smudge of what I hope is dirt from his temple to the edge of his jaw as he comes face to face with a pissed-off Ronan.

Dread pools in my gut. They're so close, and Ronan might as well be wearing the omega's slick on his skin with how strong her scent is on him. It's left a trail down from the driveway to the house. One whiff will be all it takes for Jasper to lose his mind if she's—

Ronan tears past him, shoving his way into the house and out of view. I jog after him and pass through the doorway without Jasper blocking the way.

"Where's Landon?" Ronan grits out.

Jasper is at his side now, unmoving. I hold my breath, mentally preparing for the shit storm that's brewing as he grips Ronan's shoulder and fists his shirt to haul him closer.

"What is that?" he groans, a stuttered, rough purr kicking up in his chest.

Ronan lets him paw at his clothes, their height similar enough that they're nearly nose to nose. I inch toward them, trying to keep my steps as silent as possible. While we do get classes on omegas in school, we're not exactly taught how to handle shit like this. I assume interrupting them right now isn't the best course of action.

There's a wildness to Jasper now as Ronan tilts his head and bares his neck, welcoming our packmate to get more of the omega's scent into his lungs.

"It's what you think it is," he grunts.

His pissed-off stare finds me over Jasper's shoulder, attempting to pin me into place. I don't stop moving.

"Where is she, Ro?" Jasper asks, curling his fingers into his shoulder while he attempts to pull himself away. It doesn't work. "*Who* is she, and why isn't she here?"

His voice is weak, the words spoken with a plea that cuts clean through me. He's never hidden his desperation to find an omega, but now, hearing him like this, it's painful to not be able to hand him what he wants. It makes me feel like I made a mistake not allowing Ronan to bundle her up and haul her back with us.

"Ask Dash," Ro grunts, standing stiff as a board.

Jasper whips around, and fuck me, the emotion written all over him nearly undoes me. His scent spikes, filling the living room with the comfort of warm, fresh laundry. The most sensitive alpha I've ever met stares at me with a hope so intense he must be able to taste it and waits for me to speak. Suddenly, it's the last thing I want to do.

"Tell me she's outside waiting," he murmurs.

Fighting back a wince, I say, "She's not."

Ronan growls. "She's alone instead. All by herself in the same building my family lives in."

"Why? She belongs here with us," Jasper croaks, a hand shaking as he lifts it to push his dirty-blond hair back. His laundry scent shifts, the sharp bite of leather drowning it out. "Let's go get her. Bring her to the pack house so we can all meet. Why didn't you do that in the first place?"

"Because of Landon," Ronan snaps, eyeing the staircase that leads to the second floor.

Our bedrooms are all upstairs, including Landon's. But I'd bet he's not hiding away up there. When he's home, he's in the basement, busying his mind with another workout that pushes his already fatigued body to its breaking point.

"He made the call to leave her behind?" Jasper asks with a wince.

There's a shift in the air the moment Ronan opens his mouth to reply. I prepare myself for his anger, knowing that I can't blame him for his emotions.

Only the voice that appears isn't his. And I think that might be even worse.

"Who the fuck brought an omega into our house?"

MONTGOMERY PACK

Landon

THE VOICES from upstairs draw me out of the gym. I'm tense, my neck stiff with tension that I can't get stretched out. The tweaked muscle in my knee hurts like a mother right now as I try not to limp.

Last game was shit. I hit the ice more times than I think I have in the entirety of my career. The medic warned me to take it easy, but I couldn't stop myself from heading into the gym the minute I got home from practice tonight. An ice bath will help enough to take the pain away, but I don't know for how long.

Exhaustion has me in the worst mood. I haven't gotten more than a handful of hours of sleep for weeks, and it's wearing on me.

Breathing in, I stumble, the toe of my running shoe catching on the edge of the top stair. I shoot my arms out and brace myself on the walls, my chest caving in. Lust zaps through me, an invisible hand reaching between my legs to squeeze at my knot. I grit my teeth and drop my head forward, muffling a groan by burying my teeth in my tongue.

Fuck, I can't do this anymore. These phantom whiffs of her have kept me up at all hours of the night and distracted me so badly I'm injuring myself on the ice. The omega is everywhere. Even after paying a detailing company thousands to rescrub the interior of my SUV three times, she's still there. In the cracks of the upholstery, the air vents, and, for god's sake, even lingering on the breeze that blows in through the open windows.

I don't know what else to do. Even here, in the empty stairwell two weeks later, I smell her just as strongly as that first and only day. Lemons follow me everywhere, the sweet aroma of warm cookies lingering in my hair and on my skin.

My cock is raw, rubbed to death by my palm three times a day in hopes of easing the insistent fucking pull in my groin and chest that demands I go back for her.

I've lost track of the number of times I've convinced myself that even if I did, the odds of her being there are slim to none.

My desire shows no sign of calming, so I push out of the stairwell, focused on getting the fuck into my bedroom and a cold shower.

I don't make it ten steps before my chest rumbles with a weakly contained growl. The omega's scent is too strong to be memory. It makes my scent gland pulse in time with my knot, my vision darkening around the edges.

She's here. The omega is here.

Unable to fight the pull, I tear into the living room, lip curled to bare my teeth. "Who the fuck brought an omega into our house?"

It's Ronan who turns to me first. The storm in his eyes is vicious, the kind that sinks ships and destroys neighbourhoods. An irredeemable cruelty.

If I weren't so worked up, I'd have taken a step back at his reaction. There's no hope in doing that now. Instead, it feeds into my rage and releases the chains I keep on my dominance, encouraging it to break free.

He doesn't heed the warning I offer him with my delayed response to his feral energy.

"How would you even know what an omega smells like anymore?"

I roll my jaw to hide my initial reaction to him catching my slip-up. "It reeks in here. I could smell whoever she is all the way in the gym."

"Whoever she is," he echoes lowly. "She's our omega."

"We don't have an omega," I hiss.

I'm aware of Dash and Jasper watching, lingering closer to Ronan than they are me. The pang in my stomach is shoved away just as quickly as it appeared.

Ronan doesn't back down. "I do."

"You don't smell it too, Lan? Clearly, you smell something," Jasper says.

A dark laugh from Ronan, taunting me. "Oh, he fucking does. You're bursting at the seams, Landon. How does it feel? Your instincts are screaming at you to go find her. Come here and get a better whiff of it before you try telling us that we can't complete our pack."

"Ronan," Dash warns, planting himself between us now. "Let's just sit and talk. As a pack."

Jasper is silent, and when I look at him, the reason why is obvious. He's always been the smartest of us all. If there was one member of our pack who could have taken the leader position from me based on intelligence alone, it would have been him.

My stomach drops between my knees.

"Have you already met her? Do you know whose scent this is?"

Dash's eyebrows fly up his forehead while Ronan seethes, hands buried so deep into his pockets that he's sure to bust holes in them.

I don't lie to my pack. They're my brothers. My family. Everything I've gone through in my life, they were there to witness. Whenever I've faltered, it's Jasper who ducked beneath my arm and held me up. Ronan's protected me our entire lives. And Dash has listened to every complaint, every rant. He's never judged me for anything. Not once.

But this? This isn't a situation where I can trust Jasper to take his place beneath my arm and hold me steady. Ronan won't ever forgive me for how I treated the omega he already sees as his. Dash's beta instincts keep him more level-headed, but will that be enough to keep him from abandoning me too?

The lie tastes like bile in my throat. "No. I have no idea who this omega is. And I don't want to, either."

Jasper flinches. "You can't possibly know that without meeting her."

"It doesn't matter who she is. She's not for us. We don't *need* an omega," I declare through my teeth.

"It's not only up to you," Jasper says.

I narrow my eyes on him. "You haven't even met this woman."

"No, but I can smell her. And she smells like she could be mine, Lan. Ours."

"Don't let your desire for an omega confuse you. She's not ours."

Ronan laughs again, this time making sure it's loud enough to make us pay attention. My chest caves in when he shakes his head and walks right past me. His shoulder slams into my body with a strength that creates an ache deep in my muscle, not bothering to speak another word.

I stand in place, quieting my alpha when he demands I follow him. To make sure he's okay and warn him to be careful.

There's only one place he's going, and I want to tell him not to go. Our conversation isn't over. If he leaves now, I risk him slipping even further out of my grasp.

I stay silent.

Dash looks in my direction, a plea for me to speak up glaringly obvious in every twist of his features. I've grown so used to disappointing these men that it's almost instinct to do it again.

"You're going to let him walk out of here like that?" Jasper asks, his disappointment a knife in the gut.

"If he wants her, he can have her." Every word tastes like poison.

Jasper doesn't let it go. "You don't mean that. I can see how off you've been recently. You might not think that we need an omega, but we do. The pack is crumbling, Landon. You're just too stubborn to figure out how to go about facing it."

The air is too tainted with her. Ronan's gone, and she's still all I can smell. All I can *think* about.

I ache to follow Ronan so I have even a slim chance of seeing her again. My centre of gravity has been rotated, and everything leads to the woman I don't even know where to find. I've never felt anything so manipulative. My own mind has turned against me, and now, my pack.

"I don't want her. Not now, not ever. Have at it, Jasper. Find whatever it is you're looking for because I want no part in it."

Dash sucks in a sharp breath, and I'm moving, leaving before I have to deal with the repercussions of my words, both with them and myself.

I don't stop until I'm stepping into the shower and cranking the water to ice-cold, letting it soak through my clothes. Teeth clattering, I tilt my head back beneath the spray of water, letting it rain down on my face.

Ronan will be fine. They all will be. I'll protect them the way I always have, and when they realize that the omega they thought they knew was nothing more than the one person who could tear us apart, it'll be me who gets them past it the way I did my father.

They'll get past it because I'll be here. That's the one thing I can promise them.

13

Briar

"Are you aware that phones exist, Bee? I'm this close to taking back your best friend status at this point," Clover threatens, pinching her thumb and pointer finger together but keeping them from sealing completely. "This is the second time you've left me hanging."

"I didn't think that a phone call would have done what I need to tell you justice."

"Well, you're right. But I still would have liked to know sooner."

"The morning after isn't good enough?" I tease between sips of the green smoothie she handed me a few minutes ago.

It tastes like ginger and grass and not like anything I'd prefer to ingest at eight in the morning. Clover is nothing if not overly considerate when it comes to those she loves, though. At least she's stopped "accidentally" buying too many groceries every week and filling my fridge when I'm capable of doing that myself. I shouldn't complain about a green smoothie.

The small café we've met at today is only a block from the office, and with back-to-back deliveries today, I know this is the only chance we're going to have to talk about more than placentas and breathing exercises.

And I really, *really* want to talk about the men from last night. So, I do, and the details of my meeting last night come spilling out.

Clover stares at me blankly, ripping off a piece of her gluten-free muffin. "How are you even here today? You're seriously telling me that you met your scent match last night and you're not at his place banging his brains out already?"

My face flames as I keep my immediate reaction to that suggestion subdued. Considering that I've gone through all of my clean pairs of thick panties already and there weren't any available to wear today, I doubt the old couple a few tables away from us wants to smell just how much I wish I could be with Ronan right now.

"It's more complicated than that," I say.

She frowns. "Scent matches are supposed to be the least complicated thing in the universe. You smell each other, you realize that you're all but fated to be together, and then you fuck until you can't fuck anymore."

"Do you have to say it like that? And so loudly too?"

"It's true, though, isn't it? Tell me that you didn't want to climb the guy's body like a squirrel up a tree. This is monumental news, Bee. You're being too calm about it."

"Ronan, Clover. His name is Ronan."

Even just simply saying his name has an effect on me. In a blink, I have my cardigan off and hanging over the back of my chair to try and cool my spiking temperature.

"Ooh, that's a sexy name," she coos.

It's an innocent comment, but in a matter of seconds, I've got my eyes narrowed and a tension in my muscles that's completely unnecessary.

Noticing all of this, Clover smirks. "See? I bet this wouldn't have happened if you'd slept with him and got those first-meeting jitters out of your system."

"Really? I'd have thought it would have made it worse."

"Maybe. I'm probably not the best omega to be giving you

advice on this, though. I don't know shit about scent matches outside of what we've learned at work. Have you told your mom? I bet she'd know what to do."

I wince, shaking my head as I relax into my chair again. "No. Not yet. There's more to this story than you know."

"Do you want me to beg for more details? Because I will."

"As entertaining as that would be," I start, glancing around the café as it fills table by table, "I don't think everyone around us needs to hear about my love life."

"Fair enough. So, what's wrong with him?"

I huff a laugh. "There's nothing wrong with him, Clo."

"Then what's the problem? It's not his smell, clearly. Does he have a super-small head and a massive body or something?"

"He has a pack."

There's a moment of heavy silence while she swallows and readjusts in her seat. "I still don't see what's wrong. You've always wanted a pack."

"I do. I really, really do. It's not that I'm upset about it. I'm mildly freaking out—in a good way! There's a beta—"

"A beta?"

"Yeah. Dash. I thought . . ." I spin my plastic cup, swishing around the melting smoothie as I force the rest of the sentence up my throat. "I thought he could have also been a scent match."

Clover leans over the table, confusion swirling in her eyes. "He wasn't? I didn't think that was possible. Have you heard of that before? Just one pack member not sharing a scent match compatibility with an omega?"

"I don't know enough about it. He smelled amazing to me, and I know I was busy trying not to lose it over Ronan, but there was a pull between us too. Or I thought there was. He didn't seem to think so."

"How did Ronan react to that?"

"I don't know. He didn't show a reaction."

"Well, it's unusual in the first place to have a pack with only two alphas, but considering one is a beta, maybe that's just how it is," she offers, putting a considerate amount of effort into reassuring me.

It's not that simple.

"There are two others," I blurt out. "Alphas."

Her mouth falls open. "Four?"

"Four," I confirm.

It's almost . . . exciting being able to say that. But I hold off on getting too worked up over it. There's no telling what could happen with the other two men. If they're like Dash, I'm almost too terrified to think about what that would mean.

Scent matches are so easy that they're complicated. Sure, if we allow biology to take the driver's seat in situations like this, there wouldn't even be a second to doubt or worry. Unfortunately, I'm not that type of person. I think too much to simply hand over control to the omega inside of me and present for a stranger at the drop of a hat, scent match or not.

And knowing that I could potentially have three alphas as mine, along with a beta who didn't seem all that impressed with that idea, completely freaks me out. Suddenly, dreaming and yearning for a pack of my own has gotten a lot more complicated.

"And? Tell me about them, Briar. What are their names? Are they hot? Who am I kidding? They obviously are," Clover states boldly.

Pain spreads in my chest. Last night, it kept me up for hours. It's sharp enough to steal my breath as I swallow a hiss.

I work past it, hiding as much of it as possible. This is another complication that I'm learning comes with finding a scent match. After meeting the strange alpha in the restaurant, I've gotten weird phantom aches, but nothing quite like these. I push those ones aside, knowing they're probably unrelated due to their lack of severity. It turns out there was nothing there, even if for a moment, I wondered.

Now, the initial connection I've made with Ronan is trying to bring us back together. My body craves him, even if my mind hasn't quite caught up yet. Every hour that we're apart becomes more draining on me.

"I know their names, but they're strangers," I admit, my voice cracking on the last word.

The emotion that rolls over me is alarming but not even unexpected at this point. I sniffle past the burn in my nose and take an angry sip from my smoothie.

"I'm so confused right now," Clover admits.

"That makes two of us. I didn't have much time to ask anyone anything before Dash was pulling Ronan away from me. He barely managed to give me his number first," I snip, my sadness morphing into anger.

Clover watches me closely, elbows on the pastel blue table. "Have you texted him yet? Maybe he could help with your confusion."

"I don't even know what to say," I admit.

"You could start with hello."

I twist my lips before sighing. "Help me, Clo."

"I know you're nervous, sweetheart, but this is literally something all omegas dream of. You've got this, and I'll be here to help anytime you need me."

Half my mouth lifts into a thankful smile as I hand her my phone and watch anxiously as she types my password in.

"I'm honestly a little surprised that he didn't demand your number before he left. That seems like a very un-alpha thing to do," she says while her finger swipes down my screen.

"I think we were both too overwhelmed to think of much more than what we were feeling. It was a lot."

Her eyes lift from the phone, finding mine. "But amazing, right? Everything you'd dreamed of?"

"He was everything and then some," I murmur, letting my emotions free for a moment.

The disbelief and awe when I saw him and the utter obsession that followed the first whiff of caramel. His intense eyes and the way they fell upon me so gently, like a caress of fingertips. Being in his arms was the safest I've ever felt. One moment with them around me and I knew he'd take care of me forever.

Maybe that's why I'm so scared.

Once I send this first message, I'm accepting what fate has handed me. My life won't ever be the same again.

But . . . hasn't it already changed? It would be a waste to continue pretending that it's the same as it was before last night.

Darting my eyes to the window, I gaze out at the busy street and roll my thoughts around in my mind. A tall, ruggedly built man is standing across the road, startling me. Brown hair buzzed short, he's wearing a similar leather jacket to the one Ronan had on last night, but surely that isn't him. I blink, keeping my eyes shut for a second longer than normal before opening them again.

The man is gone, if he was ever there in the first place. Another pang explodes in my chest as I look back at Clover.

"I can see it on your face, Bri. He must have been something special," Clover agrees, her voice a soft hum.

I tuck my hair behind my ear and prop my arm up on the table. "It doesn't feel real."

"Well, it is. And the quicker you text this alpha, the sooner you'll get to see him again. After we're done with today, you'll need a break. I can't think of a better way to spend it than with your scent match."

"Don't get ahead of yourself," I say, rolling my lips to hide a smile.

"Oh, I'm not. It's called being realistic, sweetie. Now, what do you think about a simple 'hey, hottie'?"

I all but lunge over the table to try and snatch my phone from her. She pushes her chair back with a laugh, holding the phone in the air and out of my reach.

"I'm kidding, I'm kidding," she says through a laugh.

"You better be. Don't embarrass me with this."

"Me? I'd never. Even though it's probably impossible to embarrass yourself in front of a man who would quite literally do anything for you."

"We hardly know each other. Let's try to keep things the tiniest bit realistic here for now."

She narrows her eyes. "I don't like seeing you so self-conscious. Is this because of that asshole alpha at the restaurant?"

I might as well be standing directly in the sun with how quickly I heat up. Only this time, the red on my cheeks is for an entirely different reason.

"How am I supposed to forget that happened? It wasn't that long ago."

"Briar, that guy was a goddamn fool, okay? Honestly, he probably knew he couldn't handle you. One look at you and he was hit with the realization that he's a total loser and would forever suffer with feeling inadequate."

"It doesn't matter the reason. His reaction to me is branded into my brain. I'm pretty sure I'm going to be having nightmares about it for months still."

"No, you won't because you'll be too busy getting railed by your pack. Trust me, in a few days, you won't even remember that douchebag."

Clearing my throat, I nod. The only thing that will come from me continuing to pout about what happened is a lingering sense of shame. Clover's right. I have better things to focus on, even if they share the hell out of me.

"Hand me my phone," I say.

She does immediately. My palm is sweaty as I grip it tight and bring it in close. Ronan's name is simple on the screen but still makes me shiver.

"Just be yourself. You're amazing that way."

My head swims as I type out a simple message and send it before I can delete it.

> Hi, Ronan. It's Briar. Do you have time to talk sometime?

14

Ronan

I WANTED TO COME ALONE.

Fuck me, I almost got away with sneaking away undetected. If Jasper hadn't been so antsy to leave after practice, he wouldn't have caught me on my way out of the arena.

We're only a few days from heading off on an away game, and the only thing I want—the only person I want—is the beautiful omega waiting for me at her place.

Ever since her text appeared on my screen this morning, I've been fighting back the urge to ignore all my responsibilities and go straight to her. But Briar has a job too. She made it very clear that we would meet tonight, and I couldn't risk upsetting her already. I'm already hanging on by a thread; I can't imagine how out of my mind I'd be if she didn't want to see me because I screwed up.

Jasper was never a part of the plan, though.

He sits behind the wheel of his car, tapping his fingers on the steering wheel at a quick, off-tempo beat. We've been lurching down the road every few minutes when he gets restless and presses too hard on the gas pedal. If I didn't hate driving in such a confined space, I would have kicked his ass out of from behind the wheel already.

"Tell me again what she's like," he begs, tugging anxiously at his hair before gripping the wheel with both hands again.

I swallow, staring straight ahead. "Perfect."

"That doesn't help me. I want to know something about her. Something important."

"I don't know anything more than that."

"You didn't try to learn anything when you were texting? Please, Ronan. I can't mess this up. I can't."

Sighing, I shift in the leather seat, making it creak. I'm not lying to him. Everything I know, I've learned from being a fucking stalker.

"She's . . . tiny."

"Tiny? Really, Ronan? Every omega is tiny compared to us."

"Well, fuck. I've only seen her twice."

Well, a few more than two. Technically, I've only spoken to her twice, but I've seen her more than that. Following her to and from work and everywhere in between has become a bit of a habit of mine. It's only so I can make sure she's safe. Protecting her is my job.

"That's twice more than I have!"

"Let it go," I grunt.

"No, I won't let it go. This is my omega we're talking about. It's important that I don't make a fool of myself in front of her today."

"She's *our* omega," I correct him, not bothering to mask my growl.

"Semantics. My point stands."

"You weren't even supposed to come with me tonight."

He whips his head to glare at me. "That narrative isn't helping at all."

"Sorry."

"I'm terrified, Ro."

I ditch the scowl. "Why?"

"What if she doesn't like the way I smell? I've only smelled her on you, but even that was enough to make me sure about who she is supposed to be to me. She could feel differently, couldn't she? Or she could hate the way I look. Or speak. Maybe I breathe too loudly, and she hates loud breathers," he rambles, nerves bringing his tone up a pitch.

"You're freaking out over nothing. I'm pretty sure it's unheard of for only one half of a scent match to feel the pull. And you breathe quietly."

His exhale is strained as he releases a hand from the steering wheel and scratches at his neck. Anxiety doesn't look that great on him. The vein in his forehead is going to explode any minute, and I'm positive Landon's would, too, if he found blood on the seats and had to get yet another vehicle detailed.

"Tell me what she looks like," he says, his voice softer now.

I swallow. "You're going to see her in two minutes."

"Tell me anyway."

"Her eyes are blue. Pale, like if you dropped blue paint on a plate and added too much white. There's a tiny stud in her nose, and her hair is a deep brown, so dark it's almost black like Landon's. She only reaches my shoulders, but she pushes up on her tiptoes to try and appear taller every chance she gets."

That's something I've noticed by . . . keeping an eye on her. Yeah, I'll go with that.

Fucking stalker.

"What else?"

"You can see for yourself. Pull over here."

The car jerks to the right before he finds a parking spot along the curb. The engine runs quietly while he shifts into Park and then grows still in his seat. I unbuckle my seat belt and stare at him, waiting for a sign of life.

"You can't meet her sitting in the car."

He turns to me, eyes fear-stricken. "This is the moment I've been waiting for my entire life."

"I know."

"Do you think she's been waiting for us too?"

"I hope so."

"You get out first. I need a minute," he says, loosely flinging his hand toward the door.

"Thirty seconds, Jasper. You don't need longer than that."

Stepping outside, I hesitate to shut the door, worry bunching in my gut as I stare at my packmate. He blows out a heavy breath and swipes his hands over his already perfectly swooped-back hair. The shake in them doesn't go unnoticed.

Before I can order him to stop fussing, he turns the vehicle off and pushes his door open. In a matter of seconds, he's meeting me on the sidewalk and locking the doors behind us.

"Do you need to text her first to let her know we're here?"

"I was just going to buzz her apartment."

He blinks at me. "Yeah, that works too."

I slip my hands into the pockets of my jeans and try to calm my own nerves. I'm not as open with them as Jasper or Dash are, but that doesn't mean they're not there. At least I know that Briar feels the same about me as I do her. That makes this a bit easier to handle. Jasper has none of that reassurance.

With a slap of my hand to his back, I lead the way up the side-walk. Jasper fidgets with his hands the entire way inside before taking a deep breath and forcing himself to stop.

"You haven't been in her apartment before?" he asks.

The wall of apartment numbers and their call buttons have his attention as he stares at them all. For the first time ever, I don't press on my mom's.

The loud ringing of our call to Briar's apartment fills the entrance as I say, "No. I haven't."

I've only seen her front door a million times. Passed by it, unknowing as to who was waiting behind it.

Jasper nods, appearing relieved. "Okay."

The door in front of us buzzes when it's unlocked. I reach ahead of Jasper and pull it open, waiting for him to pass first.

"You're Jasper Montgomery," I remind him.

He glances at me, smiling softly. "And she's our forever, Ro."

My throat grows sticky. I don't reply, not trusting myself enough to. Instead, I zone in to what we're about to do.

Her apartment door is almost visible from the entrance of the building, but it's tucked slightly off-centre, keeping it a bit hidden. From the street, you can't see too far into the building, and I made damn sure nobody could see Briar coming and going from her apartment door. Not like anyone but me has been perched on the street watching.

Jasper sucks in a few breaths and straightens his shoulders as I lead the way down the hall and to where the door to her place waits. He tucks a finger into his shirt collar and tugs, trying to get some air beneath the fabric.

"You didn't have to wear a dress shirt," I tell him.

"I need to make a good impression."

We stop in front of a wood door with the number 100 on it, and I bring my knuckles to it, knocking twice.

"You will," I assure him.

He nods jerkily and stares at the door, waiting. "She knows I'm coming, right? You told her it wasn't just you?"

"Not exactly."

He gapes, turning his entire body to face me at the same time the door opens. Briar appears in front of us, eyes clear and bright, cheeks the slightest bit red. Dressed in a pair of straight-legged jeans and a shirt cropped just above her waist with the hem frayed, she stares at the both of us, taking in our presence.

"Hey, Petal," I rumble, keeping my hands hanging loose at my sides instead of reaching for her like I ache to let them do.

Brown lashes flutter as she tucks her lip in between her teeth and focuses on me. The scent dampener in the vents hides the full blast of her lemon and cookies, but being so close to her home offers me a tease of it. I breathe it in, relieved when I feel that same tightening in my gut that I did the first two times I was this close to her.

She rolls her lip, bringing more colour to it as she says, "Hi, Ronan."

The hands she has folded in front of her are pressing hard into her belly. A nervous tell, maybe.

Slowly, her eyes flick to the right before expanding in size. Still the same beautiful blue shade, they focus completely on Jasper, raking up and down his body like she's trying to burn him into her memory with only one glance.

"I'm Jasper," my packmate exclaims, his face redder than a fresh burn. He's leaning toward her, stealing the space between them inch by inch, almost unknowingly. "You're Briar. Our omega—I mean, you're *an* omega. My scent match."

Briar drops her eyes for half a second, laughing so softly I almost miss the twinkling noise. When she looks at Jasper again, she's grinning at him.

"It's nice to meet you, Jasper. I am an omega. And you're an alpha."

I press a hand to his chest when he rocks forward on his toes. "Can we come inside?"

"Oh! Yes, of course," she says, stepping back to make room for us to slip past her.

Jasper follows me, nearly tripping over my heels. I'd laugh at his overeager attitude if I weren't so on edge with the lack of Briar's scent. Being so close so soon after finding her and having scent blocker scratching at my nose unsettles me. At Mom's, the lack of scents doesn't bother me. But here? I want it everywhere. Hers and mine. Jasper's too.

It doesn't feel fair that he's meeting her without the same openness that I did, either. They can't smell each other properly yet.

I step into the small apartment and frown. It's cluttered with her furniture, not one specific piece having enough space. They're all high-quality, probably nicer than the stuff we have at home.

The fridge is old and yellow, and the tiles in the kitchen are peeling up at the corners. It looks like she tried to DIY some renovations in the kitchen but didn't finish entirely. A strip of greenish-brown granite cuts through what should be a butcher-block countertop, and one of the silver knobs on the cabinets has fallen off, revealing the brown paint around the screw hole where the rest is white.

Colourful magnets hold up an assortment of photos and a brightly filled-in calendar on the fridge. I want to read what she's written on it, but I'm pretty sure that would cross me fully into stalker territory, and I'm already too close to that.

"I should have told you I wasn't coming alone," I say, twisting away from the fridge.

Briar rushes around the living room, picking up and fluffing all the thick accent pillows on the couch. Her exhale is forced when she finally leaves the decorations alone and adjusts her shirt, tugging at it when it rides up.

"It's okay. I need to meet everyone eventually, right? I'd prefer to do it now. Do either of you want anything to drink?"

Jasper's swallow is audible. She passes by us in a flash, her energy all over the place. The intensity in the way Jasper stares after her is like looking in a mirror. He hasn't even gotten the chance to touch her, and he's ready to hand her his heart.

"I'm okay. What would you like to drink? If you give me a tour of the place and tell me where you keep your glasses stored, I'll get you something. You don't serve us, Briar," Jasper says, grabbing hold of himself enough to follow her.

My alpha demands I join them, but I don't. I grit my teeth and press my back against the wall instead, thinking of my pack-mate and what he needs.

I've had my time—for now. He's already here, anyway. It's only fair I share our omega for a few minutes.

**MONTGOMERY
PACK**

Jasper

BRIAR.

Her name is as perfect as she is. The way it falls off my tongue has my skin tingling and the hairs on my arms rising. She spins to face me in the kitchen, causing a burst of lemon to pass between us. I grip the countertop for balance as my knees wobble, balance non-existent.

"You don't have to get me anything, Jasper. This is my house, and I'm capable of serving guests," she argues with no real venom in the words.

"I don't doubt that you're capable of doing anything you want to."

Surprise flicks across her face, and I think about that too much. What did I say that was so surprising? Has she been told the opposite?

"That's nice of you to say," she murmurs.

With my fingers still clutching the counter, I hold her stare. "I know this is sudden. Really sudden. Ronan should have let you know that I was coming with him so you didn't feel bombarded. You've already opened your home to him, and I don't want to overstep. I'm a stranger to you."

"I can't smell you in here. Not very well."

I furrow my brows. "Do you . . . want to smell me?"

"Don't you want to smell me? You're just going off a hunch here, aren't you? Hoping that you'll like me because Ronan does?" she asks.

"I'm already familiar with how you smell, love."

"How?"

"Ronan came home filling the air with your sweet lemon and warm cookies. I knew right away what you were to me. Who you were. The only thing I don't know is if you want me the way I want you."

I'm more than aware of how biology works for us. Scent matches are a rare and beautiful thing, but omegas themselves are something precious. An alpha will stop at nothing to be the one whom the omega decides is perfect for their pack. Now add in a scent match, and there was never a chance I wasn't going to declare this perfect, beautiful omega as mine. I've spoken to her for five minutes, and I already can't stand the thought of leaving without her.

How Ronan did it, I'll never understand. And how Dash can deny what I know must be there somewhere . . .

Landon is something completely different altogether. He refuses to accept her without even a single glance. The past he's tried so hard to forget is damaging his future, and I wish I knew how to shake some sense into him.

We need Briar, whether he and Dash are ready to accept that or not. She's the gravity that could realign our scattered pieces, and now more than ever, I worry what will happen if that shift doesn't start.

Briar's gaze is heavy, thoughtful as she stands across from me. The silence is nearly too much with all the chaos in my head, but I'd suffer beneath it for hours if it meant I could stay this close to her.

"Do you want to step outside on the balcony with me, Jasper?" she asks, almost in a whisper.

"You have a balcony down here?"

"It's not a balcony as much as it is a small dug-out patio, but I like to think it still counts. And there isn't de-scenter out there."

I nearly combust. "Yes, I'd like to join you on the balcony."

"It's this way, attached to my bedroom for some reason," she explains, moving to slip by me.

I zero in on the lack of space between us as I forget to step back, blocking most of the walkway. Briar notices too, but not until she's already attempted to pass. With her back pressed against the counter, she stares up at me, her throat slightly exposed. My shoulder is right in her face as I accidentally trap her.

My heart jumps, lodging itself in my throat when she reaches out with a hand and lightly touches my back. In a blink, all my blood rushes to press against the skin beneath her fingertips, making it come alive in a way I've never felt before. She might as well be branding me, claiming me with a simple touch.

"Jasper," she whispers, pressing her front closer to my side as if pushed by an invisible hand.

Her scent is trapped in the apartment, subdued but not invisible. The ballooning of her pupils comes a second before a fresh wave of shortbread cookies hits me. It's somehow more decadent, sweeter. Strong enough to completely cut through the scent blockers that I want to stop blowing into this apartment immediately. My alpha snarls at her scent, knowing without a doubt what it is.

Our omega is perfuming for us.

15

Briar

It didn't take smelling Jasper to recognize who he was. Just like the first time I saw Ronan across the yard outside the building, I knew he was mine. Call it intuition or omega instincts, but there was no mistaking that ruthless yank in my belly that seemed to connect us.

Jasper, with his mossy green eyes, blond hair thick with streaks of brown throughout that make it appear a shade darker than it actually is, and a warm, comforting aura to him that immediately makes me feel at ease, is perfect. His soft voice, which I have no doubt could comfort even the most terrified omega, strokes delicate fingers down my spine, urging me closer.

It's our close proximity that short-circuits my brain. I reach for him on instinct, too busy contemplating the quickest and easiest way to turn around and present for him in this tiny walkway to think properly. Feeling the strong muscles in his back makes everything *so* much worse. Yes, he's tall and broad, but I didn't expect him to feel so . . . hard.

I release a weak breath and whisper his name, feeling my head cloud, thoughts scattering. My scent grows thicker in the small space as I shiver, drawn closer to him. I'd give anything to smell him right now. To turn him around until we're chest to chest and pull myself up his body, bringing my nose to his throat.

A tight, gruff puff of air escapes him before he's twisting, a hand moving to grip the countertop directly beside me. His pinky brushes my hip, sending a wave of arousal pulsing through me. I blink up at him lazily.

I need him. I need both of them.

A dull ache grows low in my belly as slick fills my panties. The scent of warm, clean laundry manages to swirl around us before a sharper bite of leather appears. I whimper without thinking, my first whiff of his scent sending me into a tailspin.

It's Jasper. *My* Jasper.

A purr rattles in my chest as I breathe him in, leaning away from the counter to smush us together. He groans when I wrap my arms around him, dipping his head to bury his nose in my hair.

Everything feels stronger today than it did when I was in this position with Ronan. I've been alone without him too soon after we met. Everything is more intense now, a storm of desire trapped for days with no escape.

Jasper brings a hand to my spine, stroking a hot line up to palm the back of my neck. "You smell so good. You're perfect for us. We're pack."

I moan at his words, rubbing my cheek against his sternum, marking him. He doesn't so much as sway when I press against him, searching for more of his scent and growing frustrated when it's not as strong as I need it to be. The blockers in the air are wrong. They make my skin itch where it should be buzzing.

"I want more," I demand, pushing up on my toes to chase the tease of his scent. "Please."

"Want more what, love? Tell me what you need."

My chest tightens, a swell of emotion suffocating me as I paw at him. "I need more of you. All of it. *Please.*"

I can't smell Ronan, but I know he's joined us. His energy is dark, but I welcome it with open arms, knowing I'm safe, protected. It should be mortifying to be having such a visceral reaction so quickly to these men and to be able to trust them the way I do, but that's what biology does. It takes control when our mind flounders, second-guessing the good things we've been handed.

And these two alphas are the *best* things.

"It's the de-scenter," Ronan grunts, his voice tight. "She can't smell you properly."

My eyes burn as I whine, "You either."

Ronan starts smoothing his hand down my hair. Through heavy-lidded eyes, I examine the strain pulling at his features. His eyes are so dark they're nearly black as he watches me.

"The balcony is in the bedroom, right, Petal? Can we take you there?"

I nod, gripping Jasper tighter. He must have heard what I said to Jasper earlier.

"Yes."

There's a moment of silence while the two men stare at one another, a silent conversation happening that I can't listen to. I trap a moan in my throat when Jasper shifts and a thick bulge brushes my belly.

"Hold on, love," he murmurs before I'm being lifted into his arms.

It's unnecessary, but the move pleases my omega. I clutch onto him and nuzzle against his shoulder while we move through the small apartment. My bedroom door is already cracked open when Ronan pushes it aside and hangs back, waiting for Jasper to bring me in first.

As soon as we've passed him, Ronan's heading for the balcony door. He slides it open with one pull while Jasper sets me down on the bed. I close my eyes and wait for the breeze to come.

"Is that better?" Jasper asks, a cautious note to his tone.

I keep silent as the fresh air blows through the room, clearing out the de-scenter enough to give me what I want. The full force of their scents hit me a second later, yanking a needy noise up from deep in my chest.

Words are too hard. Leather and whiskey mix with that soft, warm laundry scent before a hint of coffee swirls around it. My eyes roll back behind my lids as I curl my fingers in the comforter beneath me and gasp, that low pitch of arousal flaring into an inferno beneath my skin.

A gravelled noise appears in front of me, and I swallow, desperate to get a hold of myself. My heat isn't here. This is something different. A tease of what's to come now that I've found them.

It's a good sign.

"What do you need, Petal?" Ronan grits out.

I breathe deeply. "Can you . . . touch me?"

They don't reply with words. Instead, I feel their fingers on my arms, my shoulders and legs. I soak my panties further, perfume pluming in the room.

"You're in control here, Briar. Tell me what you're feeling. What's happening?" Jasper asks.

Their lack of omega knowledge pleases me. It means they don't have much experience with them. I could be the only one.

"I think it's a heat spike. Scenting the both of you together has triggered something," I explain, my speech thick with lust.

Ronan grunts. "So that's why you smell so fucking good."

"Would you prefer us to go, love? We can give you privacy," Jasper offers.

I snap my eyes open, shaking my head furiously. A sharp yearning punches straight through me. "Don't go. I just need . . ."

Ronan licks his lips, expression tortured. "You need to find release. Will that help? Will coming help the spike?"

Oh, my god. I moan loudly, my muscles turning to jelly.

"This wasn't supposed to happen yet. We haven't spoken at all," I whimper. "You don't have to do this."

"We have time for all of that. Right now, you need to find

relief. Do you want us to help you? We won't touch you without permission," Jasper declares.

"Yes! Yes, I want you to help. Please, touch me. Help me before I go up in flames."

They pounce.

Jasper settles on the bed beside me while Ronan gathers me in his arms and lifts me before taking my spot. I know before we even start that this will be quick.

Now seated on Ronan's thick thighs, I wiggle, anchoring my arms around his shoulders. They don't make a move to shed their clothes and instead focus on mine. Ronan brings his face to rest against my throat while Jasper plucks at the button on my jeans and slides the zipper down. I expect them to be pulled off completely, but Jasper only wiggles them down enough to make some room near my groin.

My heart flutters with both excitement and nerves as I continue to burn. The ache in my belly grows in strength, making me hiss. I drop my head and watch what's happening between our bodies.

Ronan's coffee scent sweetens with caramel before I gasp, two curious fingers slipping into the opening of my jeans. It's distracting enough that I don't realize Jasper's begun peppering soft kisses up the side of my throat. I shiver, bucking against Ronan's fingers as they explore my bikini line and blaze further down.

"Still okay, Petal?" the gruff alpha asks, halting his movements.

Jasper sucks gently at the underside of my jaw while cupping my breast over my shirt. My nipple aches against his palm, hard and sensitive.

"Yes. Yes, it's okay," I breathe out.

Ronan's chest rumbles with a deep noise, and then his fingertips are brushing over my clit, never slipping beneath my panties. I cry out at the touch, so overly sensitive that it's almost painful.

"So wet," he rasps.

All I can do is nod. My hips lift, forcing my pussy harder against his fingers. It won't take much to orgasm. I just need a little bit more . . .

Jasper takes my nipple between his fingers and plucks it before squeezing. "You're safe, omega. We've got you."

I let out a high-pitched, pleasured noise and dig my nails into Ronan's back. He applies more pleasure between my legs and starts to roll circles around my clit. My panties are drenched with my slick, no doubt wetting his fingers, but he still doesn't slip them beneath the fabric. It's not necessary.

With Jasper's mouth latched around my scent gland and Ronan's breath on my cheek, I push into the fingers and roll my hips. The orgasm is quick but strong, expelling every last breath from my lungs and weakening me to the point I collapse against Ronan.

He slips his hand out of my pants and curves an arm around my back, holding me steady. Jasper places a lingering kiss on my cheek before pulling back and tucking my hair behind my ear.

I fill my lungs again with their scents. My omega knows we're safe to stay in our alpha's arms, but Jasper wouldn't be included then, and I want them both around me right now.

"I'm sorry," I whisper, slowly peeling myself away from Ronan.

"Don't apologize, love. I think it's normal for scent-matched pairs to feel like this. It's an intense connection being activated all at once," Jasper says.

Ronan strokes a knuckle down my jaw. "Safe to say you're officially pack."

The confident statement makes me feel uneasy. Am I really pack? How is it possible that they're sure about that already, especially when Dash doesn't share the same connection with me that they do?

"What's wrong?" Ronan asks sternly, most likely scenting my anxiety.

I look up, focusing on the soft pink shape of his mouth. He

has perfectly symmetrical lips, somehow made better by the white scar that cuts through the very corner of the bottom one.

"You said there are two other members of your pack. Jasper is one, but so is Landon. And Dash . . . I'm not his scent match. How is this supposed to work?"

Ronan's mouth tips down into a scowl before Jasper takes my hand, flipping it over to trace the lines in my palm.

"We would need to discuss Landon. He's our pack leader. And Dash . . . that's another discussion to be had. All we know is that you're a part of us now. There's no changing that."

"What do we do, then?" I ask.

Ronan tips my chin back with the pad of his finger, forcing my eyes to clash with his. "Now, you tell us everything about you, and we answer all of the questions you want an answer to."

It sounds simple, perfect. All I have to let myself do now is trust that when I crack myself open, they'll stay true to their word and keep me forever.

16

Ronan

Briar tucks her legs beneath her body on the couch and hums as Jasper drops a hand to her knee. I take a seat on her other side and lean as close as I can without hovering. The windows are all open now, airing out the chemicals clogging the air even after turning off her vent system. Her perfume lingers in the living room, but it's easier to handle now, her needs sated.

I've never experienced that strong of a physical reaction to someone before, even the first time I was here, racing toward her on the grass. Yeah, I knew it was possible with matches like ours, but to feel it in real time? To have my body physically ache for someone so strongly that it shoved my mind into the back seat the way it did for Briar is wild. Fucking out of this world.

I want to know more about scent matches. Everything I learned at school was only the bare-minimum information needed to make sure we had some semblance of an idea of what could happen for us. The instant attraction, sense of rightness, and desire for a mating mark. Rejection of a match was touched on briefly, but beyond the knowledge that it can be a painful process, I don't remember shit.

What I need to know is whether it's possible for her to only mate half of a pack, and if that's the way things go for us, what will happen to Landon and Dash?

"What do you do for work, love?" Jasper asks, his gentle voice managing to smash through my thoughts.

Briar's hands fall to her lap, eyes glowing with excitement. I make note of her reaction to that question.

"I'm a doula. My best friend and I run a birthing clinic."

"A doula . . . that's a birthing partner, right?" Jasper asks.

"Yes! Clover is an OB/GYN, so she handles the babies and all the medical whatnot, and I focus more on the moms and their experience. Childbirth can be as traumatic as it is beautiful, and the omegas we help often don't have any form of support with them. That's where I come in."

"Incredible," I muse, pressing my arm against hers. "You like doing that?"

She sets her chin on her knee and looks at me, a tiny smile on her lips. "I love it. And I should mention that if any of you want me to quit to stay at home, I won't do it. I want to be clear about that now."

Jasper's mouth drops as I stiffen, adjusting my position until my spine is snapped straight.

"We'd never ask that of you, Briar. If you love what you do, then that's that," Jasper says.

"Really? You don't want your omega to stay at home and pop out a million babies for you?" she asks quizzically.

I scoff. "No."

"What Ronan means is that no, we don't need you to do that. If babies were ever a possibility, we would figure it out, but you'd never have to quit your job. Seeing you happy is all I want. All we *both* want," Jasper adds with a quick roll of his eyes in my direction.

She tongues her cheek, inspecting the both of us as if she's trying to detect a lie in what we've said. Or more like what Jasper's said. I'm not the best with words.

What feels like an hour later, she relaxes her stare, seemingly believing him. "Alright, good. What do you two do for work?"

"We're on the Rayton Riptides hockey team," I say, stretching my arm along the couch behind her. "Do you watch hockey, Petal?"

"Uh, you mean, like, the NHL team, the Rayton Riptides?" she squeaks.

Jasper laughs, squeezing her knee. "Yes, the NHL team."

"Truthfully, I don't watch hockey, but my dads do. They're not Riptide fans, unfortunately. I've heard more complaining about a Landon Montgomery and his special treatment than much else when it comes to that team. Are they right about him? I assume this all makes him your Landon?"

Jasper does a better job of hiding his amusement than I do. A gruff laugh escapes me instantly, filling the apartment. My throat aches from the power of it.

"Oh, fuck. He'd have a fit hearing that from you," I manage to say.

She flushes. "That's a yes, then?"

"Yes, he's our Landon," Jasper confirms.

I play with a strand of her hair where it's draped behind her shoulder. "The special treatment isn't always true. That's just the complaint everyone who hates the team uses instead of accepting that their favourite team isn't as good as we are."

"He's the son of one of the greats. It puts a target on his back," Jasper adds.

"I can understand that. Does the attention bother him?"

I pause for a beat, registering her question. Jasper stares at her with a depth that I know borders on obsession. I feel the same way.

She's a miracle.

"I don't think any one of us has asked him that in a long time," he murmurs.

Briar frowns. "Well, someone should. I don't have a lot of

experience with famous parents or unholy expectations, but I assume it's probably really suffocating."

"Maybe we'll keep it for you to talk to him about," Jasper suggests.

She nips at her cheek, eyes dropping to where Jasper holds her knee. "I don't know if that's really a first-meeting topic. He isn't interested in having an omega, right?"

"He doesn't think we need one," I say tightly.

"And Dash? He's close to Landon?"

Jasper answers the question. "Dash cares the most about the pack dynamic. He's stubborn enough to put aside his desire to have an omega in the pack if it means Landon doesn't leave."

"And you think Landon would leave if I became pack?" she asks, her voice timid as her scent sours.

I trap a growl in my chest, thinking twice about what I should say next so I don't scare her away with a declaration she isn't ready to hear yet.

Jasper fills my silence, jumping in with his well-thought-out words.

"He wouldn't leave. Landon is pack leader, and he loves us more than he'll ever admit. He has his reasons for why he's so reluctant to find an omega, but once he meets you . . ." He pauses, tipping the corner of his mouth up into a soft smile. "He'll change his mind. It will be impossible for him not to."

"That's if he recognizes me as a scent match," Briar whispers.

I cup her shoulder, pulling her to lean against me. She moulds into my side like she was always supposed to be there.

"He will, Petal."

"How can you be sure? Dash—"

Jasper shakes his head, tongue slipping along his bottom lip. "Dash is wrong."

The light chuckle that escapes her releases some of the tension in my muscles. I let loose a huff and nod at Jasper.

"I wish it was that easy," she says.

"It can be. Give us a chance to prove it to you," I all but beg.

Jasper spreads his fingers on her knee, touching more of her leg. "Come to the house and meet them properly. We can do this the right way and make the rest of the decisions from there."

"Landon will be okay with that?"

No. But there's not a fucking chance I'm letting him ruin this for us all. "Yes. He'll be okay with it."

Briar unfolds her legs and drops her feet to the floor. She folds her hands in her lap, fingers tapping her knuckles. While she's looking down at them, I meet Jasper's eyes, hoping he can read what I'm thinking.

Landon won't agree to a meeting willingly. Especially not at our home.

He runs an anxious hand through his hair and sighs softly. I know immediately what he's thinking.

We're screwed.

"I'd be up to coming over. At least to see how things go," Briar says, looking up from her hands. Her eyes pass between Jasper and me, looking more shy than before. "Like I said the other day to Ronan, this isn't a done deal. I know scent matches are pretty set in stone, but I don't want to only be with someone, especially a pack, because that's what our biology says we should do. Having done what I do for work, I've seen the negative, painful side of a scent bond, and I refuse to feel pressured into anything. I want a choice."

Jasper nods immediately, rubbing slow circles on her leg. My chest pounds at her bravery and certainty. My alpha purrs in approval, blood rushing to my groin.

"We completely understand. All I want is for you to know that we're very interested in having you be our omega. The final decision will always be up to you," Jasper promises.

"Told you the first time I saw you that I'd court you. I'm still going to do that," I add.

Jasper crosses his ankles and smiles approvingly. "How about we start with dinner on Saturday? Let's say six?"

"I'd like that," she murmurs.

"Until then, you should call your landlord and have him permanently turn off the scent blockers in your apartment. They can't be good to inhale twenty-four seven," I grumble.

"It's easier than taking suppressants. I'd prefer not to have to start again. Especially not . . ." *Now.*

Jasper's brows furrow. "How long were you taking them before?"

"For a while. They made my heats more manageable, but my doctor warned me that prolonged use could cause more damage than they'd end up helping," she explains.

Worry gnaws on my stomach. "My sister's on suppressants."

"You have a sister?" Briar asks, intrigued.

"She's eighteen."

"Well, suppressants are normal for omegas in their most hormonal years. It's the same thing as rut blockers for teenage alphas. I designated at fourteen, and without suppressants, I wouldn't have been allowed within a foot of an alpha. Your sister should be just fine."

I take her reassurance and bundle it deep, using it to calm the protectiveness that I can't ever seem to shake.

"Thank you, Petal."

"You're welcome, big guy. And I will call my landlord. Maybe he can just turn them down a bit so it isn't so overwhelming the next time you come over."

The next time.

A rumble sputters to life in my chest, and Briar giggles, brushing her palm across it. Jasper watches me with an open expression, letting me see the adoration that's swelling inside of him. This right here means more to him than anything else, past, present, and future. Briar has given him the world, and they've only just met.

It's all I've wanted for him, and I'm going to do everything in my power to make sure he gets to keep this forever.

17

Dash

"We don't have to go to this, Lan," I offer for the third time in the last ten minutes.

Ever since he came down from his room dressed in the typical slacks and button-up that his father demands we all wear during dinner, he's been uptight to the max. It's somehow worse than normal but not completely out of character.

He's always standoffish during the nights our attendance is demanded at his parents' home. I think we all hoped it would get easier to go spend the evening with his parents as we got older, but nope. The tensions continue to run high.

Landon adjusts his tie, staring at his reflection in the hall mirror. "If we don't, I'll hear about it for weeks. It's easier to give him what he wants."

"At whose expense?"

"Not his, that's for sure," Jasper says, joining us with a tinfoil container of what I really hope are his famous potato skins.

Ronan steps into the hall, still refusing to dress up for these dinners. Every inch of him screams *fuck you* and *what you think you can make me do.*

"The only reason he wants us there is to warn us not to embarrass the Riptide legacy."

"The Montgomery name comes with a reputation. The world is watching," I mock, dropping my tone to match Dean Montgomery's.

Landon tongues his cheek before turning to face us. The bags beneath his eyes are almost staggering. His black hair makes the pale shade of his skin appear worse, almost sickly.

"When's the last time you slept, Lan?" Jasper asks.

"I don't remember."

"Yeah, we can see that," I mutter. Concern jabs deep. "Are you sure you don't want us to stay home? Last chance to change your mind."

He lifts his keys and jingles them around. "We're going. I'll sleep later."

"I'll make some tea when we get home. It might help," Jasper says.

Landon acknowledges the offer with a weak nod and turns his attention to Ronan, staring him up and down. His following sigh is heavy.

"He'll hate those fucking jeans."

"Good," Ronan says bluntly.

Lan lets it go, knowing there's no point in pushing. "I don't want to be late."

We make it out the door and on the road quickly, not wanting to push him right now. It's only been a few days since our blow-up about the omega, and things are still tense. Tonight is the first time we've all been together like this since Landon walked out the door instead of facing what's happening to the pack head-on.

It's concerning, to say the least. Landon isn't the guy to run away from his problems. There's a reason he's pack leader, and it isn't just because he's the biggest of us all and can command nearly any alpha to follow his directions with a single bark. He has the natural leadership needed for the position, and we've all witnessed it more than a dozen times.

The topic of an omega has ruffled him more than he's letting on, and I'm feeling hopeless to fix everything.

We don't speak much on the drive to Landon's family home. I'm no alpha, but even I can smell the lingering cleaning products on the upholstery. Even with Landon's window rolled down and the sunroof open, it refuses to disappear. Whatever happened to make him take such drastic efforts to clean this thing is beyond me. By the time we're pulling around the circle driveway, I'm pretty sure my face has windburn.

"Last chance to back out," Jasper says, leaning up between the front seats.

Landon turns off the engine and pushes his door open. "We won't stay long."

"Works for me. As long as I get some of Jasper's potato skins, I'm good," I say.

Jasper shakes the tinfoil container. "Potato skins? These are stuffed mushroom."

"Wash your mouth out with soap, Jas. You wouldn't dare."

"Back me up here, Ronan. You saw me cutting them this morning, right?" Jasper asks the grumpy ass leaning against the SUV.

"Yeah. Smelled 'em too."

"Don't joke about potato skins. Especially not in the same breath as the mere mention of mushrooms. In what world does eating fungi sound healthy for anyone, let alone humans?" I ask, shivering.

"Pretty sure wolves eat that shit right from the ground," Ronan grumbles.

I tug my brows together in disgust and blink at him. "It's a good thing we're not wolves, then, isn't it?"

Jasper chuckles, cracking the corner of the tinfoil just enough to expose the cheesy potatoes inside the container. The smell of bacon and green onions makes my stomach scream for food.

"No mushrooms here, Dash."

"Are you done?" Landon asks, his tone exposing how stressed he is.

It sobers the rest of us up.

"We're right behind you," I say.

He exhales, taking another look at the three of us before leading the way to the front door. His stepmom is already there waiting for us.

"Boys! Come, come. You're right on time. Dinner's just about done," she exclaims, ushering us in one by one.

Landon bundles her into his arms for a hug, lingering there while we shuffle around the grand foyer. "Hey, Daph."

The tiny omega with a short red bob and lipstick to match squeezes him tight before pulling back to look him over. Her worry is to be expected. We all feel it.

"You look terrible, Landon. Let me feed you before you wither away to nothing. Have you been eating at all recently?" She flashes quick looks at the rest of us with enough ire to make us straighten. "What use is a pack if you don't look after one another? Hmm?"

Jasper offers a soft smile. "We've been trying, Mrs. Montgomery."

"Stubborn male," she chastises her stepson. When she releases him, Landon stares down at her sheepishly. "To the dining room. We'll eat immediately."

Her soothing lavender scent runs rampant through the extravagant home, burying all hints of Landon's father. For as long as I've known my packmate, it's been this way. I think it relaxes everyone. Landon's father smells angry all the time, even when he isn't.

"Christ, Landon. You look like you need a coffin to sleep in," he grunts, appearing at his wife's side dressed in light grey slacks and a deep green polo that coordinates perfectly with her dress.

Landon settles between me and Ronan, saying, "So I've heard."

"How is your knee?"

"Good as new," Landon lies.

I've seen the limp, and yeah, I've kept up with his physiotherapist. Sue me.

His knee is recovering fine, but it's nowhere near good as new, especially with how hard he's pushing himself.

His dad jerks his chin. He inspects the rest of us and scowls when he sees the ripped jeans Ronan chose to wear tonight.

"I see the dress code has gone . . . *forgotten*, once again," he notes.

Ronan grows taller somehow. "All of my slacks were dirty. My apologies."

"Let's not worry about that right now. Scoot into the dining room and sit for dinner," Mrs. Montgomery orders.

I pat Landon's back when he leads the charge, Ronan falling into pace beside him. Jasper tugs at the collar of his shirt and walks on my right.

Landon's father doesn't wait for us to sit before speaking again. "Congratulations on the last win. It was too close, though. Florida doesn't have the power to be outshooting you by fifteen shots. If it weren't for Dash, you'd have lost that one."

It's not a compliment, and I don't take it as one.

Ronan's the first to sit at the long table. It's already been set with expensive china and glasses topped with chilled water. The plum-coloured table runner matches the fabric napkins and curtains hung over the tall windows. The properness of this place is intimidating but also just. . . unnecessary.

Our pack is the opposite of all of this.

We don't even have a matching set of plates at home. Everything has been collected randomly over the years. Ronan's mom is the only reason we have any semblance of decent furniture because she took his bank card the day after we bought the house. It's still hard to believe that Landon grew up here in this mansion fit for royalty.

"Tomorrow is a new game. We'll work out the kinks," Jasper says, taking the spot on Ronan's left.

I find my usual seat across from him while Landon sits beside me at the furthest place from his father. Mr. Montgomery lowers himself in the head chair across from where his wife will sit.

If there's one person who that guy loves enough to warm even slightly, it's Landon's stepmom. The omega he found after losing the one who put on the greatest act in history.

"I sure hope so. Everyone expects the Riptides to make it to the Stanley Cup finals. There's a lot riding on this season," he says.

Landon pulls his chair in, clearing his throat. "We'll do it."

A nod of acknowledgment from his father. "That's right. And you'll start sleeping. You've been slugging down the ice every game."

"I'm fine. Just feeling a little under the weather."

I whip my head to look at him, frowning. "Why haven't you mentioned anything?"

His jaw tenses. "Because it's nothing. Some aches and pains. I'll survive."

Jasper and Ronan look at me at the same time. The concern from earlier doubles in size.

"You should make an appointment at a clinic. Something could be really wrong," Jasper suggests.

I nod along with him. "When's the last time you went into a rut?"

He rolls his shoulders out, unease tugging at his features. Quite possibly because I just asked him about a rut in front of his parents.

Oops.

"I don't remember."

"See the team doctor, Landon. Your health is important. The team needs you," Mr. Montgomery chimes in.

I have to stifle a groan at his lack of awareness. The last thing that matters right now is hockey.

"Who's ready to eat?" Mrs. Montgomery sings, bouncing into the room with platters full of food.

She starts setting everything down on the table around Jasper's tinfoil container. The smell of ham, potatoes, and mac and cheese fills the air, ramping up the grumble in my stomach.

"Why didn't you ask me for help with this, Daph?" Landon's father scolds lightly, disappearing out of the dining room, more than likely in search of more food.

Mrs. Montgomery rolls her eyes. "Such a busybody, that man."

"You deserve the help," Landon says, his voice low.

"If I had someone help me with everything I did, I'd grow bored. Taking care of all of you is what makes me happy."

Landon's smile is genuine, bigger than I've seen it in weeks. "I know."

"Well, dig in. Your father will only find fresh rolls and vegetables left in that kitchen. Everything else is already here for you. There are no bonus points for waiting any longer," she says with a wave of her hand.

"Fine. But only if you sit and dish up first," Landon barters.

While reluctant, she does as he says and makes a show of digging the big metal spoon into the potatoes to take a heavy helping that she probably won't end up finishing. Only once she's plopped it onto her plate do the rest of us follow suit.

Landon nods to himself, content with the knowledge that she's taken care of before he's filling his plate. His care for his stepmom is reassuring to see after watching him be so void of emotion the past couple of weeks. The overprotective, caregiving alpha that we've all grown to know and love is still in there, just buried beneath secrets I need him to spill.

The dinner this weekend that we've yet to tell him about may very well be our best chance to do just that. All we've got to do now is break the news to him that the omega he's so dead set on ignoring exists is coming over, whether he likes it or not.

Goody.

Briar

CLOVER BOBS ON HER ROLLING STOOL WHILE TYPING away on the computer. The notes she's taking range from everything to Sadie's everyday pregnancy symptoms to an overview of what she wants for a birthing plan. This is our third meeting together but the first where we're starting to nail down every detail needed to ensure the best delivery possible. She could go into labour any day now.

"How intensive is the restraining order?" Clover asks.

Sadie pats her thighs anxiously. She appears a bit less nervous today than in the previous meetings, but there's still an edge to her that I want to smooth.

"It's strict no contact. No personal visits or even a text message."

"In that case, we'll have extra security monitoring the clinic before, during, and after delivery. Our medical staff here is incredible, so I don't want you to worry about your care at all. If it's okay with you, I'd like to have Briar, myself, and one of our labour nurses in the room during the birth. Then, once you and baby are cleared to go home, we'll continue providing as many visits and checkups as you wish to have for as long as you need them. Do you have anyone to help you at home?"

Sadie stares at Clover, cheeks tinted pink. The glassy look in her eyes calls to my omega, causing me to reach for the hand on her thigh. I take it in both of mine and squeeze.

"That sounds okay. The three of you, I mean. And my mom may come down to help. I've asked a few times," she murmurs.

Clover swallows the anger flashing across her face. "If she's unable to come, I do encourage you to reach out to us. We can work out a visit routine for the first few months until baby is a bit easier to handle on your own. Our home nurses are some of the best in the country."

"I'm always available as well. Anytime you need me, just call. You're not alone in this. Being a new parent is one of the most challenging moments in our lives, and while I don't have any children of my own, I've been privy to quite a few other omegas' parenthood journeys. It can feel very intimidating and isolating, but we're here to remind you that you have us at your disposal. That's what Harbour of Hope is all about," I say, keeping my voice soft but firm enough to get my point across.

"Thank you. That's . . . that's very generous," Sadie breathes out.

Clover pushes closer to us on her stool and crosses a leg over her knee. "I know this most likely isn't a topic you want to discuss, but we do need to give the security team we've called in a heads-up on what they need to expect on the job. They would prefer to hear a briefing from you directly, but Briar and I have spoken to Duke, the team lead, and he has given us the go-ahead to relay the information to him. If you don't want us to do that, we don't have to, but I thought maybe it would be easier for you," Clover says.

Sadie's face blanches. "How much detail do you need?"

"Enough for us to best protect you if need be," I answer, squeezing her hand again.

She exhales. "How many domestic abuse cases have you handled before?"

"A few," Clover confirms. "All of which have been handled differently depending on individual circumstances."

"Thorne is possessive. He believes I'm his property and, since he's the father of my baby, also thinks he has ownership of her. The pack is small. Thorne is lead alpha, and Sebastian follows him regardless of what he wants. Out of the two of them, it's Thorne I worry most about. His temper makes him terrifying, but his ego is what sets him off. Once he sees there's security keeping him from us. . ." She trails off, roughly biting her lip.

Clover nods as I blink past the pathetic burn in my eyes. The warm scent of brown sugar fills the office, meant to calm Sadie but doing the same to me. If it's unprofessional to feel so strongly for the omegas we help here, then I'm as bad as they come. That's who I am, and I won't change for anything. I like to think my compassion makes me a better doula and human being.

There's a lack of empathy in the world right now. Too many people have become afraid to care for others and instead fill their hearts with cruelty. It might be easier to feel nothing, but if that's the kind of person someone chooses to be, I pity the day they seek help from others and are met with the same disregard they offer to those who deserve better.

Caring deeply for others isn't a flaw in your molecular makeup. It's the opposite.

"We'll take care of it, Sadie. You can put your trust in us here. We won't take it for granted," Clover swears.

Sadie smiles slightly. "That's why my brother sought you out."

"Are you safe right now? Have there been any breaks in the restraining order?" I ask.

"No. They've stayed away for the most part."

"What falls into the 'most part' category?" Clover asks, shifting forward slightly on the stool.

"I've seen Thorne lingering across the street from my place, but he hasn't crossed the road or attempted to contact me."

Clover hides her concern behind a well-crafted mask of calm, but I know her better than to fall for it. "Would you mind sending over a picture of the restraining order when you get home? I'll pass it to the security team and have them read over the details for their plans. Starting today, they'll be monitoring the clinic off and on until you go into labour."

If Sadie's alpha is already stalking her outside of her home, it makes me nervous that he'll escalate once she goes into labour. Keeping an alpha from his offspring isn't an easy task, let alone one who's legally required to keep his distance. Add in his tendency for violence, and we need to make sure we're prepared.

"Yeah, of course. I'm going straight home from here anyway," Sadie says.

Clover drops her leg to the ground and leans over her knees, holding Sadie's timid gaze. "I'll have my phone on me every day. I'm serious, if you need anything, you let me know."

"So will I," I add.

"Every day but Saturday," Clover corrects me with a stern look.

Despite my best efforts, my stomach erupts with butterflies at the reminder of my plans. In just two days, I'll be having dinner with my potential pack. The first of what I hope can be a million more to come.

Clearing my throat, I nod, knowing this isn't the time to give details. Looking at Sadie, I say, "Every day but Saturday. *However*, if it's an emergency, Clover will let me know, and we'll both be there no matter what."

"I appreciate both of you being so dedicated. Truthfully, I didn't know what I was expecting when my brother told me that he'd made me an appointment," Sadie admits, rubbing soothing circles over her belly.

Clover beams. "It's what we do. And I'm grateful he knew that."

"Still. I've never been great with putting my faith in other people."

"We're excited to prove ourselves to you, Sadie. You deserve a support system," I say.

"What about a friend? Or two?" Clover asks.

Sadie's eyes widen, betraying her surprise. "I don't expect anything like that."

"I know. That doesn't mean we can't give it a try, anyway. Do you have dinner plans tonight? I can make a mean and clean chicken casserole. Baby girl will love it," Clover says, going completely off book.

I don't remember the last time we invited a client for dinner. It's not a bad thing, just unexpected. Clover has a heart ten times too big for her tiny frame, but she guards it from those she doesn't know well.

"You're sure?" Sadie asks cautiously.

I laugh. "Trust me, she wouldn't offer if she wasn't sure. But she is overselling the casserole."

"Ignore her. I even have a few mocktail mixes I've been needing an opportunity to use," Clover muses.

Sadie keeps a hand on her belly. "Well, in that case, I'm sold."

"Perfect! I have two more appointments this afternoon, so how does seven sound?"

"Seven works for me. Just don't take it personally if I start drowsing off on you afterward."

I watch the pregnant omega smile, proud of Clover for reaching out. "We'll be right there with you. I'll send you a text with Clover's address once we're finished here."

"Thank you," Sadie says.

Clover grips her knees, straightening her spine. "Alright, first, we need to get on with the actual appointment before we get too distracted. If you can get up on the bed, we'll take a listen to baby's heartbeat."

Sadie's expression explodes with interest and excitement. My heart warms at the sight while I stand and make my way to the door. The waddle Sadie has makes me stifle a giggle behind my fist while stepping out of the room.

I'm not needed in here for this part of the appointment, and now that I know we have plans for tonight, I have a one-track mind set on ordering dessert from my favourite bakery.

Baked goods are the key to solidifying any new friendship, and something tells me that Clover won't stop until we've done just that with Sadie.

MONTGOMERY
PACK

THERE'S A VERY distinctive feeling that comes when someone's watching you. Whether it's from afar or only a few feet away, that prickle on your skin and drop of a pebble in your stomach is unmistakable.

As I remove my key from the doors of Harbour of Hope, I know there's someone somewhere nearby with their eyes on me. Breathing in, I slowly adjust my hold on the key to rest between my fingers and slip my hands into my jacket pockets.

Clover left half an hour ago to grab the order I made at our favourite bakery while I offered to stay behind to lock up. We got lucky with not having any emergency deliveries tonight, and I let her go early with genuine excitement. I've never minded staying behind to lock up, and tonight, the lead of the security team we've "rented," as Clover would say, is still here, adding to my ease.

Duke's standing beside me now, his back to the doors and eyes on the street. His rigid posture isn't that alarming . . . right? We've worked with him and his company since we started the clinic, and he's always a bit stoic.

"Everything okay, Duke?" I ask softly.

The mammoth of an alpha with shoulder-length red hair and gnarly scar from his left ear to the corner of his mouth grunts in response to my question. "I'll walk with you to your car."

"Just to be a gentleman, right?"

"Yes."

"You're not selling it very well."

He drops his eyes to me, expression flat. "Let's go."

I nod, sucking in a calming breath. It's probably just a homeless person who's gotten lost. We're only a few blocks from the closest shelter, so it's not that far-fetched.

Scanning the street, I don't see anyone. Not even a stray animal.

"Did you get a chance to look at the restraining order Sadie sent over today? Clover said she forwarded it to you."

Duke hovers a hand over my back without touching as we head for the parking lot. His respectful nature is one the entire team shares.

He picked every member by hand when he first started his company, and they all follow very firm safety precautions considering the work they do around omegas. Duke is the only alpha on the team and is on a constant prescription of rut suppressants. I've seen him go as far as to use nose plugs in a situation where he couldn't replace himself with one of his highly trained betas.

Safety is a priority for us here, and it's a relief to be able to put complete faith in the team of outsiders we've involved in what we do.

Duke keeps his eyes trained forward. "I have."

"And?"

"And I'm starting to draft a safety plan."

"Have you dealt with this before? Two alphas stalking their runaway omega while a restraining order is in place. Should we be worried?"

"We'll take care of it, Briar. You and Clover don't need to worry about a thing."

I huff, releasing the key digging between my fingers. "You know that's not possible, right? We're going to worry no matter what."

"I'll protect Sadie," he says, or swears, rather. The certainty in his tone is steely, confident to the max.

I lift a brow. "Oh, *you* will, will you?"

"We will," he corrects himself.

My car isn't anything special, and I almost cringe when we stopped at the driver's door. I focus on the duct tape keeping my side mirror on. Yeah, one small ding and it just fell off—a total manufacturer problem.

"Keep us updated with the details of your plans, please. Sadie could go into labour any day now, so if you can put a rush on it?"

Duke peers into the back window, checking it before doing the same to the front. "I'll have it finished by tomorrow. For now, keep her vigilant. Remind her that she doesn't have protection when she's outside of the clinic."

"Well, she'll have it tonight while we're with her."

"You and Clover need to take my advice as well."

I frown. "We've never had reason to worry for ourselves before."

"You've also never had these exact circumstances to deal with before. Nor have you made it your mission to befriend an omega seeking help from the clinic."

"Is there a lecture coming, Duke?" I ask, palming my hip.

"No. I'm just making sure you're careful. If either of you ever feel unsafe outside of the clinic, let me know, and we'll get something figured out. The same goes for Sadie."

Surprise swells in my chest. "You're offering personal favours to an omega in need now?"

"Get in the car, Briar."

"Not when this is getting so juicy!"

He pushes forward and opens the door for me, staring pointedly at me to get in. "Now."

"You do know that we pay you, right? It's rude to order your boss around."

"You enjoy my company too much to fire me," he mutters while I reluctantly slip into the front seat.

"Or maybe you just know we're the best ever and that you'll never find a business like this again, so you work your booty off to make sure we don't stop hiring you."

"Sure," he deadpans.

"Don't try to deny it. Have a good night, Duke."

"Stay safe."

He shuts the door and backs up enough to break the spell of safety I was under. Without it, I'm quick to lock the doors and turn the car on.

Unease drips like cold water down my spine as I pull out of the lot and toward Clover's place. For the first time in my entire life, I keep an eye out on the road behind me to make sure I haven't been followed.

19

Briar

Clover's already two mocktails in by the time I arrive.

The giant pitcher of pink juice sits on the centre of her kitchen table as she slips a cheese-sprinkled casserole into the oven.

"Am I allowed to have a real cocktail, or am I also stuck with a mocktail?" I ask, dropping my keys beside the pitcher.

Sadie's already here, too, and from the soft smile she wears while sitting at the table, it's clear she's been having a pretty alright time thus far.

"I think you both deserve a real drink," she says.

Clover spins away from the oven and points lazily at me. "Briar won't agree with you there."

"Don't try it, Clove. We both know you have always done what you want, when you want to. It's what makes you such a force to be reckoned with. I only want you to be safe when you're drinking on your own, out in a place that isn't meant to be safe for us," I say, trying my hardest not to lecture her but sounding exactly like I am anyway.

Sadie takes a sip of her drink before asking, "Has there ever actually been a place meant to be truly safe for us that isn't an omega-specific building?"

"That's a great question. I'm afraid the answer is most likely no. At least, I've never found one." Clover reaches into the cupboard above her fridge and pulls out a small bottle of vodka. "I'll pass on this, but I think you deserve something hard, Bee."

Sadie watches me closely, her expression more open than it has been in the past, but still not to the point where I know she's completely comfortable around us yet.

"What's going on?"

I take the seat beside her at the table and sigh, rolling out my neck. Usually, I'd be open about this sort of thing in this sort of environment, but with Sadie, I don't know what is okay to say and what isn't. It doesn't feel right to talk about an alpha around her, let alone a pack of them, considering everything that's going on in her life.

I'd like for her to be a friend eventually, and starting off that friendship on the wrong foot isn't ideal.

Reading all of that on my face, Sadie adds, "I can handle talking about men, Briar."

"I believe you. I guess I just don't want to overstep. To be honest, we've never done this kind of thing before," I tell her.

Clover joins us at the table, a hand falling to rest on my shoulder once she's set the alcohol bottle down. "The whole inviting clients thing over for a girls' night is probably frowned upon in the professional world. But I can't say that I regret it. Maybe it's just easier for us to say that we don't know what you're okay with hearing about. Give us your boundaries, babe. We want to make sure we can be the best friends possible if you end up wanting that kind of relationship from us."

"I do want that. I don't know if it's obvious, but I'm not the most outgoing person. Friendships have never come easy to me. Even as a kid. I think it's gotten harder in my adult years, though," Sadie reveals, tapping a blunt nail against her dewy glass.

I think there's edible glitter in her drink. A closer look at the pitcher tells me that I'm right. Clover really went all out tonight for her.

"We have more in common than I thought, then. Making friends has never been my specialty. That's always been something I left up to Clover," I say.

Sadie nods, a small smile curling her mouth. "In that case, I guess, my boundaries are only that neither of you treat me like I'm glass. I haven't been easy to break in a long time."

"I have no doubt about that. From the moment you walked into my office, I knew you were strong as hell," Clover says.

Some of the tension drains from Sadie's posture as she settles in the kitchen chair and focuses on me. "It's settled, then. Tell me about why you need a splash of vodka in your drink now."

Clover winks at me before pushing away from the table and busying herself with dinner plates and the silicone oven mitts on the counter.

I reach for the glass already set out on the table for me and fill it nearly to the brim with the glimmering pink mocktail. Before adding the vodka, I take a sip of it. Watermelon erupts on my taste buds, followed by a heavy hint of mint.

"My dear Briar is having knot-related problems," Clover says while I'm busy twisting off the cap of the vodka bottle.

A laugh slips up my throat. "I wouldn't exactly say that."

"What would you say?" Sadie asks.

"I'd say that I'm struggling the most with the only member of my potential forever pack who *doesn't* have a knot."

Sadie's brows shoot up. "A beta's being the complicated one?"

I finish pouring the vodka and set it aside before swirling my drink around to mix it in. Once I've taken the first sip, I answer.

"It's odd, right? I mean, there are problems with the last alpha in the pack, don't get me wrong. He's the only one I haven't met but already know doesn't want me around, which isn't great. I guess I just didn't expect to have the designation closest to us as omegas to be the one who was so . . . standoffish with me."

"He thinks he's not her scent match, regardless of the fact two of his alphas have made it very clear they are. They even went to Briar's place and—"

I cough to cut Clover off. "I think there's a block keeping him —us—from feeling the pull of a bond."

"Which is ridiculous. I know that betas work a bit differently than omegas and alphas, but to ignore a scent match?" Clover adds.

A timer goes on her phone, and she's quick to silence it and pull the casserole from the oven. The cheesy top is now perfectly golden brown and crispy, which will make it a bit easier to convince myself that it's not fake vegan cheese.

There's a cautious touch on my wrist, and I snap my eyes down to stare at it. When I see they're Sadie's fingers pressing against my skin, I offer her a smile, warmth blossoming in my chest.

"What about the other alpha? The other one who's causing problems?" she asks softly.

"I think Landon is closest with Dash, our beta. That could be what's causing so many issues with our bond, but I can't be sure. At least not yet. I'm supposed to go to their house for dinner, and maybe then I'll get more answers."

"Pack bonds are . . . intense. Loyalty is something that can be both a blessing and a curse. I don't have any experience with betas, though," Sadie says.

Clover tugs open a drawer to grab a spatula before attacking the casserole. "All I know is that with or without a knot, they can keep up just fine with what an alpha can offer."

"I'm in the same boat as you, Sadie. Dash would be the first beta I've been with before." I take a long pull of my drink and try and cool my temperature before it can spike. "If that even happens."

Sadie squeezes my wrist before pulling her hand away. "If it doesn't, he would be a fool. The entire pack would be to let you slip away."

"Thank you. That's sweet."

"You're welcome."

"Okay, how hungry are you? Tell me before I pile too much food on your plates," Clover says.

From what I see when I look at the three plates on the counter beside her, she's asking a bit too late. The tower of food on the furthest plate is intimidating.

"I'm pretty sure I could eat a value-size box of Lucky Charms at this point," Sadie states while rubbing her belly.

The stretched material of her shirt shows the outline of her belly button. But it's the movement happening above that tiny swell that steals my breath.

"I think baby likes the idea of that," I murmur.

Sadie follows my gaze and pokes the top of her belly. "Oh, I'd say so. They've been one of my cravings. Well, Lucky Charms and strawberry milk."

"Clove, the baby's dancing right now," I tell her.

"Ah!" She whips around so fast the spatula in her hand falls back into the casserole dish with a splat. "Let me see!"

"You can feel if you want," Sadie offers once Clover's dropped to a crouch beside her. "I think we're past that stage by now. You too, Briar."

Tears prick my eyes as I nod and join Clover. I set a hand beside my best friend's on the area of Sadie's belly currently rippling with movement.

"This is their foot," Clover explains, slowly prodding down the side of Sadie's stomach and to the bottom curve before settling. "So active. Do they do this all the time?"

"Pretty much. It's usually more when I've had something sugary."

"Like Lucky Charms," I note, cracking a smile.

Sadie laughs, light filling her eyes. "And a watermelon mocktail."

"Well, I can't say that they'll be my biggest fan once I've gotten some real food into you. I guess I'll have to be the buzzkill aunt," Clover teases.

Sadie looks at the two of us, something like hope sparking. "I don't think they'll mind. At least, I won't."

A rush of excitement shoots through me. It's probably too early to be making plans with a new friend, but something tells me that Sadie won't be going anywhere. At least not if we have anything to do about it.

She may not have come to Harbour of Hope in search of more than healthcare, but oops. We're more than happy to give her more than that, and soon, baby too.

A night like this makes it hard to worry about my romantic life. It's relieving and exciting and exactly what I needed.

20

Jasper

I enjoy cooking, but it's not a passion of mine. Taking care of the pack, however, is. That includes several things I'm not the biggest fan of but do regardless.

Growing up, my mom worked the night shift, which left me in charge of feeding a pack of three starving alphas when they got home a few hours after she left. Weekends were the only times I ever managed to slip out of the house to do my own thing.

Being raised in a pack household instilled more than a handful of habits in me. A true pack dynamic can't be taught in a classroom or a video online. You learn by living in one.

It's the small things, like nobody eating until all members are at the table, chores being done by everyone and rotating every week, and no singular event or hobby taking precedence over the others, that keep a pack together. I lost track of the number of shinny games and musicals I was taken to during the weekends and over holidays, sometimes back to back to back.

A pack only works as well as the effort put into it, and mine now? It's hardly hanging on.

Ronan is the only one of us who never grew up in a pack. He's had to adapt to the life and open himself up to the changes required to make one work. But as the years have gone on, it's become obvious where the biggest kink has come from, and it has nothing to do with him.

Without an omega, we're stars in our own orbits, drifting without a central force to pull us together. It's hard for a pack to make it work without one, but I didn't think it was possible for us to be affected so deeply so soon.

Tonight could be the ultimate turning point for us. Briar's about to change everything.

"Have you seen Landon?" Dash asks, cracking open his third Coke Zero of the day.

As he stands in front of me in the low kitchen lighting, it's obvious that he's put in more effort tonight than I was expecting him to, considering his "lack of interest" in Briar. Personally, I think this has all to do with Landon and little to do with his beta instincts. The carefully styled hair and fresh shave don't make him appear nonchalant.

"Ronan said he was headed home with him a few minutes ago," I answer, glancing at the timer on the oven.

The homemade pizza is simple, but with how intimidating it must be to meet an entire pack at once, I figured simple was best. She doesn't need anything else to overwhelm her, even if I want to impress her in every aspect possible.

"Did he get lost, then? I haven't seen him since this morning."

"He'll be here."

"We're in for a shit storm when he finds out she's coming and we kept it from him. You know that, right?"

"If we'd have asked, he would have said no."

It's a terrible reasoning. We're betraying him, and I've had to convince myself that it's for a good reason. If he accepts her, it won't matter what we did prior.

My mom would smack me upside the head if she knew I was hiding behind a possibility. I was taught to never do this exact thing my entire childhood. But it feels like the only option I have left.

I'm not allowing Landon to destroy our chances with Briar without at least meeting her face to face.

"You're right, but that doesn't make it any better."

"I appreciate the comforting talk, but I'm not really up for it right now," I say, sarcasm tweaking my tone.

"Sorry. Everything just feels so delicate."

I shove my sleeves up to my elbows, suddenly hot enough to wish I'd worn something with less fabric than this sweater. The scratchiness I could overlook, but the last thing I want is to greet Briar with pit stains.

"It is delicate."

"Especially with you and Ronan being dead set on her already," he adds, attempting to be nonchalant but eyeing me a bit too closely.

"Is there something you want to say?"

His tongue swipes along his bottom lip. "Is she worth it, Jas?"

"Is she worth what, exactly?"

"Destroying the pack. Pushing Landon too far."

A tortured kind of pain explodes behind my ribs, spikes impaling deep. "We're already there. I don't want to hurt Landon, but I can't feel this emptiness anymore, Dash. That omega you're asking about is worth this risk ten times over. You might not feel it yet, but you will. Give yourself the chance to get to know her without the worry of Landon clawing at your back, and you'll be right where I am."

"It doesn't make sense. I'd have felt it regardless," he argues weakly.

"Not necessarily. If there's a block, it could be affecting every-thing, even her scent."

"And how long am I supposed to wait to see if that's the case? Weeks from now? Months?"

"I don't know the answer to that. What I do know is that you're not helping yourself by arguing on his behalf. Landon is a grown man. We chose him to lead this pack, and he needs to show us that we made the right choice all those years ago."

Dash rolls his shoulders, as if attempting to wiggle free of the shackles keeping him stuck in his current mindset. I reach out and palm his shoulder.

"Follow our lead. Try to go into dinner without worrying about Landon. He's going to be angry, and honestly, I'd rather have him angry than how numb he's been recently."

"Fuck, Jas. I don't know how we got here."

"What if this is where we're supposed to be?"

He knits his brows. "What do you mean?"

"Briar was meant for us. Broken or whole, we're her pack. I have to believe that she was always supposed to find us, even if we're not perfect."

"You don't think she'll take one look at us like this and decide we're not worth the trouble?" he asks, a tease of nerves slipping through.

"No. And even if she did, I'm prepared to prove to her that we're still worth it. Are you?"

Dash doesn't look away from me. The glimmer of certainty in his eyes is exactly what I'd been hoping for.

"Fuck, I'm in. But I'm sending Landon straight to you when he realizes what's happening."

I don't hesitate. "I'm ready for him."

Even if ten minutes later, Ronan texts me to let us know they're not going to make it home before Briar gets here. Whether that's a purposeful move on Ronan's part or a sheer coincidence, I'm positive we'll never know. I wouldn't put it past him to have delayed them on purpose. Not when we all knew there was a chance Landon decided Briar wasn't welcome here at all.

Regardless of anything else, it's obvious that this is the worst news we could have gotten. It's my fault we left everything up to the last minute, but I wasn't expecting him not to show at all. There's no telling how he'll react to seeing her here with no warning, even if only a few minutes' worth of it.

"What did Ronan actually say?" Dash asks, leaning over my shoulder to look at the texts.

"Be home in twenty."

"That's it? Ask him why."

I type out a message and send it quickly, my stomach hanging between my knees.

Why? What's going on?

Dash groans. "How long do we give him to answer before we call?"

"Maybe we should do that anyway. It gives us a chance to warn Landon."

"So what? He can demand they go anywhere but home?"

"Everything is going wrong. This isn't how tonight was supposed to happen," I say on a tight exhale.

"Fuck it. Just call, and we'll risk him not showing up at all."

"You sure?"

Dash opens his mouth to reply when my phone buzzes in my hand.

Lan insisted we stop by the rink. Needed to talk to the doc.

"The doctor? Is this about him not sleeping well?" I ask no one in particular.

"Speaking of his lack of sleep, are we going to talk about what he said at dinner?"

My chest pangs. "Which part, exactly? The aches or the sickness?"

"Both. He never mentioned anything to me."

"Me neither, but I'm not surprised. He feels what's happening with us more than we do."

"How do we help, Jas?"

"I don't think it's us who can help."

He pauses, stare heavy. "The omega?"

"She's here now for a reason, Dash. Even if you don't believe that the way Ronan and I do."

"It's not that I don't believe it. I just don't feel the pull like you and Ronan do. I'm not dumb enough to think that if Landon were anyone else, you wouldn't already have her moved in here and attached to your hip. My hesitation isn't anything against her. Maybe things are just different for betas."

I don't bother lying and telling him he's wrong about me and Ronan.

"You know that's not true. Betas have scent matches the same way alphas and omegas do. There are differences, but not ones that big. Just because you don't feel it to the extent we do yet doesn't mean it isn't there. If you open yourself up to the possibility instead of putting all your focus into Landon, maybe you'd be surprised."

"And if I do open myself up and still don't feel it? Then what? Do you have a plan for what happens if Landon ever did accept her and I still don't feel a bond?"

"No, Dash. I don't have a plan for that," I bite out, my frustration bubbling over.

He sighs. "I'm sorry. That was unfair."

"It wasn't unfair. I just don't have an answer for you. I'm still trying to keep us all together right now while also grasping onto Briar. It won't be possible to choose between the pack or her," I say, defeated.

"You have my word that I won't make you choose. Mate or not, she'll be pack in my eyes no matter what happens."

"Do you mean that?"

He clasps my shoulder. "We're family. Of course I mean that."

"We'll convince Landon. Even if it takes weeks," I swear.

"Can you picture us with an omega? God, what do we even do with one?"

I laugh hard enough for it to transform into a cough. "She's not a stray pet."

"That's not what I meant!"

"It's what it sounded like."

He releases me with a shove. "I meant that none of us have been on a date in years, and now we're supposed to court an omega? How are we going to convince her to choose us when we can hardly even keep our pack together?"

"There's a reason omegas are the heart of a pack, Dash. I think if we give this a chance, we'll be surprised with how we come back together."

As long as we can get Landon on track.

Once we do that, we have a real chance at this. At convincing Briar that we're the pack for her the way I know she is.

Briar

I'm going to hyperventilate.

I've never been so nervous for anything in my life. Not when I got my first Pap smear or was called to speak at an omega health conference last year. Regardless of how old I get, my nervous system still lacks the ability to be able to tell the difference between meeting my potential packmates for dinner and being held at gunpoint.

My scent is charred enough to choke me in the small confines of my car. It's a good thing I told Clover not to chauffeur me around today because if she had, there would be one more person to witness how terrified I am. At least on my own, I can pretend to everyone else in my life that I handled tonight with grace instead of buckets of under-boob sweat and a damp neck.

It's silly. Ronan and Jasper have been nothing but incredible to me. They're my mates, and no matter what happens tonight, I have to put faith in their promise to fight for me. I've handled worse people than a doubtful beta and a scorned pack leader.

Sitting out here on this goliath of a driveway in front of the most beautiful piece of architecture I've ever seen doesn't help my burning feelings of doubt or lack of self-confidence, either. I got here at least ten minutes ago, and I know how that must look to them if they're aware of that fact.

A knock on my window has me screaming. My legs kick up into the steering wheel as I smack my head on the roof of the car and reach for the automatic door locks to make sure they worked properly. They did, and the face staring at me in the window isn't one to fear.

Seems they were aware of me being here all this time...

I unroll the window immediately, struggling to catch my breath.

"I'm sorry, love. It's just me. I wanted to make sure you were okay," Jasper rambles, leaning his head into the car.

Shaking my head, I palm my throat and attempt a smile. "It's okay. Thank you for looking out for me."

"You're welcome. Although, I can't say I helped much. Can I open the door?"

"Of course." I pop the lock and inhale the spiced laundry scent of him that comes in on the breeze. "I didn't think I was so jumpy."

The door is out of the way in a blink, and then he's there, reaching for me. My nerves disappear the moment I'm in his arms. He slips a hand beside me to unbuckle my seat belt before I twist toward him and curl my arms around his strong body.

"Is it too early to say that I've missed you?" he mumbles, face finding my hair.

"No. I missed you too."

"I want to know all about how the rest of your week was as soon as we get inside. Honestly, I tried to keep from overwhelming you with texts and calls, but I wanted to reach out so many times," he admits.

"You wouldn't have overwhelmed me. Not at all."

I think we're already past that.

"I'll keep that in mind, then."

When we reluctantly break apart, our arms linger, eyes immediately connecting as the space grows. It would be so, so easy to push up and bring my lips to his for even a brief taste of him. Just this once, I wish I was brave enough to take charge in that way.

With a soft smile, I drop my gaze and shift to turn off the car, successfully cutting the tension.

Jasper lets me take charge, leaning back to give me some more breathing room. I snag my purse from the seat beside me and join him on the driveway.

"This house is incredible," I say while he extends an arm past me to shut my door.

His palm is warm as it settles on my lower back and guides me past the car. "I'm glad you like it. Really, we didn't have much to do with choosing it. Landon's father had his real estate agent send us options shortly after we made the pack official, and we just chose the one with the most room."

"I can imagine with four of you, a smaller place would have felt too tight. None of you minded that you didn't get to fully choose your pack house, though? Aren't alphas really picky about that sort of thing?"

I can't say I've ever heard of a pack allowing someone else to choose where they live. My mom and dads surely wouldn't have gone for it. A pack house is supposed to be a sanctuary of sorts. The place they bring an omega to start a family in.

My skin flushes despite my best efforts.

Jasper spreads his fingers wide, expanding his touch. "That's a great question, Briar. I've never spent much time thinking about that."

I swallow. "The last thing I want to do is overstep, but your pack . . . seems strained. Like it's been that way long before I got involved."

His steps falter briefly. "It has been, and I'm sorry you have to deal with anything less than perfection. This isn't the kind of pack dynamic I ever wished to bring our future omega into, but it's the only one I've got to offer."

The pain lacing the words is quite possibly the worst thing I've ever heard. Jasper stops walking and uses his hold on my back to spin me to face him. His green eyes beg for a pause, for me to offer him a chance to speak before making any assumptions.

He rolls his lips together while staring up at the cloudless blue sky. When his eyes fall back down to me, I don't hide from the openness in them.

"We're not perfect, love. I know you've already pieced that together, but being honest with you is the least I can offer. Our pack dynamic is weak, and our bond is fracturing. It won't be easy to convince Landon to open up to this, and I can't begin to imagine how scary that is for you. All I can promise you right now is that the rest of us are going to be here fighting for you just as much as you'll have to fight for us. And I know it isn't fair to ask you to fight when we've only just met and there's still so much we have to learn about one another. I'm just hoping that at least for tonight, you can give us a chance to show that we're worth the effort. Including Landon."

My omega whines as this alpha lays his heart out for me to either accept or toss across the perfectly trimmed yard. I can't say that what he's asking isn't a lot. It's intimidating as hell. Putting myself out there has never been easy, and given what happened with Greg and the wound left behind that still hasn't fully healed, it's even harder.

But even before hearing everything Jasper's said, I knew I would come into tonight with an open mind. Nothing good has ever come easy for anyone, so why should a scent-matched pack be any different? Just because something is meant to be doesn't mean it shouldn't have its fair share of complications.

His expression is tight, strained with stress and guilt, but as I lift a hand to palm his cheek, he shivers, everything slipping away but startling devotion.

"I want this, Jasper. As crazy as it is, I'm not going to abandon what could be because it will be challenging," I declare.

"And I'm not pressuring you into saying that?"

"No. I knew before I came here today what I was going to do and what I was willing to offer."

He releases a long breath and nods, pressing us closer with the firm hand on my back. "You're incredible."

"You don't know enough about me yet to make that conclusion," I tease, lips tugging up.

There's no tease in his words. "I don't need to. I've known you were one of a kind from the first time I laid eyes on you."

"Oh," I whisper.

He chuckles, sweeping his hand up my spine before bringing it back down again. "Let's go inside. Ronan and Landon aren't home yet, but Dash is waiting. I hope you like pizza."

"I love pizza."

"If Ronan had it his way, we'd have prepared a five-course feast for you, but I figured starting easy might be the better option."

Jasper pushes the door open and makes room for me to walk inside first. My steps are uneven, sandals scuffing the floor as I try to perfect my walk. The strength of the scents hitting me in one thick cloud steals my breath.

Caramel coffee, rich chocolate swirled with peanut butter, spiced leather with an undercurrent of warm laundry, and vanilla, the kind straight from the bottle. My eyes close, a sharp pain clawing at my stomach.

The hard chest pressing against my arm draws a moan from me. I don't have a chance to be embarrassed before Jasper's holding me, allowing me to lean against him.

"I know it's a lot, love. If you need to step outside, we understand," he murmurs.

"No!" I exclaim, appalled at the idea. "I want to be here. I like it. I can smell all of you."

Dash is across from me, lingering on the balls of his feet. The blue in his eyes is so bright I might as well be looking up at the sky as we stare at each other.

"We were hoping the pizza might help mask some of our scents to make them easier to handle," he says softly.

"I don't want them masked. I'm okay. It's just the first time I've smelled them all together like this."

I know better than to assume they can't scent how affected I am by that, either. Scent-masking panties or not, I'm all but dripping. Every inhale I take makes it worse as I try and pick the scents apart to get the full depth of each one.

Coffee is Ronan, chocolate and peanut butter is Dash, and the cozy scent of laundry is Jasper. The vanilla, though . . . that's got to be Landon. I can't fight the pull to inhale deeper, subtly drifting further into the house.

"Landon smells like vanilla," I breathe out, hardly able to think over the pulse pumping in my ears.

Jasper stays close, following me as I move like he's scared I'll run. "He does."

The hair on my arms stands, memories flashing. There's hardly a trace of cinnamon, but finally, I find it and the slight burn hanging on to it.

I'll never forget the mortification I felt while standing at the entrance of that restaurant with spaghetti sauce staining my fingertips and tables full of people watching an alpha who smelled just like this command me to leave him alone.

Oh god.

Things couldn't have been worse than this. Dread pools like tar in my belly as I turn to face Jasper. Words get caught in my constricting throat.

"What's wrong?" he asks, frowning deeply.

I shake my head, my emotions spiking too intensely to make sense of them.

"Talk to me, love."

"Did we do something wrong?" Dash asks, appearing beside Jasper.

My scent sours, and I lose the vanilla and cinnamon. Something inside of me cracks for the second time since that day as my omega recoils at the idea of missing out on it again. My instincts demand I focus enough to find it again, but that only makes it worse.

"Okay, maybe we need to go outside," Dash adds, taking charge when Jasper freezes, his nostrils flaring.

I want to crawl into a hole and die because it's obvious what he's smelling. A terrified omega's scent mixed with the slick she's hopeless to hide.

Pupils expanding, Jasper lets loose a rough sound and nods, smoothing his hand down my arms.

"Outside," he echoes.

There's no time.

It's impossible to mistake the sound of footsteps on the porch steps for anything else. I hold my breath and keep staring at Jasper, trying to find solace in the way he watches me like I'm something precious he's not willing to let go of regardless of how confused he must be right now.

"Ronan said we were having pizza. Sorry we're late."

My eyes roll back into my head at the sound of that gruff voice. Goosebumps cover me from head to toe, and I reach for Jasper on instinct, curling my fingers into his shirt. His body hides my view of the man who spoke, but as heavy footsteps continue our way, I know it won't matter.

"Jesus, what's that smell? It's . . ." The footsteps stop.

I see Ronan first when he moves to the side, eyes already on me. It takes all I have in me not to run toward him.

"What's wrong, Petal?" he asks, voice low.

There's only one man the stranger could be. Landon's voice is a whip across the room.

"You brought the omega *here*?"

A whine gets caught in my throat, and I risk a breath, allowing it to escape. The other men in the room take it as a sign of distress, but it's not a fearful noise.

I push myself out of Jasper's arms and avoid the ones Ronan opens for me. My head swims as I step into the open, searching for Landon and finding him frozen a few feet away. Too far from me.

"You ran from me," I croak, eyes burning as I blink profusely.

The same alpha from the restaurant stares at me, blue eyes as vivid as they were the first time I looked into them. Everything about him is the same as it was that day, but without the suit, he doesn't appear as scary. Even with his towering height and wide, bulky shoulders, I know he isn't a danger to me the same way I thought then.

His jaw is tense, teeth grinding as he watches me step toward him. I don't stop, even when he narrows his eyes in warning.

"You *ran* from me," I repeat, harsher this time.

Jasper sucks in a breath while Landon slips his hands into the pockets of his jeans, his expression smoothing to paint a picture of pale-skinned ease. A complete façade that I don't buy for a minute.

"I did."

"Why?"

"I don't want an omega."

It's a knife in the softest part of my chest. "Why? You don't even know me."

I get lost in the perfection of his facial features, so close to him now that I can make out every indent and curve. It's like he's been created in my mind from dreams I've had ever since I was a little girl. I couldn't find a flaw if I spent hours searching for one.

I ache so deep inside that I have to plant my feet harder on the ground to keep from jumping at him. The last time I did that, he left me standing alone, rejected.

The words he speaks now may be worse.

"I don't need to know you. I don't *want* to know you. I thought I made that clear when you destroyed my dinner and embarrassed the both of us. Now, if you'll excuse me, I need to go," he says sharply, each word a well-aimed bullet.

"Watch your mouth, Landon," Ronan snarls, suddenly at my side. "What are you talking about right now? You've met before?"

His hand steadies me, and I'm too desperate for his support to push him away right now.

Landon keeps his glare focused on me, somehow making it cruel enough that I flinch, my heart all but bleeding in his clenching fist.

Slowly, he drags his eyes to Ronan, the blue burning like a flame. "Do not blindside me like this again. I told you all my stance on this. It won't change. Not for her or for any other omega you find."

Dash passes me with a knuckle gliding over my bicep. "Don't be cruel. That's not who you are."

"Isn't it? Ask your omega how we met, and then decide if you still believe that," Landon bites out.

"Don't leave like this again, Landon. We'll stay down here, just go upstairs or to the gym. But stay here," Jasper pleads.

Landon hesitates, something heavy passing between them. "Tell me when she's gone."

When Jasper warned me that this very situation could happen, clearly, I didn't take it seriously enough. I hoped that it wouldn't be as bad as he made it out to be. That maybe Landon would see me and change his mind. But now, knowing that their Landon, the leader of their pack, was the one I met three weeks ago and wondered if maybe he could have been my scent match . . .

I was so, so very wrong.

This is much worse than I ever thought it could be.

22

Landon

One more second in her presence and I would have gone into a rut. I'm clawing out of my skin as I heave over my knees at the top of the stairs, needing to get that lemon scent out of my system.

Her voice twinkles up to the second story as she vaguely explains how we met, her voice strained enough to betray her hurt at my actions.

Fuck, I can't stay here.

The others don't know how affected I am, and I want it to stay that way. With my eyes closed, I see her again. Every curve of her body and glimmering strand of brown hair almost the same shade of black as mine. The same nose ring I remember from that night is still there, a tiny little diamond twinkling.

I've never cared much about the clothes a woman wears, but how the fuck am I supposed to pretend that seeing her in a tiny little sundress the identical pale blue colour of her eyes with lace tights didn't nearly push me over the edge?

The omega is stunning. Beautiful beyond human comprehension. The earth shook beneath my feet when she stared up at me, her chin lifted in determination. She wasn't supposed to be here, and she certainly wasn't supposed to hold such power over me with little reason. We're not pack, yet she feels like it.

That immediate draw is the worst part of it all. It's a trick played by our instincts to try and control us.

Chest caving in with the force of my breaths, I lean against the wall and, despite my desire to leave, linger at the top of the stairs.

"I'm sorry," she murmurs.

"You have nothing to apologize to us for, Petal," Ronan reassures her, but his voice is tight. "I had a fucking feeling. My gut's never wrong."

I expect him to be the first to seek me out, the soothing tone of his voice long gone and replaced with a venom that I'd bet he wished could fill my bloodstream.

Nobody would blame him if that were the case.

Jasper speaks next, feet shuffling. "It doesn't matter who knew what. Come with me, love. You need to eat. We can talk more about this after."

"I'm not really hungry," the omega argues weakly.

"I know. At least let us try to feed you. If you end up not eating, I'm sure Ronan will have your portion," Dash barters.

It's not very common to have a beta in an all-alpha pack. Nobody I knew growing up had one in theirs, and I'm still unsure why. When I met Dash, we were just kids with no idea how or when we'd create an official pack.

It was fun to play around with the idea and make imaginary plans for our future. Not even one of us thought it was weird or out of place to have Dash be a part of our family when the day came to make things official.

My father didn't agree and made sure to tell me his opinion on it several times over the course of my life, but it didn't make a difference.

When you meet your packmates, it's forever. You feel the pull, and that's that. In a perfect world, I would have taken one look at Briar in that restaurant and inhaled her scent before deciding the same thing.

Every instinct I have is telling me that the gorgeous omega downstairs is my scent match, but I know how easy it can be to let desperation drive you. The last time I watched that happen, I was on the outside looking in as my father and his packmates doted on my mother for half of my childhood as alphas mated to their scent match would. Nobody was expecting the truth to come out after they were so sure about it. The marks on my mother's neck were nails in a rotting coffin.

She was nothing more than a con artist, and she played everyone. Even me. Neither my father nor his prior pack ever met their scent match. The woman who I call my mother was after them for one thing, and it wasn't love. She did everything possible to convince them otherwise, and it worked. A bottle of custom omega perfume and my father's pack was a lost fool for her. Everything fell apart after that.

I refuse to allow myself to fall into a similar trap. Even if not being with Briar is killing me slowly. The pain now is better than the possibility of destruction later.

They continue talking as I push off the wall and silently creep down a single stair. The metal railing is cold in my hot palms, and I grip it tight, swallowing a hiss when it digs too deep.

Our main floor is made up of an open living and dining room, a kitchen facing the backyard, three full bathrooms, and four bedrooms we use as an office and storage rooms. The stairs look out at the kitchen with the living room beside them, and the openness allows me to see Briar where she stands at the wide island, her back to me as Jasper pulls two pizzas from the oven and sets them on the stovetop.

Ronan and Dash are seated on bar stools on either side of her, both staring like they're scared if they look away, she'll disappear. Jasper makes a joke, and Dash laughs, the sound so nice to hear that it's grating. I hate how badly I want to be there with them. It's been months since we've laughed together like that.

I could hold a pity party for myself, but what good would that do? If I want to protect our pack, that means inserting myself into situations where Briar has them all by the balls. Leaving them alone with her won't do me any favours, even if being close to her could be worse for me than distance.

"You know what? On second thought, I'm starving," I announce, steeling my spine as I join them downstairs.

Briar jumps, her hair whipping through the air as she turns to look at me. Her naturally pouty pink lips part around nothing.

"Great. You changed your mind just in time," Dash tells me.

Ronan narrows his eyes, trying to read my blank expression. "You're not welcome here right now."

"Ronan," Jasper lightly scolds.

"Are you going to say something if I stay?" I dare him.

"It's okay. Hi again, Landon," Briar says, mouth curling at the corner.

It's a fake fucking smile.

I pass them all and open the fridge, digging through it for the last blue Gatorade. Cracking the lid, I close the door with my hip.

The drink smells strong, but it's still not enough to hide the sweetness of her lemon cookie scent. My cock twitches, growing stiff in a fucking blink behind the zipper of my jeans.

"We were just about to start comparing schedules. I suggested Briar come to our next game," Jasper says, being the first of my pack to speak to me without outright malice.

I choke on the Gatorade and set the bottle on the island. Frustration bubbles in my gut, but I ignore it with a clearing of my throat.

"Great."

"I'm not much of a hockey fan. I hope that's not a deal breaker," Briar warns.

My brow shoots up on its own. "Why not?"

It's silent for a moment, nobody answering me before she does, those pale blue eyes too curious for her own good.

"Sports aren't my thing."

Jasper sets a pile of plates beside the cutting board he's using to slice the pizza. "What sorts of things do you enjoy?"

"I haven't really had much time to find many hobbies, but I've always liked bundling up in front of a fire or on a porch at night and doing those paint by numbers. There's something really calming about spending a few minutes doing something simple like that. It helps with anxiety too."

Can't say I saw that one coming.

"I don't know the last time I painted anything," Ronan grunts.

I spin the cap on my bottle tighter than necessary. "Probably when you were a child."

"If you ever find yourself wanting company while you paint, I'd love to give it a try," Jasper offers, stroking a knuckle over the fingers she has resting on the quartz countertop.

Briar flushes, lashes fanning as her stare falls to where they touch. Jealousy sizzles beneath my skin, pissing me off further.

They seem so close already after only seeing each other a couple of times. It's just another reason why a scent match bond shouldn't be so blindly trusted. Who's to say that they won't get sick of one another in a couple of weeks? There are still too many unknowns. We don't know anything about this woman other than her enjoyment of painting.

"I like painting," Ronan says.

It takes everything in me not to laugh. "Since when?"

His glare is vicious. "Since I fucking said so, asshole."

"Jasper was telling me earlier about when you chose the pack house, but I wanted to ask when you actually all became pack?" Briar asks, changing the subject.

Dash leans forward on the island and beams at her. "Well, we all met when we were kids, and I think we knew even then that we were supposed to be pack. When we all designated, it seemed to just click into place. We held the ceremony when we were all eighteen."

"I don't know much about pack ceremonies," she admits.

Jasper nods, beginning to cut the pizza up. "I wouldn't really say it's a ceremony per se. At least what we did wasn't anything like that. We filled out all the legal paperwork joining us, took Landon's last name, and had a party. That's really what it is for a pack without an omega."

Ronan eyes me up, daring me to be a jackass and add something unnecessary. If it weren't for Briar's genuine interest as she listens to everything we have to say, I would have made sure to remind her and everyone else that we're not in the market for one, either.

It seems fucking impossible to spout my mouth off as they continue talking and Briar rests her chin on her fist, nodding along with every word spoken to her. Jasper gets dinner dished up for everyone the way he always does, and we sit at the table for the first time in months.

I take the furthest seat from her and adjust my crotch beneath the table. Jasper sits beside me, noticing the move but leaving it alone.

"Tell us how work's been, love."

"Well, we have a few patients that we're watching closely as they're due to go into labour any day now. I don't think I've gone this long without checking my phone in a few days," Briar says between bites of pizza.

Jasper wipes his mouth with a napkin. "If you need to check, please do. We don't want you to miss out on anything."

"I have my ringer on and a special ringtone set for work. I'm doing just fine without looking," she says, smiling brightly.

"You're a doctor?" It comes out much harsher than I meant it to, but I don't apologize for it.

"I'm a doula," she corrects me.

I tap a finger to my bottle and say, "I'm not familiar."

She doesn't react with anything but calm understanding, features relaxed. "I work alongside an OB/GYN during baby deliveries and offer physical and emotional support to the moms doing all the hard work. I've never had a desire to become a doctor."

"Briar co-owns a birthing clinic with her best friend," Jasper boasts, chest puffed.

It's confirmation that there's already more to her than there ever was my mother, and I hate it.

Gritting my teeth, I let the conversation drop. I don't need nor want to hear anything else.

"You've been busy, then?" Dash asks after swallowing a bite of pizza.

I stare down at mine and poke at the golden crust as my stomach swirls. I've hardly eaten these last couple of weeks, and apparently, that isn't changing tonight.

"Very. Clover, my best friend and business partner, has been keeping us on our toes with a new patient. I think she's trying to shove our friendship down her throat, but Sadie's been a real trooper about it. We made her a truly awful chicken casserole the other night, and she swallowed it down without a single cough."

"Sounds like when Dash makes a friend and Ronan attempts to cook," Jasper teases.

Dash pinches his pizza and shakes it in Jasper's direction. "Don't take shots at me because I'm the only one in this pack who knows how to have a conversation with someone new instead of just grunting at them."

"Why am I catching strays?" Ronan asks around the rim of his beer bottle.

"I never said you were the one doing the grunting. You guessed that all on your own," Dash sings.

Briar's giggle has everyone falling silent. Jasper grins wide enough to show both rows of his teeth while Ronan stares bluntly at her, his eyes all but twinkling.

Dash is the only one of them who tries to hide his reaction. He glances at me and offers a wince-like smile that I immediately look away from.

"What about you, Landon? Do you cook?" she asks.

It takes me a moment to realize I'm the Landon she's talking to.

"Not often," I reply bluntly.

"Who does, then?"

"If anyone, Jasper does."

She tips her chin, ripping a piece of her crust off. I stare at her plate, a brow sliding up as I examine her food. The cheese is gone, along with the majority of the crust, while the actual pizza remains intact, uneaten.

Dropping her eyes to where she can see me looking, she freezes with the crust hanging between her fingers.

"I've always eaten pizza like this," she tells me.

"Why?"

She cocks her head, examining my plate. "Why aren't you eating at all?"

Jasper clears his throat, frowning at me for a beat. "Landon hasn't been feeling well recently."

"In what way?" The alarm in her tone makes my alpha preen, the smug bastard.

"Don't worry about it," I grumble.

Dash keeps pushing. "What did the doc say today?"

"To sleep more."

And to start taking care of my body before it gives out on me. His warning was grim, and I'm not up for repeating it. The only thing that'll do for me is make the rest of them hover.

"That's incredible medical advice if I do say so myself," Dash mutters, sarcastic as fuck.

I feel Briar's eyes on me, forcing mine to lift to meet them. Something shifts in my chest at her concern, a piece of me that aches for her attention and care. From across the table, I feel the ghost of her touch on my skin lingering from that night three weeks ago. My nails dig into my thigh, the pain doing nothing to faze me.

I inhale through my mouth to avoid her scent, but I taste it instead. It's thick, intoxicating. My chest begins to rumble as I stiffen, cock throbbing so intensely it's painful.

"Is there anything anyone can do to help you, Landon?" she asks, her voice a purr stroking around my swelling knot.

"No," I croak.

A dainty finger reaches up to tuck a chunk of hair behind her ear, lingering behind the delicate curve of it. "Are you okay?"

I drop my hand to my lap and grab my cock, pressing down hard. My vision grows dark around the edges momentarily before I release myself and jolt to my feet.

"I need some air."

Jasper stands, moving toward me to help, but I'm shifting out of reach before he can make it two steps.

"Alone," I snip.

"I'm sorry if I overstepped," Briar rambles, hopping out of her seat. "I know it's not my business."

"It is your business," Ronan says, reassuring her with a brush of his hand across hers.

Dash scrunches his features. "Do you need someone to come with?"

I smell the spike in my scent at the same time everyone else does. The scorching cinnamon clinging to a thick vanilla smothers the table before four sets of eyes drop to my crotch.

The only set I care about are the ones that widen to the size of saucers before shooting up to the ceiling. Briar turns redder than the spaghetti sauce it took two showers to get fully out of my hair.

I'm out of there before any of those fuckers have a chance to say anything to me about what they saw. I know it's coming, and regardless of how I feel about the omega, there's no need to embarrass her any more than she already is.

With my dinner untouched and still on my plate, I rush away from the table and straight out the front door. My sock-clad feet pound against the driveway as I take off into a jog, content to run until my legs give out.

Maybe by then, I'll be calm enough to show my face again instead of on the brink of yet another rut.

23

Ronan

"Well, that was fucking awkward," I grunt.

It's the first time anyone has spoken since Landon took off a few moments ago. I wish it hadn't been me to break the silence. Jasper pinches the bridge of his nose and sighs.

"So, I think we need to talk more about what happened when you and Landon met," Dash states.

Briar looks like she wants to be anywhere but here as we all turn to look at her, searching for any hint of how she's feeling with all of this.

Jasper clears his throat, releasing his nose. "Are you up to it, love?"

"It seems only fair. Especially given Landon's obvious feelings toward me."

"Don't take them personally. His opinion on pack omegas is very different than ours," Jasper says.

I roll my jaw, shoving away my immediate frustration at his use of that excuse. It's not enough for me. Landon's not one to be so vicious, and I'm not a fan of the version of him I've been seeing, let alone in Briar's presence.

Hearing her tell us that she met him previously was enough of a strike against him, but to know he rejected her right then and there?

My fingers curl as I struggle to keep my cool.

Not accepting her when I first laid eyes on her was never a possibility. The pull was too strong, and I felt it in my goddamn soul who she was to me. *To us.* I'll never understand how Landon was even able to walk away, let alone in such a mortifying situation.

"How was he able to leave you there?" I ask roughly, desperate for an answer.

Briar worries her lip, eyes low. "I mortified the both of us. Not to mention completely covered him in food. I always thought he couldn't fully pick up on my scent. I've never left the house without scent-blocking perfume."

"Honestly, I doubt it. I thought it was weird when he had the SUV detailed for so long, but now . . . it makes sense that he was trying to get rid of your scent," Dash says.

Jasper huffs, glaring at him when Briar stiffens, face paling.

"I never went into the car," she whispers.

"Did you touch him? Or touch each other? If you had even the slightest scent spike, it could have clung onto his clothes and onto the car seats," Jasper says.

"Yes. I . . . I tried to clean him off before he left."

Dash runs a hand through his hair, tussling it. "This could all explain his current state. The pains, inability to sleep, and lack of hunger. His body is rejecting him rejecting her."

"It's my fault he's not feeling well?" Briar's face crumbles. "I didn't mean—"

I cut her off with a firm shake of my head. "No. This is not your fault. He's the one who left you."

"I've never known an alpha who has experienced bond rejection sickness without a mating mark already in place," Jasper mentions, face scrunched in thought.

"It's most likely not to the full extent of most cases *because* of the lack of a mark. Landon isn't a regular alpha, Jas. He's a pack leader with the most sensitive senses I've ever seen in another alpha. We've witnessed it his entire life. He can't stand being in the dressing room with the rest of the team and couldn't even handle the mild scent of Briar in the SUV to the point he had to get it removed. Look at how strongly you and Ronan felt the pull. Landon's definitely feeling it even stronger."

"Why is he fighting me so badly, then?" Briar asks softly.

There's a gnawing in my gut that I can't shake.

"He doesn't trust omegas, Petal."

"How do I make him trust me, then?"

I reach for her hand on the table and cup it between mine. She releases a breath at the contact while I hook a foot around the leg of her chair and pull her closer. When her head rests against my shoulder, I turn languid.

Jasper watches with a soft expression. "Are you saying you still want to try?"

"If I'm ever going to be a member of this pack, I don't want it to be broken. Landon doesn't scare me, and neither does hard work. I'm willing to give it a chance. Give it all a chance. And if he doesn't let me in after I try . . . then at least I'll have known that I didn't walk away too early."

"Thank fuck," I declare, nuzzling my face in her hair.

Jasper extends a hand over the table, palm up, and waits. "You have no idea what you're offering all of us, Briar."

Briar gently pulls her hand free from between mine and rests it over Jasper's. Dash eyes us with caution from beside Jasper, and Briar meets his stare head-on.

"I'm not giving up on you, either, Dash," she declares.

I hold my breath, watching them.

His throat bobs with a swallow. "You'll be pack, Briar. No matter what."

It's the closest thing to acceptance as I know to expect just yet. And it's more than enough.

MONTGOMERY
PACK

"I DON'T NEED an escort home, Ronan," Briar teases, lingering at the side of her car.

The entire vehicle is a danger, and I'm one more creak from the breeze from hauling it to a junkyard. It's so tiny I doubt I'd fit properly, let alone Landon or Jasper. I'll be listening to the engine to tell just how much work I'll need to get ordered on it this week.

My bike is already on the driveway behind us ready to go. "It'll settle me."

"I suppose I'll have to get used to these sorts of offers, right?"

"Would that be hard for you to do?"

Her lips lift into a teasing smile. "I think I could suffer with them."

"Suffer," I echo, drawn closer to her.

She tips her head back, resting it against the door as our gazes lock. I press a hand to the body of the car, the tip of my thumb grazing her ear.

"Is this also something I'll have to get used to?" she whispers.

Her hair blows in the breeze, and I welcome the burst of her scent that follows, wrapping around us.

"What do you mean, Petal?"

"Being this close to you and feeling like . . . like I should and could stay here forever?"

My heart pounds. "You stay right here forever and I'll die a happy man."

"We're still strangers."

"Fuck, Briar, we're the furthest things from strangers. I might not know every corner of your mind just yet, but our souls have known each other for decades."

Her face flushes as she shivers, chest arching to meet mine. "Aren't you supposed to be the grumpy one?"

"It's who I am."

"You don't seem very grumpy to me."

"You're the exception," I declare.

"It will be easy to fall for you. For all of you."

It's impossible not to smirk at that, even if it is small. "That's the plan."

The burn in her eyes dulls enough to spook me. It's the only sign I find that something's wrong.

"I'm sorry it won't be easy."

"This isn't on you. None of it is," I declare, bringing my other hand to hold her cheek. My skin sizzles where we touch, a blast of heat shooting up my arm. "Pack is for life. And if you choose to be a part of ours, we'll show you every day why we deserve you."

"I've always dreamed of having a pack of my own."

"Did you grow up in one?" I ask, unable to take the opportunity to learn more about her.

She nods, pressing her cheek into my hold. "I did. My mom and dads are all scent matches."

"So, you know a lot about pack dynamics."

"It's all I know, really. Which is one of the reasons why I've wanted a pack of my own for pretty much as long as I can remember."

Curling a piece of her hair around my pinky, I hum. "You and Jasper have a lot in common."

"I don't with you?"

"I've only got my ma, dad, and younger sister."

She frowns, her bottom lip jutting out slightly further than her top in a way that I've become completely enamoured with.

"That still sounds like a pack to me."

I inhale deeply, dropping my head to bring our foreheads together. She grazes her fingers across my chest, eyes sliding to focus on my mouth.

"Yeah, Petal. You're right. They're all I've ever needed outside of the guys inside."

"What are they like?" she asks, speaking softly enough for her words to blow away on the breeze, here and gone in a blink.

"Can I kiss you?" I ask instead.

She laughs, gaze flicking back to hold mine. There's no annoyance there. Just the desire to do the same.

"Yes, Ronan. You can kiss me."

One brush of our mouths, and I can nearly taste the future. Lemon and caramel mix in the air around us as I press my lips over hers in a firm kiss. She exhales in my mouth before raising an arm to curl around my shoulders, pulling me close.

Her confidence turns me on, lust clouding my mind. I plaster our fronts together, swallowing a possessive growl at the feel of her against me. I memorize the feel of her soft belly, the curves of her heavy breasts, and the thigh that parts from the other, inviting me to move between them.

We fit perfectly, my bulk swallowing her frame and allowing me to protect her from anyone and anything that could be lurking nearby. And as I shift my hips, the thick length of my cock digs into her belly, expelling a groan from my chest.

She answers with a low whine that tightens every muscle in my body. Perfume fills the little space between us, sweet enough to make my teeth ache. I stroke the underside of her jaw, teasing her scent gland.

"Briar."

It's a warning and a promise.

"I know," she gasps, eyelids fluttering as she pins me with pale blue. "It's intense."

"Gonna need you to get in the car now."

The sweet scent bitters quickly, and my head clears immediately. She swallows, as reluctant to release me as I am her.

"We're not there yet. I want to do things right. Show you who I am before I bury my face between your thighs and taste how sweet you are," I add.

"I know you're right. It just doesn't feel . . ."

"It feels like fucking torture."

She's slow to slide her hand from my shoulders to my wrist, lingering there. "When can I see you all again?"

"We're on a small road trip this week, but we'll be back Thursday."

Fuck. Having to be away from her for five days makes me feel sick to my stomach. Is this how Landon feels every day?

Briar nods. "Can we call or something while you're gone?"

"Always. We're going to court you, Briar."

"I have no idea what to expect with that," she admits, her spirit lifting bit by bit.

"Good. We'll have fun surprising you."

"Does following me home tonight count toward your courting?"

"Nah, baby. That's just an alpha taking care of his omega."

It flows off my tongue like butter, and by her pink cheeks, I don't think she hates it too much.

I grasp the door handle behind her body and linger, unable to be the one to back away first.

Keeping her back to the car, she slides a foot to the right, giving me the space to open the door. The creak of its hinges isn't incredibly reassuring, but when she ignores it, I keep my mouth shut.

I'm not entirely sure if buying someone a new car counts as a good courting gift, but maybe I'll give it a try anyway.

Once she's in the driver's seat, I wait for her to buckle the seat belt before kissing her again. She sighs when I pull back, brows furrowed.

"Don't speed, Petal. I'd love chasing you too much."

Her laugh burrows itself in my chest. "Noted."

I close the door and wait for her to turn the engine before taking slow steps backward. It's just about as bad as I knew it would be, the heavy ticking noise burning itself into my brain.

"Thank you, Ronan," she calls, poking her head out of the window as I straddle my bike.

"Always."

Like a good girl, she never goes above the speed limit the entire drive to her apartment. I linger on the street while she pulls into the resident parking lot and steps into the warm night, knowing that if I get close to her again, I won't be able to leave again.

She stands on the grass a beat later, staring at me. Her fingers wiggle in a wave, and I flick my visor up so she can see my eyes as I lift a hand in a wave.

Once she's inside, I stay rooted in place. My bike rumbles beneath my body, comforting me as I straighten and look out at the street. The neighbourhood is as familiar as the one I live in now, but I've never seen this specific red car parked out here before. Especially not one with blue LED headlights that could blind someone looking directly at them from a kilometre away.

Suspicion bites at me. I narrow my eyes and stare at the car, trying to see inside but meeting dark tint instead. The sound of a sawed-off exhaust fills the street when it starts to move, crawling toward me at a snail's pace.

I track it, keeping my posture rigid as they pass, the feeling of someone staring directly at me making my skin prickle despite not being able to see who it is. Once they're gone, I look back at the apartment building and turn the bike off.

I keep my ass planted here all night, watching the front doors until dawn.

24

Briar

WITH AN OAT MILK ESPRESSO WITH EXTRA CARAMEL in my hand, I hum the melody of my latest favourite song on my way out of the parking lot. It's stickily hot this morning, but not even that can sour my mood.

While it's been a whole three days since I've seen the Montgomery pack, the distance has been easier to handle with their sporadic text updates. I've even been added to a group chat that sees more daily activity than the one Clover started with me during her last night out without me. It's impossible not to giggle thinking about the conversation I woke up to see this morning.

Lightning Daddy: Who changed my name? This is so weird.

RoRo: Don't pretend it wasn't you, Dash.

Lightning Daddy: It wasn't! I bet it was Landon *finger pointing emoji*

Jasper Cullen: I don't know if I should be offended by this or not.

Queen M: What does the M stand for?

Queen M: By the way, Jasper Cullen's really good looking in an I'm going to drain you dry type of way. Don't be offended.

I wasn't expecting the name they chose for me, but being labelled as a queen isn't anything to complain about.

RoRo: I assume the M is for Montgomery.

Lightning Daddy: I'm jealous of a vampire now.

Jasper Cullen: Where's Landon? It's looking more suspicious the longer he doesn't say anything

Lord Grumps A-Lot: Get off your phones before Coach sees you.

RoRo: Oh fuck. So it wasn't Landon. Nice name choice Dash.

Lightning Daddy: Ooooooops.

It's only one of the few times they've chatted in the group, and while I'm not ready to actively participate too much yet, I really appreciate being included. Regardless of how long we've known each other, I miss them like crazy already.

"Cross the street and speak to me properly, Sadie. Enough of this! You need us!"

I cut off my humming in response to the harsh male voice. The serrated edge to it is almost as alarming as the sight of Sadie frozen on the sidewalk only a few steps from the doors of the clinic.

She's a deer in headlights staring out at the man, an arm wrapped protectively around her belly. I'm moving instantly, adrenaline pumping in my blood.

"You'll talk to us sooner or later!" he yells, louder this time.

I glare at the guy watching her like he has every right in the world to be making demands and huddle close to her side. He's tall, maybe the same height as Jasper but without the outrageous good looks. There's a wideness to him that tells me he's an alpha, but he's leaner than you'd usually see. He's tucked his hair beneath a black beanie, yet I can still tell it's long and, from the looks of the curls hanging out, a dirty-blond colour.

"Who is that?" I ask her, not wanting to assume.

The clinic door whooshes open behind us, and heavy footsteps clunk on the sidewalk.

She leans into me. "Thorne."

Rage swells inside of me before Duke is there, every thundering inch of him moving at a quick pace down the sidewalk and across the street. Thorne flashes his gaze toward me, a darkness there that sends ice water down my spine.

"Come inside, Sadie," I whisper, sliding my arm around her back to slowly turn her. "Duke will take care of him while we talk."

"I'm sorry. I didn't know he was following me here."

"It's not your fault. Let's just get inside. We got a new flavour of hot chocolate in yesterday that I think you'll love."

"What flavour?"

"Cinnamon sugar."

I open the door for us and usher her inside. The look I sneak behind me doesn't settle any of my anxiousness. Thorne doesn't back down as Duke towers over him, his expression hidden.

"I've never known anyone to have as many flavours of hot chocolate and tea as you and Clover do," Sadie says weakly.

"Clover doesn't drink coffee, so I think we're all stuck drinking hot cocoa for the rest of time."

High heels clap on the floor before Clover's voice drifts down from the hall. "Don't act like I pry open your jaw and make you drink it. You literally have a coffee in your hand right now."

I wave it around, the ice inside my reusable cup clinking. "I'm almost done it."

Our receptionist, Alicia, laughs while sliding a black binder across her hefty white desk. "Duke left this here for you before he stepped out, Clover."

"Did he say what it's for?"

"It's regarding Sadie."

Most likely the first draft of our safety plan. "Thank you, Alicia."

I take the binder before Clover has a chance to snatch it and rejoin the group. We let Sadie inside the office first. Clover takes the rear, closing the door behind us.

"How are you feeling today, Sadie? Any pain, cramps, or

discomfort that's unusual?" she asks, falling into her doctor persona.

I take one of the two seats in front of Clover's desk while Sadie slowly lowers herself into the other. Clover perches behind her desk and smiles sympathetically before taking the binder from me.

"No. I'm just exhausted. When I take the few steps up to my bedroom, I feel like I've run a half marathon. I don't suppose you can help with that?" Sadie asks.

"Unfortunately not. The finish line is so close now, though. You've already done such an incredible job, Mama."

"I know it doesn't help how you feel, but you're glowing," I add.

Sadie rolls her eyes, adjusting her position on the chair. "You're trying to butter me up, and it's working."

"As your OB/GYN, it's actually my job to cheer you up, especially when we're this close to baby time," Clover says.

"I don't want to open that binder, but we should before I get too freaked out," Sadie suggests, palming the middle of her belly.

Clover looks at me. "Do you want to go find Duke?"

"He was busy the last time I saw him."

"Doing what?" she asks, immediately concerned.

Sadie clears her throat. "It's my fault—"

There's a series of rough knocks on the office door, and I stand. "Hold that thought."

It's Duke's face I see when I pull it open. His expression gives nothing away, so I don't prod, leaving that for Clover. I have a feeling bringing it up now will only upset Sadie more than necessary.

Opening the door completely, I say, "You're right on time."

He passes me, his posture perfect, like he's got a steel pipe pressed against his spine beneath his black shirt. Sadie turns as much as she can in her seat before she sucks in a sharp breath, eyes crawling up his body.

"I don't know if the two of you have been properly introduced yet, but Sadie, this is Duke. He's the lead of the security team we'll be using and the one in charge of creating the perfect security plan for your birth," Clover says, waving between them. "Duke, this is Sadie."

"The omega with a giant watermelon attached to her front," Sadie adds.

"How do you feel?" he asks, voice gruff and low.

Sadie's inhale is quick but easy to disguise as a moan of discomfort. Duke lurches forward in response before stopping himself, his dark eyes growing more focused than I've ever seen them.

Curiosity has me watching them a bit closer. The de-scenter in the air won't allow them to get a good whiff of one another, but the interest between them is obvious. At least it is until Sadie seems to realize the same thing and visibly retreats.

"I'm fine. Very pregnant," she says before turning back around to stare at Clover. "You were talking about a safety plan?"

My best friend buys the sudden change as little as I do. Her eyes find mine for just long enough for me to read the meaning behind them.

Are they for real right now?

I roll my lips to hide a smile and let it go.

"Yes, I was. Shut the door a bit, please, Duke," Clover says.

He does as she says before leaning against it, arms crossed.

Clover opens the binder and starts to go through the well-labelled list of precautions Duke's made, as well as a few of the names of the men he'd like to have on call for when Sadie goes into labour.

It's a simple protection detail with two guards outside the front and one at the back, just in case. Dramatic as it may seem to plan this detailed of an assignment, it's a necessity in these situations. Alphas kept away from their babies, especially when they can't be near their omega for comfort, can be incredibly volatile. Combine that with Thorne's natural aggression, and there could be the potential that he goes haywire and attempts to come get them regardless of the restraining order.

Duke and his team will ensure that doesn't happen. And once Sadie and the baby are ready to leave, we can only hope that Thorne will have calmed enough to remember his legal obligations. As much as it may bother me, once she's gone, we can't do much to help her.

Maybe that's why Clover has made it her mission to befriend her. Even after Sadie's gone, we'll still be in her life and therefore still able to provide some sort of protection.

My phone buzzes repeatedly in my pocket, so I slip out of the office, grateful that I was there to hear most of the important parts.

Jasper's name being the first thing I see on the screen is like an electric paddle to my chest. I answer the call with a cheek-splitting smile.

"Hi, Jasper."

"Hello, love. I hope I didn't interrupt you at work. We're just leaving practice, and I wanted to sneak a few words in before we hit the media room."

"You didn't," I lie.

"Great. How has your morning been? Did you get a hold of your landlord?"

"Not yet. I tried calling when I was getting coffee, but he didn't pick up. I'll try again when I'm off work. How was practice?"

My landlord's been dragging his feet when it comes to cutting off the de-scenter from my ventilation system. On the one hand, I understand that it's safer to have it blowing everywhere all at once, but on the other, it's really started bothering me.

Every night when I get home, my skin itches deeper, and my nose burns. Maybe it's because I've recently found my scent matches, but either way, I need it to stop before I can't stand being at home anymore.

"Pretty good, actually. Dash has been on fire this season."

"And Landon?" I ask. Hopefully, my concern isn't too obvious.

Jasper lowers his voice slightly. "He's the same as he has been. We all miss you, Briar."

"You're back in two days, right? I know Ronan mentioned me coming to your next home game . . . is that something all of you would want?"

"I'll buy you season tickets if that'll mean you're at every single game, not just the next one."

I nip at my cheek. "I guess that's that, then."

"Not yet. There was something else behind the reason I called."

"What's that?"

"There should be a delivery arriving for you any moment now."

"What? Where?"

"At the clinic. I sent you a bit of a present. One of many you're going to receive from us."

I nearly drop the phone in my rush to the front doors. Alicia stops talking mid-sentence, the clinic's phone pressed to her ear. I wave a hand at her and force myself to slow down before I scare the delivery man and he reports back to Jasper that I'm an absolute nut.

"You good, Briar?" Alicia asks.

"Yep!"

Jasper's chuckle is as smooth as the whiskey in his scent. "Swap to FaceTime. I need to see your excitement for myself. Hearing it isn't enough."

My stomach flips. I bring my phone in front of my face and, with a tap of my finger, watch as the screen turns black. He answers instantly, and I chomp down on my tongue before blurting out something embarrassing.

Hair damp and cheeks pink, Jasper stares at me, mouth split in a smile. I didn't think it was possible for teeth to sparkle on camera, but I was wrong.

"Is it there yet?" he asks.

I look over my phone at the glass doors, finding a white delivery truck parked out front, a tall man walking around the hood with a medium-sized brown box in his hands.

"I think so."

"Is that Briar?" Ronan's voice draws my gaze back.

He's just as wet and red as Jasper but somehow more alive. Like he thrives on physical activity. Goosebumps lift all over my skin as I stare at the two men, wishing I was there.

"Hi, Ronan."

His gaze is intense. "Look at you. Fucking gorgeous."

"Don't try to show me up," Jasper mutters.

"Step up your game, then."

"I didn't see you calling her."

"Because you did it for the both of us."

"Guys," I interrupt, rolling my eyes. "I'm about to get the box."

They stop bickering as I pull the door open for the delivery man and take the extended box from him.

"Briar?" he asks.

"That's me. Do I need to sign or anything?"

"No. Have a great day."

"You too," I say half-mindedly, staring down at the package. "Can I set this on the desk, Alicia?"

"Go for it."

"Show us you opening it," Ronan says.

Jasper snorts a laugh. "Please, Briar."

I balance the phone on the desk against the stapler and set the box down, peeling up the corner of the tape with my nail.

"Do I get a hint as to what's inside?" I ask.

"I can't wait to see you wearing it," Jasper teases.

My mind explodes with possibilities that make me glad the descenter in here is even stronger than the stuff at my apartment.

Once the tape is gone, I slowly peel the box open and stare inside with eyes growing glassier by the second. The bright blue arms of the hockey jersey are fit with a number 1 while the white back of it has Montgomery stitched in the same shade of blue.

It's simple but thoughtful. Something that I wouldn't have felt comfortable asking for yet would have hated not having while watching their last game on TV.

"Number one doesn't belong to any one of us, so we figured it would be perfect for you," Jasper explains.

I run my fingers along the silky fabric and the letters that spell the name of their pack. "It's beautiful. I've never had a hockey jersey before, let alone a custom one."

I'd recognize Ronan's purr anywhere, and even hearing it through the phone is intoxicating. It sends flutters through every inch of me.

"We were hoping you'd wear it to our next game," he says.

Grabbing my phone, I bring it close and murmur, "I'd love to."

"Sounds incredible. And we'll see you before then," Jasper swears.

"I'll be waiting."

And honestly, while patience isn't my forte, I'm growing to realize it's well worth it when it comes to these men.

25

Dash

We're all sore and exhausted when we get home. Jasper's moving in hyper speed to get our luggage in from the car and up to our rooms before Briar arrives while Ronan disappears to shower.

My stomach still hasn't settled from the flight, so I make a beeline for the kitchen to grab some water. Landon's following me, but I don't have the energy to start a conversation right now. When he doesn't speak, either, I assume we're on the same page.

Only as soon as I start filling up a glass, his sharp tone cuts through the kitchen.

"What are your plans with the omega?"

"Her name is Briar, Landon."

"Fine. What are you doing with her here tonight?"

I turn off the tap and face him, my back pressing against the countertop. Landon watches stiffly, his lean off-centre as he takes as much weight off his right knee as possible. He played fine the last three games and was good enough to escape the scathing judgment of fans online and the press up in their boxes, but still, he wasn't at his peak. His passes were loose, backcheck slow. It was so unlike him that I spent every second I wasn't defending the net watching him.

"We're just hanging out. Ronan and Jasper missed her."

"They missed her? Not you?"

Something about the question makes me snap. "Didn't you? Or are you still pretending that you don't care?"

"I don't care about her, but I do care about my pack. I'm trying to find out the plans for the night so I know if I need to stay and keep an eye on all of you."

"We don't need you to watch us, Landon. You're not our father, and we're not children. Briar isn't a danger to anyone, let alone us," I argue, releasing a sigh that gives away how tired I am. "You weren't clever joining us for dinner the other night as if you weren't only there to make sure we didn't what, mark her?"

His lip curls slightly, anger mixing with something deeper, painful. "You've all started trusting her too easily."

"She hasn't given us any reason not to trust her. I know why you feel differently, and I respect you and your feelings, Lan, but you being such a hard-ass isn't helping. I've taken all you've said to us over the years into consideration, and it's why I've moved slower than Ronan and Jasper, but there's no stopping them. They're going to bond her someday, and if you want this pack to stick together, you need to stop using your distrust in Briar to drive a bigger wedge between us. What do you think will happen when she goes into heat? We've been lucky as it is that she hasn't already."

Landon's shoulder droops, a soul-deep exhale escaping him. The deep blue beneath his eyes is almost as concerning as the tweak of pain that travels across his expression when he leans forward with his hands on the island.

"You're not pulled to her?" he asks, his voice weak.

I reply carefully. "She smells really, really good to me, but something is missing."

"Why?"

"I'm not sure," I lie, leaving out Jasper's theory. It'll do no good to bring it up without any proof. "Just go up to bed, Lan.

Take some melatonin and try to sleep. Stay out of the gym, or I'll put a lock on the door."

He lets his head fall between his arms. "If you need me . . ."

"I'll get you," I finish for him. "But we won't. She's an omega, not a villain in a superhero movie."

"She could be pretty close."

"How's your knee?"

The question flops between us, remaining unanswered as he straightens out and starts to leave like I knew he would. I snort before draining the rest of my water and ditching the cup in the sink.

It's better Landon has this conversation with me than any of the others. Ronan would have told him to suck it the hell up and pull his head from his ass, and Jasper would have tried reasoning with him before inevitably giving up when Landon refused to give an inch.

With a yawn, I leave the kitchen. It's silent in the house, everyone having abandoned me to do their own thing. Jasper should be down soon, and I need to change before I'm saying hi to Briar in sweatpants with a hole in the knee and a shirt I cropped as a joke a couple of years ago. They're the only clothes I had with me in my travel bag, and I couldn't stand wearing my suit for another minute once we got on the plane to come home.

I'm the only one in the pack who changed, but I know Ronan would have if he hadn't been trapped in the window seat beside Landon.

I'm nearly to the stairs when there's a knock on the front door. It's gentle, almost like the person doing the knocking isn't sure if they want anyone to answer it.

They knock again, a bit stronger this time, and I unlock the deadbolt before tugging the door open. A set of cautious blue eyes stare up at me as Briar keeps her hand in the air, her fingers curled into a fist.

Guess ratty sweatpants and a cropped shirt it is.

"Hi," she squeaks, arm falling.

I'm suddenly almost self-conscious of what I'm wearing and how beat down I know I look. Briar's far more done up than I am, wearing a black, knee-length skater skirt, a cropped blue top, and a pair of biker boots with chunky heels that I know Ronan would blow in his pants if he saw. The last time she was here, she wore a dress, and now I'm having trouble pinpointing what exactly her style is. In all honesty, it's almost fitting, considering I haven't been able to figure her out, either.

I haven't tried.

"Hey. Come in."

She slips past me and starts to toe off her boots when I stop her with a hand on her arm. It's bare and warm, silky beneath my fingertips. I know I should retreat when she drops her eyes to stare at where we touch, but I linger, intrigued by the tease of a sizzle shooting up my arm.

"You should leave them on to show Ronan. He'll lose his mind," I say, my stomach suddenly settled.

"Really?"

My thumb swipes a hot line across her bicep, and I focus on the lift of the thin hairs there more than the way mine do the same.

"Motorbikes, leather, and boots are his favourite things. Such a typical bad boy."

"Don't forget the scowl," she teases.

"Ah, yeah. He's perfected that by now."

"Speaking of Ronan, where is he? I'm not early, am I?" she asks, nervously eyeing the living room behind us.

"No. We got home a few minutes ago, but if we're being totally open right now, we're all exhausted. Road trips are always more tiring than usual."

She nods, twisting her mouth as her stare slips back to me. "If someone had told me, I would have made dinner or something. Are you hungry?"

"You don't have to cook for us. We usually just order in on nights like this."

"That was before you had an omega who was offering to make you something to eat," she says before her eyes flare wide. "I mean, not like I'm the pack's omega or anything. What I meant is that I'm *an* omega, and I'm here offering to make something."

I crack a slight smile. "I knew what you meant."

"So, can I?"

"You're not going to let it go, are you?"

She laughs softly. "No. I'm not."

"Then the kitchen is this way."

Removing my hand from her arm is like trying to peel apart two pieces of paper that have been glued together. It takes a hard yank that no doubt makes me look incredibly odd before I can drop it back to my side and lead her through the house.

My head starts throbbing with a hunger headache again while my stomach does summersaults with nausea. Airplane sickness is a real thing despite what the guys on the team say, and it's a constant reminder that I may have chosen the wrong profession. If I didn't love hockey so damn much, I would have chosen something that wouldn't involve going thirty thousand feet in the air every few days.

I swallow past the bile creeping up my throat and focus on not collapsing onto the floor.

"I'm not sure what we have to cook with. We always let the fridge go empty before a road trip," I warn Briar, keeping my eyes forward.

"I can figure something out."

"Alright," I mutter.

The lights are still on in the kitchen when we enter. I immediately collapse on the closest bar stool at the island while palming my forehead.

"Are you okay?" I hear, Briar's voice twinkling in my ears.

With my eyes squeezed shut, I grind my teeth to try and curb the wave of nausea.

Inhaling, I pick up the fresh scent of lemon with the slightest note of sweetness. I can't help but take in another deep pull of it before releasing the pressure I'm applying to my forehead. The gentle yet steady press of her hand between my shoulder blades halts the rolling in my stomach.

She slowly starts massaging my tight muscles. "Does it help when I do this?"

"Yes." It's a throaty noise more than it is a verbal reply.

"I'll keep doing it, then."

"Why?" I blurt out.

Her hand stalls for half a second before continuing its movements. "Why what?"

"You don't owe me anything. We're not mates."

"How can you know that already, Dash? We've only known one another for a month. Less than that, really."

Instead of nausea, it's unease that creeps into my gut. "It should have been immediate. I would have recognized you, and you would have recognized me. That's how it works."

"According to who? My omega loves how you smell, even if your scent is a little more subtle than the others, and I feel . . . comfortable with you. How do we know that beta and omega bonds don't take longer to snap into place than alpha and omega ones do?" she asks.

In the back of my mind, I know she's right. Everything she's saying makes sense. Especially when I take the break in conversation to realize that my nausea hasn't just eased; it's retreated completely with her closeness. Not only that, but my headache is also gone. I open my eyes and blink, taking in the empty kitchen before turning my head to glance at her.

Her beauty is almost startling. Up close, her freckles are more distinguishable, and the dip of her full upper lip is a defined V rather than a soft U. Black makeup clings to her lashes, framing her eyes and contrasting the pale blue within them.

When I don't reply to her, she breathes in a long exhale and, with her voice steady, adds, "I know you and Landon don't trust me, and I'm really trying not to take that personally. What happened with him in the past is his business, and I can appreciate your loyalty. I guess I just want to reassure you that I'm not here to try and further divide your pack. I'm the outsider here, so I'm just trying to see where I could potentially fit in. Being here with all of you and offering to take care of you, even if just to cook a simple meal, is my way of figuring that out."

Guilt is a sharp and unforgiving emotion, and when it strikes, you oftentimes will bleed. Right now, I'm drowning in it, iron tangy on my tongue.

"We eat a lot," I say, slowly extending a branch for her to take.

She doesn't ignore it. "So do my dads."

"Jas keeps the pantry stocked pretty good regardless of how much we're planning on being home because we're snackers. If there's nothing in the fridge, I'd check there next."

"I'll do that, then. Thank you," she says, eyes brightening.

"Am I good to stay here? I'm still recovering from the flight, and sitting here helps."

Yeah, sitting here with her nearby. That's a good sign. Maybe she's right after all and this is the way things are supposed to be. If not, at least we can be sure that we could get along.

I'll take the small win.

26

Jasper

"Do you like to cook?" I ask, focused solely on Briar the way I have been since I found her in the kitchen.

An hour later and I'm still watching her as intently as I was when she was moving around my kitchen, cracking open every cupboard and drawer in her search of supplies. The chicken soup cooling in the bowl in front of me smells better than anything we've ever made in this kitchen before.

Ronan dives into his immediately, the steam swirling above his bowl not deterring him. Briar's eyes twinkle with hope as she watches him.

"I enjoy it. Usually more when I get to cook for other people. Clover hogs that responsibility most of the time, so I'm stuck creating meals for one," she answers me, still eyeing Ronan.

He's like a dog who hasn't been fed in weeks. My mouth is gaping as he plows through the soup, barely chewing the chicken and vegetables before swallowing.

"I think it's safe to say that you can cook for us anytime you want. If you give us the chance to do the same," I say.

Ronan blinks, seemingly realizing how feral he appears and making a show of chewing his next spoonful. It's comical the way he tries to tame himself around Briar, as if she wasn't watching him with complete devotion while he tore into his food.

I dip my spoon into the hot soup and load it up with a bit of everything before bringing it to my mouth. The immediate burst of flavour on my tongue makes it easier to understand Ronan's lack of table manners.

"This is really, really good," Dash tells her, speaking my thoughts out loud.

"You didn't have all the normal ingredients I would have used, but I tried my best. Maybe next time I come over, I can bring some of my own groceries?"

I swallow my mouthful and clear my throat when my stomach growls, demanding more. "How about you just give us a list of what you need, and we'll make sure it's here for you."

"That goes for anything," Ronan adds.

Briar kneads her lip with her teeth and darts her eyes between all three of us. "I'll keep that in mind."

"Are you sure you don't want to have any? We'll devour the leftovers, but I don't want you being hungry," I say.

"I ate a big dinner, actually. Is Landon hungry? Or has he already eaten?"

My chest pangs. "He hasn't eaten."

"Do you know where he is? I don't mind bringing him something to eat."

"You don't have to do that. I can," Dash offers.

Briar shakes her head, determined. "No, I will. Where is he?"

"I told him to go to bed, but I didn't think about him being hungry," Dash says, wincing as he stares down at his bowl.

"He does need sleep. At least, he did the last time I saw him. Is it worse?" she asks, setting a hand over Dash's and squeezing.

It's such a subtle way of reassuring him. A very omega way of offering support that means more to Dash than he'll ever know how to explain.

Ronan sets his spoon in his empty bowl as I slip mine back into my mouth.

"Yeah, it's worse. He'll crash out hard one of these days," he grunts.

"Where's his bedroom?" Briar asks.

Swallowing, I accept that she won't let this go. If we're being realistic here, she may be the best person to go up and see him right now, anyway. While alphas can be overbearing and demanding, we're not the top of the food chain in our society. We're naturally weak for omegas. Our desire to provide for them and make them happy overpowers our natural need for control and power.

Landon can pretend he's unmoved by Briar, but I feel it in my gut that he'd be the first to sacrifice himself for her.

Ronan meets my stare from the opposite end of the dining table, and I know he's thinking the same thing I am. We can only shove our instincts down so far before they come rushing back with a vengeance that we have no chance of stopping, and Landon might be closer to that outcome than he's ready to accept.

"When you get upstairs, go straight down the first hall. His room is on the left," I explain.

"Thank you."

She releases Dash's hand and moves to me before kissing my cheek and stepping up to the stove. There's an empty bowl already on the countertop, and she fills it to the rim.

With a spoon in her other hand, she turns to us, eyes falling on Ronan and his outrageous pout. The corner of her mouth twitches before she goes up to him and plants a dramatic kiss on his cheek, like the one she laid on mine.

"Better?" she asks teasingly.

He makes a low noise in response and snakes a hand up to hold her waist, keeping her beside him. When he stands, her head falls back on instinct.

"Almost," Ronan mutters.

Instead of accepting her initial kiss, he takes her jaw in his hand and lays one on her mouth instead. She falls into it without hesitation, and while I wish she were kissing me too, I don't feel the sharp teeth of jealousy. Instead, it's yearning that overwhelms me.

With pink cheeks, Briar pulls back and adjusts her hold on the hot bowl. Ronan keeps his dark eyes pinned on her, a million promises written within them that I'm sure both Dash and I feel as well.

"I'll be back," she squeaks, voice thick before she clears it.

I nod. "We'll be here if you need us."

"I know."

And her confidence in us—in me—is more than enough.

MONTGOMERY
PACK

Briar

I FEEL as hot as the bowl I'm holding when I head up the staircase. Kissing Ronan is indescribable in the best way, but doing it in front of both Dash and Jasper somehow ramps up the intensity. Especially when neither of them said anything against it and instead . . . watched with a shared intensity that was more attractive than anything I've ever witnessed before.

In pack relationships, obviously I know that sharing is a common thing. But not once in my life have I gotten the chance to experience that. During my heats, I've always gone to a clinic and requested a single alpha as opposed to one of the omegaless packs that volunteer. I wanted to save that experience for my pack instead of wasting it on a group of strangers who wouldn't find anything special in it.

My nipples peak in my bra as I try to control my breathing. Lingering at the top of the staircase, I sniff the air to make sure I haven't started perfuming too badly before attempting even one more step. Perfuming in front of Landon would actually be my worst nightmare.

Luckily, my scent is only a bit sweeter than normal, so I keep walking. The soup in my hands isn't anything special, but I couldn't not offer Landon anything. My omega wouldn't stop clawing at me the entire time I was cooking it, trying to get me to find and feed him.

I want to take care of Landon, even if he doesn't want me to. That either makes me naïve or dedicated. I'm not sure which is more accurate quite yet.

My heart rate kicks up with every door I pass. Most of them are open, allowing me a brief look inside while the others have my mind running quickly to try and guess what's hidden out of sight. I wish I wasn't so on edge because I'd love to do a bit of snooping to see which room belongs to which alpha.

Last room on the left, Briar. Focus.

I've got this. Landon might be ready to draw my blood at any given moment, but at least . . . No, there's not an at least here.

I stop in front of the door Jasper told me was Landon's and gulp when his scent grows stronger than I've ever smelled it. My head swims as I lift a hand and rap my knuckles across the door.

There's not a single noise from inside the room. I wait for another minute before growing worried. With a glance back down the hall, I look at the rest of the doors, curious if I chose the wrong one. Surely, I didn't. This is the last door on the left, and there was only one hallway to take.

I knock again, a bit harder this time. The inside of my cheek burns when I bite down on it hard enough to taste blood when he doesn't answer again.

It's possible that he didn't go up to his room like the others thought, but there's a force at my back, softly nudging me to go inside to make sure. I squeeze my eyes shut and drop my hand to the doorknob before giving it a test twist. It goes all the way, unlocked.

With a gentle push, I open the door enough to get hit with a wall of vanilla and cinnamon. My grip is slick on the doorknob as I grow hot beneath my skin. I release it and rub my palms on my skirt.

Landon's bedroom is exactly what I would have expected a grumpy alpha's would look like. The lights are off, but that doesn't affect my ability to see the dark grey walls, drawn blackout curtains with the slightest gap between them, and gigantic bed pushed against the far wall. It's fitted with a thick, black duvet thrown aside messily from the two singular pillows, as if someone jumped out from beneath without tucking it back in.

A small sliver of light spills onto the floor beside the bed, acting like a beacon. I glance down at the bowl of soup in my hands and then to the two-door nightstand on the side of the bed with the thrown-back duvet. Tossing all caution to the wind, I set the bowl down atop it and head for the light.

My socks cushion my steps on the hardwood as I creep toward the cracked open door and pause, my eyes catching on the reflection in the mirror hung on the wall beyond it. Breathing is suddenly a foreign concept.

Worry mixes with desire so sharp I can taste it. I battle off the latter and step inside, focusing on the man asleep in the tub.

"Landon?"

It's hot enough in the bathroom for steam to appear thick in the air as I move to the soaker tub planted in the centre of the room. It's impossible not to blush as I keep my eyes above the clear water.

He shouldn't be sleeping in here. Especially when he's alone on the second floor with nobody to keep an eye on him. It's reckless, and as my frustration blooms, I have to focus on not waking him up and demanding he go to his bed.

But how am I supposed to do that right now? When for the first time since I've met him, he isn't scowling or demanding I leave him alone?

His eyes are shut peacefully, and the frown lines that live in his forehead are smoothed out for once. The lips that are always formed around his blunt, cold words are relaxed, parted with his steady breaths.

The hard edge of the tub digs into the back of his neck, but I doubt he feels it. I'm not sure he feels much of anything right now. With his black hair and naked upper chest completely dry, it doesn't look like he got much washing done before he fell asleep. If that was why he got in the bath at all.

Continuing to keep my gaze above the water, I take the chance to simply stare at him without his eyes on me, too intense to handle without growing nervous.

With his shoulders as wide as the tub, he has his arms draped over both sides of it, big hands hanging loose. One knee is bent, popping out of the water. The purple and yellow bruises mottling the otherwise pale skin are concerning, and before I can talk myself out of it, I'm reaching out to touch them.

My breath hitches when my fingertips brush the hot skin. Despite the dark hair, it's smooth. I force my hand back to my side and stare at the small stool in the corner of the room.

It's like I'm running on autopilot as I grab it and set it beside the tub, sitting beside the alpha who every cell of my genetic makeup says is mine.

As if sensing that he's not alone anymore, Landon sighs in his sleep, his fingers flexing and reaching through the air. I swallow, my throat tight and dry when they narrowly miss my bare calf.

It's completely silent in the bathroom besides our breathing when I dip my fingers into the tub by his shoulder to test the temperature of the water. I'm relieved that it's still warm.

As long as he isn't alone, he should stay asleep for as long as possible.

His head rolls along the back of the tub toward me as he groans again, this time sounding like he's in pain. The scrunch of his nose and brows poke at something sensitive between my ribs.

It's a summoning that I'm too weak to ignore. With bated breath, I bring my fingers to his hair, giving the thick strands a test stroke. They're silky and strong, curling between my fingers and tickling my palms.

"Briar," he mumbles, the sound of my name on his lips shooting like an arrow through my chest as he relaxes once again.

I freeze, a hand still buried in his hair. A moment passes, then another without him moving before I can get myself to continue. He doesn't really know I'm here, even if his subconscious recognizes my touch.

Inhaling, I let his scent wrap around every inch of me, inside and out, bottom to top. The peace that greets me is yet another reminder that I'm exactly where I need to be.

I have to believe that there will be another chance for us to be close like this again when he's awake and can witness how good it feels to accept the pull that keeps trying to yank us together.

Once he does . . . everything will change.

27

Briar

"I'M STARTING TO BELIEVE THAT THIS BABY WILL NEVER come out," Sadie moans, collapsing on the arena seat between me and Clover.

"I'd prefer not to induce you, so as long as everything keeps looking as great as right now, we'll keep you cooking the little girl for a bit longer," Clover says.

She gently pats Sadie's swollen belly and offers her a sympathetic smile.

The pregnant omega sighs. "It could be worse, I guess."

"That's the spirit," Clover cheers.

I shake my head at the two of them, too nervous to add anything to the conversation. I'm not only at my first-ever hockey game, but the star players are also my future packmates.

Getting dressed this morning in the custom jersey Jasper sent me felt like a dream. It's a claim that's obvious to me but subtle to those who don't know me or them. The giant number 1 and letters spelling out Montgomery on my back make my skin tingle beneath the jersey. Even sitting only a few rows from the ice, I'm burning up inside, my skin damp and mouth dry.

It helps having Clover and Sadie here with me for support. The shy omega we only met a few weeks ago seems to be the perfect fit for our small friend group. She's the only pre-existing hockey fan out of us three and was gracious enough to give me a bit of a rundown on the rules and positions on the way here.

"You look like you're going to crap your pants, Bee," Clover says, leaning over Sadie's lap.

"I'm just nervous."

"Why? Do you think they'll lose?"

"No. They're good, right?"

"The Riptides are doing well so far. They've been better, though," Sadie says with a hand buried deep in the bucket of buttery popcorn she's balancing on her belly.

I'm more concerned about Landon's knee than I am the team's standings in the league. From the look of his bruising, he's been in a lot of pain for at least a week. I'm not sure continuing to play with an injury is the best choice.

"Do you know how Landon hurt his knee?" I ask.

Sadie nods. "It was a knee-on-knee hit with another player."

"That's allowed?" I ask, sucking air between my teeth. Another flush of heat races up my spine as I try not to outright pant.

"No. The hit came in the middle of a game a couple of weeks ago. Orlovsky is a dirty player and got kicked out for it."

My stomach turns, cramping slightly. "That's good, at least."

"The team wouldn't let Montgomery play if they thought he could worsen his injury," someone says from my opposite side.

Our seats are close to the rink in a section reserved for omegas. That doesn't change that the man standing beside my seat is clearly an alpha. He's wearing a Rayton Riptides jersey, and after studying the numbers of the Montgomery pack earlier today, I know the 5 on his shoulder belongs to Ronan.

"I think you're in the wrong section," Clover snaps.

The anxious vibes coming off Sadie right now are strong enough to make my nose burn with her scorched scent. She agreed to come out tonight knowing that we would be in the omega-only section. I'm still shocked she said yes even with that reassurance.

"The seats here are better than they are on the other side. That's not very fair, is it? We all pay the same to watch these games," he states nonchalantly.

Still standing beside me, he stares down at us with intrigue. It's the same look that's responsible for the special "Omega Only" sections in most public spaces. Some alphas don't know how to properly behave around an unmated omega, and that makes them a danger to us.

After having so many accidental matings over the past decade, all omegas must be given the opportunity to sit in omega-only areas. Usually, Clover and I don't bother, but with Sadie in attendance, we figured we'd give it a try. It seems that now it was just a waste of a few extra hundred bucks.

"Do you want me to call security and have them haul you out of here?" Clover asks, pushing to her feet.

We're all small in comparison to this guy, but Clover's the tallest of us and has the sharpest bravado. I've seen her intimidate alphas far bigger than this one in less busy spaces.

I sneak a glance at the seats around ours and relax slightly when I see the number of empty seats. Apart from our small section, everyone already sitting on this side of the arena seems to be focused on the ice and where both teams are now skating around the boards for their warm-up. I try to search for one of the Montgomery alphas but flinch back into my seat when a firm hand touches my head, stroking my hair.

"Hands off, fucker," Clover hisses at him.

He glares at her. "Settle down, omega. I'll warm this seat here for whoever it belongs to."

I don't jump out of my seat the way I want to. Sadie was supposed to have a fun night out before baby comes, not get caught up being accosted by a no-good alpha like the ones she's currently trying to avoid. I'll happily be a buffer between her and him until security realizes that they let an alpha in.

"You're all unmated. Why not give a guy a chance?" the alpha asks, his grin making bile crawl up my throat.

If his receding hairline wasn't bad enough, his strong rubber scent would be. I want to run away from him, but I stay in my seat and reach for Sadie's hand, finding it fisted in her lap.

This is the last situation I wanted to be in tonight. Calling attention to myself while attending my very first hockey game is a complete nightmare. I don't want a single member of the Montgomery pack to think I'm trying to embarrass them or that having an omega is more work than it's worth.

"Who said we're unmated?" I ask, cocking my head.

His eyes fix themselves to my throat, and he inhales deeply. "Where's the bite, then? You smell good enough to eat, omega."

"Don't you know that there are far more interesting places to be marked than the throat," I retort.

It's the wrong thing to say. Instead of respecting that I could be mated, he grows more interested. His eyes slip down my body at a snail's pace, lingering on my chest.

"Do tell this lonely alpha where you've been bitten, beauty," he drawls.

"Briar," Clover says.

I ignore her, narrowing my eyes on this guy. When I push to my feet, his expression shifts, growing darker.

"Unless you want me to scream for help, you'll leave us alone. I'm sure you're aware of what happens to alphas who find themselves threatening the safety of an omega in a public space," I warn, voice low in an attempt not to call any more attention to us.

"Briar," Clover repeats my name with more force behind it this time. "Look—"

The alpha extends his hand and tucks a finger beneath the collar of my jersey to try and expose my shoulder. I flinch, his touch ice-cold. There's a bang from the boards a breath later that sends him stumbling.

I step back and nearly fall onto Sadie's lap before Clover's catching me, standing at my back. As I whip my head to the ice, my heart skips several beats.

Electric-blue eyes catch mine from where Landon stands at the plexiglass. My inhale is shaky and sharp as I take in the sight of him wearing bulky padding, a jersey with the number 29 and a C on the chest, and skates that add a few inches to his already towering height. His nostrils flare as he wets his lips and darts his eyes to the alpha beside me who's frozen in place, still lingering.

The growl that escapes Landon is feral, cold enough to chill someone right down to the bone.

He punches the glass with a gloved hand and flashes twin rows of white teeth as he snarls at the man, who takes another careless step in our direction. The gasps from around us don't faze me. I'm trapped in Landon's orbit, too busy preening at his protectiveness to worry about what other omegas are thinking.

He's my alpha, not theirs.

Oh, god. I'm hot all over again, this time in addition to a tightness in my belly that shouldn't be there yet. I keep waiting for another sign of an impending heat to come, but nothing does.

My temperature dies down before I can smell a change in my scent, the pain disappearing. *False alarm.*

"Landon Montgomery," the alpha beside me blubbers. His large body suddenly stumbles over the empty seats in front of us and down to the glass, where he continues speaking. "Can you toss me over a puck? I'm a huge fan! Do you think you could get Ronan to give me a stick?"

The warm-up music blaring through the arena speakers hides Landon's reply, but slowly, I watch as the alpha fawning over him takes a step back from the ice, back ramrod straight. His heel catches on the empty seat behind him before he flops back onto it.

Landon pins him in place with a predatory gaze as I pull away from Clover and use the steps beside her seat to go down to the ice. My throat is dry as I pass by a row of women and keep my eyes in front of me instead of looking to see if they're watching.

I blink, and then Ronan's on the ice in front of me, his stick held at his side as he hangs back behind Landon. Dash appears on Ronan's right, both of them watching with strained expressions. I flash them a thumbs-up, and Dash nods, nudging Ronan's shoulder.

There isn't time to properly appreciate how good they look in all their gear right now, but I make a promise myself that I will once I've spoken to Landon.

What I'll say to him . . . I don't know yet. Thank you? Does this mean you're starting to like me?

By the time I get to where he's still standing on the opposite side of the plexiglass, the stranger is gone.

"What did you say to him?" I ask, clasping my hands at my middle and pressing them against the boards to avoid palming the glass.

He rakes his gaze over me from head to toe, as if doing a check to make sure I'm okay. It's less savage than it was a few seconds ago, but there's still a wicked gleam in the bright blue that feels like a rough touch on my body.

"Who was he?" His voice is almost garbled, the words tangled in a web of rage.

"I don't know. He showed up a few minutes ago."

Gosh, he's like a goliath right now. All of that messy black hair is poking out from beneath the back of his helmet, and damnit, he looks tired again.

It's been two days since I sat beside him in the bathroom, and the bags beneath his eyes make it appear like he hadn't slept at all.

"Have you been sleeping?" I blurt out.

He flexes his jaw. "That's not your concern."

"Isn't it?"

"Do you think one night of you invading my personal space to watch me sleep is an invitation into my life?"

I press my lips together hard, trying not to let my hurt show on my face.

"How did you know I did that?"

He laughs, but there's no humour in it. "Your scent was everywhere. Including my hair."

"You could have drowned. Weren't you ever told not to sleep in the bath?"

As his laugh dies off, he pushes closer to the plexiglass and narrows his eyes on me. "I don't need you to look after me. If I want to sleep in the bath, I will. And next time, I'll make sure to lock the fucking door."

"I'm trying here, Landon," I push, hating the quiver in my voice as I plant my hands on my waist and lift my chin. "What can I do to prove to you that I'm not as bad as you think I am?"

Even with the wall between us—both physically and emotionally—I still want to touch him. Want to be with him in any way possible. And I've never felt weaker in my life for it.

"Nothing," he grits out, tightening his grip on his stick. "You can wear the jersey and make yourself comfortable in my home, but you won't be my packmate, let alone my omega. I have enough packmates, and I've never wanted an omega."

I shake my head, pushing harder. "I don't believe you. If you didn't feel anything for me, you wouldn't be here right now, inserting yourself into a situation that didn't involve you at all. And when I sat beside you and kept you company for an hour in the bathroom, you wouldn't have called out for me and leaned into my touch like you knew I was there.

"I want to know what it is that's keeping you from giving me a chance. Unless you tell me what I'm up against, I won't be able to help change your mind, Landon."

He turns his head to the right and then to the left, checking his surroundings before focusing the full weight of his attention on me again. I don't bend beneath it.

"If you want to help me, you'll sit back down and forget about what just happened. It was a mistake to come over here."

And just like that, the slimmest glimmer of light is blocked out. Landon turns around and skates off before I can get another word out. I'm silent as I avoid looking at the other guys on the ice and return to my seat.

Silent and with a fake smile.

Ronan

I SHRUG OFF ANOTHER HIT AND STRAIGHTEN OUT, focusing on the player trying to escape me. His glare is vicious behind his visor, but it has nothing on mine. I'm vibrating, adrenaline flooding my veins as I stalk him, forcing his teammate to abandon him and pass the puck off to someone else in a game of keep-away.

Jasper comes sweeping up from behind me and steals the puck before it meets the tape of the waiting player's stick. His pace is unbeatable. Here and gone in a flash, he carries the puck out of our zone and into Nashville's.

Spinning in a half circle, I slip past the forward I just blocked from getting a shot off and chase after Jasper. Dash claps his stick against his crossbar behind me while Landon tears his way up the ice across from Jasper, waiting.

He's not as fast as Jasper, but he's close. Even with a sore knee.

The Nashville defensemen pop up beside me, flanking both of my sides as they try and catch up to my packmates. I grin on instinct, loving the thrill that follows the chase. Skating full speed down the ice is the closest to flying I've experienced outside of an airplane.

Jasper and Landon stop in front of the Nashville net as

Jasper sets up for a shot. He flicks the puck off his stick, but it bounces off the upper corner of the goalie's shoulder. It slides away from the net enough for Landon to scoop it back up and evade the second Nashville player who pushes past me, trying to take it.

The first player doesn't make it past me before I shoulder him into the boards. Stick out and ready, I catch the puck Landon shoots to me and send it to Jasper before the player I'm watching has a chance to steal it.

Landon is battling against a defenseman a few inches taller than him, jabbing his elbows out to try and break free. I can't get to him without opening Jasper up to the guy on my ass.

The Nashville goalie tracks the puck with an ease that reminds me of the way Dash plays, his gait easy yet controlled. Jasper surveys the zone before eyeing Eklund, my defensive linemate.

The Swedish powerhouse skates through the slim gap that's been left open and taps for the pass. Jasper flicks it off to him and, in a blink, has it right back on his stick.

Landon manages to shove off the player who was guarding him and frees himself up enough to receive an expert pass from Jasper. Everything moves in slow motion then.

His aim is perfect the way it always is as he snaps a shot off and sends the puck sailing through the only opening the goalie hasn't managed to close. It sinks into the top left corner of the netting before the buzzer goes off, loud and proud.

Red light flares as he does a lap around the back of the net and glides to the bench without celebrating. His stick drags behind him on the ice while he stares out at the stands where I know Briar's sitting wearing the jersey we got her. She's been there from the moment we hit the ice for warm-ups, but fuck, there's something off with her.

I know it has to do with Landon, and honestly, I'm struggling to keep from giving him a very public beat down right now. I've had enough of his attitude, and seeing Briar hardly managing to clap to celebrate Landon's goal is my last straw.

From the quick push of Landon's skates as he hops over the boards and onto the bench, I'm positive it's his as well.

Jasper joins me as we follow our pack leader and leave the ice. Coach slaps me on the back while speaking to one of our rookies sitting on the end of the bench.

I drop my body on the opening beside Landon and lean my stick against the boards. "You're not in it again."

"Don't lecture me."

"You deserve one," I bite out.

The puck drops for a faceoff, and our second line sets out to try and add another goal to our three-to-nothing score. Landon ignores me, fixing his attention on the ice.

I jostle his leg with my knee. "What did you say to Briar?"

He grabs the squeeze bottle of water offered to him by a member of the coaching staff and squirts it into his mouth. It's obviously a stalling tactic, but as the whistle blows and an offside is called, the window we can use to talk grows larger.

"Did you know about her being in my bathroom?"

"Yeah. You're lucky she didn't drown you with how shitty you've been to her."

"She had no right to bust into my space," he snaps.

"Is that what you said to her? You gave her shit for looking after you like a sorry fuck?" I ask, exasperated.

Landon tosses his water bottle beneath the bench and spreads his legs as wide as possible. His exhale is angry.

"They were supposed to be in an omega-only section. Why was there a fucking alpha there talking to her?"

A light bulb glows in my head as I watch his possessiveness flare. "You told him off, right?"

"Yeah. I got rid of him."

"So why did she deserve your shitty attitude?"

He stretches his leg out and hisses, glaring at his knee. "She didn't."

"You can apologize tonight, then," Jasper says, hovering over us from behind.

"She's coming to the house?" Landon growls.

Jasper lifts both of his brows. "What's wrong with that?"

"Nothing. I'll be in the gym burning off the rush."

"No. You'll be with the rest of us doing whatever it is we decide to do," Jasper states.

Landon's lip curls slightly before he rolls his jaw. "And what are you going to do?"

"Montgomerys, get your asses on the ice now. Enough gossiping," Coach demands, waving a hand over the boards.

We rush to listen, conversation abandoned for the time being. Something tells me there won't be any reason to revisit it after we're done here. Landon's growing more bothered by Briar as the days go on. His ire toward her is dulling, and I'm fucking excited to see how weak he grows tonight.

MONTGOMERY
PACK

"Are you sure you don't want us to drive you?" I ask, hovering in front of my omega.

Briar offers me a soft smile and nods, stroking my bare arm. My dress shirt was left abandoned in my bag in exchange for a plain shirt.

"How about you bring me home on your bike later instead?"

"Fuck, Petal. Don't tease me."

"Would I do that?" she teases, batting her lashes.

I want her to come home with us right now, but Clover, the omega who's currently trying to intimidate me with a narrowed gaze, is adamant about being the one to drop her off at our place. The pregnant woman beside her is shy, cowering slightly.

Jasper, Dash, and I keep a healthy distance away from her.

I tug at the hem of Briar's jersey, rock hard in my slacks with how perfect she looks in it. "When will you be done?"

"I'll have her to you as soon as we've dropped Sadie off," Clover answers for Briar.

"We'll wait as long as it takes," Jasper says, stepping up to press a kiss to Briar's cheek. "Being with you is our only plan for tonight."

She flushes, that warm lemon scent sweeter than I'm used to. "Are you sure it won't be too late? I can imagine you're all tired."

"We'll survive," I grunt.

Clover snakes an arm around Briar's. "On that note, it's time to go, Bee."

"I'll text when I'm on my way. You all played amazing, by the way. I wasn't expecting you to be so fast, considering how big you are," Briar rambles, looking at all three of us.

My knot swells, precum soaking into my briefs as I nod in response to the naturally innocent compliment. I'm still ramped up with adrenaline, and with her so close, wearing our pack name on her back, I'm already close to falling into a rut without hearing how fucking big she thinks we are.

I take a step back before my scent shifts to expose my arousal and hold myself in check.

Jasper's voice is deeper than normal as he says, "Thank you, love. We'll see you soon."

Yeah, he's fucking hard as shit too.

Our perfect omega nods excitedly and allows her friends to tug her away and toward the hall that will take them back up to the public exit. I swallow past the lust that's grown thick in my throat.

"Landon's outside already?"

Dash sighs. "Yeah. He was the first one out."

"What did he say to her on the ice?" Jasper asks.

I tame my anger with a deep inhale. "Not sure. But he was an asshole."

"Do you think tonight is still a good idea?" Jasper leads the way to the player-only exit, where our SUV is parked.

"We need to give him a nudge," I state.

Jasper slows his pace slightly, matching mine. "How?"

"He wants her. His denial is bullshit," I say.

Dash hums his agreement while Jasper shifts to stand in front of the both of us. We freeze in the parking lot, waiting for him to speak.

"What do you suggest we do?" he asks, hope bright in his eyes.

I wet my lips, glancing at where our SUV sits, the engine running and headlights illuminating the parking lot.

"We know his routine. Let's use it to our advantage."

"Be careful, Ronan. We can only push so far," Dash warns.

I shake my head, anger beating at my chest. "I think I'm about done with being careful. If my option is having Briar be a member of our pack or pushing Landon an inch too far, I'm going to choose the first option. Pack leader or not, he doesn't control us. Briar is my fucking omega, and I'm not waiting around for him to pull his head out of his ass and risking losing her because of it."

"I'm willing to give it a try," Jasper agrees.

I clasp a hand to both of their shoulders. "Fucking good. Tonight will either change things for the better or for the worse. I'm ready either way."

29

Briar

THERE'S A DIFFERENT ENERGY TO THE GUYS TONIGHT, most likely because of their incredible game tonight.

Maybe I'm biased because it's the only one I've been to, but I enjoyed it a lot. The score was high, with the Riptides scoring five goals, and Ronan was in the penalty box once for a tripping call. It almost looked like he enjoyed being in there too, which didn't surprise me. Something tells me that Ronan is fully aware of every move he makes that could lead to being sent away for two minutes.

Dash had a shutout game, which I learned from Sadie before we dropped her off means he didn't let the other team score. Jasper skates faster than what should be humanly possible, and Landon . . . well, it's obvious why he's the captain of the team. Not only does he carry himself with a proud sense of leadership, but his ability to take control on the ice while under pressure is admirable. It's obvious he's someone who can think well on his feet.

I've been on the receiving end of his quick thinking a few times already, but not a single time have I enjoyed it.

Wiggling into the couch cushion beneath me, I blink at the movie playing on the flat screen and swallow a sigh. I chose which one we're watching, but I haven't been able to focus on it once. My brain keeps going back to the only person not here on the couch with me.

Ronan stretches his arm where it's draped over my shoulder and runs his curved nails up and down my bicep. Tonight is the first time I've gotten a chance to really examine the tattoos that cover the length of his arm. He has a full sleeve, but every design feels important. Like he had each one designed with a story to tell.

The first one—my favourite—involves four stars that circle a planet. It feels like a call-out to us, even though he must have gotten it inked a while ago, long before I came along. Then there's the hockey stick with the number 5 on the blade and two women's names, along with a bolded Montgomery.

I settle further beneath his arm while Jasper nuzzles his cheek against my knee from his place on the floor in front of me. He kisses me there, and my chest tightens, the obvious affection from the two men causing my heart to swell too big.

Dash is on my other side but hasn't made a move to touch me yet. At least his scent is soft and rich, which I've taken as a good sign.

"He's down in the gym, Petal," Ronan whispers, leaning close to my ear.

My pulse skips. "Who?"

We've avoided talking about Landon all night. When I arrived an hour ago, he was already hiding away. His scent was strong, though, which told me he was still at home.

"Go talk to him. We'll be here waiting."

"He doesn't want to talk to me."

Dash makes a humoured noise in his throat while Jasper palms my ankle, stroking the bone with a slow touch.

"Landon spends hours in the gym after a game. It's not healthy. Maybe you can help convince him of that," Jasper suggests.

"I think the last thing he wants is me to convince him of anything," I argue.

Dash turns his head, taking me in with a worried expression. "Would you check on him instead? For us?"

It's worth a shot. His lack of acceptance shouldn't mean that he's left to struggle alone.

"I'll try. Don't get your hopes up, though. I'm the last person he wants checking on him."

Ronan releases a gruff noise and tugs me into his side. I fit into the curve of his body perfectly, like I was always meant to be right here.

"Call for one of us if you need anything. I'll come running," he promises.

I smooth a hand down his thigh, feeling the muscles flex and strain beneath my touch. "Okay."

His breath catches on a low groan while Jasper slides out from between my legs. My skin flushes at the sound before I'm standing and taking quick steps away from the couch, knowing if I don't move fast, I'll wind up stuck here, pinned between two alphas and a curious beta.

"I'll be back, then," I rush out, slick pooling in my panties.

Ronan jerks his chin in a forced nod while he grips the arm of the couch. Dash glances at him before Jasper's shoving pointedly at his knee.

I slip out of the room while their attention isn't on me and make a beeline for the basement. I've only had a brief tour of this area of the house, but as I start down the dimly lit staircase, I let my instincts guide me forward.

The basement is huge, with a couple of bedrooms, a storage room as big as my entire apartment, and the home gym, which rivals any public one I've ever been to. Each door is open besides the one I stop in front of, the scent of vanilla and cinnamon slipping through.

Music pulses behind the door as I hesitate to enter. Somewhere deep inside my chest, I know this should be the last time I try with Landon. If he doesn't let me in even just a little after this, he probably never will, and forcing myself to believe otherwise isn't healthy.

I'll still be able to have a pack of my own, even if it's not complete.

With a swallow, I glide the door open and step inside. I don't see him at first. The room is a bit overwhelming with workout machines I've never used and racks upon racks of weights. Mirrors are hung on the opposite side of the room while two swinging bags dangle from the ceiling.

My sock-covered feet sink into the black floor as I sway further inside, drawn by the tether in my chest. The hairs on my arms stand up as my skin pebbles. A turn of my head and I'm lost. My knees lock up, forbidding me to run as I stare across the room.

Landon hasn't noticed me yet. He's too focused on his exercise.

Large puffs of air escape him as he glares at the ceiling and lifts the weight bar above his chest. His naked, gleaming chest and the carved abdominal muscles that might as well be winking at me as they flex. My eyes struggle to focus as he lowers the bar and grunts, spreading his legs further and digging his heels into the floor.

Again, he lifts the weights. His biceps are thick and round and so damn *hard* as they carry the weight. I don't have to feel them to know that. I've never seen arms or a chest like that.

His shoulders are wide enough to hang over the bench in a way that I would assume isn't all that comfortable and despite being half hidden in a pair of loose basketball shorts, his thighs are unbelievably muscled.

Heat crawls up my spine and throat before painting my cheeks red. I feel the burn so deep I know there's no chance of dousing the flames before an ache builds in my belly. Gritting my teeth at the discomfort, I press my thighs together and release a weak breath.

The wall is behind me, too far to lean back against as I gasp, throbbing between my legs. Pressure rises, my scent spiking and flaring wide in a call meant for him.

Another jab goes through my middle, forcing my eyes closed while I wince. There's a loud clang that rattles in my ears and pricks at my skull. Suddenly, I'm too sensitive, every inch of my skin buzzing.

I choke on the air, Landon's scent battling mine with an intensity that doesn't seem real. It just makes everything worse. The yearning in my chest, the throb in my core, and the slick pouring out of me faster than water in a faucet.

"Briar." His voice draws a moan up my throat. "Get out of here."

I shake my head, opening my eyes to find him right in front of me, and *oh, god.* Craning my head back, I trail my eyes up his entire torso. Over the ridges of the abs still glistening with sweat, the sharply contoured pecs and broad shoulders pushed back with dominance. My pussy throbs so fiercely I flinch before finally meeting his blazing stare.

The heat rippling off him is still nowhere as intense as the gleam in his eyes as he grinds his teeth. Veins strain beneath the thin skin of his throat before he speaks again.

"You need to leave."

Panic explodes inside of me. "No."

Slowly, he looks down. The heat beneath my palm has me doing the same, only to find my hand planted firmly on his chest. I hold my breath and press harder, watching in fascination as his muscles ripple in response.

"Why are you so warm? Your scent is wrong," he hisses.

I wait for him to step back or push my hand away in disgust, but he doesn't. Pupils expanding, Landon leans forward, close enough for my elbow to bend at our proximity.

"Wrong?" I whisper.

He inhales, body quaking. "You smell like you're—"

"In heat."

The growl that escapes him should send me running in terror.

It's deep and raw, aggressive but somehow comforting to the omega inside of me. Fear is the last thing I feel right now.

"Are you?"

"Not yet. I can't be."

It has to be another spike. My next heat cycle is closing in, but surely, I have at *least* another week to figure out what I'm going to do. I'm not ready for it yet, and the signs haven't started yet other than for brief moments. My stomach swirls at the thought of sharing my heat with anyone but a member of this pack.

As if sensing where my mind has gone, Landon shocks me by snapping a hand out and cupping my face. It swallows the side of my head in a strong, possessive hold that I can't help but wish was between my legs. The pre-heat hormones twist me up inside, forcing all my innermost desires to the surface regardless of how much force I apply to shove them back down.

I need Landon. Need him on me, with me, inside me. Yes, inside me. He'll know how to help. We're mates. I'm his to soothe.

"Please, Lan," I plead.

His expression shudders and cracks. The mask he wears disappears as he strokes his thumb over my chin and below my jaw to where my pulse thrashes.

"Please what, Haven?"

My heart beats wildly. "Please help me."

"You have no idea what you're asking for."

His cinnamon scent is on fire. I lean toward him, bringing a second hand to his middle and slipping it around his back.

"It has to be you," I state through the fog in my mind.

He hisses a breath and tightens his hold on my face, fingers threading through the hair behind my ear. Lips grazing my forehead, he shifts his hips, letting me feel the hard press of him in his shorts.

"It won't mean anything."

"You're lying."

"Get one of the others to help," he demands, not moving away.

I splay my fingers on his abdomen and stroke the firm muscles. "Touch me, Landon."

"Jasper would be better to you," he argues, sounding weaker with every word.

"Is that what you want? Someone else to do your job for you?"

It's a lowball shot, but I'm desperate. Every moment I don't get relief, the pain grows more intense, threatening to steal the air from my lungs. I could leave, but my body wants Landon right now. Needs him more than it needs anyone else.

Sparks fly in his eyes. "Nobody could do as good of a job as me."

"It's fine. I'll ask Ronan." My body cries in outrage as I release him and take a single step back. "He's already—"

Suddenly, Landon's hands are all over me. One second, my feet are on the ground, and the next, they're in the air, and my back is planted on the same weight bench, still warm from his body.

My entire body shakes in anticipation as the emptiness inside of me grows more painful. Landon drops to his knees at the end of the bench and grabs my thighs, yanking me toward him. His nostrils flare as he inhales and paws at the hem of my dress. It's high on my thighs but still hides my panties. I shed the jersey earlier, and I'm grateful for that now. It would have been too thick. Too bulky and in the way.

"It's my turn," he snaps before my dress is shoved up to my belly, my slicked panties exposed. "You can scream, omega. Let *Ronan* know who's making you come now."

Coherent thought escapes me. The only thing I can do is nod and fall into the promise of relief. My eyes roll back as the band of my panties snaps and the soiled material is peeled away, baring me completely.

"I'll be the first one to taste this pussy, Briar," he spits, angry at me for something I don't care to learn the reason for yet.

"Yes," I moan.

He shoves my legs up and away before diving between them. His tongue draws a hot line up my pussy before he sucks at me and fills the gym with a rattled curse. My vision disappears as the pain eases, replaced with a blast of pleasure that makes me jerk against the bench.

"Call my name," Landon demands, tongue lashing my entrance.

A thick finger slides inside, filling and stretching. I push up with my hips, searching for more.

"Landon," I breathe out.

"*Louder.*"

He adds a second finger while pulling my clit into his mouth, teasing it with his teeth. I reach down and grab at his hair, needing more of a connection with him. His responding groan shoots through me. Two fingers curl with every thrust, dragging across the spot that blackens my vision.

"Landon!"

"That's it. I'm the one easing your pain. You needed it this way, right? Needed me." His voice drops, darkening. "Wanted me."

"Wanted you," I repeat mindlessly, chasing the relief dangling above me.

"Fuck. You're gushing on my tongue. Slicking me up, Haven. This room will smell like you for weeks."

I nod, reaching behind me for the bench, needing stability. His hair is so soft that it pains me to pull on it as I thrash below his mouth.

My lemon scent swirls around vanilla and cinnamon until they become one. It's still not enough. Nothing is enough.

"Please, Landon. Please," I cry out, tears flooding my eyes.

My alpha pushes harder. I hardly register each flick of his

tongue as he drives me closer to release, fingers pistoning inside of me.

"Give it to me, Briar. Let this perfect pussy come for me."

Time freezes. Landon's eyes snare mine, brutally beautiful and cruel. He snarls as I come, slick pouring out of me and into his mouth. His fingers don't slow as I quiver around them.

"Landon," I whimper, the heat not breaking the way it's supposed to.

Another slash of pain moves through my belly, bringing a second wave of tears to my eyes. Frustration and fear make it hard to think clearly.

Bright blue eyes blink up at me from where he kneels on the floor and slowly eases back, fingers slipping free. "Go, Briar. Leave."

"It's not getting better. It should. It's just a spike," I ramble, voice lifting with worry.

The next wave of pain has me pushing up and away from him. My dress falls to cover me as I breathe in through a constricting throat.

Concern twists his expression. His mouth is still wet with my slick, lips glossy and swollen.

"What do you mean it isn't getting better?"

Sweat breaks out on the back of my neck. My nipples are so hard they're painful as they brush against my dress, attempting to cut right through the fabric.

"Touch me again, Landon."

"I can't."

I whine, heart crumbling. "Why not? You just did."

"What do you need? Another?"

"Maybe. Yes. I think so. I don't know. It's just—" My stomach cramps, and I lean over my thighs, breath pitching. I slur my next words. "Please, Landon. Just . . . just give me your knot."

"No. You're not getting that from any of us."

His rejection hurts worse than the cramping. "Why don't you want me?"

"Ronan!" Landon booms. When his eyes fall on me, he lowers his voice and adds, "You're not in heat. It's important to wait until then with the guys."

"It doesn't matter when it happens!"

"Yes, it does. You need to wait to be sure—"

"You still don't believe me?" I attack, looking up at him.

He doesn't hide from the question. "Not yet."

"What do you need from me? Go ahead and mark me, Landon. Do it and see for yourself."

I bare my throat for him, unashamed of the desperation tainting my words. There's no reason to pretend I'm anything but desperate right now. He already doesn't want me. Not for anything more than a quick heat spike relief session. Anything more than that and I might as well be proposing.

He focuses on my throat, head shaking. "Don't offer that to me. Even out of frustration. You can't take back a mating mark."

"You can. And I could," I threaten, knowing I'm playing with fire.

Insanity flashes in his eyes. "If you wore my mark, it would stay there for the rest of eternity. Long after we were both six feet under."

"Nobody is biting anyone," Ronan snaps from behind Landon.

"Ro," I whimper, my anger melting to make way for the desire clawing at my insides.

He lurches into action, lunging past Landon. I spread my legs in preparation, but suddenly, he's stopping. Inhaling, he focuses on Landon, staring and staring . . .

"What's going on?"

I claw at the top of my dress when it grows impossibly tighter, suffocating me. "I need more."

"More what, Petal? What did Landon give you?"

"You know what I gave her. Finish the job," Landon snips, avoiding my eyes.

Ronan keeps his sights set on his pack leader. I gush slick onto the weight bench, but I'm too drunk on desire to care. Let them see it. Maybe they'll finally come back to me.

My dark and broody alpha points a finger at Landon. "She needs you. You're doing this to her."

"Her heat's coming soon. Any day, if I had to guess. Keep an eye on her until it does," Landon demands.

How does he know that? Has he slept with that many omegas in heat?

I whine so loudly it burns my throat.

"You know what? I will. But you'll help."

Landon hesitates before releasing a warning growl. "Ronan."

I pant heavily and tug down the top of my dress to bare my chest. The heavy weights of my breasts bounce free before I dip a hand between my legs and swirl a finger through my hot, slick flesh. Pleasure bursts behind my eyes as I moan, eyes drifting shut.

The sound of a zipper sliding down floats into my ears before Ronan's voice calls out, encouraging me to open my eyes again. When I find him standing beside me with his jeans open, my mouth waters, hands reaching for him.

"There are plenty of ways to satiate an omega in pre-heat, Landon. If you're not up to be the one to help her, then stand there and fucking watch me do it for you."

30

Landon

HER TASTE LINGERS ON MY TONGUE LIKE A TEASE FROM the devil himself. I'm ten seconds away from taking her hand from where it's playing with her pussy and licking her fingers clean. Being on my knees has never felt as right as it does when I'm between hers.

Breasts hanging free, nipples hard and pink, she gapes up at Ronan, pleading with wild eyes. My packmate drops a hand to her head and strokes her hair before knuckling her chin and tipping it back further.

Briar pulls frantically at the waistband of his jeans and briefs, another pained noise balling up in her throat. I want to be the one to help her. To please her the way I did just minutes ago.

It should have been enough. An orgasm is always enough to help soothe an omega in pre-heat when their body is preparing them for the real thing. Yet it wasn't, and instead of giving her more, Ronan will do my job for me and make damn fucking sure I know it.

So why can't I leave?

My cock pulses, knot swelling to the point of discomfort as Ronan thumbs her parted lips and slowly sinks it inside her mouth. Briar sucks the digit, rosy lips sealed around it while his jeans fall to his knees.

She releases his thumb with a gasp and stares wide-eyed at his cock. It's got to be at least nine inches long and thick enough that she'll struggle to fit it into her mouth, but I'd bet it's not either of those things that have her so awestruck.

The black piercings running up and down the shaft are responsible for that.

"Like them?" Ronan asks, stroking her face and neck.

Briar moans, sliding her ass to the edge of the bench. She brings the tip of one finger to touch the bottom rung of his Jacob's ladder. Ronan hisses, thrusting forward slightly.

"Do they hurt?" she whispers.

"No."

Growing more confident, Briar leans into his groin and sticks her tongue out. Ronan's fingers curl in her hair when she brings the tip of it to the bottom rung.

"Count them with me, Petal."

She moans, flattening her tongue before circling both metal balls. "One."

I swallow thickly and release a harsh breath. There's a burn in my chest as I watch them. I'm not jealous. There's no place for jealousy in a pack. This is worse. It's a soul-deep desire to join them that's responsible for the inferno inside of me. Every second that I reject what my body and instincts demand that I do makes my yearning stronger.

I fear the day I won't be able to deny it anymore and my body gives out.

"Two," Briar whispers, having slid her tongue up to the second set of piercings.

Ronan's throat strains as he says, "Good girl."

Our omega preens at the praise, her body shaking with a shiver. The knot beneath her chin is as swollen as mine, and I watch with narrowed eyes when she wraps her hand around the bottom of it and squeezes.

Without realizing that I've grabbed myself, I feel the bulge of my knot beneath my palm and quickly replicate her squeezing movement. I lose the breath in my throat and freeze, focusing on the mix of relief and pleasure.

"Keep going, Briar. Don't get distracted now."

Focusing back on them, I whisper a curse. Briar's abandoned his knot in exchange for taking his shaft into her hand. Tongue lapping at the third rung of his ladder, she guides his cock toward her, the tip leaking so fiercely cum leaks down to pool on her tongue.

She pulls it into her mouth and moans, eyes closing. "Three."

"One more, Petal. One more and you can have more cum in your belly."

It's all she needs to hear. When her tongue meets the fourth set of piercings, she moves so close to the edge of the bench her ass hangs off. Sparks fill Ronan's eyes as he steers her by the hair to take his tip into her mouth.

"That's four. Now, take what you need, omega."

In a blink, she sinks down the first few inches. A gag fills the air before she shifts, a hand wrapping around Ronan to grab at his ass.

"Oh, shit," he grunts, palming the back of her head.

I squeeze myself again, wetness building inside my underwear. My balls ache, the weight of my knot nearly unbearable.

Briar sucks on the cock offered to her, gaining another inch every time she lowers her head. Tears leak down her cheeks, and the wet sound of her mouth fills the air. Ronan's caramel scent is strong, trying to smother my vanilla. Neither of us is any match for the sickly sweet lemon-sugar scent coming from Briar.

Each inhale makes me gush more, my knot expanding too big for its constraints. Ronan knows it too. He tenses his jaw and glances at me while encouraging Briar to take him deeper, the third rung of his ladder disappearing into her mouth.

"You're doing so good, Briar. I know what you need. My sweet little omega wasn't satisfied with just an orgasm, was she?

You need a belly full of your mate's cum to soothe you. Landon just wasn't up for the task."

A feral noise builds in my chest and escapes before I can stop it. The challenge bites at me as the vision of my omega choking on his cock burns my eyes. It should be me feeding her what she needs.

Scent-matched pairs are said to have so many benefits that I forgot about this one. I've spent so long refusing to believe that she could be mine—*ours*—that I let her needs escape me.

An alpha's cum has substantial benefits to their omega during heat, providing not only comfort but hormones meant to soothe, heal, and give enough sustenance to keep energy levels up without needing to break for food.

I never thought she would need that already or that it would even work. But if Ronan's helps, then . . . Fuck. No, I'm not going there right now.

Briar whimpers and rubs her thighs together. I don't need to look between them to know she's soaked, slick dripping onto the floor. The scent of it is everywhere, trying to coax me to join them.

"You're gorgeous, Briar. I look at you and can't believe you're our omega. Never imagined you'd be here sucking my cock and needing me the way you are. The way I need you," Ronan murmurs, dragging a hand to her throat, over the bulging muscle. "Don't stop. I'll give you what you need. What only I can give you."

It's another dig.

"She needs to come," I snap, gripping my shaft in a brutal grip.

"Does she?"

Briar makes a needy noise and buckles down, taking even more of Ronan's cock into her throat. She strokes what she can't fit and traces nails along his knot, teasing him.

"I'm busy," he adds when I don't answer.

I roll my jaw, fully aware of what he's doing but unable to help myself. "Move her."

"How?"

"Put her on her back."

He smirks, knowing he's got me hooked. Even as he eases Briar from his dick and she cries out at the loss, he doesn't hide his smugness.

"Don't stop," she slurs, shaking her head.

The dazed look in her eyes would be concerning if it weren't for the heat spike. It'll only get worse when she's in heat for real, and fuck me, I know I can't be anywhere near her when that happens.

Ronan lifts her off the side of the bench, and she clings to him immediately, nuzzling her face in his neck. He groans, and I watch as she sucks at his skin, tongue swirling.

"Smell so good," she mumbles. "My alpha."

I watch Ronan when he inhales a deep breath and keeps his lips shut, a battle of wills being fought within his hard stare. Unlike me, he's battling his instincts but not refusing them entirely. Just enough to keep from burying his teeth in her throat and marking her right here and now.

"We'll take care of you, Petal."

"I know," she purrs.

Laying her lengthways on the bench, similar to how I had her earlier, Ronan pulls her along it until her head hangs off the edge. She paws at him immediately, taking his cock back into her hand before kissing the tip and licking up the cum collecting there.

"Yeah, take it back down your throat, Briar. Nice and deep for me," he instructs, reaching over her to palm one of her round tits.

The blushing pink nipple disappears beneath his palm as he squeezes the soft flesh and plucks at the other, making her writhe on the bench.

"Landon's going to lick your pussy again, Petal. Be a good girl and spread your legs for him."

I don't ask how he knew I'd already tasted her. Falling back to my knees is easy. Briar parts her thighs, and I smooth my hands up the soft skin of her calves and knees. When I reach her inner thighs, I slow, my palms growing slick.

"Fuck," I spit.

Ronan stares at me. "She's wet, isn't she?"

"Soaked. She's dripping, Ro."

I drape my torso over the bench, possessed by the sight of her swollen pussy and the way it shines in the gym light. I've never loved lemon more than right now as I shove her dress the rest of the way up her stomach and draw a hot line up her lips with my tongue.

She tastes sweet, like temptation and sin and every fucking perfect thing in the world wrapped into one. I trap her beneath my mouth and get to work.

Her cry is muffled by Ronan's knot as he plows deep, her throat bulging. She takes my two fingers easily, already stretched out and so wet I doubt I'd find much resistance if she were still as tight as earlier.

"Tell me how she tastes," Ronan barks.

There's a feral edge to him now that I've only seen a handful of times on the ice after a fight. With one hand buried in his hair and the other alternating between pinching and tugging our omega's nipples, he grinds his teeth and struggles to control his breathing.

I move my mouth to her entrance and lap at her slick, teasing him but also trying to satiate my own needs. Every fibre of my being begs to get as much of her as possible.

Fuck her. Knot her. Bite her. Make her mine.

Every demand plays on repeat in my mind.

"She tastes like ours, Ronan. Sweet as sugar but with lingering lemon. Perfection."

"Fuck yeah, she does."

Briar humps my mouth, twisting and rolling her hips as I bring my tongue to her clit and flick it with a quick pace. My fingers are soaked as I drive them into her faster, working every inch of her in the hope of making her come.

Ronan tenses, his thrusts gaining in intensity. Briar jerks in time with his movements, bringing her onto my mouth at a pace that twists my thoughts.

"Gonna come, Petal. Keep sucking just like that and I'll fill you full of it," Ronan warns.

I bring a hand between my legs and cup my cock, massaging my knot as Briar tightens around my fingers. She bucks against my tongue, and I growl, feeling her pleasure as if it's my own. Tingles break out up and down my spine as I squeeze my knot and gasp.

Ronan pushes inside one last time before stalling and jerking into her mouth. "Swallow, baby."

I scrape my teeth over Briar's clit as Ronan comes, pushing her over the edge. She gushes onto my face and cries around the mouthful of cum he's giving her, forcing some to leak from her lips.

Another squeeze of my cock has me joining them. I press my mouth to Briar's pussy, silencing myself as I throb in my briefs, coating them in cum that I wish was joining Ronan's. My entire body flushes as I give in to the sensation, feeling more alive than I have in weeks.

"That's it, Petal. That's it."

Ronan pulls free of Briar's mouth and immediately drops to his haunches. He strokes her face, over her pink cheeks and swollen lips, still wet with his cum. She closes her eyes, inhaling heavily, chest rising faster than normal but her scent dulling.

Knowing that she's okay now, I back up, removing myself from her entirely. A gnawing in my gut has me hesitating to leave, but I push past it, knowing damn well if I don't leave now, I won't at all. And fuck, these two are in their own world.

I refuse to hang around to watch them fall further in love while knowing I won't ever get there with her. My steps are near silent as I creep away from them, a pit of emptiness growing in my chest.

"Landon," Briar whispers, stopping me. "Thank you."

I straighten my shoulders, evening out my expression as her appreciation strikes me deeper than I imagined it could.

There's nothing that I can say right now that won't betray me, so I stay silent, nodding once instead. Ronan meets my gaze, tilting his head slightly.

I don't know what happened and what it means. All I do know is that I need to be alone somewhere I won't be reminded of her everywhere I turn and with every breath I take.

So, I turn and leave before either of them can try and convince me to stay.

31

Briar

I DRIFT OUT OF SLEEP WITH THE LOW SOUND OF MALE voices in my ears.

It's too hard to open my eyes, so I keep them closed and burrow further into the chest of whoever's holding me. I'm weightless, my legs dangling free as I'm carried in strong arms.

Slowly, conscious thought comes back to me. I remember where I am and that the subconscious feeling of safety I have is because I'm surrounded by my mates. I must have fallen asleep after Ronan helped me back upstairs and tucked me beneath a blanket to finish the movie.

It's Dash's voice I hear first, the soft rumble comforting me. "Are you sure she'll be okay with sleeping here?"

"Heat spikes are draining. She needs sleep, and I'm okay risking it so long as she gets as much as she needs," Jasper whispers.

The chest beneath my cheek is firm, the arms steadfast. I know that even if the world shook beneath us, they'd stay banded around me.

From the intensity of the warm leather and whiskey in the fabric of the shirt rubbing against my cheek, it has to be Jasper carrying me.

There's a beat of silence before Dash speaks again. "Should we check on Landon too?"

"I already did. He's asleep in his room."

"What?" He sounds as shocked as I feel.

"Whatever happened downstairs between them seemed to help him," Jasper states.

"That's good, right? We're good?"

"Maybe. I hope so. We won't know tonight."

I wish he did. Falling asleep knowing that Landon was closer to accepting me would be a dream come true. Although, after what we did earlier, I'm positive the change has started, even just barely.

I've never felt so . . . cherished as I was spread out between Landon and Ronan. There wasn't even anything romantic about what we did. It was purely a necessary burning of sexual tension and need, but somehow, it felt more beautiful than any other experience I've had.

"How do you think he'll react when he finds out she stayed the night in the nest?" Dash asks.

My ears perk up, sleep fading fast.

Jasper jostles me slightly before we start ascending a set of stairs. "That depends on if you mean how he truly feels or how he pretends to feel."

"There's a difference?"

"Come on, Dash. You don't actually think he's truly this against her, right? His mother has put this constant doubt in his mind that makes him act out in fear of reliving what his father went through. It's not Briar who scares him but the possible future of what could happen to us because of her. If we had met anyone else, it would have been the same. We'd still have been in this exact same situation," Jasper says, voice harder, stern.

"His mother was a poor excuse for an omega, Jas. He can't be comparing what happened with her to Briar. It's not fair."

Jasper adjusts me and runs a knuckle behind my ear as his steps even out, telling me we're done with the stairs now.

"It's *not* fair. I've been saying that the entire time. I'm hoping that the more time he spends with her, the easier it will be for him to see that too."

Another pause before a door creaks open. "Do you think she'll like it in here?"

"I hope so. For now, let's get her tucked into bed."

It takes everything in me not to insist they both stay with me once I'm lowered onto a soft mattress. The sheets feel like silk against my bare toes as I stretch out and grasp at Jasper's arm. He drops the fluffy comforter over me and hovers, trapping my hand beneath his.

"What's wrong, love?" he murmurs.

When I crack my eyes open, he's the first thing I see. Even in the low light from the hall, he's so incredibly handsome.

"You can stay."

His mouth tips up at the corner. "Not tonight."

"Another night?"

"Absolutely."

I smile through a yawn and rub my face into the silk pillow-case before remembering where I am. The mention of a nest sears into my brain.

"Am I in the nest?"

The mattress shifts at my feet. I peer down to find Dash perched beside them, a hand hovering over my calf.

"It's the nest. We've had it for years, but there's never been anyone in this bed. I didn't even know we had sheets for it until right now."

"I put them on earlier. Just in case," Jasper says sheepishly.

I hum, my chest warming at his honesty and consideration. "They're nicer than the ones I have at home."

"We could get you a pair for your place if you really like them. You deserve good sheets no matter where you sleep."

Dash nods along with his packmate before his hand finally falls to touch me. "What's your favourite colour?"

"My favourite colour is pink. The pastel kind. But you don't need to buy me fancy sheets. They can just be a special part of staying here. A bonus."

"I'd hope that you would eventually move out of this bed and into one of ours. If that's something you ever felt comfortable enough to do," Jasper murmurs, running steady fingers through my hair.

The repeated motion is almost enough to send me toppling into the exhaustion that's stinging my eyes. I let them shut. Just for a minute.

"Do you have silk sheets on your beds?"

"Of course," Dash guffaws.

"Such spoiled hockey boys," I tease softly.

Jasper presses his lips to my forehead, lingering. "We'd love to spoil you."

"Can I have a first request, then?"

"You can have anything, Briar," he whispers, lips moving across my skin.

I keep my eyes closed, grateful that I can hide because of my exhaustion instead of revealing my nerves.

"Can both of you leave something of yours in here before you go?"

"You want our scents around you?" Dash asks.

It's too sterile in this bed. I'd usually say that's a good thing because it means they were truthful about me being the only omega who's been in this nest, but I'm close enough to my heat that I'm getting the itch to start my nesting process.

Obviously, I don't know if I'll be spending my heat in this room, but for tonight, my omega needs the reminder that they're here close by.

"Yes, please."

Jasper leans away from me and, a second later, sets a ball of fabric beside my head. I inhale the clean laundry scent and snap a hand up to grab the shirt, holding it close to my chest. Dash shifts by my feet before I get a strong whiff of peanut butter and choco-late. I clutch at the soft shirt he sets on my chest and sigh.

"Do you want something from Ronan too?" Jasper asks, tucking the sides of the comforter tight against my sides.

It's such a childish thing to have done, but it makes a difference to my omega. The snugness of the comforter in addition to their shirts settles me, making room for sleep to sweep me away.

I manage to get a few slurred words out before the world turns black.

"Don't forget Landon."

MONTGOMERY
PACK

THE SHRILL SOUND of my phone ringing wakes me up from a dreamless sleep. Panic sets in when I come to enough to realize it's Clover's ringtone. Not even the strong scents of all four of my guys can soothe me the way they did when I fell asleep.

I search for the lit screen in the dark room, finding my phone plugged into a charger on the nightstand. My voice is thick with sleep when I answer the call.

"What's wrong?"

She answers in a frazzled rush. "Those cursed alphas have been banging on Sadie's door for the last hour."

"What?"

I'm already out of bed and crossing the room by the time she replies.

"I told her to call the police, but she doesn't want to deal with their questions tonight. I'm on my way there right now."

"What are you going to do against them? Just wait for me. I'm coming."

"You didn't even text me when you got home last night! I'm assuming that means you're still at the packhouse."

"It was an accident. I fell asleep."

She huffs, a door slamming nearby. "It doesn't matter."

"What's the plan for when we get there? These aren't kind alphas, Clover. Do you really think they'll care if we show up?"

"I can't just do nothing."

I open the door and hesitate, stealing a final glance behind me. In the dark, it's hard to pick apart the different aspects of the nest apart from the massive circular bed that looks bigger than it felt when I was asleep and the gauzy curtains draped around it.

"We don't do noth—" I turn forward and gasp.

Ronan reaches for my arm, steadying me when I rock backward. He moves closer and pulls me into his chest. I melt into the embrace and take a long, deep breath.

"I'll be there in a few minutes, Clover. Just wait for me before you go all Superwoman on those guys," I say.

Clover snorts, and I can imagine her shaking her head. "We'll see. Hurry, Bee."

The dial tone follows her flippant agreement. It's not incredibly comforting, but I don't have time to stand here and contemplate whether she'll listen.

"I have to go," I tell Ronan, hating every second of leaving his arms.

"I'll drive you. Tell me where we're going."

I look up at him, surprised. "What? It's the middle of the night. You should be asleep."

"You don't have your car, Petal. I'll take you where you need to go while you tell me what's going on."

The pet name reminds me of what happened earlier, and I flush, my core tightening. It's not the time or place, but I can't help it.

"I know," he rasps, reading my mind. "It kept me up for hours after you went up to bed."

That tidbit of information doesn't help calm my hormones one little bit. It takes every ounce of restraint I have to separate my thoughts and veer around the desire swirling in my belly.

"Sadie, the pregnant omega who was at the game with me and Clover, is in trouble," I force myself to say instead of begging him to take me back into the nest and stay with me for the rest of the night.

Instead of his shirt, he could cover me with—

His muscles stiffen, scent sharpening. "Let's go."

"You wouldn't mind dropping me off? I know it's got to be late."

"I'm not going to drop you off, Briar. I'm going to go with you to make sure everything is okay. You're my omega, and I'm going to take care of you."

He takes my hand and leads me out of the nest and down the hall. His legs are longer than mine, his strides larger, but he keeps his pace in time with mine. It's something so subtle but thoughtful. Like Jasper's constant concern and Dash's habit of waiting to touch me until I have a chance to tell him not to. As if that's ever a possibility in my mind.

Landon can act as nonchalant and unfeeling as he wants to, but I see the lingering, reassuring looks and the new hesitation to walk away.

I let my lips turn up in a small smile. "Thank you, Ro."

"I would do anything for you," he declares without hesitation.

I clutch onto his hand. "I'm starting to learn that."

"Learn it, memorize it, believe it, Petal. I'm going to do everything I can to convince you of it sooner rather than later. Starting tonight."

32

Ronan

I DON'T LIKE THE THOUGHT OF BRIAR ANYWHERE NEAR danger. But I really fucking detest the idea of her being near it without me. At least with me at her side, I can protect her. Nobody she doesn't want close will get within a foot of her if I can help it.

From what she's told me so far about these two alphas, I'm ready to insert myself whenever possible.

"They wouldn't have dared try this at the clinic. It's pathetic that they've decided to harass her at home in the middle of the night," she rants in the passenger seat of the SUV.

I'd have taken her out on my bike if it weren't three in the morning and the wind wasn't strong enough to rock the vehicle every time we're on a straight road.

"She's got a restraining order?" I ask, reaching across the dash to hold her thigh.

"Yes, but it doesn't seem to be helping."

"They've broken it by approaching her apartment like this. If she got the police involved, they'd be arrested."

Her sigh betrays her exhaustion before a yawn does. Fuck, she's adorable. The scrunch of her nose before she closes her mouth nearly does me in.

"I know. Sadie doesn't want that mess tonight, though. I'm not going to make that call for her, either. Not if she's against it. That's why Clover and I were going," she explains.

Eying her in the darkness, I try not to look as dumbfounded as I feel. "What were the two of you planning on doing on your own?"

"I don't know. Anything, I guess. She deserves better than this. Clover will want to check on her and the baby now, anyway. It's safer that we go."

"I'll take care of them tonight, Petal. But from now on, she'll need to be okay with calling the police. It's not safe to have aggressive alphas hanging around her."

She drops a hand over mine and laces our fingers. "I know. Thank you for coming. It means a lot to me."

"Just promise me that if you ever see them without me, you'll call. It doesn't have to me, but make that call to one of us. Your safety is our priority."

The thought of her being accosted by these men on her own is enough to drag clawed nails down my spine. It's not going to happen. Not in this life or the next ten.

"I promise. You don't have to worry about me."

I let out a disgruntled noise and follow the instructions on the GPS when it tells me to turn right. We're in an okay neighbourhood. It's better than the one Briar and my family live in. Another thing I don't like.

"That's Clover's car. You can just park behind her," she instructs, already unbuckling her seat belt when I pull along the curb.

I reach for her hand when she tries to dive outside, halting her. "Wait for me, Petal."

"I will. I'm just—I need to get outside."

"A few months ago, Dash was subject to a cruel article about his place in our pack," I start, hoping to fuck he won't care about me sharing this with her. Briar turns her head to look at me with a hand on the door. "As a beta, he's always under more scrutiny than the rest of us are, even if he pretends otherwise. Usually, he can shake it off. That specific article just got under his skin, and seeing him so upset snapped something inside of me. I found the same reporter who published it outside of our next game and threw his camera at a wall so hard it shattered. Landon had to write a big cheque to get him not to pursue legal action."

"You care about your packmates, Ronan. That's not a bad thing," she murmurs.

My appreciation for her multiplies when she doesn't sound like she's judging me at all. The immediate understanding does things to me that should be terrifying.

"It's not. I'm just saying that I get it. But it doesn't always matter what our intentions are. Things can backfire anytime. And if you charge into Sadie's place right now, we'll both be dealing with the aftermath, prepared or not."

She nods, flipping my hand and drawing a line up my palm with a rounded nail. "Is Dash okay? I've never thought about what a beta would have to deal with from the public when it comes to being in a pack."

"He's okay. If you asked him, he'd tell you anything you wanted to know."

"Really?" It's a shy question.

I grunt. "He's coming around to you quicker than I expected."

"Alright, I will ask him, then. Are you ready to go up now?"

Turning off the SUV, I shove open my door. "Let's go."

"I'm going to apologize ahead of time," she says while climbing out of the vehicle.

We meet on the sidewalk before I rest a hand on her lower back and walk in step with her toward the duplex. "For what?"

Ahead of Clover's tiny blue car sits a familiar, lowered red showpiece with windows tinted so dark they're black. My hackles stick straight up as I shift closer to Briar, guarding her as much as I can without taking her into my arms and tossing her back in the SUV.

"I feel like I've brought a lot of drama into your lives in such a short time," she starts, either not picking up on the change in my demeanour or ignoring it before it can affect the moment. "With Landon and now this tonight."

"Landon's actions aren't your problem, Briar," I say immediately.

"Aren't they, though? He's not just the lead alpha of your pack, but he's supposed to be . . . We're connected, Ronan. I feel it so deep inside of me that I swear my entire molecular makeup has shifted these past few weeks. When I'm with you, Jasper, and Dash, I feel incredible. Like I'm breathing fresh air after spending my life in a cloud of pollution. But there's still something missing. Someone."

I roll my jaw to keep saying anything against Landon that I'll regret. Briar sighs heavily and leans against my arm.

"I don't want you to think I'm not happy or that I won't be happy if Landon never comes around. The three of you could give me everything I'd ever need," she adds quickly.

"You'll have us all, Petal. Every fucking one of us," I declare, the unbreakable promise thick in my words.

It's obvious from the quick smile she flashes me as we move around to the back of the building that she doesn't believe me completely, and that's fine. I've never had an issue with proving myself to anyone before. The only ones I've cared enough about to do that for are the same men she's talking about. She's the perfect addition.

"Sadie's place is just around the corner. She has the back . . ."

Her voice dies off when we turn the corner. My first instinct is to shove her behind me, but she's too quick.

My omega takes off toward the three people facing off in front of the front door. Clover stands firmly in front of two males— alphas, with her arms crossed and feet planted wide. The largest alpha towers over her and sneers at her. Sadie is nowhere to be seen. That's for the best.

"Get the fuck out of the way, omega."

"No," she snaps. "You can feel free to leave before I call the cops."

"If you were going to, you would have already."

I rush after Briar on full alert. Panic threatens to shackle me, but I ignore it. Fear has never done anything for anyone but make them sloppy.

She stands right beside Clover and squares her shoulders. "Thorne, I'm assuming? You're not allowed to be here. Do you not care about Sadie's well-being at all? She's nine months pregnant. This stress isn't healthy for her."

The shorter alpha beside this apparent *Thorne* looks Briar up and down, his eyes a bit too narrowed for my liking. Fuck, any amount of eye contact from either of them in her direction is too much. Depending on what happens next, maybe I'll get to rip them out and eliminate their looking entirely.

"She's nine months pregnant with my baby. It's my right to check in on her whenever I please," Thorne hisses, inching forward.

I'm there before he can get any closer. He can be taller than my omega, but he's not fucking taller than me. Our height difference is so large that it startles him. He falters, jumping back the step he's just taken.

"I don't recommend getting any closer to her," I warn lowly.

His eyes are almost black as he braves a full glance at me. "I didn't know Sadie was making so many friends."

"Is the red car out front yours?"

"Depends. Is that omega behind you yours?"

I pause, considering how to handle this. The sheer possessiveness in his stare is coming from one place, and it isn't because he wants Briar. No, he wants to know if she's mine so he can eliminate me as an object in his way of Sadie.

Pushing forward, I force him to move further back until the women aren't directly behind me. "If that car is yours, I want to know why the fuck it was parked outside of my omega's apartment building."

"Your omega," he echoes, relief blooming as he gets approval that I'm not seeking out Sadie.

The relief evaporates when I curl my fingers in the top of his shirt and yank. He curls his lip at me and struggles, trying to get away. The fight only makes me tighten my grip.

"Answer me," I demand, a bark lingering at the back of my throat.

"I have no idea what you're talking about."

I slide my eyes to the alpha beside him. He's too fucking quiet while his packmate is making a complete fool of himself. Does he always stand by while he acts out? Encourage him even?

"What about you? Are you capable of speaking?"

He swallows, glancing at Thorne for confirmation before speaking. "There are plenty of red cars in Rayton."

My laugh is hollow as I shove Thorne away, enjoying the sight of him stumbling over his feet. "Not enough to keep me from picking out yours. If you go near her again, a visit from the cops will be the least of your worries."

"She shouldn't have taken Sadie as a patient if she didn't want us hanging around," Thorne snaps back, teeth clacking.

"If you're going to make a threat, make it obvious. Come out with it loud and proud. I'm more than happy enough to beat your ass into the ground right here, right now instead of later."

Thorne lifts a hand to fidget with the hoop in his earlobe, an anxious tell that I latch onto. "Sadie belongs to me."

To *him*. Not them. Not herself. The sense of ownership has unease coiling low in my gut.

Suddenly, there's warmth seeping into my body, soothing me. Briar's lemon scent hits me before I sense her pressing against my back.

"She does not!" Clover screeches, stomping to my side.

Thorne turns his nose up at her, ignoring her declaration. He's too focused on me, reluctance beginning to build in his expression.

"I *will* see my daughter," he promises.

The sharp hiss of breath behind me doesn't go unnoticed.

"How do you know the gender?" Clover shouts, pouncing at him.

An arm snapping out from behind me tugs her backward before her nails can make contact with his face.

Thorne glares daggers at her, shoving a hand through his messy hair. "I'm not sure such a violent person should be in the room with my omega when she's giving birth."

"That's not your call. Just go," Briar says.

I glance beside me and get a blast of pride deep in my chest. She might be small, but she's braver than someone triple her size. I don't ever want to be the one she's glaring at so fiercely.

Thorne shifts from one foot to another before stealing a look at the window behind us. "Tell Sadie she can't hide from us forever."

Clover laughs darkly. "She's not hiding. You know exactly where she is and can't stand that she won't give you the time of day anymore. After what you put her through, you're lucky you're still able to smell the breeze tonight."

He snarls one final time at her before shifting his attention to me. "We'll see the both of you again."

"Only if you have a death wish," I threaten.

The alpha beside him pales and waits for Thorne to start to leave before following him like a well-trained pet. Only when they disappear behind the corner of the duplex do I let my shoulders drop an inch.

Briar clutches my arm and spin to my front, resting her forehead against my chest. She doesn't speak, and I don't blame her. I don't know what to say, so I follow her lead. Shit, I never know what to say on a good day, let alone after all that.

Clover doesn't have that same issue. "Well, he's downright awful."

I grunt in reply. Briar shakes with a quiet laugh, and I set my hands on her waist, needing the connection.

"Would it be weird if I said he wasn't as bad as I was expecting?"

"Were you expecting the actual devil? That guy was a piece of garbage, Bee."

"I know. I just thought he'd try tearing past us to break the door down or something instead of just standing there talking."

Her confusion makes sense. Alphas aren't known for their habit of speaking about their issues instead of taking action, especially when we're feeling territorial and pissed off. Add the other issues Thorne has, and his behaviour was odd.

A pit grows in my stomach. It's almost like he was testing us.

I pull her flush against me and narrow my eyes on the corner of the house. "Be careful, Petal."

She nods, lips drifting over my shirt. "I will."

That has to be enough for now. Until we can handle this situation as a pack.

All five of us.

33

Jasper

THE HOUSE IS ALWAYS SILENT THIS EARLY IN THE morning.

Dash could sleep until noon every day of the week, Ronan doesn't like to converse with anyone until at least nine, and Landon's usually already either on a run or down in the gym and won't come up until we've all scattered, going about our day.

I'm a morning person. There's something special about being awake to watch the sunrise through the tall windows in the kitchen with a hot cup of coffee in my hand. For an hour every day, I feel completely at peace. Before meeting Briar, this was the only time I could have that.

Now, she is my sunrise.

Tucking her into bed in her nest was even more amazing than I could have dreamed. The last thing I wanted to do was leave the room once she dozed back to sleep, but I knew there would be time for us to spend long nights tucked up beneath the same covers, her body tucked into the curve of mine. I'll do anything to make that happen.

I take a sip of my coffee and stare out the window at the pink and orange, cloudless sky. The sweet taste warms my stomach as I get lost in a world of possibilities. With Briar, we could do everything we've ever wanted to. The dreams we had could include her, and I don't think there's anything better than that.

The thought of waking up before dawn's cracked to find her beside me, her eyes closed and lips parted on soft, even breaths, feels closer than it did even yesterday morning.

Finally, we'd have some use for the giant custom bed in the nest. I had it crafted with the hope that five of us would one day get to use it together, as long as our omega approved of that, of course. Briar calls the shots, and I'm more than happy to give her full control over every aspect of our relationship. Emotionally and sexually, we're hers to command.

Having her asleep upstairs as I sit down here alone in my thoughts is a tease worse than any other. I came right downstairs once I woke, knowing that if I checked on her in the nest, I'd end up stuck there watching her sleep. It's too early for her to think I'm such a creep.

I blow out a breath over my mug and watch as the surface of my coffee ripples. It's enough of a distraction that I almost miss the sound of the front door clicking shut. Turning on the bar stool beneath me, I set my mug down, waiting.

Ronan's slouched frame comes into view when he starts my way. I know he hasn't realized that I'm here, and that makes it easier to examine his demeanour. It's the deep blue bags beneath his eyes and the way he rolls his neck to work out either a knot or lingering tension that concerns me most of all. His clothes are wrinkled, and despite Landon constantly harping on him about wearing his boots in the house, they drag on the floor. At least they look clean.

He stares at the ground and reaches up to wring the back of his neck. I watch, confused as to where he was and why he's only coming home at six in the morning. My gut tells me that it wasn't for anything good.

"Want a coffee?" I ask.

Eyes flying up, he jumps, scared by the question. He blinks quickly and drops his hand.

"Forgot how early you're up in the morning."

"Is that why you didn't use the back door to sneak inside?"

"Are you going to ground me?"

"I'll let it go this time," I tease, lifting my mug. "So, coffee?"

"Coffee," he confirms.

I get off my stool when he takes the one beside me and move to the fancy coffee machine Dash bought for himself last Christmas. The expensive pods are perfectly organized in the drawer beneath it—Landon's doing—so I grab the darkest blend and slip it into the machine.

"At least you were quiet coming in. Briar needs sleep after last night," I say, sliding a matte-black cup off the rack beside the machine and clunking it in place before the coffee starts spurting out.

"I'm not sure she got any. I took her out in the middle of the night."

Spinning around, I press back against the counter and frown. "Why?"

"Did her phone ringing not wake you up?"

"No. I had the sound machine on."

The guys tease me for it, but I've always had problems sleeping in the silence. There's a time and place for it, and apparently, for me, that isn't after. I save that for my mornings.

Ronan shakes his head, eyeing the stream of coffee coming out of the machine. "There was an emergency with Sadie, and she needed to go to her place. I brought her there and then home to her apartment."

I shove the disappointment away that springs to life as I realize I missed out on a chance to be with her. "When was this exactly?"

"A little after two."

"And you're just getting back now? What happened?"

My hand shakes as I tug his mug away from the machine and rest it on the countertop. I rip open the fridge door and grab the milk with a sweaty palm.

"She's okay, Jas."

I nod stiffly and focus on not spilling the milk all over the place as I pour a splash into his mug. "What happened?"

"You remember Sadie, yeah?"

"Her friend from the clinic, yes."

"Yeah. She's got two alphas who can't comprehend the meaning of a restraining order. They showed up at her place and tried to bash the door in before we got there."

"How is she? I imagine that was stressful, especially for a pregnant omega."

"I didn't ask. Should I have?"

I give his coffee a stir with the spoon I used for mine and sigh before glancing at him over my shoulder. "What did you talk about after, then? Tell me you at least asked Briar if she was doing okay when you dropped her off."

"'Course I did. Fuck, I'm not a total idiot. She assured me everything was fine."

"And you believed her? Tell me exactly what happened."

I bring his mug to the table and set it in front of him before sitting back on my stool. Despite the temperature of it, he takes large gulps and shuts his eyes, exhaustion hanging heavy from his slumped posture.

When he sets the cup down, all that's left inside is a few dark drops. If I didn't think he was ready for bed right now, I'd offer him a second cup.

"Just bullshit about Sadie belonging to them and that they were adamant about seeing both her and the baby. Briar pisses them off because she won't allow them to. That's my concern."

I nod. "Do we need to get involved?"

"I'm already involved now." He taps the counter, his jaw tightening. "I recognized Thorne's car tonight."

"From where?"

"It was outside of Briar's place the night she came for dinner at the pack house, and I followed her home. I marked it when I was waiting for her to get inside, and it drove away soon after. It was fucking weird, but I didn't make the connection then."

A cold sense of dread drips down my spine. "Do you think he's been following her around since then?"

"I don't know if it was only that one time or if it's a constant thing. Either way, he had to follow her home once to know where she lives. I don't fucking like her going anywhere on her own."

"We can't bundle her up and refuse to let her live her life, Ro. That's not what we're here for," I argue, cautious not to sound too scolding. He has a fair point.

"We're supposed to protect her. She's linked to these fuckers now, and I don't want them anywhere near her. If they so much as get close enough to look at her, I'll make them regret it."

I palm my mug, humming in agreement. "We need to talk to the others before we start making any sort of decisions. Including Briar."

"And until then? I'm not leaving her alone for longer than absolutely necessary. We should ask her to stay here."

"Without talking to Landon and Dash first? You know that isn't how things work. It might make everything even worse, and I don't want to move Briar from one tense environment to the next without a concrete plan. The last thing we need to be doing is acting impulsively. The ice beneath us is too thin for desperate moves."

Ronan stops tapping the countertop and curls his fingers into a fist instead. "I'll be spending every free moment I have parked outside of her place, then."

"When do you plan on sleeping?"

"I'll figure it out."

"We're in the final stretch before playoffs. If we win our next two games, we could clinch a wildcard spot. You can't be running off hopes and dreams and risking an injury."

"Then she needs to stay with us here," he argues, as stubborn as he's always been.

He knows just as well that I'm equally as stubborn when it comes to things I care about.

"Not without speaking to the others."

Clacking his tongue to the roof of his mouth, he stands from the stool and grabs his cup. He lingers there, staring down at me with a straight-lipped expression.

"Then we're at a stalemate."

"Just . . . please give me a few days to figure everything out."

"Why should you be the one figuring everything out? Isn't that Landon's job?" he asks, the words sharp.

I meet his hard gaze with one of equal determination. "The two of you need to make amends."

"I'll make amends when he figures out his shit," he grunts, abandoning me at the island to bring his cup to the dishwasher.

The sound of the door swishing open and the top drawer sliding out fills the kitchen, swallowing the heavy sound of my exhale.

"You never shared what happened between the three of you downstairs last night."

"I figured it was obvious."

"That's what I thought too, but considering how you're acting right now, I'm wondering if I was wrong."

When he sets his mug on the rack, he does it hard enough for the other glasses to rattle. He spins around to face me and crosses his arms.

"What happened between us should have been enough for him to snap out of this. Having our omega in such a vulnerable position like she was, bringing her pleasure and having her eager to return it, damn well should have made the bond he's so fucking sure doesn't exist snap into place. He's so determined not to accept her that he's going to wind up more broken than he already is," he snaps.

While his words are angry, I'm too familiar with Ronan's emotions to miss the hurt there. And the frustration. I feel all of it too.

"We have to be patient," I mutter, trying desperately to believe what I'm saying.

"I've just about run out of patience, Jasper."

"I know."

"I'll give him three days. If he still hasn't figured himself out by then, I'm asking her to stay with us regardless."

It's pointless to push him for more time. We've already given Landon two months. Any longer and I worry the rest of us will run the risk of losing Briar.

"Three days, Ro."

34

Briar

"WHEN ARE YOU COMING TO VISIT? WE MISS YOU, darling girl. You haven't even called me often. This is the first time in nearly a month," Mom says, pushing harder than the last five times she's called asking me to come over. "Your fathers have been even antsier than me."

"I'm sorry. Tell them that I'll come by soon, I promise. Life has been crazy."

"Oh? And why is that? Do you have hot tea to spill?"

I recoil at her use of tea and spilling. "Who taught you that saying?"

"I saw it online. Did I use it right?"

"You did, but maybe you shouldn't say it. It sounds wrong coming from you."

"I'm too old to be hip, Briar."

"I didn't say that." *Not exactly.*

She huffs dramatically. "Fine. I'll keep the tea spilling to a minimum if you tell me what's been keeping you so busy that you can't come visit your parents."

Sitting in the back lot of my apartment building, I shake my head at her subtle guilt-tripping. My mom has always had a habit of laying it on extra thick, so this isn't that surprising. Back when

I first moved out of the pack house, I would come visit every weekend. Things have changed over the course of the last couple of years, and I don't really have an explanation for that. I love my mom and dads. Life is just . . . hard sometimes. Nothing is ever as simple as you'd hoped it would be.

I rub my lips together while butterflies fill my stomach. "I've met my scent matches."

"What? Briar Meadows! Excuse my mouth, but are you shitting me right now? When did this happen? Are you bringing them home with you when you come?"

It's impossible not to laugh at her eagerness.

"Slow your horses, Mom."

"You had a chance to tell me when my horses were slow, and you didn't take it, so now you get my fast ones."

"Oh, god. You're killing me with these sayings."

"Don't try distracting me!"

"I'm not, you're just being too antsy!"

She takes a very vocal few breaths. "Okay, I'm better now."

"You sure?"

"Yes, I'm sure. Out with it, Briar."

"Fine, since you asked *so* nicely," I tease, adjusting the heat I had blasting so I don't sweat to death in here. "There are four of them."

Her squeal is so high-pitched it makes my ears ring. "Four! Oh, sweetie. I knew you'd find them. It's a Meadows specialty. Did you know that both your grandma and great-grandma had scent-matched packs?"

"Yes, Mom. You told me that all the time growing up."

"Well, I'm saying it again. I remember when you used to stay up past your bedtime asking Rodger if he thought you'd find a pack like ours."

"He told you about that?" I ask, cheeks hot.

"Of course he did. At first, he swore up and down that he'd never allow it, but I know he eased into the idea the older you got."

Rodger is one of three alphas in my mom's pack. We've never known which of them was my biological father, and honestly, it's never mattered to me. They're all my dads. Growing up as their only child meant that I got too much attention, good and bad. It was a lot easier to get approval for things I wanted but a lot harder to hide when I messed up.

"Well, I hope he's eased into it enough because they're not really the types to let anyone tell them whether or not they can be with someone," I say.

"Is that so? They're tough, then. That's good. You need tough."

"What does that mean?"

She hums. "Nothing bad, sweetie. Just that you can be a bit . . . shy at times. You don't like causing waves, and that means that you can let others walk all over you. Having a pack who isn't afraid to stand up on your behalf isn't a bad thing. They say we find mates who fit with us perfectly."

"You're right. There have been a couple of those times already."

I purposely leave out the most recent example of that from two nights ago when Sadie's mates showed up at her place. Without Ronan there with me, there's no telling if things would have gone the way they did. Knowing he was there to stand up for not only me but Sadie and Clover, too, was everything I didn't know I needed.

I even saw him hanging around outside of my apartment building last night. While he never said anything to me about it before or after, I recognized him and the bike he sat perched on. The only explanation I have for his secret appearance is that he still felt uneasy after our time with Thorne. If I find him there again tonight, I've already promised myself that I'll go down and invite him inside. I should have done that last night, but when he didn't tell me he was there, I didn't want to be clingy, thinking he was there to see me. Now, it seems ridiculous to have thought that way.

"And? Did you say thank you, at least?" Mom asks.

"Before and after, since you're so curious."

"Oh, don't give me that. I'm just excited for you. What are their names? How old are they? What do they do for work? Do they live in Rayton?"

"You're asking too many questions at once again, Mom," I chastise lightly.

My butt aches from sitting on it all day in an office chair and now here in the car. Paperwork days are my least favourite, but they have to be done. We haven't had a patient give birth in a week now, and I'm starting to get antsy.

Sadie, while stressed and anxious to the max, was still not anywhere close to ready to pop the other night. She begged Clover to check her cervix, but she didn't show any signs of her labour coming soon despite her due date being only three days away. All I could do to help was send all of my suggested ways to naturally induce labour and hope for the best.

At least Thorne and Sebastian haven't attempted to pound their way into her place again.

I turn off my car and pop open the door before stepping out into the warm evening.

"Okay, first of all, tell me their names," Mom begs.

"Ronan, Jasper, Dash, and Landon. They're all the same age."

"And that is? Don't tell me they're much older than you. Your dads will have a total fit if you're mated with men more than ten years older than you."

"They're only two years older than me."

"Twenty-seven isn't bad. Do they have money?"

Shoving my door shut with my hip, I let out a loud, snorted laugh. "Mom!"

"What? I just mean it would be nice if they were well enough off to be able to take care of you."

"I don't need anyone to take care of me."

Mom clucks her tongue. "Briar. Work with me here."

"Alright. Yes, Mom. I think they're well off."

"Thank you. That wasn't so hard, was it?"

"I'm walking up to my building right now. Keep teasing me and I'll hang up on you before I get there," I warn, locking the car doors.

"Since you brought it up—you need to move out of that place."

"How many times are you going to tell me that?"

"As many as it takes! That place is very unsafe."

"You haven't been here in months. Maybe it's better now."

"Well, is it?" she counters.

I pause, opening up the heavy front door. "No."

"Exactly. Do me and your fathers a favour and move in with your pack instead. Surely, they have somewhere better for you to live. *Safer.*"

"You'll be pleased to know that it's very safe."

My keys jingle as I pull them out of my purse and use my fob to open the inside door. The lock clicks before I shove it forward and then pull it shut behind me. The hallways are empty, and the de-scenter burns my nose after my first inhale.

There's a tingle in the back of my mind as I head toward my apartment, but I ignore it, chalking it up to exhaustion after a long day.

"That's a relief, at least. Will you be doing as I want and moving in with them, then?"

"You make it sound so easy. Did you forget what it was like when you first started dating the dads?"

"Now that you mention it, I remember a bucketload of courting gifts. Tell me that your scent matches have been spoiling you. That's the best part of all this. Alphas are stubborn, arrogant creatures, and the courting phase makes it worth all the hassle they bring."

The three steps down to my apartment appear in front of me as I swap my phone to my other hand and get ready to unlock the door.

"I got a delivery the other day with a custom jersey to match theirs," I tell her before pushing my key toward the handle.

There was no point. I nudge the door with my toe and watch with a cement block filling my stomach as it floats open, the cheap wood floors inside appearing.

"A jersey? What kind? Did you suddenly start watching sports?"

"It's a long . . . story . . ."

My entire body seizes up when I stare down at my broken door handle.

I gulp despite my dry throat and push the door open further. Words are a foreign concept. I blink a few times and rub at my face as if I'm imagining the colossal mess in front of me and it'll magically go back to the clean state I left it in this morning.

"Briar? Hello? Are you still there? You can't ignore me and hope I'll just drop the subject."

A minute passes with the state of my home not changing.

Fear strikes deep when I take a longer look around and realize how much damage has been done. With fist-sized holes in the wall, my couch cushions slashed, and all of the food from inside my fridge dumped out, it looks like a wild animal tore through here.

I shouldn't go any further inside. Not on my own.

But this is my home. My safe space. The looming danger of whoever did this still being here only makes me want to go inside more.

"I have to go, Mom," I ramble, unable to hide the fear in my voice. It's wobbly and weak, and I know she can tell.

"What's wrong? What happened?"

I hang up before her worry convinces me to ask her to come help me instead of who my instincts are demanding I call.

Still standing outside of my apartment, I fumble with shaking fingers to pull up the name of the person I know I need right now.

Every second the dial tone rings, my heart rate speeds up.

He sounds surprised when he answers. "Briar?"

"Lan—Landon? I—" My words get swallowed in a frantic inhale. "I need you."

"Where are you?"

I grasp my throat. My skin is ice-cold. "My apartment."

"I'll be there in five minutes."

"That's not possible," I whisper, sinking against the wall behind me.

"It is for me. What's wrong? Are you safe?"

"I don't know."

A muffled curse comes before he says, "Can you get safe?"

I'm unprepared for the swell of emotion that hits me. I suck in a sharp breath and pull the phone from my ear, holding it to my chest as I gasp in breaths. It's embarrassing, maybe even a bit pathetic at how deeply his concern affects me, but I can't help it.

This man, this emotionally unavailable alpha who seems so sure that we're not meant to be together, is worried enough about me to drop whatever he was doing and come to my rescue without even knowing what's wrong.

Blinking away the burn in my eyes, I slowly bring my phone back to my ear. "I think they're gone."

"Who?" he snaps, but there's no bite to it.

"Whoever broke in," I whisper.

He releases a rough exhale. "Alright. I need you to go up to the second floor of the building and to apartment 203."

"Why?"

"Ronan's family lives there. If you tell them who you are, they'll let you in, and I'll come there as soon as I get to the building."

"His family?" I echo, shock settling over every other emotion trampling over me. "I didn't know they lived here."

How didn't I know that? Why didn't he tell me? God, I've totally messed this all up.

"You can take that up with him later. Just go, Haven. Now."

"You'll be here soon?"

"I'll be there soon. As fast as I possibly can."

35

Briar

Apartment 203.

A simple set of gold letters and numbers is more intimidating than ever despite the bright flowery wreath partially concealing them. There's still a shake to my hands when I raise one to knock on the door.

"I just knocked," I whisper into the phone.

Landon's voice is loud over the constant drone of the busy road he's on. He must have been moving at superhuman speed because before I could ask if he was on his way, doors were slamming closed, and I heard an engine turn over.

"Do you want me to stay on?"

"No. No, I'll be okay."

"I'll be there before you know it."

Footsteps on the other side of the door have me blurting, "Someone's coming."

"Ronan's family are good people. Call me back immediately if you need me," he demands.

"I will."

"See you soon, Briar."

I jump when the door opens. Before I can say a proper

goodbye to Landon, I'm panic hanging up the phone and letting it hang at my side.

The woman who appears in front of me is familiar, every feature on her face replicated in Ronan's. Deep brown eyes fix themselves on me as she pushes out a hip and leans against the door.

While I've never asked Ronan what designation his mother is, it's easy to tell she isn't an alpha. Not only are female alphas uncommon, but as I breathe in, there's no scent jumping at me. Even with the chemicals in the air, I should be able to smell *something*. My guess is she's a beta.

"Hello. Who are you?" she asks, not unkindly but suspiciously.

"I'm Briar. Ronan is my—I'm his . . ." I roll my lips, frustration blooming in my chest when I can't wrangle together the right words.

The woman I assume to be Ronan's mother tries to hide her surprise in response to my jumbled mess of words, but the upward tweak of her brows is impossible to miss.

"You know my son?"

"I do."

"Come in, then. You can tell me more about how you know each other inside."

I puff out a breath of relief and step through the open doorway. The de-scenter is strong in here too, but it's not enough to hide the new hints of fresh bread and blueberry in the air. The scents must belong to the sister Ronan mentioned was taking suppressants.

Ronan's mother shuts the door while I linger in the entry, unable to keep from looking at the dozens of photo frames hung on both walls. Some of them seem more recent, with more vibrant colours and a much older-looking Ronan in them, while others are faded. The second frame is the largest of them and easily snags my attention.

Ronan has to be around ten years old in it. He's rocking a full mullet while the younger girl—his sister, I assume—is on his back, using his hair like horse reins.

"He hates that I have that photo up," his mom says, moving to stand at my side.

There's a peaceful aura about her, and I really, really needed that. Maybe that's why Landon sent me here in the first place. As if simply having company while I waited wasn't enough.

It's easier to pretend everything is fine now that I'm here. The lingering fear of what I'll find once I start examining my destroyed home takes a back seat.

"I didn't expect him to have ever had a mullet."

"He hated it. The one and only time I tried to cut his hair, I butchered it."

"Is that why he has it buzzed now?"

She huffs a laugh. "There's probably a direct correlation between those two things, yes."

There's a lull in conversation as I turn to her and attempt my best smile. If she knows I'm putting on a brave face, she doesn't let on.

"I know it's sudden to show up here like this. Landon suggested I come up while I wait for him to get here."

"This sounds like the beginning of an interesting story," she says with a wave of her hand in front of us. "Do you like tea? Are you hungry?"

"Thank you, but I don't know if I'll be here too long."

I could be for only a handful of minutes or for hours, depending on whether Landon was being sincere in his worry. My gut is telling me I'll be gone soon.

"Well, alright. If you change your mind, just let me know."

We walk out of the front hall and into the living room. It's warm in this room despite the windows being open, and I'm suddenly not all that upset about being stuck in the basement suite. Hot air rises, and I'll happily be cold from time to time if it means that I don't have to sweat to death in the summer.

I hesitate to move further into the room once I reach the

couch, another wave of unease approaching. It's not the same kind of feeling as before I noticed my front door had been opened by someone else, but like I'm . . . trespassing if I go any further.

Without Ronan here, it feels like an invasion of privacy. I want to be here *with* him, knowing that he wants me to meet his family.

His mom smiles at me and slowly sinks into the couch. She's dressed in a pair of white-washed jeans and a flowy yellow top that accentuates her dark brown hair. I notice her mismatched polka-dotted socks—one yellow and blue and the other pink and green—and hide a smile.

Does Ronan share this quirky trait? If I looked in his sock drawer, would I find a bunch of mismatched socks?

"I'm Kira, in case my son failed to share that information with you. Considering he kept his mate from me, I'd say that's fairly plausible."

My lips part on a silent gasp. "You know who I am?"

Leaning back into the couch cushions, she crosses one leg over the other and cracks a soft smile. "As I'm sure you're aware, Landon doesn't get involved with many omegas. Him simply instructing you to come up to see me, regardless of the reason behind it, tells me everything I need to know. Add in that I can smell my son on you, and I knew who you were the moment I opened the door."

"I smell like him?"

God, I didn't know it was so obvious. Ever since the night I spent at the pack house, I've been going to work with a chunk of each of their shirts on me. Either in my purse or my jeans pocket, I've needed to have them close. It's my nesting instincts, and I've been coming to terms with the fact that I'm going to be going into heat any day now.

"You smell like all of them. And by your surprise, I'm also assuming that everything is still fairly new."

"You could say that," I say before huffing a soft laugh.

"Landon may be here soon, but for now, sit beside me. Tell me about yourself, Briar."

I don't make her tell me twice. The couch is one of those old ones with the thick, velvet cushions that they just don't make the same anymore.

"Well, what do you want to know?"

"What kind of person are you? Do you have many similarities to my son?"

The questions surprise me. They aren't what I was expecting. Usually, all anyone wants to know about you when you're an omega is what you do for work and if you want kids. I can't say I've ever had a stranger ask me about who I am instead.

"Honestly," I start, folding my hands in my lap, "I don't think I'm anything like Ronan. You weren't wrong about everything still being very new, but I think I have a pretty good sense of the man he is, and I've had twenty-five years to try and figure myself out.

"Ronan is gruff where I'm soft and brave when I want to cower. He's had my back every single time I've needed him to, and I like to think that I've been able to give him a safe space to be himself in return. With him, I can feel my backbone becoming a bit stronger. I know there are a million things we still have to learn about one another, but I'm having a really great time doing that so far."

Kira's upturned lips settle some of my anxiety after blurting out so much about myself to her.

"I always had a feeling that he'd find someone a bit warmer than me and his sister, Ciara. Someone like his father. That man prefers to crack jokes over serious conversations any day of the week. Giving Ronan a hard time with just about everything is something his sister and I can't help ourselves with, and he's grown a thick skin because of it. I think you'll help soften it up a bit. So long as you still promise to give him a hard time when he deserves it. Lord knows that boy has a habit of grunting a few too many times instead of making proper conversation. The best love is the kind where both people have the safety and support to learn and grow."

I nod, absorbing her words. "You don't think we're already too different?"

She lifts a brow. "Is there such a thing as too different? I couldn't be further from my husband in most things, but our key values are the same."

"You're right. I just—this whole situation has been, well, over-whelming," I admit sheepishly.

"Please tell me if I'm overstepping here, but I also know how pack life works. Ours here is small, but again, the core values are the same. Will you be the pack omega? Or are you and Ronan . . .?" she asks, slightly wary.

My eyes blow wide. "Oh! No! I'd never make him leave the Montgomery pack. I'm—" I pause, my cheeks burning as I take in her expression, searching for any sign of discomfort or judgment. There's neither. "We're scent-matched."

She sips in a sharp breath, a hand lifting to cup her throat. "Oh, that's even better than I was expecting. I knew it was serious, but a scent match? That's . . . that's incredible."

"I'm glad you think so. I do too," I murmur.

"My boy has found his mate."

A feeling of weightlessness comes over me at her support. It's like getting a passing grade on the test that will determine whether you get held back a year or not.

"Now I understand why you mentioned it being overwhelm-ing. Just the thought of having four mates gives me a headache, so I can't imagine how it feels to actually have to deal with such a change in your life," she adds, softly touching my arm.

"I've been handling it okay. Trying to, at least."

"Have they been good to you?"

The way she asks the question is like she's already contem-plating the fastest and most efficient way to deliver a scolding to four grown men.

"They have. Ronan and Jasper have welcomed me with open

arms and haven't stopped trying to make me feel like a part of the pack from the moment I met them."

She frowns. "And the other two?"

"Uh . . . it's just been a little hard to handle for them, I think."

"For them? What about you? An omega who's been thrown into an already established pack of three very successful, larger-than-life alphas? If that's an excuse they're using for treating you poorly, Briar, don't you allow it," she says firmly. The hand on my arm shifts to cover both of my hands. "If Landon is the root of this, I need you to know that it isn't because of anything you've done. That boy needs a smack upside the head."

"How do you know it's Landon?" I whisper, unable to be any louder as spikes spear my chest.

Somehow, hearing that someone who hasn't even seen me and Landon together is able to pick up on the fact we aren't as connected as the others . . . it hurts. Is it really that obvious?

"I've known your mates for as long as Ronan has, and we're well over a decade now. Ever since Landon's mother was kicked out of his father's pack, he's been so grey, the vibrancy he had as a child dulled completely."

My surprise must be obvious because she gives my hands a squeeze and tips her chin.

"He wasn't always so closed off," she confirms.

"Why was his mother kicked out? What happened?"

"She—"

The sound of the front door opening cuts her off. There's a slam before footsteps head in our direction, their pace frenzied. My stomach flips, anticipation rolling through me as I slide to the edge of the couch cushion and stare at the opening in the wall.

Nothing else matters once I see him.

Breathing frantically, Landon strides my way. He fixes a shuddering blue stare on me beneath knitted brows as I hold completely still. If I move, he might disappear.

"Did you just slam my door shut, Landon Montgomery?" Kira asks.

She doesn't get an answer.

Landon physically shakes when he gets close enough to smell me and, without hesitating, scoops me off the couch and into his arms. My eyes burn as I curl myself around his body and cling to him, the distraction from earlier disappearing and making way for the reality of why I'm here in the first place.

The de-scenter in the apartment tries to hide his vanilla, but that doesn't stop me from searching for it and the slight edge of cinnamon that I just *know* will be there right now. I take advantage of the low cut of his T-shirt and bring my nose right to his throat, breathing him in like I'm scared it'll be my last chance to do so.

"Are you okay?"

His hands dig into my thighs as I tighten them around his waist. The low, husky sound of his voice is downright sinful. I like it far too much. Almost as much as I like the way he pulls back and inspects me, the eyes I'm so used to seeing closed off in my presence dimmed with worry.

Is there an answer to that question that won't make him drop me right now?

"Yes."

"Time to go, then."

"You could stay," Kira suggests, but something tells me she doesn't really mean it. "Or you could take your omega home."

"Home," he snaps, the facial hair he's been growing out scratching at my neck when he lowers his chin to my shoulder. "Thanks, Kira."

"Mm. You're always welcome here, Briar. Next time, bring my son so I can tell him exactly what I'm going to tell you, Landon."

The alpha holding me grows still, fingers clenching around my thighs.

Ronan's mother's touch is gentler than Landon's as she pats the back of my head affectionately.

"Life is too short, and scent matches are too rare to ignore.

The past has no place in our futures. If you mess this up, you won't get a second chance. It's one in a billion."

Landon doesn't reply with words. The dark rumble in his chest presses into mine, a silent vow.

One that I'm not sure he means to make but that has me gliding my mouth up his neck and to the shell of his ear.

"I knew you'd come."

36

Landon

I KNEW YOU'D COME.

Her faith in me is undeserved. I've done absolutely nothing for her to think that or to have called me out of all the guys when she was in danger.

Yet, she did call me, and I have this unyielding desire to give up the predetermined and unfair opinion of her that I've made so that she always will.

I never have my phone on me when I'm at the rink. It's kept tucked inside my bag because the only people who ever contact me are at my side on the ice. But it was another strike of perfect timing that had me changing out of my gear early to meet with the team physio when she called.

The terror I felt when she first said my name could have debilitated me had I not been shot up with adrenaline. I pulled on my workout clothes and tore out of the dressing room without a care as to how slick with sweat I was or how deep the ache grew in my knee. The pain disappeared the moment I heard her say she needed me.

I'm a shitty driver on a good day, but our mailbox will be full in the coming weeks with more red light and photoradar tickets than I've ever received.

The weight of her in my arms as I carry us through Ronan's family home is like finally holding something I'm never supposed to let go of. Like releasing her will rip something vital from my chest.

I clutch onto her a little tighter, hoping she doesn't notice. Kira doesn't need to keep pushing me on accepting my omega. It's not as simple as forgoing all of my propositioned feelings and jumping headfirst into a courtship.

I want to believe that acceptance isn't in the cards yet, but continuing to refuse what my mind and soul are telling me feels wrong. That much has been made clear with how one simple plea to come to her rescue has me here right now, unsure what my next move is and how I'll take it.

Briar has had me upside down and backward since the moment we met, and I don't know how much longer I can take the world no longer making sense.

"I hope I didn't ruin your day."

Her soft, hesitant voice wedges the dagger that's been living between my ribs deeper, moving it side to side.

"Practice was already over when you called."

She nods into the crook of my neck, the ghost of her lips skating over my throat makes my arms shake. The reactive squeeze of her thighs around my hips when I start down the stairs has me on a fucking hair trigger.

"How's your knee?" she asks.

Gritting my teeth, I turn my head to the side and breathe in the chemical-ridden air. "I can't feel it."

"Is that a good or bad thing?"

"Neither."

"You can set me down now."

The thought alone pisses me off, so I ignore it. "What did you and Kira talk about?"

"You want to hear about our gossip?"

"Why wouldn't I?"

"You don't seem like the chitchat type," she states.

It's blunt but honest, and I respect that more than if she'd cushioned her words for my benefit. Outside of my packmates, it's hard to have a genuine conversation with someone without feeling as though they're constantly trying to pat my ego.

I have no doubt that's one thing I'll never find with Briar.

"I'm not," I confirm.

The ground floor of the building is silent as I move us around the corner and toward the entrance to her apartment. Not going there the moment I stepped inside felt wrong, but not being at her side as fast as possible was worse.

I could have called one of the other guys to check out the place while I went up and got her, but I couldn't risk losing this time with just us. It couldn't be more obvious how fucked up everything is when I would rather risk running into danger with her behind me than see her falling into arms that aren't mine.

My packmates aren't my competition, but right now, anyone who could steal her attention is.

"So, I'm going to take that as I help bring out your talkativeness, then," she says, slightly teasing.

"If I confirmed that, you'd never let it go, would you?"

"Nope."

"Figured as much."

A moment of silence passes before she crosses her feet at my back and pulls her face out of my neck. With her soft hands pawing at my shoulders, she fixes pale blue eyes on my darker ones and quirks her mouth into a smile. The soft indent in her right cheek is barely a dimple, but it's the cutest thing I've ever seen.

"We were talking about you. Me and Kira," she reveals, expression completely open.

My throat tightens up, a tug growing deep in my chest. "What about me?"

"I want you, Landon."

Four words.

They rip through me, tearing through flesh and blood and

imbedding themselves into my bones. Briar's name joins them, a permanent brand like the one my teeth ache to give her throat.

"Don't tell me that right now," I half snarl, half beg.

The wall next to her doorway meets her back as I slam us against it, rattling the boring, cheap paintings hung close by. The harsh movement has her jostling against me, her thighs tightening despite the way she slips down my front. The length of my stiffening cock presses against the thin material of my workout shorts, and I know the moment she feels it digging into her.

I bite down so hard that my gums pulse as I press myself flush to her front and adjust my hold higher up her thighs. The backs of my knuckles meet the curve of her ass.

She gasps, her scent ripening until it's so sickly sweet I pick it up over the chemical de-scenter.

"It's true. I want you, and I know you want me. Whatever it is that's keeping you from accepting me, I want to know so I can help convince you how wrong you've been. We're meant for each other, Lan. Biology doesn't lie," she declares fiercely—so fucking beautifully.

"You can't rely on biology for everything," I argue. It's a pathetic attempt at it.

She touches my face, palming my scruffy jaw with a gentleness I've never felt before. "Not everything. Just this."

"I admire your loyalty."

"Stop that. Don't try to diminish what I'm saying. Whatever it is that's keeping you from trusting fate, let me change your mind."

"How do you plan on doing that?"

Her lashes flutter when she leans in close and murmurs, "Kiss me."

I nearly choke on a moan, knot throbbing. She wiggles her hips, encouraging our middles to meet, her leggings hot in the centre. I'm trapped in her hold, fully aware that I could set her down, but with limbs refusing to do just that. One thrust and I'd be grinding against her pussy.

"What will a kiss prove?" I ask, voice full of smoke.

"Everything."

She pulls my face close until the rounded tip of her nose rubs along the bridge of mine. I can taste her perfume in the air, and my head fogs, an intense drive to give in to her poking and prodding at my brain.

"One kiss will do that?" I ask.

"Maybe."

It's enough for me. Fuck, is it ever enough.

I grab two handfuls of her ass and press her harder against the wall before slanting my mouth over hers and tasting her lips for the first time.

The world keeps turning, but it's different. The air brushing my skin is crisper; every sound is louder, clearer. My heart beats the same, but it's steady, like for the first time in nearly three decades, it's finally figured out the perfect tempo, and while it'll thrash again, it won't be as out of control, searching for a person who I hadn't found yet.

Briar tries to pull me closer, but it's impossible. The only way we could be closer is if we were naked, my cock inside of her and my knot—

A low grumble spills from my mouth into hers, and she's ready for it, swallowing it immediately.

My ears prickle, an awareness there and gone as I pin her against the wall with my hips. She nods in response, nails digging so sharply into my shirt that they pierce through to scrape at my skin.

"Inside," she whines.

I sink my teeth into her bottom lip, balls pulling up in pleasure. "One kiss."

"Not anymore."

No, not anymore. I'm not sure it'll be one kiss ever again.

"Inside," she repeats when I don't move.

It's a reminder of why I'm here.

There's a crack in my resolve as I lower her to her feet, hating every second that it takes to peel her off me. Especially when she tightens her grip on my shoulders and shakes her head, eyes half-closed and dazed.

"Nobody is going inside until I make sure it's safe," I soothe her. Or try to. Shit, my voice is cracking. "I need you to be safe."

She sighs, head rolling back along the wall behind her. "Hurry, Superman."

"Funny," I deadpan.

"Mm, not funny enough to make you laugh."

I leave her where she is and use the toe of my sneaker to push the door the rest of the way open. It already being cracked and unlocked for anyone to help themselves to her place doesn't sit well with me. It may piss me off more than her living in his apartment building in the first place.

Before I enter, I look at her over my shoulder. Her eyes are still on me, simmering with a need I want to sate.

"Do you want me to laugh for you, Briar?"

She shrugs, trying to play it off. "I don't think you've even smiled at me before."

Regret is an emotion I've grown familiar with when it comes to Briar. It still hasn't gotten any easier to swallow.

"I'm ticklish," I blurt out.

Her brows fly up. "What?"

"I'm ticklish. Everywhere. My armpits, thighs, feet."

"Are you— Do you want me to tickle you? Is this an invitation?"

It might not be the full thing, but the noise that escapes me is as close as I've gotten in a long time to truly laughing. At least this time, I don't try and stifle it. The crook of my lips pulls at my cheeks, using weakened muscles.

Briar's answering grin is everything I needed to see.

"Give me a minute to clear the apartment, and then you can try and give it a shot," I say.

"I'm pretty sure the place is empty."

"I'm not risking anyone but me smelling you like that."

She glances down her body, cheeks pink. "Like what?"

"Like you meant what you said back there. That you want me."

"I'll prove it to you," she dares.

I squeeze my eyes shut and fight back the visceral reaction that nips at me. "Don't move."

"You got it, Superman."

The nickname doesn't bother me. It might be the best one I've ever had, if only because she gave it to me.

Leaving her alone is hard, but I make my inspection of her place as quick as possible. It's a disaster, personal belongings destroyed and walls punched. My gut screams at me that this wasn't a simple robbery. The shredded curtains, slashed couch cushions, and the spray paint on the bed make this feel personal. Even her nest, or what's left of it in the corner of her bedroom, has been upturned, and I'm hoping she didn't see that when she first got here.

An open desk drawer in her bedroom calls my attention, and I find folders belonging to Harbour of Hope patients inside of it, a few papers scattered atop the dresser. The name on the top folder makes me curse.

Leaving them there, I join her again, a new tension in my shoulders alongside a gnawing sensation that I've been kept out of the loop about something.

Her eyes latch onto me when I step into the doorway and hover there, my expression plain.

"Did you find a burglar under the bed?"

"Has your friend ever been here before? Sadie?" There's no teasing quality to the questions, only a firm demand for answers.

She swallows, dread creeping across her features. I don't miss the realization, either.

"No. Why?"

"The files in your room were messed with. You mentioned her at dinner last week."

"She is a patient. We're waiting for her to go into labour any day now. I had her birthing plan in my desk drawer because I like to take them home and study them to make sure I know everything off by heart."

My feet carry me to her. She holds her breath as I approach before releasing it all out in one long, forced exhale.

"You're coming home with me," I state, leaving no room for argument.

"Uh, okay. Yeah, I don't think I could sleep here tonight, anyway. Not with the state of it. I'll have to, what, file a police report first?"

"No. I mean you're coming home with me, and you're moving in. I'll handle everything else from here."

She snorts a laugh, shaking her head in disbelief. "I'm serious, Landon. I should file a police report and get a cleaning crew in. I've got renters insurance, so hopefully I can get most things replaced that were destroyed."

"If you think I'm going to watch you walk back into this place when someone targeted you . . ." I swallow, nostrils flaring with a deep breath. She watches me with beautiful wide eyes as I trap her against the wall again, this time stealing her move and taking her face in my hands. "We'll take care of you. Take care of all of it. Just move in to the pack house."

Her lashes flutter with slow blinks as she asks, "You want me to live with you?"

"With all of us. Everyone's been keeping things from me, haven't they? That's why you aren't surprised that Sadie's information was touched. You know who did this."

The pink in her cheeks pales. "I assumed Ronan would have told you what happened."

Fucking Ronan.

"Tell me everything while you pack."

A single eyebrow curls upward. "I haven't said I'll move in yet."

"What do you need from me to say yes?"

"You already know the answer to that."

I dip my head, bringing my mouth to the underside of her jaw and nipping at the soft, smooth skin. "Say it."

"Finish what you started."

37

Briar

Landon follows me inside, keeping his pace slow with too many steps between us. It feels like a tease, a dare for me to turn around and tell him to hurry up.

I won't be doing any more demanding. I've done enough of it. It's his turn now.

His prior mention of my messy desk is enough to keep me from leading us into my bedroom and instead keep to the main room of the apartment. The inside of my place isn't sexy on a good day, but especially not when there's furniture overturned and fluff from the couch cushions thrown about.

Still, none of it matters right now.

The de-scenter is still strong as it continues puffing through my ventilation system, which would have annoyed me had it not also been the only reason for the lack of foreign smells that would have been lingering from the break-in.

All I want is to be surrounded by Landon's scent, his arms, and feel the burn of his lips on mine again. A whine builds in my throat at the reminder of our kiss and the disarray it left me in. Perfection would be an insulting description.

I let the noise out, unashamed of the way he makes me feel. After all, it's natural, despite his bullheaded belief that we're not scent matches. A belief that I can see crumbling further with each moment we spend together.

"It's not pretty right now. Is that a deal breaker for you?" I ask without turning around.

"Are you asking if I'll only touch you in a pretty place?"

Heat slides from my neck to the base of my spine. "Yes. I guess I am."

"Was my home gym a pretty place?" he asks, his tone dripping in dirty reminders and promises of what's coming.

"Your home is beautiful."

"Our home."

My toes curl as I give my thighs a subtle squeeze together. "Don't taunt me with a future you don't want to give me."

"Haven," he calls softly. I don't look back at him. The sting in my eyes keeps my attention forward on the mess cruelly left for me to find. "I don't know how to give you what you want."

"Why not?"

"It's not a story for today."

"What about tomorrow? Or the next?"

He hesitates, and my stomach pinches. I can feel the walls between us coming back up, growing taller than before. I panic, spinning to face him. Shoulders pulled back, I try forcing my way inside his mind. The barriers are thick, not impenetrable. Not like they were before.

"When are you going to realize that you can't push me away? I'm not a hockey fan parked outside of Surge Centre, hoping for a brief hello and a wave. We're scent matches, Landon. Just admit it already."

Lightning flashes in the deep blue of his eyes. He takes two steps in my direction.

"And then what? If I admit it, you'll take everything from me. One mistake and we'll be left broken without you. Our pack will crumble, and we'll be—" He cuts himself off and lunges another two steps before jerking back, as if remembering why he's keeping his distance. "They're my family. I can't lose them."

Some of my anger shifts, making way for pain. "I'm not going to leave you broken. Do you think that I want to feel like that, either? That I'm not scared too? The four of you could just as easily break me!"

"But we wouldn't. Don't you get that? Jasper and Ronan would burn down the fucking world for you already, and it's only been a few weeks! Dash might act like he's unaffected, but he's tripping over himself in silence."

"And you?"

He rolls his jaw. "What about me?"

"You haven't said what you'd do."

His breath comes out sharp, controlled. "I wouldn't burn the world down. I'd remake it. I'd tear it apart thread by thread until nothing existed but you, me, and our pack. I'd pull the stars from the sky and shatter time itself before I let anything take you from me."

I'm moving before I can comprehend how. I reach him in three large strides, and he scoops me into his arms, bouncing me up his body as our lips meet. Teeth clink and lips grow sore, the swelling tension so close to exploding that for a moment, I worry what the aftermath will look like.

At least the place is already destroyed.

Landon storms through the apartment, not stopping until we're in front of the couch. He spins us and then drops to the shredded cushion, keeping me planted on his thighs.

Warm, long fingers slide through my hair. He holds the back of my head and tips it back before gliding his tongue between my lips and into my mouth. I drop down fully onto his lap, my hips rolling forward on instinct.

"Oh . . ." I moan, repeating the movement.

His shorts are thin, hiding nothing as I rub along his hard shaft, my eyes crossing when my clit bumps his knot. It's been months since I've spent a heat at a clinic and even longer since I've taken a knot that wasn't made from rubber. I clench around nothing, slick gushing into my panties.

"We're saving that," he rasps, tugging softly at my hair, guiding my head back further. When his tongue swirls over the side of my exposed throat, I preen, grinding down on him. "You'll get my knot when my teeth dig into your throat."

I cry out, gasping a weak "Promise?"

He palms the dip of my waist and pulls me closer, demanding more and more from me. When I press down now, his cock is right . . . right there.

"I promise, Haven."

"Make me come, Landon. *Please*."

Alarm floods his eyes when he stares at me, but I shake my head and start working his shirt up his torso.

"It's not here yet. I just want you. Just once before you change your mind," I ramble.

I'm so wet I know he can feel me soaking through my leggings and into his shorts. My pulse is loud in my ears, matching the frantic tempo of my heart.

"There is no changing my mind now. I'm damned one way or another."

I press forward, stopping my hands where they rest clenched at his shoulders. "Nobody has to be damned. Just happy."

"Happy," he repeats, as if it's the first time he's tasted it on his tongue. His forehead meets mine, softly pressing as I lean close, trying to chase his mouth. "It sounds so simple."

"Why does it need to be complicated?"

"I've always seen mating bonds that way."

I answer by shoving his shirt up, and he reacts swiftly. Lifting his arms above his head, he lets me work it off before setting it on the couch and bringing my palms flush to his chest.

"You're beautiful," I whisper, watching in awe as his breathing kicks up and each muscle flexes beneath my fingertips.

"So are you."

My lips spread in a lazy smile. "Take my clothes off, Superman."

His eyes darken, pupils swallowing the colour as he obliges, never looking away. One piece at a time, he works me out of my shirt before wiggling down the band of my leggings. I wait for him to take them off completely, but he removes his hands when they bunch at my knees.

My curiosity is sated when he says, "I don't deserve you yet. Not like that."

"Are you planning on courting me?" I sound as confused as I feel.

"Should I not be?" His hand swallows my thigh, gliding up over a million goosebumps. I struggle to breathe, losing my inhale when the tip of his finger glides between the wet flesh between my legs. "It feels like you want me to."

I whimper, holding still. "I do. I want you to."

"What do you want me to do, Haven? Court you? Or sink a finger inside your slicked pussy?"

"Oh, god," I croak.

"Try again."

He swirls his finger around my clit, avoiding applying direct pressure. I let my head fall back and gulp in air. The fire in my lungs rages higher.

"Both! I want you to do both!"

Inch by inch, his finger breaches me, gliding all the way to the knuckle. I jerk against him, hands swiping at his shoulders before latching on with a clawed grip.

"Good girl, Briar. You deserve it all. From me and your pack."

Emotion clogs my throat. Every slow retreat of his finger makes the pleasure hot enough to burn. "It was your pack first."

"And it's yours for the rest of time. I was just taking care of it until you arrived."

"I won't lose you. Not any of you," I declare, riding the motion of his thrusts. "We'll talk it out together. Work through everything."

"Yeah, Haven. We will."

When he adds a second finger, I drop a hand between us and palm his erection, more slick dripping down his knuckles.

"*Christ*. You can't touch me like that. I've been close to a rut for weeks," he spits, pleasure soaking his tone.

I grip him tighter, working him beneath his shorts. His head hits the back of the couch before his eyes close, the speed of his fingers growing in intensity inside of me.

"Baby—" He chokes on whatever he was going to say when I shove my hand beneath the waistband of his shorts. The bare length of him is hot and thick, pulsing beneath my fingers. "Fuck. Take me out and spit on it, then, Briar. Get it wet."

Excitement jolts through me as I follow his orders and shove his shorts down enough I can pull him free. My eyes widen on the monster in my hand. Veiny and so thick it's a struggle for my fingers to touch around the girth of him, his cock is beautiful. The precum on the tip makes me moan.

Slowly, I push back on his thighs and lower my head before spitting. The clear liquid drips over my fingers and down the smooth skin of his cock.

He pistons the two fingers inside of me now like a reward. I grind against his palm, searching for pressure on my clit. He pushes into the roll of my hips and gives me what I need.

"I'll come too soon," he warns when I use the slickness of my saliva to stroke him.

The bulge at the base of him bumps against my hand, and I clench around his fingers, wishing he could push it inside of me.

"Me too. I'm—I'm close already. Just a bit . . . more. It's so good," I slur, my eyes unseeing as they roll back.

He curses low, throat straining. It's unbelievably sexy how vocal he is, each moan and shuddered breath driving me closer to an orgasm.

His scent explodes, and then I'm choking on vanilla and cinnamon. I lean forward and kiss him, needing to taste them on my tongue. It's like a hit from a drug. A fix for me alone.

"Get ready," he warns, teeth skating over my lip.

I go still, pleasure blooming in my belly before growing claws and tearing its way through the rest of me. My vision goes white before I cry out, starting to shake.

Landon throbs in my hand as I squeeze him hard and push down, aiming him directly between my legs. When he comes, I feel it. Not just as he pulses in my hand but as I tug his fingers from inside of me and the hot splashes of cum paint my pussy instead, covering me in him.

"Oh, fuck. Look at you," he pants, watching in bewilderment.

His fingers return to where I'm slick in both of our releases and play with me, never slipping inside. When he finally lifts them, they tap my lips.

I stick my tongue out without being asked, and he slides them along it, going deep enough I worry I'll gag before retreating. Then, he does the same, our eyes clashing as he sucks his fingers clean.

Words evade me. All I can do is relax in his lap and feel the comedown, knowing he's here, even if just for right now. And when he coils his arms around my back and holds me close, I believe that he'll be here for a while yet.

38

Dash

After disappearing into thin air, Landon sent a text to the group chat letting us know he was on his way home with Briar. That's all the warning we got, and that was well over an hour ago.

Coming back to the dressing room after practice to find him and his stuff gone with no explanation was alarming, to say the least. Jasper scoured the arena from top to bottom in search of him before we got to the parking lot and realized the SUV was also nowhere to be seen.

One tense Uber ride later and I was pacing the kitchen, threatening to call the police. Ronan quickly shut that idea down, reminding us that he hadn't even been missing for an hour.

"Does he think that's enough? Just that he's on his way?" Jasper asks.

Ronan grips the counter until his knuckles are white. "Did he take her somewhere?"

"Would it even matter now? It's too late to try and get any warning. He could have at least left us a way of getting home instead of abandoning us completely."

There are three open beer bottles on the counter, two full and the third empty. I'm the only one of us who gulped every drop of one, needing it to soothe some of my anxiety.

"Am I the only one concerned about what they were doing together? This is out of character for him," Ronan mutters.

I frown. "He wouldn't hurt her."

"I didn't mean like that. Just that he's been pretty fucking rude to her in the past."

Jasper leans his forearms on the kitchen island and blows out a breath. The stress lines in his face aren't the most comforting. "We need to have a pack meeting. How we've been recently . . . things can't stay like this. We'll collapse."

"I agree," I say.

Ronan taps his fingers to the countertop. "What do you think a meeting will do? Are we going to host an intervention?"

"It's worth a shot. I want us to be happy, Ro. All of us together. Not just those of us who are prepared to welcome Briar into the pack. We need to figure out a path forward together," Jasper declares.

Ronan doesn't seem convinced. "Landon's the only one with the issue. He needs to figure his shit out for the sake of all of us."

"We're pack. It's our job to help him with that. And Briar needs us to as well. We can't pretend that her heat isn't coming any day now. If we don't get things figured out before it hits . . ." Jasper's words trail off, and a collective fog of dread hangs above us all.

I swallow, tasting the bitter beer that's lingering in my throat while staring at Ronan. "He's right. We need to discuss things with Briar and figure out what she wants to do once that time comes. I'm assuming you and Jasper will be the ones involved."

"Not you?" It comes from Jasper.

It feels wrong to say no, but there's no way she'd want me there with her during her heat when I've been so adamant that she's not my scent match.

"I don't see that happening," I say.

Ronan chuckles lowly, not a hunt of humour in the noise.

"Maybe if you stopped thinking so much about what Landon wants and focused on yourself, you wouldn't be left out."

"What's that supposed to mean?" I ask roughly.

"You're no better than Landon. This loyalty you feel to him has blinded you."

"Just because I don't feel the same way you do—"

Ronan pushes against the edge of the island, eyes narrowed and gaze cold. "Don't. You sound like a fool when you say shit like that."

I don't have a reply. His words sink in as I stand there, marinating in the frustration he has toward me. When I pull my gaze away and to where Jasper watches us, I hate that I can see the same feelings written all over his face.

"Landon's gone to battle on my behalf, and I owe him my loyalty," I try and argue.

Jasper nods. "I know. Ronan and I do too. There's a reason we chose him to be the leader of the pack. But at what point do we have to question if he would want us to lose our chance at our one-in-a-trillion omega because we're too focused on keeping the pack together."

"We deserve a chance with her. She's my scent match and my mate," Ronan snaps.

Jasper smiles faintly. "As she's mine."

"She's all of ours."

Surprise flashes across my packmates' faces, and I spin around, following the shift in their attention. When I do, Landon stares back at me. I can only gawk at the sight of his arm behind Briar, a hand seemingly resting on her back as they lean close.

The beautiful omega blinks up at Landon, a lip nestled beneath her teeth. There's a glow to them, a sign that something happened while they were gone. Something that's brought the colour back to Landon's face and a warmth to the dark eyes that have been slowly dying the last few weeks.

Ronan, seeming to pick up on the same things I have, grunts, "What happened?"

"I should be the one asking you that," Landon snips, his peaceful expression slipping. "Living room. *Now*. We're having a pack meeting."

"That was our plan as well," Jasper puts in.

Briar smiles at him, reluctantly stepping away from Landon. She lingers near me on her way around the island to Ronan, and I breathe through my mouth to avoid inhaling her lemon scent.

Now isn't the time to be trying to figure out if I've been a fool all this time.

The rejection that fills her eyes bites, but it's better than taking attention from what Landon wants to talk about.

"Hi, Dash," she says.

"Hey."

"I like that colour on you."

Jasper chuckles as I glance down at the peachy T-shirt I threw on after practice. It's got a lame quote on it that says, "Need Vitamin Sea?" with a cartoon starfish waving an arm. I'm pretty sure it was a gag gift at Christmas a couple of years ago.

Still, the compliment makes my chest swell. "Thank you."

She slips past me, disappearing and leaving me with nobody to look at besides Landon. His glower is intense, almost threatening.

I lift a brow in a silent question. *What?*

Careful, his glare says.

It's clear what happened between them changed more than any of us are prepared to learn. I'm happy for him, but if he's decided to accept Briar, where does that leave me?

I'm not only the only beta in the pack but the only one of us without a scent match.

The demons I've been ignoring from the moment I said yes to joining the Montgomery pack howl in triumph. The deep-rooted doubts of not belonging somewhere I need to be eat at me no matter how many times I tell myself that I'm here for a reason.

"Come with me," Landon says, the demand shot in my direction.

I push away from the island without looking to see which man Briar's gone to first and trail behind him as we move between rooms. By the time we reach the living room, my chest is tighter than it has been in a long while.

"Do you want to tell me what's going on?" he asks, taking a seat on the sectional.

The living room is wide and open with a skylight in the ceiling above us. If it weren't after sunset, I'd be able to feel the warmth from the sun on my face when I sit beside him.

"Do you?" I return.

Even his posture has loosened, his shoulders dropped and jaw relaxed.

"You're the one staring into space like you're waiting for a miracle to pop out in front of you."

I lick my lips, shaking my head. "Have you ever wondered why I was in our pack?"

"Are you being serious?"

"I am."

"Fuck, Dash. You're in our pack because we're brothers. It was set out to be this way from the moment we were born."

"If that were the case, I would have designated as an alpha."

Landon spreads his legs before leaning over them, elbows digging into the meaty part of his thighs. "Why does it matter what designation you are? Alpha, beta, fucking labradoodle, you're pack. That's never going to change."

"I'd have recognized her, Lan," I croak.

"Not if you didn't want to."

I drag a hand through my hair, meeting his stare. "What do you mean?"

"Do you remember when we were in twelfth grade and the four of us were asked to go to Kale River's house party?"

"He was a weasel."

Landon chokes on a laugh. "Yeah, he was. That's not what I'm getting at, though."

"What, then?"

"When we got to his place, you went to greet him and overheard him talking shit about my dad. He was running his mouth about his washed-up career and how I was wasting my time on the ice trying to be better than him."

I remember every word that guy said and the fight that broke out afterward.

Landon continues, not giving me a chance to interrupt.

"You were never the guy to cause a scene. It was always you, the three of us, and the computer you spent two summers of savings to buy. But that night? You stormed over to Kale and bull tackled him in into his pool."

"I never wanted to be friends with that guy, anyway," I say.

"No, but if you hadn't tackled him, you'd have gotten a chance at checking out his gaming room, and I know you wanted that bad at the time. It's the only reason we went there in the first place."

"A gaming room was never more important to me than you, Lan. Like you said, we're pack. Even back then."

"Exactly. Over and over again, you've given up things you've wanted because I've either had a negative interaction with someone or lost out on an opportunity that they opted out of offering me. Your loyalty is unshakable. Back then and right now."

I shift on the couch. "Is there a point to this walk through history?"

"Yeah, smartass. You're too busy worrying about me and how I feel that you're not thinking of yourself."

"You're the second person to say that to me now," I say.

"And are you listening?"

"You want me to give her a chance when you've been doing the opposite for weeks."

He nods, not hiding from the accusation. "And I'm dealing with that now."

"Why the change of heart?"

"That's what I want to talk to all of you about."

I lean back, relaxing slightly. "I can accept that."

"For what it's worth, Dash, I'm sorry for getting between you and Briar."

"Why should you apologize? I inserted you there all on my own."

"So, you're admitting it, then," he says far too smugly.

I chuff a laugh. "Have you known this entire time what I've been doing?"

"For as long as you've been doing it. I couldn't face it without owning my own shit first."

"And you're ready for that now," I say, trying not to sound sceptical but failing.

"Yes. You could say that."

39

Jasper

Having Briar back in my arms is like breathing freely after having a bag over my head. I inhale her lemon shortbread scent and hum in satisfaction as she hugs me tight and nuzzles her head beneath my chin.

Ronan watches us with a sharp longing in his eyes despite just having her smothering him with love a moment ago. I can't judge him for that. I'm pretty sure separation anxiety is a struggle in all scent-matched packs.

The only thing that might help is a set of mating bites imprinted on her skin. Alongside her bite on ours, hopefully. If that's something she'd be interested in. I can't even think about it without my dick throbbing. The possibility of that kind of connection threatens to unravel me thread by thread.

Before my scent can betray where my thoughts have gone, I kiss the top of Briar's head and inch her back enough for our eyes to meet. I've never loved the colour blue as much as I do the pale shade of hers.

"It seems you have plenty to talk to us about," I murmur.

"Are you upset?"

Ronan's the one who speaks, but I'm sure my confused expression says enough.

"Why would we be upset?"

She rolls her lip between her teeth. "I'm assuming Landon did leave practice early, even though he said he didn't. I don't want anyone to get in trouble because of me or anything like that. It was just instinct to call him."

"No, love, we're not upset. I don't know what happened yet, but if you called him, I'm glad he left. Landon's priorities were right."

"So he did leave early," she says, latching onto that tiny tidbit of information.

"Yes and no. He was cleared to leave so he could go see the team's physio. That's where we thought he was before we realized he was gone," I explain.

"For his knee? He told me he couldn't feel it earlier."

Ronan clears his throat and swoops in to drop an arm around her shoulders. His mouth moves to her temple before he says, "He was lying, Petal."

She lurches forward, knocking his arm off before Ronan moves with her, leaving me to catch up behind them.

"I'm going to go ask him about that. If he's injured, he needs to be taking his recovery seriously and not being so careless."

"I've been trying to get that into his head since he hurt himself. Maybe he'll listen to you," I say.

"He won't have a choice."

Amusement sparks in Ronan's eyes when he glances at me. His smirk is dangerous, betraying how much he loves our omega's fire.

The flames lie dormant behind the veil of sweetness and thoughtful instincts, but they're constantly on the prowl, waiting to be stoked. Landon seems to be the one who lights them up faster than anything else we've seen.

"By the way, Ronan, your mother is amazing," she pipes up before slipping fully out from beneath his arm and speeding out of the room.

Ronan's steps stutter. "What?"

She's already disappeared, leaving his question unanswered. My packmate turns to me dumbstruck and blinks.

"Don't look at me. I have no idea what went on today," I defend myself.

"Are we about to be completely fucking railroaded here?"

I debate the question. "I'm going to assume yes."

"Great," he huffs.

When we enter the living room, everyone else has already taken their preferred spots. The sectional that eats up most of the space in here is huge. It's a full U with cushions big enough to fit two grown men on each one, yet as I stare at it today, it feels even bigger. On the rare occasion that we're all home and together long enough to sit and watch a game, there's always so much space between us, both physically and emotionally.

Today, Dash, Briar, and Landon have squished themselves on a cushion and a half, and by the look on Landon's face as he ignores our entry and watches Briar with a desperation that I recognize immediately, I feel the dwindling hope in my chest take flight.

We could leave this room today as a healing pack.

"We haven't missed the discussion, have we?" I ask.

The closest spot to Briar is on Landon's side, so I snag it before Ronan can. The broody alpha rolls his eyes at me and, instead of taking the spot beside me like I expect, drops to the floor in front of her. He presses his toes to the bottom of the couch and his knees against the cushion while leaning forward and palming her thighs. His gaze is intense, but it doesn't seem to bother her.

She covers his hands and squeezes. "And here I thought pack meetings involved everyone."

"They do. Which is why you just used their absence to lay into me about my knee instead of something more serious," Landon drawls. His body language is odd, a mix between uneasy and confident. Like he knows what he has to say but is nervous about how we'll react. "We haven't had a real pack meeting in a long time. I wouldn't be surprised if none of us remembered how they worked."

"We have time to fix that," I offer.

Ronan isn't as forgiving. "Not sure that's anyone's fault but yours, Pack Leader."

"Don't, Ro. Not right now," Dash says with a heavy exhale.

Landon slowly peels his eyes from Briar and settles them on each of us, lingering longer on the pack member who's had the biggest issues with him recently. Ronan's pride goes toe to toe with his, and it's kept them in a constant power struggle. That, and the kind of alpha energy that can turn every room into a battleground.

I don't think Landon's ever taken for granted that he has Ronan's approval to be pack leader. If he ever changed his mind, the foundation of our pack would be forever shifted.

It's some higher power that's responsible for their ability to overlook their battling dominance and love each other the way we all do. We're better off together than apart, and that's been obvious from the moment we met.

"No, get it out of your system, Ronan," Landon encourages.

Ronan wets his lips and holds Briar's thighs tighter. "We're pack. One person's selfishness isn't supposed to threaten the happiness of everyone else. Yet you let that happen without a care for how the rest of us would feel."

"Just because you've never had a reason not to trust Briar doesn't mean that I haven't, either. You can't begin to understand why I made the choices I did," Landon explains tightly.

Dash leans past Briar to stare at Landon. "So explain to us why. We've been ready to listen for weeks, Lan."

"I'd like to know as well." Briar releases one of Ronan's hands to steal Landon's.

Finger by finger, she uncurls his fist until she can bring his palm to her lips. I feel at peace watching her kiss his hand and bring it to rest against her chest.

Landon gazes at her, his expression wavering slightly. "I have never trusted an omega. My mother ruined that for me."

"She's been out of your life for a decade now. You can't let her ruin your life now the way she tried to ruin your father's," Dash says.

Landon keeps his eyes on Briar. "My father met my mother when he was twenty and new to the NHL. He hadn't met his packmates when he was a kid like I did and had only started getting to know them. They met when he entered the league, and only two weeks later, my mom came around.

"It was impossible not to know who my father was if you were a hockey fan, and while she wasn't a fan, she did know who he was. When they met, my dad explained it as being a miracle. He took one look at her, and he swore something awoke inside of him. Once he smelled her, he swore she was his scent match, and the entire pack agreed. Two months later, she was bonded to them and pregnant with me."

A dull ache grows behind my ribs as I listen and watch Briar lean her head on his shoulder, keeping their hands against her chest.

Landon buries his face in her hair and inhales, his throat bobbing. When he pulls back, he sets his chin on her head.

"When I was old enough to go to school, she started disappearing for long periods of time. Dad always told me she needed "Mommy break time," and I believed him. Every time she'd come home, I would smell her and get this churning sensation in my stomach like I knew something wasn't right. That was when I realized I had an ultra-sensitive sense of smell. It turns out that every time she was off on one of her breaks, she was running off to her real scent match. When I was seven, I smelled him on her for the first time."

Nobody speaks when he halts his explanation, working through a lifetime of betrayal that he's never actually completely dealt with. It's not just him, either. His father hasn't bothered helping himself or his son at all. They've let their relationship fall apart instead, an intimidating distance between them that they don't know how to close.

Ronan shifts his hand from Briar's leg to Landon's knee, giving it a firm pat. "Your mother was cruel, Lan."

"She was. Briar, you have to understand that it was never about you," Landon chokes out, pale and frazzled.

She strokes the back of his hand with her thumb. "Keep explaining it to me so I can understand."

"I tried to hide what I'd learned, but there were three alphas in our house, which meant once they picked up on my new discomfort around her, they didn't let it go. Stubborn as fuck, they demanded I tell them what was wrong, and once I did, they called a pack meeting and asked her about it. She denied it, but I think they already knew. I remember watching them spend less and less time with her and wondered how that was even possible if they were bonded scent matches. The emotional distance should have been killing them, but instead, they were happier when she wasn't around."

He swallows loud enough for all of us to hear, and I touch his shoulder before Dash reaches behind Briar to do the same with his other one. The joint connection with each of us soothes him enough that he can continue.

"When you're bonded to an omega . . ." he starts.

"You share one soul. Their emotions are yours, and you have access to every nook and cranny of their mind," Briar finishes.

When his lips part on a silent question, she smiles softly before answering, "I grew up in a pack. My mom has three bites on her neck."

It's both a reminder that we still have so much to learn about her and a reassurance I didn't know I needed from her.

"Yes, you all but share a soul. Even after they kicked her out of the pack, she still wore those bites, and the pain that followed tore them apart piece by piece. My childhood home heard more fights than it did anything else, and it wasn't long after the divorce was finished that the pack broke apart. They lost half of everything to her when she left, and my father spent every spare minute he had at the arena. I always say I grew up in a pack, but the truth is that I didn't. Not even close."

"I forgot about some of that," Ronan says.

Landon winces. "I wish I did too."

"How did she manage to pull off that good of a performance? Pretending to be someone's scent match? That's—well, that's insane," Briar whispers.

I nod, understanding where she's coming from. "Scent masking was only just becoming a more known thing back then, but it was also a lot easier to pull it off before more and more scent matches started finding one another. There's been a twenty percent jump in successful pairings over the last ten years alone."

"Okay, Mr. History," Dash teases.

It's the lighthearted comment that slices through the heavy energy around us. Briar giggles and in turn brings some light back to Landon's expression. Ronan kisses both of her knees, unabashedly obsessed with her. I watch them all in awe.

"It's true. My mom waltzed into my father's life with a dream and came out on the other end successful. The rest of the pack and me? We were just casualties on her stride for a big payout."

"Have you seen her since?" Briar asks.

"No. And some days, I forget I knew her at all. I don't miss her, even if I should."

Emotion wets Briar's eyes. Landon's thumb is sweeping beneath them to dry each tear before it can get beyond her lower lashes.

"Are you trying to say that you want to move past what happened with your mother? To accept Briar?" Dash asks.

Landon keeps his thumb on her skin but soon adds the entirety of his hand to cup her cheek softly. For a man who's been so afraid of the complications that come with intimacy for so long . . . these soft touches say more than words could. I hope Briar knows exactly that.

"It's not that simple. We still need to court her properly. Spoil her and finish the nest that's been sitting incomplete for years. We haven't earned her as our omega yet," he declares.

Ronan makes a deep sound in his chest. "Some of us have been courting her for a while now."

"So keep going." Landon speaks to Briar now. "We have more to show you than we have so far. Our pack has been balancing one-legged on a tightrope for a while, but if you'll give us a shot—a real one—we'll do right by you. *I'll* do right by you. Even if I'm not perfect."

Briar's lips quirk at the corner as she looks at each of us. "I've never needed perfect. Just contentment and happiness. Support from those who I'm meant to spend forever with. Being courted is the norm, but I just want to see that you can give me all of those things. Gifts have never been all that important to me."

"You'll get gifts," Ronan states bluntly. "A fuck ton of them."

Her cheeks warm. "I won't say no to that."

Landon releases her face and straightens, speaking to every member of our pack. "So? What do you say? Are we doing this?"

"We've been waiting for you to catch on," I say with a bump of our shoulders.

Ronan agrees, and Dash . . . he simply nods.

I eye him a bit longer than I do everyone else, but soon enough, he's grinning and joining the new conversation. It's all very lighthearted for a change, all of us finally on the same page.

Landon clears his throat after a few minutes, suddenly serious. I tense up, a bad feeling—

"Now, who wants to tell me why Briar's apartment was broken into and why everyone seems to know who's responsible for it but me?"

40

Briar

"WHAT DO YOU MEAN YOUR APARTMENT WAS BROKEN into?" Ronan snaps, an angry shade of red slowly creeping up his throat.

"That's where Landon's been. I called him when I saw my door open and went inside—"

"You went inside alone when you saw your door was open?" Jasper asks, still scolding but not as ruthless as Ronan.

I try not to waver beneath their worried words and keep strong. If I let them railroad me now, they won't know where my boundaries are. "Stop ganging up on me, or I won't tell you anything."

All four of them keep silent, but it's Ronan's chest that won't stop rumbling. I take the small win and hold back a smile at his protectiveness. It's not a new development by any means.

"She went up to your parents' apartment while she waited for me," Landon says, eyeing the grumbling alpha. "And I don't think you're in a position to be growling at anyone, considering you didn't share that there are a pair of alphas dangerous enough to pose a threat to our omega lurking around."

To Ronan's benefit, he doesn't look taken aback by Landon's chastising. Sure, his anger isn't specifically directed at him, but it may as well be. Landon's like a dog with a scent, and after semi-successfully avoiding his interrogation on the ride here, I knew it was only a matter of time before he brought his questions and suspicions to the rest of the pack.

I do feel guilty for not sharing what happened with Sadie's alphas with the rest of the pack, but it all happened so fast, and I didn't think a text was the way to handle it. In a way, I guess this is a blessing.

Landon's taking care of it now.

I never thought I'd be able to say that after how things were before today.

"I only met the two alphas the other night," Ronan says before glancing at Jasper. "And I wasn't the only one who knew."

Landon's energy shifts, his scent sharpening. "So, both of you knew and didn't speak up. You shouldn't have gone anywhere you thought could have been dangerous without backup. We should have dealt with whatever happened together."

"Would you have even come if I'd asked? And I didn't set off to tell Jasper. He was up when I got home the morning after," Ronan defends himself.

I lift a brow and stare down at him. "You mean after you stayed parked outside of my apartment all night?"

His mouth slants into a smirk, knowing he's caught. "It wasn't the first time, and it won't be the last."

I don't know if he means to, but Landon clutches my hand with a python grip, as if he needs my support to continue this conversation.

"I know you don't think much of me anymore, Ro, but yes, I would have come. You're my family, and I'd do anything for any one of you, Briar included. Which is also why I've asked her to move in with us."

"What?" Dash guffaws. When I steal a look at him, he's wide-eyed.

Is it really that surprising? Or is he upset?

Some omegas move in with their scent matches after the first time they meet them. My mom was mated and bonded a week after first scenting her mates.

"That's the best call you've made in months," Ronan tells Landon, inching forward and dropping his lips to kiss both my knees. His eyes blaze when they meet mine. "You belong here with us. Safe and cared for."

"Yes, you do," Jasper adds.

He's sitting too far away, but the steady warmth of his hand on my back helps with the distance.

Dash doesn't have a chance to say anything else before Landon's bringing the conversation back to the break-in. His leadership is shining through right now, and I'd be lying if I said it wasn't extremely sexy watching him take control of the pack.

"When I was looking inside of Briar's place, I found a bunch of Harbour of Hope folders open. Most importantly, Sadie's. It was empty. Now, is there a reason Sadie isn't with her alphas? And why has Briar been brought into what's going on with them? I need to know everything that happened the other night and over the last few weeks."

"Thorne and Sebastian are the only two in the pack, but they're not her alphas anymore. Not really. She already left them and has filed multiple restraining orders, with the most recent being heavily detailed. They're not supposed to be within six feet of her, but they've been constantly appearing outside of the clinic and as of the other night, trying to get into her house. Our security does a great job of keeping them away while she's at the clinic, but other than that, we have no jurisdiction," I explain.

Landon hardly contains a growl. "Which one of them is the father?"

Ronan strokes my legs in soothing movements. "Thorne. He's the one stirring the shit. When I drove Briar to Sadie's the other night, it was him who was trying to get inside of her apartment. They're bonded, and he feels like she still belongs to him."

"His instincts aren't going to allow him to pretend his baby doesn't exist. He won't leave her alone," Jasper adds tightly.

Dash clears his throat. "Briar needs to be our focus. Especially if they're now targeting her."

We're pressed so close together that our arms and thighs touch, and when he grows stiff, I feel it. He might doubt our slow-growing bond, but I know it's there, and every moment we stay this close, it becomes even more apparent. His scent is subtle but delicious. Good enough to eat, really.

If he would only give me a chance, I know we'd be great together. The small hints of his humour and jokester personality intrigue me. Dash is like a glass of cold lemonade on a sweltering day, and I'm desperate for a long, refreshing gulp of it.

"I would say I'm a target less than I am just someone in their way. They want to know details about Sadie's birth that we—*I*—refuse to give. For as long as she's a Harbour of Hope patient, Sadie will have around-the-clock protection at the clinic and top-of-the-line care. That means Thorne can't just walk in and demand answers. Yes, breaking into my place was a poor decision, but he's desperate. This isn't about me at all," I say.

Landon forces out a harsh breath. "It doesn't matter if this isn't about you. The moment he brought you into this, he made himself an enemy of the Montgomery pack."

My heart lurches, wings flapping in my stomach. Twisting, I peer up at him through my lashes. "And what does that mean exactly?"

Jasper curls his fingers and draws five soft lines across the length of my shoulders while Ronan sweeps his hands up to the tops of my thighs.

Dash swallows and digs his eyes into the side of my face while shifting his hips and spreading his legs, a knee digging into my leg beside Ronan's hot fingers.

My senses become overrun with their touching and the swell of scents around me. I try to breathe in each one, but as I peer into Landon's electric gaze, the best I can do is sip on hot air.

I wait anxiously for him to join his packmates in touching me, but he makes me wait for it. My breasts heave, nipples hard and sensitive in my bra. Every second it takes for him to put me out of my misery is another I can feel myself growing wetter between my legs, slick filling my panties.

When Landon finally brings an arm into the space between us, I'm parting my legs, inviting Ronan to slide his hands further. For some godforsaken reason, he doesn't.

I don't realize why until Landon shakes his head and gently pinches my chin, a calloused thumb stroking the dip in the centre of it.

"The Montgomery pack is yours, Haven. Anyone who threatens, hurts, or so much as looks at you the wrong way won't be given a chance to apologize. You're ours to protect, and we won't let you down. *I won't*. Not again."

A shiver runs down my spine. A fourth hand joins the others, and I fling my head to the side to see Dash joining in. The cautious, soft pressure of his fingers around my waist fills me with blinding pleasure.

I moan breathlessly, relaxing back into the couch. Landon doesn't allow me much space and strokes his knuckles down the side of my face, keeping the consistent fever running hot. The bubble around us thickens, becoming impenetrable to everything outside of it.

"What do you want for your heat, love?" Jasper asks, his voice muted behind the sound of my pulse.

Landon uses the tip of his finger to trace my lips. "*Who* do you want?"

"It's coming soon," I whisper, shutting my eyes.

The burn simmering beneath my skin is only a taste of what's to come. And for the first time in my life, I'm excited for an incoming heat. Not just for the endless pleasure that I know will come but because I'll get to spend it with them. My mates.

"Even I can smell how close it is," Dash notes, his voice deeper, strained.

Jasper hums in agreement. "We need to get the nest ready."

"You need to decorate it, Petal. Fill it with everything you've ever wanted."

"Jasper should take you shopping," Landon says, his scent more cinnamon than vanilla. "He knows the most about nesting. I've seen his bookshelves."

Jasper's fingers climb from my shoulder up my neck and twist in my hair. "Dash knows more about designations than I do."

"Not omegas," Dash adds gently.

"I'd like both of you to take me," I gasp when Jasper tugs on my hair hard enough for me to feel it between my legs. "And all of you involved in my heat."

"Even me?" Dash asks, almost timidly.

"You're my scent match. I know you are."

"Then we'll all be there," Ronan promises.

His hand slips along the inner side of my thigh, slowly crawling toward where I'm hot and damp. The brief press of his pinky to my seam causes me to jolt.

"Easy, beautiful. What I said earlier stands. We're going to wait until your heat," Landon purrs in my ear.

Dash thumbs the pulse point in my wrist. "Think about what you want from us when the time comes. Not just sexually but emotionally. We've never done this before."

"It's an honour for you to be our first," Jasper declares.

It's Landon who gives me what I'm too scared to dig for. He has a deeper insight into my mind than I could have ever expected.

"And only. You'll be the only one."

I force my eyes open until I can focus on each of them. "Is that a promise? I take my promises seriously. If you say yes and then break it—"

With a ferocity that muzzles me, Landon swoops in and kisses me. He forces the worry from my consciousness and replaces it with a declaration of forever.

"I promise, Briar."

41

Dash

I ESCAPED INTO MY ROOM AS SOON AS I COULD. As much as I want to be around my pack, I just can't right now. I need a distraction. A break from the sweetness of Briar's scent and the reminder that I messed up. Not only with her, but with Landon, Ronan, and Jasper too.

They needed my support just as much as Landon did, but I chose him over them. I chose him over Briar.

My head is a mess as I tighten my grip on the Xbox controller and lean over my knees, keeping my eyes on the TV. I'm not playing goalie today and instead opted for a defenseman so I could have an excuse to digitally beat someone up. It's not as good as doing it for real, but I've never gotten into a physical fight anyway. I'd wind up minced beta meat beneath a heavy fist if I attempted it.

Ronan's the fighter out of the four of us. He always has been, although he's settled more over the years. His anger was ramped up during his teen years because of the rush of alpha hormones and his natural distaste for most people, so there was never a need for the rest of us to practice.

With everything coming to light about the danger Briar's in, maybe we should have tried anyway.

I zone out, relying on muscle memory to control my fingers as they dart around the controller, pressing buttons that lead my player into a brawl with a random defenseman on the other team. My headphones are snug to my ears and the top of my head, blocking out all noise from around me so I can focus on the bass-heavy song playing.

My throat is sticky, the tightness in my chest not loosening even after my player gets placed in the penalty box and a loading screen appears in front of me.

I skip through the replay footage of the fight and settle back for my next shift. Even virtually, it feels wrong not playing as a goalie. For twenty years, I've played that position, ever since my dad enrolled me in hockey when I started elementary school. It's in my blood. Sometimes, I feel more at ease with a big-ass helmet on my head and a pair of pads on my legs. It's my armour.

My next shift starts, and I skate up the ice, ramming into everyone that comes close to me. It's something that would only be allowed in a video game, and right now, I take advantage of the lack of whistles.

I'm staring hard enough at the screen for my eyes to water when there's a tap on my shoulder. I watch in slow motion as my controller slips through my fingers and soars through the air, whacking the front of my dresser. Its back tab opens, and the batteries scatter across the hardwood before rolling onto the rug beside my bed.

I jump off the couch and whirl around, surprise controlling my limbs. It's so goddamn dark in here just the way I like it while I play, and that doesn't help. The person standing a few feet back is masked in shadows, and only when they rush forward with their hands up do I settle.

"Briar?"

"I'm sorry, I didn't mean to scare you. I said hi and knocked, but the door was open, and I saw you had headphones on. I'm heading to bed and just wanted to say goodnight," she rambles, voice higher-pitched than usual. "Maybe I should have taken your concentration as a sign to leave you alone."

"No!" It tears past my lips, and my cheeks heat with embarrassment. "I mean, it's all good. I was just playing."

She looks past me at the TV and the game that's paused itself due to my controller batteries being on the carpet.

"You like hockey enough to play it in your free time on top of how often you're on the ice?"

I gnaw on that. "Haven't you ever loved something so much that you never get bored of it?"

"Outside of work? I love to paint, but I wouldn't say that I've never gotten bored of it before."

Nodding, I sit back down and wave to my couch, silently offering her a seat on it. She smiles and joins me, leaving only a couple of inches between our bodies.

Her scent is still sweeter than usual, a sign that her heat is approaching fast. There's a restlessness in my chest, a flutter kicking up behind my ribs that demands I get closer. It could be the pull of her incoming pheromones or . . . something else. Something that I've been denying myself.

"The only thing I've ever felt that with is hockey. But I guess that's what happens when you grow up playing it. It's engrained in me," I say.

She folds her hands in her lap. "Did you always love it?"

"I think so. The first time I was in a pair of skates, I was two. I didn't start playing until I was five."

"Two seems really young. I imagine you were quite adorable in tiny skates, though."

"I'll have to show you my mom's old videos one of these days. I was a mess," I confirm with a low chuckle.

"Well, you aren't anymore. I don't know much of anything about hockey, but you play with grace. It doesn't seem possible that you could be a mess now."

"That depends on the game. I may not slip and fall anymore, but I have my fair share of bad games. It's hard to work through those ones, but I've got the guys with me. Not every goalie is as lucky as I am to play with his entire pack on the same team."

"Oh, I assumed it was mandatory for packmates to have to play together. Are there many packs in the league like ours?"

Ours.

The others would turn halfway feral if they heard her say that. Shit. There's a stiffening in my jeans that's nearly painful. I shift in discomfort, her claim on us having a terrifying effect on me.

"No," I choke out, trying to subtly grab a deep breath. "Only a handful, and other than just one, all their members are separated. Finding a team that's okay with keeping a large group of their players tied to heavy, long-lasting contracts is rare."

"Will Rayton keep you together forever?"

I strangle my knee with a sweaty grip. "We hope so. There's still five years left on our contracts. We've got time to figure that out or what comes next."

"And in five years, where do you think you'll be? In your life, I mean."

Her sincerity is adorable. And refreshing. Really refreshing. The more time I spend with this woman, the easier it is to see why the other three are so obsessed with her. Even Landon, who I didn't think would ever let an omega in, has shocked me and done just that.

I'm surprised she's even here talking to me right now instead of with him. Or Ronan. Hell, even Jasper. Do they really not care that she's going to spend another night alone in the nest?

"Why are you here right now?" I ask, immediately wincing at the roughness to my voice. "You could be with any one of the others."

I keep my eyes fixed to the TV, unable to force myself to look at her. If I saw the shine of realization or regret in her gaze, I think it would hurt more than I'm prepared for.

Her hand falls to cover the one I'm using to crush my knee. Stroking my knuckles, she murmurs, "I know I could. But I'm pretty content right here."

"We're not doing anything."

"We're talking, aren't we? Getting to know each other?"

I laugh without meaning to before finally looking at her. The slight curve to her mouth settles me instantly.

"And you wanted to know where I see my life in five years," I state.

"I do. Because I have a pretty rough draft of what I want in my next five. I'm curious if our plans match up at all."

"Is that a deciding factor for you?"

She tips her head, her smile sliding higher. "We'll see."

"You know, usually it's me that's teasing everyone."

"Would you like an invitation to tease me, Dash?"

Tightness grows in my groin as I stop fighting my instincts and fall more into myself.

"I wouldn't mind one, Bright Eyes."

"Bright eyes? That's a new one."

I lean slightly in her direction, easing into the space between us until the sudden tugging sensation in my chest relaxes. "Nobody's ever called you that before?"

"Not until now. I guess it makes sense. My eyes are pretty light."

"That's not why I chose it, Briar."

She pauses, curiosity lighting her expression. "Are you going to tell me why, then?"

"Not yet. I thought you wanted to know what my five-year plan was."

"That's not fair," she huffs.

"You're beautiful even when you pout."

Her eyes flick up to mine. I swallow, debating between kicking myself in the ass for saying that or being proud of my honesty.

"You think I'm beautiful?" she asks softly.

I furrow my brows. "Yes. Are you not aware of how gorgeous you are? I thought you'd have dealt with guys staring at you everywhere you go."

"None of them are you or the other men outside this room right now."

"You're perfect, Briar."

"So, why are you still pretending you don't feel the same way I do? I don't care what your designation is, there's no way you aren't aware of who we are to each other," she declares, going right for the jugular.

There's no point in continuing to hide from this. If everyone else can be brave, why can't I?

"At first, I didn't want to push Landon. When I met you, I knew Landon wasn't ready for an omega. His history with his family wasn't a secret amongst us, and Landon . . . he's my brother. Not in blood, but by choice. He chose to have me in the pack and accepted me for who I was, designation and all, despite the backlash he got from too many people who haven't outgrown the old way of thinking.

"It should have been obvious to me that there was a block between us. I put it up before I'd even met you, and the night Ronan came home smelling like an omega . . . Fear is dangerous, but so is hope. At least with fear, you always expect the worst. Hope sets you up for heartbreak. A brief period of bliss, and then with one strong wind, you're tumbling off a cliff with nowhere to go but down. What if I'd been open from the start and Landon hadn't changed his mind?"

I focus on the warmth of her hand and clear my throat when it grows tight.

"The draw to you is there, Briar. I won't deny that. The way you smell and feel when we touch like this—" I slip my fingers through hers and bring our joined hands to my lips, kissing her soft skin. "—it's right. All of it is right. There's a tug in my chest that guides me to you, but I can't—I can't get past the wall completely, even now. Maybe I've waited too long."

Twisting beside me, she settles on her knees and leans into my side. Before I can snag her hand again, she places it back in mine and brings the other to rest on my shoulder for balance. Even in this position, I'm taller than her, but the difference isn't so bad now. Her mouth is level with mine, teasing me.

"There's no timeline on this. In case you haven't gotten it yet, I'm not going anywhere. I was prepared to fight for Landon, and now, I'm more than okay with waiting for you, Dash. I know what I feel, and that's that you're mine. Whether that's today, tomorrow, or a year from now."

I wet my bottom lip, and she lowers her stare, watching my tongue move. My voice drops an octave, dark with anticipation. "We don't deserve you. Not a single one of us."

"That's okay. I like knowing that you're going to have to work hard to keep me," she drawls, her teasing tone returning.

Bit by bit, she leans closer to me until her chest presses against my shoulder and her hand has slid along my collarbones. The light scrape of her nails against my shirt feels euphoric. I burn beneath the touch, wanting—needing—more.

"You have no idea how hard," I rasp.

Her smell intensifies, swirling around us so strongly that it makes my head swim despite having a weaker sense of scent than the others do. I feel it clawing at me, demanding I give us what we both want on a deep, biological level.

"Tell me your five-year plan."

I nod, humming so quietly it might possibly be silent. "The only thing I want is for my pack to be complete. Healed."

"That's really the only thing?"

Time stands still when she brings her lips to mine but hovers them a breath away, offering me only a brief taste of her.

"How could I ask for anything more than seeing you spend the rest of your life as a member of the Montgomery pack? That seems like the perfect way to spend the rest of my years, Bright Eyes. The next five isn't nearly enough for me."

42

Briar

"For a man who was so confident in being too late, you don't talk like you believe that," I whisper.

"I'm just being honest."

Dash says I'm beautiful, but I wonder if he's ever taken a good look in the mirror. While he's the more boyish-looking of the pack, he pulls it off perfectly. The hints of charm and humour that have briefly appeared in our conversations fit his appearance to a T. His deep pink lips that have a natural lift at the corner and the sparkle in his eyes that doesn't dull regardless of how tense the atmosphere gets are two of my favourite features. Wrap all of those things up in a pair of ripped jeans, a brightly coloured shirt with a cheesy joke front and centre, and a pair of skater shoes, and you've got one hell of a perfect beta.

His fears are valid. I'm not the person to tell him they're not. Nobody gets to decide that but him. But that doesn't mean I'm not going to try and prove him wrong as many times as it takes until he believes me.

"I like honest," I say, our mouths so close to fusing together.

He grabs my waist and tugs. "What else do you like?"

"Wouldn't it be more fun if you had to figure that out for yourself?"

"Are you giving me permission to do just that?"

I bite the inside of my cheek as my lips quirk. "Yeah, I'd say so."

"Then I'll stop stalling."

I let him move me until both of my knees dig into the couch and his lap is beneath me. Dash is the last one I've been intimate with, and the anticipation is eating me alive. The only other man in the pack who hasn't initiated much with me is Jasper, and I'm trying really hard not to take that to heart.

He's been very open about how he feels about me, and I need to be patient. Once my heat arrives, what we have and haven't done will be the least of my concerns.

Regardless of Dash's designation, I know he can smell how turned on I am. How could he not when I'm perfuming on his lap?

His eyes turn glassy as he breathes in and plants a second hand on my waist. Lips slightly parted, he presses forward and finally closes that gap between our mouths. Chocolate and peanut butter explodes around us as I grapple at his shirt and lean forward. My breasts are squished against his chest, my nipples hard and sensitive.

It's the taste of him that draws that first cry up my throat. His kiss satisfies a purely primal need inside of me, the part of myself that has been kept at bay until the first day I met Landon. This kiss confirms what I've been saying all along. Dash is mine, and there isn't a single part of me that can deny it. My heart, mind, and soul all agree.

My instincts were right, just like I always knew they were.

Heat nips at my spine as I slide a hand behind his neck and tug at the short hairs there. He meets my passion with a force of his own, a steady hand pressing into my lower back and urging me closer. It's still not enough.

There's a call inside of me trying to reach him, and I shudder at the intensity of it, already preparing myself for the blast of need that attacks my belly. I gasp, forcing our mouths to separate.

"Briar," he groans, eyes flashing open.

I yank his head further back until his throat is exposed and scoot down his lap to get a better angle. He spreads his legs and drops his hand to hold my ass. My lips meet his throat before I jerk in place, my pussy clenching around nothing while dripping steadily.

"I need . . ." I can barely think. Speaking isn't working.

He tilts his head and digs his fingers into me. "You can have whatever you need. Just wait to sink those pretty teeth into my neck until we're ready, okay?"

I bring my nose to his throat and inhale, frowning at his words. He smells *sooooo* good. How can he not want me to bite him yet? To mark him as mine?

I whine. He strokes the back of my head and shushes me, his touch crawling further down my backside.

"You're okay, Briar. I know. I know what you're feeling. Tell me what you need."

"I need you. Finally. I just need you."

His exhale is ragged. "Where?"

"Everywhere."

"Narrow it down for me before I decide that I'm going to risk pissing everyone else off and be the first one inside of you."

I nod rapidly, flicking my tongue up his throat. He may as well be sweating peanut butter with how strong his scent is. I can't get enough.

Without thinking twice, I slide my hands down between our bodies and tug at his jeans. The belt buckle is a pain in my ass, and I nip at his throat in punishment.

Lust drowns out the sound of his curse. He covers my hands and says my name. I melt, loving that sound too much. He says it with so much adoration and respect. Like he truly believes I'm something precious.

"Let me see those bright eyes, beautiful."

"Help me," I beg, growling when his belt buckle won't just undo already. "This is a buckle from hell."

His chuckle scrapes my peaked nipples, and I shiver, slick seeping through to wet my leggings. There's never been a chance of me hiding how aroused I am, but now? It's the most obvious thing ever.

"You're having a spike," he says, as if I need the warning.

"It's not my first one. I know what I want."

Finally, the buckle clacks, and I slip the leather through. His hands are hot and slick with sweat where they hold mine, and that's somehow really attractive to me right now.

"Briar—"

I press down on the thick length of him through the denim and purr, pleasure boiling in my belly. He's not as long as Landon or Jasper, but he's thick. As thick as Ronan, I'd bet. But I'd need to do a side-by-side comparison to be able to know for sure.

Yes, I need them all right in front of me.

Moaning, I rip at the button. Dash grunts under his breath and releases my hands to ghost his knuckle beneath my jaw. It's enough to draw my attention, my vision a bit hazy as I focus on his eyes.

"You're not thinking clearly. You came in here tonight to get to know me better, not for me to fuck you. I won't take advantage of you."

"You're not. I want you, Dash. I'm ready. Feel for yourself," I rush out.

He lets me take his fingers and bring them to my belly before slipping them beneath my leggings and between my legs. I watch for the moment he realizes I'm telling the truth. The flash of lightning in his eyes and the tightening of his thighs only make me gush again. And this time, his fingers are right there, hovering . . .

"Dash!" I cry when he swipes one through my slick flesh and gives my clit a faint brush.

The last thing I want him to do is remove his hand, but when he does so only to bring his glistening fingers to his lips, I keep my complaints to myself. With a crackling stare, Dash glides two long digits into his mouth and sucks them clean.

I'm a shaking mess. A live wire, primed and desperate for the spark that will send me over the edge.

"Like cookies, Bright Eyes. You taste good enough to devour."

"I approve," I moan, lowering myself firmly to his lap and going back for his pants.

Dash swallows and bundles my hair behind my shoulders. "I'll compromise with you."

I get the button open and tug down the zipper. At the first shove of his waistband, Dash lifts his hips for me. It's like I weigh nothing on his thighs. With the way the thick muscles strain and flex beneath me, that doesn't surprise me.

A happy sigh is all I can manage. His boxers are brightly coloured, and the dark circle right below the band has me strangling a moan in my throat.

"You need relief, Briar. Right?"

I nod, lowering my hand to cup him through the soft fabric. His dick pulses against my palm, encouraging me to continue my exploration.

"You can have it, but only my way. We'll get those leggings off you, and once you're bare, you can sit that pussy over my cock and get it nice and wet. I'll split those soft lips and glide right through, but it's not going inside. Not yet."

"Oh, my god," I breathe out, tingles erupting between my legs.

The wet spot in his boxers grows.

"Say you understand. I won't strip you until you do."

"I understand," I whisper.

"Pull my boxers down then."

I do, and I was absolutely right earlier. He's thick enough that I'm grateful we're waiting until my heat. I doubt I'd fit him inside right now.

But I will once I've gone into heat. My body will take everything he and the others will give me and beg for more. That's the thing about heats. Sometimes, you can lose sight of everything but the need to orgasm, and that's why it's always been so important to me to spend them with people I trust.

Orgasms might be the key to a somewhat manageable, pain-free heat, but being taken care of is just as important.

"I've never been with a beta before," I reveal.

He drops a hand to grab his shaft, long fingers stroking the soft skin. "I don't have a knot, but I'll still make you feel good."

"I know. You already are."

Satisfied with that, he replaces his hand with mine before starting to take my leggings off. The fabric glides inch by inch down my hips and thighs until I'm forced to balance on one leg while he strips them off completely. I don't dare take my hand off his cock, though. Not until I'm crawling up his legs and hovering above it, slick dripping down to coat him.

"All the way down, Briar. I want to feel you wrapped around me," he coaxes.

The first press of us together is wet and warm, and when I rock my hips forward, I drop my mouth to his shoulder and moan. My clit is so swollen it's borderline painful.

Dash presses a hand between our bodies and holds my breast, the callouses on his palm scraping against my nipple in the most delicious way. It's nothing compared to the bliss of him pinching it and giving it the slightest tug.

"You feel incredible," he mumbles, eyes struggling to focus.

I nod, grinding along the hot length of him. We're both wet, and I can't tell if any of the mess we've made has come from him or just me.

"Keep moving, beautiful. I know you need it. Need to come all over me."

"Give me yours too," I beg, gently biting down on my shoulder.

The shirt he's still wearing is a necessary boundary, even if it upsets my omega not to have unrestricted access to his skin right now.

"Yeah? You want my scent all over this pretty pussy?"

"Mmm."

"Won't take me long. Keep moving just like that and you'll get what you want."

Tilting my hips forward, I focus every forward glide on my clit and get the immediate response I need. A climax hovers nearby, and when he brings his mouth to my chest—

"Dash! Dash, I'm close."

His words are slightly muffled by his hold on my nipple, and that ramps up their intensity. "Soak me, Bright Eyes. This is the closest I've ever been to heaven. You're an angel."

Teeth scraping my sensitive breast, he tosses me over the edge. The orgasm is so violent that I arch my back and scream. Dash groans, low and deep, and lowers a hand to pluck at my clit while I press down on his shaft, drenching him.

"Gonna follow you, Briar," he warns, the throbbing beneath me growing in intensity.

I'm still drunk on pleasure when I scramble off his lap and, without giving him any warning, drop to my knees and take him into my mouth.

"Shit! You're magnificent," he praises.

It only intensifies my desire to have him in my mouth. As much as I'd love having his cum on my pussy, I know it'll be better this way if this spike is anything like the last. And from the heat still blistering beneath my skin after an intense orgasm, I think it is.

He gathers my hair into a ponytail and warns, "Here it comes."

I sneak in a breath before sliding my tongue along the bottom ridge of his cock and sucking the tip eagerly. He pulses between my lips and, a second later, floods my mouth.

Before meeting these men, I wouldn't have believed it if another omega told me that a scent match's scent matches the taste of their cum, but after having both Ronan's and Dash's? It's fact.

I suck harder, moaning as I swallow.

Suddenly, the heat begins to pass. I gasp, pulling back. Goose-bumps lift on my arms as my temperature falls back to normal. The shake in my fingers is nothing compared to the weakness in my legs when I try and stand.

"Stay still, Briar. I've got you."

Dash's voice soothes me. My smile is soft, maybe even a bit loopy, as he lifts me off the floor and onto the couch beside him. The second he releases me and reaches down to tuck his dick away, I snap a hand out, stopping him while my omega makes her demands known.

With a whine trapped in my throat, I take his softening length in my hand and lower myself to a lying position on the couch. He's frozen for a moment, no doubt confused about what I'm doing.

The fingers that begin running through my hair and tapping at my lips tell me when he's clued in.

"Go ahead, Bright Eyes. I'll be here."

"I like everything I've learned about you tonight," I whisper before resting my head on his groin and taking him back into my mouth.

Cock warming is something I've never done before, but the one time I saw it on a sex-positive omega blog, it intrigued me. Doing it now with Dash is confirming my immediate interest.

It's beyond intimate, and I think that's the perfect way to end what just happened between us. The instant relief that rushes through me when I don't lose this level of contact with him is everything I needed.

He blows out a breath and continues playing with my hair. "Anytime you want to learn anything else, I'm an open book."

I let my eyes fall closed and fall into a warm, inviting sense of comfort. My omega is at peace, and I fall asleep knowing that I'm not alone.

Dash is here.

43

Briar

I wake up in a bed instead of Dash's lap.

Fully stretching my limbs, I realize quickly that I'm in a giant bed. The sheets beneath my bare toes feel like the softest silk, and the comforter weighing me down is warm, like it's one of those fancy heated ones.

I squint my eyes open and blink through the sleepy haze. The nest is filled with bright light, and the sheer curtains blow in the breeze coming in from the cracked window. My smile is small but sincere. I don't think I mentioned needing to sleep with a window open to any of my guys, so it was most likely a coincidence that someone opened it while I slept. It makes me happy either way.

Sunday mornings used to be loud while I was growing up, so when I moved out on my own, it was a bit jarring for them to become silent. I expected things to be the same here, but as I sit and stretch out my arms, I'm pleasantly surprised to hear sound coming from downstairs.

The soft rub of fabric on my torso has my eyes dropping. I wasn't wearing this shirt last night, nor is it mine at all. My belly fills with flutters when I pinch the shirt and stare down at the Rayton Riptides logo on my chest. The rich scent of peanut butter fills the air around me. I grin and slip out of bed.

It's hard to keep my pace controlled as I flick the lights on in the ensuite and twist in the mirror to see the back of the shirt. Number 99 is written there in thick, blocky letters, confirming my suspicions.

I stand there staring at myself for longer than I'll ever admit to anyone before reluctantly stripping out of the shirt and hopping into the shower. I'm in and out in a few minutes and rooting through all the drawers in the vanity in search of a toothbrush.

It's surreal to search through a fully stocked bathroom knowing that it was four men who filled the drawers and cabinets. Even more so when I realize every product is one that I own and use daily.

Wait . . .

I freeze with my hand in a drawer of hair ties and bobby pins and stare at the pink electric toothbrush sitting beside the sink. *My* pink electric toothbrush.

"They didn't . . ."

But they did. Drawer after drawer, I find my things from home combined with restocked extras. Hundreds of dollars are in this bathroom, all spent on me.

I make quick work of brushing my teeth and hair before throwing Dash's shirt back on and leaving the room. On a whim, I make a detour for the walk-in closet and whistle, stopping in my tracks.

The Montgomery pack works fast.

Similar to the bathroom, the closet is full of racks of my old clothes and new ones in similar styles and colours. I trail my fingers over the sleeves of all the hung skirts and dresses and shake my head in disbelief. I've never been picky about my clothes, but I do have a specific style.

It's a mix of more relaxed fits, lace tights and undershirts, and some skater skirts that I can't seem to let go of. I like to be able to dress however I want and feel that day, and that means that I have more clothes than I necessarily need because I like options.

I don't know which guy was in charge of purchasing new

clothes for me, but they did a phenomenal job. The labels inside the shirts are fancier than any of the ones that came with me here, and even the fabric of the skirts is softer.

Despite the plethora of things to wear, I opt out of changing. Dash's shirt is massive on me and covers me down to my knees, which I doubt they'd care if it didn't go past my butt.

On my way out of the closet, I notice the tall stack of pink silk sheets all alone on their very own shelf. I press my lips together to hide a laugh while pinching the material between my fingers.

They're the exact same ones that were on the bed my first night here but in the perfect pastel pink colour. My favourite.

I didn't pay attention when I woke up, but I guarantee if I went to look, I'd find the ones that are on the bed match.

I'm giddy as I leave the closet and swipe my phone from where it rests on the dresser. The time steals my excitement momentarily, alarm making my stomach turn before I see the texts waiting on the screen.

Clove: Thanks for letting me know. Don't wake her up. Let her sleep and I'll call tomorrow for an update.

Clove: Consider this a well-deserved Friday off, Briar. Love you *heart emoji*

I run a hand between my breasts, over my heart, before opening the conversation one of the guys must have had with her last night. Dash, most likely.

The update he gave her was simple but effective. I was safe at their place for the foreseeable future after having a rough day, and I would call to give her an update when I was ready. There was nothing said about needing a day off work, but I'm not surprised Clover offered one, anyway.

And I'm also not surprised that I'm going to accept it.

Me: Love you back. Talk later, thank you xoxo

Once I send off the message, I leave my phone on the dresser and hurry downstairs. Three of the four doors I pass are open the same way they were last night. Dash must be a late sleeper.

"I think she'd like to be woken up with breakfast," Jasper says.

Hearing his voice first thing in the morning has me in knots. The good kind.

Ronan grunts deeply, and while I can't see him yet, I know he's scowling. "Or she could like her sleep like Dash."

"Only one way to find out," Landon adds.

My steps falter, and I bite down on my lip.

A part of me didn't truly believe that yesterday really happened, and I'd wake up today to the same reality I'd been living just a few days ago. One where Landon hadn't made such a drastic change and decided to give this a shot.

But he's here and, from the sounds of it, helping with breakfast?

Not wanting to announce myself yet, I creep toward the staircase and hover there, waiting to take another step.

"Pancakes, waffles, or french toast?" Jasper asks.

Landon huffs. "French toast is boring. Do pancakes and add something to them."

"Don't say lemon. I'll get a fucking hard-on," Ronan warns.

I flush and immediately try to keep my scent from exploding when I clench between my legs. This horniness is getting to be annoying. If I'm going to go into heat, can it just happen already?

Jasper's laugh is soft. "You wouldn't be the only one. I'll do chocolate chips."

"She got enough chocolate last night," Ronan grumbles.

"You're jealous?" Landon asks.

I move down the first two steps and pause, waiting for Ronan's answer.

"You know I am."

Jasper hums, and from my new spot, I can watch as he moves around the kitchen, gathering cooking supplies. "He deserves the time with her."

Landon's shirtless, in a pair of low-riding plaid pyjama pants that expose most of the V leading to his groin as he leans back against the fridge. I swear, they're purposefully trying to get my heat to come. He's so good-looking that it's a crime in and of itself, but add in his half-nakedness, and I'm drooling.

Ronan's no better. Yes, he did put a shirt on this morning, but it's torn at the shoulders and sleeveless, so really, does that count? The flex of his biceps as he stands on the opposite side of the kitchen and watches Jasper try to mix pancake batter is straight-up arm porn.

"The sooner we're all in this together, the better it will be," Jasper says.

Landon scratches the back of his arm. "Yeah, I know."

"Are the pancakes supposed to be celebratory, then?" Ronan asks.

Jasper dumps the powder pancake mix into a giant silver bowl and reaches for the milk he's set beside it. "Maybe a bit. I'm just trying to impress her and show that we're willing to put the effort in. We're already behind. If it weren't for Dash last night, we wouldn't have had a chance to get her things into the nest without her noticing."

"Best idea Landon's had in months," Ronan mutters.

It's such a small tidbit of information, but it's incredibly important to me. I move down another two steps.

Landon rests his head against the fridge and watches Jasper use a whisk in the bowl. "We have to talk to her about what she wants to do with her furniture. There's room for it here."

"We can leave it there," I say, announcing my presence.

All three of them whip their heads in my direction and smile. Or, well, Ronan smirks, more like. I've still got to get a big grin out of him.

"Good morning, love," Jasper drawls.

I hop down the remaining stairs and try not to expose my excitement by running to them. "Good morning."

"How did you sleep?" Landon asks, his voice deepening slightly.

Flicking my eyes between each of them, I bite my lip and plant my hands on the far side of the island. They watch me closely, like they're scared if they look away for even a second, I'll disappear.

I could get used to being watched like this. Like I'm the thing they cherish most in the world.

"With those soft sheets I love so much, it was the best sleep I've had in a long time. Maybe the new pink colour helped some too."

Jasper's cheeks burn a deep pink while his smile grows. "You like the shade?"

"It's my favourite."

"Thank fuck. Now he can stop being so nervous," Ronan says.

Jasper glares at him. "Ronan."

"We didn't swear secrecy."

Landon pushes away from the fridge and takes the two steps it takes to reach me. I crane my head back to meet his eyes and release a soft, happy sigh.

"Do you like chocolate chips in your pancakes, Haven?"

"As long as they aren't white chocolate chips. I've got a horror story from my childhood about those."

He gathers me in his arms and cups my face, tilting it back before kissing me. I shut my eyes and reach for him, holding him even tighter than he's holding me and pulling him close. His skin burns beneath my fingers, so hot and hard.

When the kiss ends, our mouths linger, and as he speaks, they nearly fuse together again.

"Tell me that story."

"It's not that exciting. Just traumatizing for my stomach."

His eyes don't waver. "Tell me anyway."

"He's not the only one who wants to know. Don't hog her, jackass," Ronan scolds, appearing at my side.

I move from one set of arms to another. Ronan's caramel coffee scent quickens my pulse as I make the move and press up on my toes and kiss just below his mouth. His hands find my backside before he's squeezing and using the hold to tug me against his body.

"Morning, Petal. You've got me real fucking jealous of the sleepy beta upstairs right about now."

"Because of last night?"

"That and this shirt you're wearing. There's one with a five on it waiting upstairs for you."

"Technically, it's still your name despite the number," I tease, smoothing a hand up his back.

He drops his head and chases my lips, stealing a fierce, teasing kiss that I know was meant to punish me for that comment.

It's not him who replies, though. Jasper's voice is closer now, but I can't see him past Ronan.

"If you let us give it to you, it'll be yours too."

"Either way, it's the number that's fucked me up," Ronan mutters.

I bat my lashes and press my hands firmly to his chest. "How about I wear yours next time?"

"We'll have to make a schedule at this point," Landon says.

Jasper hums. "I'll order a new calendar."

A large, firm body moves against my back, and I turn languid, melting into them. Jasper's clean laundry scent hits me when I roll my head back along his chest and moan blissfully.

Having my alphas surrounding me like this is euphoric. I feel their touches like zaps on my skin and immediately crave more. This position is foreshadowing of what's coming, and it's safe to say that I really freaking approve of it.

Jasper uses a ghost of a touch to pull my hair behind my shoulder before dropping kisses along my neck and to the shell of my ear. I stop breathing.

"Don't let them bully you into wearing their clothes," he whispers.

I turn my head until I can see him. "Do you have a different approach?"

His smirk makes him look younger, almost boyish in the way Dash is. "I would prefer you wear it when I can take it off of you."

Woah.

"When do you want to do that?"

"Soon."

"Okay."

Ronan's deep laugh pierces my chest, and I look at him with a brow lifted.

"What's so funny?"

He stops laughing. "Nothing."

"Mm, that's what I thought."

Jasper kisses my neck a final time before taking a step back and moving around Ronan. I lose sight of him a beat later, but the scrape of a whisk on a silver bowl tells me exactly where he's gone.

"Tell us your story now," he calls to me.

Ronan steals another kiss before shifting to pull a bar stool out for me. I take the seat and lean my elbows on the island, watching Jasper move around the kitchen.

The seat beside me is taken by Landon and the other by Ronan.

"Alright, but don't be disappointed when it doesn't meet your expectations," I warn.

Jasper shakes his head and sets a pan on the stove. "You could recite the alphabet and I'd be enthralled."

"Is that your kink, Jas? A good ol'-fashioned alphabet recit-ing?" Landon asks, humour heavy in the words.

Jasper sneaks a surprised look at the pack leader before rambling his response, almost like he's not used to Landon's teasing and doesn't want to miss his chance to reply. Or maybe he just forgot what it sounded like.

Have they all simply forgotten how to have fun together?

"That or a multiplication chart. Twos and fours are my thing."

Ronan chokes. "There's the nerd we know and love. Clark Kent's here in full force."

"Careful, Superman is my secret identity, right, Briar?" Landon asks, a hand falling to my upper thigh.

I can't help but poking at him. "You don't want to share?"

His eyes darken, voice smoky. "Not with that."

The smell of pancakes cooking helps keep me from slipping off the bar stool and getting on my knees for each of the men in here right now. I'm not above begging them to bend me over this island and eat me for breakfast, either, but I'm starving, and Dash isn't here.

"My mom used to bake all the time for Christmas when I was a kid," I start, hoping this will be a good distraction for all of us. "She has a habit of always overbuying things when they're on sale and filled an entire two-litre tub full of discounted, melting white chocolate. I snuck out of my room one night and went down to the kitchen and proceeded to scarf at least three cups of them. A few hours later, I was throwing them all up. To this day, I can't even smell them without getting queasy."

"It's a good thing Dash's scent isn't white chocolate, then," Jasper says, failing to hide his amusement.

I scowl lightly. "You're not allowed to tease me about this!"

Landon squeezes my leg. "We'd never do that."

"What happens if we do?" Ronan asks.

"Do you want to find out? Because I wouldn't think you'd want to risk being locked out of the nest . . ." I trail off.

He takes my hand and threads our fingers. "No teasing."

Jasper shakes his head, chuckling under his breath while flipping the first two pancakes before sprinkling in brown chocolate chips. "Do you have plans today, love?"

"Nope."

"Do you want some?"

"Absolutely," I say while my stomach growls.

"Do you have a favourite nesting store, or are you open to us choosing where we go?"

I stare widely at him before slowly looking at Landon and

Ronan. They keep quiet, but Landon's lips quirk into the tease of a smile.

"You still want to go nest shopping with me?" I wince at the surprise in my voice.

Jasper flops two pancakes onto a round plate before twisting to meet my gaze. "Absolutely."

"I'm open, then. Completely open."

44

Jasper

"THIS IS A NESTING STORE? IT'S THE SIZE OF AN airport," Briar mumbles, eyes wide as we stand in the parking lot.

Cozy Hollow is the biggest nesting supply warehouse in the entirety of western Canada, so while the overflowing parking lot makes sense, it was still frustrating when it came to finding somewhere to park. I didn't want to make Briar walk too far, so I circled the entire thing for ten minutes before finding a spot close to the front.

I've never been here before, but I know Ronan has with his sister. It would have been helpful having him here with us today, but he got called to come in for an extra practice with the defensemen. Dash volunteered to take his spot.

"It's better than an airport. You don't get sick from breathing in the air here or clipped in the heel with giant carry-on suitcases," Dash says.

Briar giggles. "Just tripped with metal carts instead."

"I'll take it. Let's go, love. We have quite the list." I offer my hand, and she takes it easily.

I peek at Dash and see him hesitating to do the same. Briar doesn't let him. She slips her arm through his and looks up at him with a sparkling grin.

"I just don't want you to get lost," she tells him.

The laugh that escapes him pierces through my chest. It's his old laugh. The one he had back before the pack started to grow strained and uncomfortable.

"We can always get back in the SUV and go to a pet shop first so you can pick out a collar and leash for me."

A car pulls into the space beside Dash, but he doesn't notice. The full weight of his attention is on Briar.

"Would you prefer blue or pink?" she purrs.

"It doesn't matter as long as it comes with one of those cute little tags with my name on it."

"I can make that happen. I'll even add a little chocolate peanut butter cup on it."

He makes a low noise in his throat and plants a fat kiss on her cheek. "Perfect."

A couple of minutes later, we walk through the automatic doors, and Briar runs to grab a cart. The black skater skirt she's wearing flares out at her thighs with every rushed step, and I blow out a long breath, still unable to keep from staring at her every moment of every day like it's the first time.

"She's incredible, Jas," Dash murmurs, doing the same thing I am.

"I've been telling you that for weeks."

"If she wasn't my scent match, do you think I would still be this interested?"

Briar pushes the cart in our direction, grinning the entire way. Her flip-flops snap loudly against the floor, but she pays it no mind.

"I think she could convince just about anyone to love her, Dash. Scent match or not, she's important to you. You're interested in her, so make that your focus. Don't spend too much time second-guessing yourself."

"I'm falling for her regardless of what she turns out to be."

I think I might already be in love with her, and that . . . that should scare me more than it does.

"Do either of you have any experience with decorating a nest?" she asks, eagerly spinning the cart back around.

Dash and I walk beside her, one of us on either side of the cart, and follow her wherever she leads, content with spending all day like this. We don't have practice until tomorrow, and I can't think of a better way to spend my free time than with her.

"I don't. Jas is the one who set up the nest the way it is right now. There's a stack of *Nesting Digest* magazines hidden in the office that you could find if you searched hard enough," Dash says.

She offers me a soft look before turning the cart to the right. "Well, what's already in the nest is perfect. If I measured, I think the bed would be as big as the bedroom in my apartment. The colours are great, and is the blanket heated, or was I just really hot?"

"It was heated. I wasn't sure if you'd like it normally, but when Dash carried you into your room, Ronan opened the window, and I didn't want you to get cold, so I turned the blanket on," I tell her, nerves wild in my stomach.

"He opened my window? I wasn't sure who did."

We turn down an aisle with pillows and blankets, and Dash stares at each one with wide eyes.

"He said you always had your bedroom window cracked open at night in your apartment," he mutters, touching one of the bright orange fluffy pillows.

Briar releases a sound of disbelief and runs her fingers along the entire shelf of fuzzy throw blankets before stopping to squeeze a pale pink one.

"I'm pretty sure Ronan was parked outside of my place watching for more nights than I originally thought he was."

"Knowing him, you're probably right," Dash says.

I focus on her attention to that specific pillow and wander closer to her. "Do you like that one?"

"It matches the sheets, right?"

"Yes. Get a couple of them," I instruct, already reaching for two.

Her cheeks glow with a fresh pink tinge. "Alright."

"It's like you said, Bright Eyes, the bed is huge. You need enough pillows to fill it, and I won't lie to you—Landon's a goddamn hog."

"Have the two of you spent a lot of nights cuddling?" she asks, teasing him again.

He scoffs and scoops another two of the same pillows into the cart. "Only every second one."

"I'm jealous." She readjusts her hold on the cart and starts pushing it out of the aisle. "But in that case, I guess five is a good choice."

"We need blankets too. Do you like any of these? Or, you know, we could head to the furniture section first instead. I just assumed you liked the bed frame, but if you'd like a new one, we can put an order in. It doesn't have to be from here, either. Is the dresser big enough?" I ramble.

My nerves aren't disappearing. It doesn't matter that I'm thoroughly enjoying my time with her and Dash; I can't shake them.

When I made the initial purchases for the nest, I knew my choices could be changed if our omega chose that she didn't like something. It's not as though I was unprepared to offer to change everything. I guess I just wanted to know that I actually did a good job with it and that without even knowing her, I could choose things she'd love.

It's ridiculous.

"Jas," she says softly, giving my hand a tug. I stare down at her and lose the ability to breathe. "Everything you chose for the nest is perfect. The bed is comfortable and big enough for all of us, and the wood finishes are beautiful. We'll add all the finishing touches today, and it'll be my absolute favourite place to be."

"You're sure?"

"My old nest was a blanket fort in the corner of my bedroom.

The one you've built for me is beyond my wildest dreams," she confirms.

Finally, relief.

I follow my instincts and reach for her. Cradling her cheek in my hand, I lower my mouth and kiss her. It's gentle, nothing more than a quiet thank you, but it still punctures me deep in the chest.

"How about we just grab a few different kinds of blankets and you can try them all out? The ones you don't like, we could always donate to the clinic. Is that something you do there?" Dash asks, pausing his examination of all the blankets beside us.

Briar slips from my hold with a fluttery gaze and turns her attention to the selection in front of Dash. "We could. I know we try to make the recovery rooms as home-like as possible instead of the sterile-looking rooms at a regular hospital, so cozy blankets could help with that. They're ridiculously expensive, though, and we like to send them home with our patients so they can keep something with them that they had during labour."

"Is there anything else you want for the clinic? I imagine it isn't easy running a business," I say while Dash begins dumping an array of blankets into the cart.

It's filled quickly, even after just adding a few pillows and blankets. They could have been at least double the size.

"You're not buying things for the clinic. But, yes, it's hard. When we first started, we didn't pay ourselves for months because we were already paying out of pocket for everything else. I've never advocated for private healthcare a day in my life, so it took a long time to get everything up on the back end, mostly with the government. We're a non-profit, so government funding and donations are what we need to keep the lights on. These omegas . . . often come to us with nothing other than the want for a safe, controlled birth somewhere safe. Being a private clinic meant charging for that. Clover and I would rather make sure we never alienated anyone because of how much money they have."

Briar keeps her head high and hums, turning the cart out of

the first aisle and down a second without waiting to see how we respond. Dash and I linger a few paces behind. The love she has for her work is incredible. Not only that, but it's admirable. She cares so much for the omegas who come to Harbour of Hope, and I'm at a loss for what we've done to deserve her.

Dash swallows so loudly I can hear it over the drone of chatting voices and pop music that fills the store. "Okay, so we're going to make it our mission to help with the clinic, right?"

"Not just the clinic. I'm going to do everything I can to give her the best life possible."

"I'm going to get another cart."

I blow out a laugh. "Grab two."

MONTGOMERY
PACK

We wore baseball caps on purpose. If it were socially acceptable to wear sunglasses inside, we'd have done that, too, if it meant avoiding being recognized in public.

Pushing three carts overflowing with home goods, we nearly make it from the entrance to the front tills successfully. I know the moment the couple we pass gasps with their eyes on Dash and me that our peaceful shopping trip is going to be interrupted.

"Is that? . . ." the woman whispers to the guy beside her.

My packmate notices them at the same time I do and is quick to intervene before they have a chance to draw attention to us.

He slows his gait a bit and lets Briar get ahead of us before flashing them a glimmering grin. "Do you want us to sign something? If we could just keep this a bit quiet, we'd appreciate that."

The man—an alpha by the size of him—rubs a hand up and down the omega's arm. "I don't have anything for you to sign— wait! What about my arm?"

"Yeah, sure," Dash says.

I stare at the woman's purse. "Do you have a pen?"

"Yes!" She pulls her hair behind her shoulders and drops her purse from her arm before starting to dig through it.

The movement exposes the two healed bite marks on her throat. I immediately look for Briar.

She's already looking at me, curious but content as we deal with the couple. The trust she has in us only makes the yearning I feel worse. I want my mark on her throat more than I've ever wanted anything before.

My hockey career pales in comparison to her.

Her brow lifts in a silent question, and I smile back, unashamed of how lovesick I must look.

"Is that your omega?"

The question comes from the woman no longer rooting through her purse. She stares warmly between me and Briar with a knowing gaze that I don't take offense from.

"Yeah, Briar's our omega. Though, I'd say we should word it more like we're her alphas. She calls the shots around here," I say.

Her face lights up. "I like that. She doesn't mind when this happens?"

"The fan interactions?"

"Yes."

"This is actually the first time it's happened."

A bite of surprise appears. "Well, I think she's just fine with it."

I find Briar again and get that confirmation for myself. When she looks at Dash. I follow her eyes and swallow a laugh.

"I'm going to get this tattooed. You're the best goalie in the league, man. I hope you get your recognition soon," the guy tells him.

Dash's chest puffs with pride while he continues drawing on the arm in front of him. It's truly terrible, a complete mess of smudged letters and a hockey stick that looks like a tree branch.

"Alright, you're done. Don't hesitate to send a photo of it to my socials when you've gotten it inked so I can see," he says before looking up to offer me the pen.

The man stares at Dash's drawing like it's a masterpiece while offering me the patch of skin just above it. My signature is much quicker and a hell of a lot neater than Dash's.

Once I've handed the pen back, we take a quick photo with the guy and then go back to our omega. She's leaning against the cart with a devious smirk.

"I had no idea I was shopping with two celebrities. Do we need security next time?"

Dash pokes her in the side, making her laugh, before pressing his lips to the side of her head. "Nah, Jasper's a big, strong alpha. We're well taken care of."

"Oh, I'm so lucky," Briar sighs dramatically, tipping her head back and fanning herself.

I roll my eyes and swat at the top curve of her ass. "Careful, love. You're stuck living at the pack house now."

"Are you hinting at something?"

Am I? In the middle of a department store?

It's a pointless question. Pressing into her side, I keep one hand on my cart while dipping my head and whispering, "Have you ever had your ass spanked, Briar?"

"No."

I wet my lips, suddenly seeing nothing but the image of her bent over my bed with her ass bright red and my palm tingling.

"Think about how you'd feel about trying it out."

She slips her fingers into the back pocket of my jeans and looks up at me coyly. "What if I don't have to think about it?"

This time when I reach to smack her ass, I keep my hand there long enough to give it a squeeze. She releases a tight breath and pushes back into my hold. I linger, not able to release her quite yet.

"Then, I'd say we have something to try out."

"Whenever you want me, Jasper, I'm yours."

They're just words, but their impact rattles me.

"Likewise, love. Likewise."

45

Ronan

I'VE NEVER WORKED SO HARD THROUGH A PRACTICE IN the eighteen years that I've been a player.

There's only one person who could make me work my ass off to get out of the arena at a decent time, and that's Briar. I'm still bitter as fuck about missing out on the day with her, but it is what it is. I've got plans for her tonight, and that's what matters. I focused on that the entire time I was skating drills.

Nudging my kickstand down, I pull my helmet off and hang it on the handlebar. The garage door shuts behind me on its own, and the lights flick on, illuminating Jasper's car and Briar's death trap with bright LEDs. Landon's SUV is still on the driveway beside Dash's, which means everyone's home.

I move quicker than I should after being at practice all day and exit the garage through the connecting door. It smells amazing when I step into the hallway, like a real home-cooked meal.

"It's an extra step, but I promise homemade sauce makes all the difference," Briar says.

I don't remember the last time Landon cooked, but I know his voice too well to mistake him for anyone else. And yeah, that's him in the kitchen.

"What happens when the sauce is done?"

Everyone is in the kitchen when I get there. Dash and Jasper notice me right away. The other two are too busy staring at the silver pot on the stove.

I knit my brows and tilt my head as I inspect the apron strings tied around Landon's back. Dash coughs to cover a laugh and nods, pointing at the pack's lead alpha.

"We still have to add the seasonings. Then once that's done, we let it simmer for a bit," Briar explains, using a giant silver spoon to stir the contents of the pot. "Can you pass me the sugar?"

"How much do you need?"

"Mmm, just hand me the container, and I'll add some bit by bit. I'm more of a season-with-your-heart kind of woman."

"That's my favourite," Dash says slyly.

Briar looks over her shoulder at him and sticks her tongue out before noticing me and pulling it back in. Then, she's abandoning the sauce and running toward me. I catch her swiftly and hold her tight, waiting for her incoming kiss. It's warm and soft, just like her.

"You're home, Ro."

And just like that, I'm at peace.

"Yeah, baby girl. I'm home."

She's got an apron on too. A pale pink one with white ruffles around the top and bottom. It's fucking adorable.

"Are you hungry? We're making lasagne tonight. I know it's taking a bit longer than usual, and you're probably starving after practice, but I figured I could teach you so you could make it sometimes too."

"You've got a tough student there. I'd have been much better," I drawl, not bothering to shed my jacket before going to her.

Landon finally lifts his attention from the bubbling red sauce and greets me with a tip of his chin. Lemon peaks over the scent of their cooking, and my mouth waters.

Briar's lips curl into a smile while she palms my chest and drops to her feet. "Don't worry, I'll make a chef out of all of you one at a time. Jasper volunteered Landon tonight."

"He's pack alpha. Seems only fair he picks up more slack than the rest of us," Jasper says in defense of himself.

Landon reaches around his front to point at him. "You just like seeing me in an apron."

"Guilty."

"It is very becoming of you, Lan. The blue really brings out your eyes," Dash says, digging further and testing boundaries that we haven't been over in years.

Landon drops his gaze to his front and turns to face us. When he looks up, he's smirking.

"I think you need a matching one."

"What about pack aprons?" Dash asks before nodding. "Yeah, we're doing it."

Landon watches me curiously. "You good with that, Grouchy Gus?"

I blink. "Did you just call me Grouchy Gus?"

"Oh, Landon, he isn't grouchy anymore. He's Sunshine Sally now that Briar's in our lives," Dash sings.

With a lifted brow, I warn, "Careful, Dash. I'm taking Briar with me somewhere after dinner, and if you piss me off, I might not bring her back."

"Oh? And where exactly are you taking me?" she asks, turning back around to resume stirring the sauce.

"That's a secret."

"In that case, how about you shrug that jacket off and come help us with this so we can leave sooner?"

Landon pushes me out from between them and palms her back. "We've got it. Ronan's as bad of a chef as I am."

"Last I checked, I was better than you," I counter.

His scowl is familiar, but also not. I slip into the fold and peer into the pot. The red sauce bubbles slightly, and the smell makes my stomach growl.

"What do you think about monogrammed aprons?" Dash asks.

Not even one of us says no.

MONTGOMERY
PACK

"Okay, I can only assume you're responsible for this new addition to my wardrobe," Briar says.

Releasing the seat of my bike, I turn to find her skipping out of the garage. At first, it's hard to look away from the clunky black boots on her feet because fuck me. She's worn them before, but tonight feels different. Like this time, she wore them just for me.

Despite the pink laces, they're as black as the night around us and go hand in hand with the new jacket hanging off her shoulders.

I've never seen anyone pull off a leather jacket the way she does, let alone one cropped just below the belly button with pink flower petals stitched over the right breast.

The boots and jacket are enough to have me spiralling on their own, let alone in addition to the skater skirt and lace tights she's still wearing from earlier. I think I'm in the middle of a wet dream.

"Why do you say that?" I manage to ask.

She stops on the cement and does a twirl for me. "Because it matches yours. Without the flowers, of course."

"I could add some."

With my bike at my back, I lean against the seat with my feet planted wide, legs parted with enough room between them for her to step in close.

She doesn't hesitate to take her place, two hands gripping the collar of my jacket. "I like yours the way it is. It suits you."

"Are you saying I have dark energy?"

Her mouth twists as she thinks. "No. More like a light grey."

"I'll take it."

"Will you tell me where we're going now?"

"Ever wanted to ride on the back of a bike?"

Excitement glimmers in her eyes. "Only yours."

"It's your lucky day, then."

And mine.

I reach behind me to the furthest handlebar and tug free her helmet. It's slick from the sprinkle of rain we got earlier, and I think that makes the shimmer I added to it more obvious.

"Is that for me?" she whispers, lips staying parted.

"Yeah. Got it custom-made weeks ago. My guy finally finished it yesterday."

With a cautious touch, she takes the sparkling black helmet from me and strokes a finger along the flower petals painted on the side. They're identical to the ones on her jacket.

"I know it's not anything you've always wanted or might even use that often, but it's—" I uncurl my fingers and press them into her back instead. "We could make memories in them. You and me. On this bike."

She shakes her head twice, a hard-to-read expression appearing on her features. I bite my tongue, growing flustered.

Did I make a bad call?

"You're softer than you let people think, Ronan."

"Is that a good or bad thing?"

Her chin falls forward as she bends over me to kiss my cheek. "The best thing. You're thoughtful and kind and gentle. Everything I've known I needed in a life partner."

"Don't forget tough. Real fucking tough."

She smiles and uses her grip on my jacket to tug me up until our mouths hover. "The toughest."

"I can't tell if you really believe that or not."

"How about I tell you once you finally take me for a ride on this bike of yours? I think I need to see how you drive to decide just how tough you are."

My pulse thrashes as I hold her by the hips. "You have to let go of me first."

"Fine."

Releasing me, she takes a tiny step back. I smirk, keeping my eyes on her face as she stares at the helmet I move between us.

"Are you going to crown me?" she teases, bending slightly at the waist.

I pull the helmet over her head and flick up the visor, revealing the soft blue of her eyes. "Done."

"Think the others will call me Biker Queen if I asked?"

"I wouldn't get your hopes up. It took me an hour alone to convince Landon that you'd be okay on my bike for a short ride."

Overprotective ass.

She watches with a sharp desire to learn as I swing my leg over the bike and sit on the leather seat, my feet planted firmly on the pavement. I free my helmet from the other handlebar and palm it.

"Does he not trust you? Are you that bad of a driver?" she asks, coming closer.

I pat the space behind me and huff a low laugh when she hesitates to hop on. "Not sure if you've picked up on it yet, but Landon's protective. The only time he'll completely trust anyone with you is when he's got you alone."

"Well, he doesn't have anything to worry about that right now."

"That's right," I say smugly.

One hand falls to my shoulder as she follows my earlier movements and straddles the seat. I grip my handlebars and steady my breathing. The firm press of her front to my back is a distraction already, and I need to shake that shit off right now.

With a few quick movements, the bike roars to life, and the scent of exhaust fills the air. Briar wraps her arms around my torso and squeezes. I cover her hands and bring them up to my mouth before letting them go to shift the bike into gear.

"Don't be nervous. Hold on to me and lean into the turns. I've got you, Petal. You're safe with me."

She leans further against me, her helmet pressing into my back. "I know."

"I think you'll like it."

"There's only one way to find out."

With a swift kick of my foot, I put up the stand and ease us into a crawl. Briar rests her head against my shoulder and keeps her arms tight around my front, trusting me.

And when we get down the driveway and onto the road, I know the moment she realizes how freeing it can be on the back of a bike. Her gasp is loud enough to be heard over the whoosh of wind.

I plan on keeping that sound with me forever.

46

Briar

I guess I didn't ever think I'd be here.

Not just on the back of a motorcycle but in a relationship with four men who also happen to be my scent matches. It's a dream, but with every day I spend with them leading up to my heat, the threat of waking up from it hangs over me, threatening to steal it all away.

I just want to get there already. It's not a matter of needing to rush as much as it is wanting to know that these men aren't going anywhere. My omega won't believe that they're here to stay until she sees it for herself. Once we've spent that time together and I wake up after a few days of pain and endless sweat to find four bite marks on my skin.

Ronan's body is firm and strong as I clutch onto him and lean with his body as we take a curve. I lost track of where we were after the first few roads we took, and now I'm just in it for the ride. It's an adventure, and I can't think of a better way to end such a perfect day.

There are still goosebumps on my skin from the last time he sped up when he cranks the gas and sends us throttling forward down the endless stretch of highway.

I lift my head from where I had it resting against his shoulder and watch the deep green trees turn into specs. The ocean air rushes past, whipping through my hair and filling my lungs.

Waves crash just beyond the guardrails as Ronan slows, and I get a chance to take in the full view around us. We're all alone on this long road, but the ocean is everywhere. I take a deep inhale and taste the salty spray. Being out here feels like a reminder of why I love Rayton so much.

It can be hard to remember that I live in one of the most beautiful places in the world when I'm trapped in the city, but out here? It's so clear.

It's green everywhere, trees and wildflowers filling acres and acres of land. The ocean is *right* there, a promise of days on the water, the scent of salt lingering in your hair, and salt between your toes. It's been too long since I've been to the beach or swimming in the water, so being here right now . . . it's more perfect than Ronan could have known.

He reaches back to hold my thigh while we pull off the highway and come to a stop in an empty parking lot. We're the only ones here, and I like this bit of privacy.

"You okay?" he asks while turning off the bike and kicking down the stand to balance us.

I eagerly jump off the bike and take my helmet off so I can get a better view of where we are. The air is so clean and crisp here. I can hear the wildlife out in the forest around us.

"I'm amazing. We're so close to the ocean, Ro."

"It's about a five-minute walk through those trees if you're up for it," he says, pointing right ahead of us.

"Yes!"

His chuckle is a low kiss on the wind. "Alright. Hand the helmet over, baby girl."

"What made you start calling me that? Was one pet name not enough?" I tease while he pulls it into his hold.

The first touch of my fingers to my hair has me hurrying to flatten out the mess left by the helmet. I blow out a nervous laugh and stare as he discards his helmet and sets it on the bike seat beside mine. Lucky guy doesn't have any hair to worry about.

"It suits you, Briar. Both of them do."

"Then continue," I sing, offering him a wink before skipping off toward the trees.

"Thanks for the permission."

"It's the least I could do after you drove us all the way over here. Have you been somehow speaking to my mother behind my back and asking her all about my favourite things?"

He catches up to me quickly and snags my hand, threading our fingers. "I considered it."

"But . . .?"

"But Jasper told me not to overstep."

"That sounds like him. My sweet man."

"Trying to make me jealous?"

I bite back a grin. "You have nothing to be jealous of. Each of you are doing a great job of earning my heart."

"Who's doing the best job?"

He's not expecting me to pinch the back of his hand. I roll my eyes up at him and let him lead the way through the forest, knowing I'm more likely to get us lost than actually find the water.

"I don't pick favourites."

"How do I change your mind about that?"

My boots crunch the twigs and bark lying on the ground as we maneuver through the trees and beneath low-hanging branches. Luckily, the sun is still hanging on to its place above the horizon, and the pretty pinks and purples paint a path for us to follow. On the way back, we might not be so lucky.

"You can't. I'm falling in love with all of you the same," I announce.

The toe of my boot catches on a turned-over rock as I stumble forward and stare wide-eyed at the sky. Ronan catches me before my knees hit the ground, and I wince, embarrassed.

"Or you can forget that you heard me say that," I ramble.

The dark eyes staring down at me are intense, focused. There's no chance for me to duck and run before I'm being picked clean up off the forest floor.

"Ronan!" My shriek gets swallowed in the trees.

"I couldn't forget those words if I tried."

I cling onto him, even though I know my effort isn't needed. He'd never drop me.

"Well, maybe just postpone your hearing of them for the time being?" I counter.

"I won't be postponing shit, Petal. Own it because I do."

My pause is heavy as I try and reason with the part of me that assumes he's saying something more than what he actually has.

"You do what?"

He shakes his head, jaw tensing as if he's angry. I don't think that's what's happening, though. Not when he's holding me so carefully, the only thing rough about him being the callouses on his fingers.

We pass through more trees in silence until finally, they part. The fading sunset hangs low over the endless blue in front of us, and I gasp at how *beautiful* the mix of orange and pink and blue is on the soft waves.

"It's gorgeous," I murmur.

"Yeah, it is."

He's not looking at the ocean or the sunset. I tear my gaze from the landscape and find his eyes waiting. They expose a fierceness living inside of him that stokes the flames beneath my skin.

I know he'd be able to handle their burn. Maybe even welcome their heat.

A knuckle traces the length of my jaw as he keeps our eyes locked and swallows. "Been falling in love with you since the moment I saw you, Briar. I've been waiting for you to take the same path."

"You don't have to say that just because I did."

"I'm not much for placating."

I can't help but smile at the bluntness of that statement. "I expected as much."

"Walk on the beach with me," he says, voice dropping low.

"I'd love to."

In a blink, I'm carefully lowered to my feet in front of him. My boots sink into the smooth sand, and I frown.

"Hold that thought," I say.

Dropping to a crouch, I unlace both of my boots, needing them off. Ronan hovers, watching as I kick them off before tugging off my socks and shoving them inside the boots.

I glance up at him, an eyebrow lifted. "Are you going to walk through such perfect sand in heavy boots? That kind of defeats the purpose of a walk on the beach, Ro."

He answers by joining me in going barefoot. I grin and move my boots to the tree line before stepping off the grass and into the sand.

It's perfect. Even with the small rocks mixed in that slip under and between my toes. Suddenly, I'm energized. I let loose a loud laugh and start to jog along the beach.

"Come on, Ronan. Run with me!"

"What do I get when I catch you?"

My stomach flutters, and I pump my legs faster. "Me!"

I might as well have lit a fire under his ass. The sand can't muffle the harsh pounding of his feet as he runs faster, growing closer and closer. I try not to smile so wide my cheeks rip.

The idea of being chased by someone hasn't had an arousing effect on me before. But right now, with Ronan . . . I can't help but recognize the pulse between my legs as just that.

Arousing.

My lace tights make running uncomfortable, but I don't allow myself to stop yet. I want him to catch me, just not yet. Not without working for it.

"I thought you hockey players were supposed to be known for your crazy stamina? Are you tired already?" I taunt, a giggle stuck in my throat.

His footsteps are so close I'm surprised he's not already pouncing on me. "If you wanted to test my stamina, there are other ways."

"You haven't earned that yet."

A growl carries on the wind, blowing through my hair and between my legs. It intensifies the lust buzzing in my chest, and I nearly trip. The slip-up gives him the opening he needs, and before I have a chance to make a sound, we're tumbling onto the sand.

Ronan's arms remain locked around me even after he's flat on his back in the sand with me above him. I blow out a laugh and use two hands on his chest to push myself up into a sitting position. His hands fall to my backside, holding firmly while I keep my eyes on his, watching.

"What about now?" he asks, voice smoky as he sucks in air.

I fidget, rolling my hips. His expression shudders, a lip slipping between his teeth. The hard length of his cock is right below me, and when I shift again—stars explode in my eyes.

He pushes my skirt up and grabs my ass beneath it, his fingers digging into the thin panties I'm wearing.

"You'll have to be more specific," I whisper.

Gosh, he feels good beneath me. It's impossible not to rock forward, desperate to feel the full size of him but unable to through his thick jeans.

"Have I earned you, Petal?"

The needy octave of his voice has a whine exploding up my throat. I lurch forward and flatten my chest to his. My hands find the soft buzz of his hair and scrape their way to the back of his neck.

When my lips touch his, I shake, overwhelmed with the need to touch him. To kiss him and just feel him all over me. Both inside and out.

Yes, inside.

"Ronan, Ronan, Ronan," I chant into his mouth as he kisses me back with the same ferocity he always has.

"I'm right here."

He tugs at my panties and peels them down until they hug my thighs. I'm dripping down my legs and through my tights, but that doesn't stop either of us from continuing. The mess doesn't matter right now.

"My face. Sit on my face," he groans, begging.

"On the beach?"

"It's private. Nobody will see you but me. Please, Briar. Please sit on my face."

I crawl up his body quickly, driven by lust and this unbearable need. He helps me get situated with ease, but I can sense his desire. It's prowling beneath his skin, his instincts demanding he abandon this idea of me sitting on his face for something better.

My face in the sand and ass in the air while he slides deep and locks us together with his knot.

"I'm going to explode," I murmur mindlessly.

"Explode for me, Briar. I'm not afraid."

Ronan grips me by my hips and, before I can recognize the sting, has my panties ripped clean off and abandoned in the sand. I scream into the ocean air as he pulls me back, and I feel the heat of his mouth on my pussy.

His tongue is feral, licking me fast and sharp as I flounder, my hands slapping out as I try and tear his pants off. He lifts his hips when I pull ruthlessly at his jeans, and I use shaking fingers to shimmy them down to his hips.

He sucks at my clit and lightly slaps my ass as I finally free his cock. The swollen, reddish-purple tip is wet, precum dripping down to coat the shaft before I wrap my fingers around the thickness and bring it to my mouth. I'm not tall enough to get more than a couple of inches in this position, and I growl, sucking harder.

His fingers part my cheeks, massaging them. He gasps for breath and rasps, "Stroke the rest."

"I want more."

He curses and dives back into my pussy, his teeth softly

scraping my flesh. I rock against his tongue and moan around his tip, drinking down what he'll give me, even if it isn't enough.

"Please, Ronan. I want you inside of me," I plead, voice cracking.

"Not here. Not yet."

"Why? Please, I need it. This isn't enough. Give me just the tip."

"Just the tip," he echoes, as if he's trying to reason with himself. "That will be enough?"

I nod hysterically, knowing I'm lying. The tip won't be enough. Nothing will until I have his knot stretching me.

"Take it, then," he demands, shifting his hands back up to my hips.

I don't need his help moving. Like I've been hit by lightning, I move in superspeed and crawl back down his body until I can feel the first press of his shaft parting my lower lips.

"Turn around."

Nodding mindlessly, I spin and stare up the length of his body at him. The black in his eyes is what I needed to see. His control is fraying, desire affecting him as strongly as it is me.

Sweet caramel mixes in with the scent of the ocean, and I drip over his groin, coating him in my slick.

"Just the tip, Petal," he reminds me.

His fingertips sear into my skin as they disappear beneath my jacket and climb to the neck of my shirt. There's a question in his stare, and I answer it with a nod.

Inch by inch, he rips my shirt open, exposing my breasts. With the leather jacket hanging open, I watch as his throat jumps, and he palms my chest, tweaking a nipple.

"This is a sight I'll never forget. You in a leather jacket, tits bare, hair ruffled, and your skirt pushed up around your waist. Those fucking lace tights are ruining me."

I moan, jerking forward and spreading my slick along his shaft. "Put it in."

He reaches between us, and I hover over his cock as he lines it up, waiting. Even just the brush of it against me is almost too much. I shake with the strength it takes not to lower myself to take the entire thing inside.

Instead, I play by the rules and lower myself only enough for the round tip to breach me, stretching . . .

"Oh," I whisper, unable to hold my head up as I force myself to stop moving.

Somehow, just the tip feels like it's ripping me open. It's a delicious discomfort, and I crave more. The ache of taking a full, thick alpha cock to the base. Ronan's cock.

"Please."

"Briar," he warns, his voice tight and rough.

I'm not above crying to get what I want. My thighs ache from how tight I'm clenching my muscles.

"Just a bit more. You feel *so* good," I slur.

"Fuck me, you're tight, baby girl. I don't know if you can even take more."

His doubt triggers something feral inside of me. I dig my nails into his chest and sink an inch lower on his cock.

"Say it again."

He tries to steady me, but I shake my head, lips parting on a soul-deep cry of pleasure.

"You're going to take the whole thing, aren't you?" he asks, awestruck as he strokes my back and belly.

"Please let me. I'm so empty, Ronan. I need you to fill me up."

His expression collapses. Eyes lifting to the sky, he wets his lips and lowers a hand to cup my pussy. His middle fingers create a V around where we connect as he presses his palm to my clit.

"Drop, Briar. If you want it, take it. You'll always get what you want when you're with me. I'm too fucking weak to deny you."

It's all I need to hear. I don't give myself a chance to be nervous about taking a dick as big as his—especially with the piercings—after going so long without anything besides fingers inside of me. Holding my breath, I dig my heels into the sand and drop.

"Yes! Oh—Ronan! You're . . . you're all the way inside."

Ronan shoots up to a sitting position and holds me in his lap. The bulge of his knot teases my entrance as I stay seated on him, holding on to his shoulders for dear life.

"Can I move?" he asks tensely.

"Please!"

I clutch onto him, rocking forward. My knees sink into the sand, the rocks moving deeper into my skin with every movement. The pain gets swallowed by the pleasure. He's so thick I gasp when I fall back and the full length of him is made obvious.

"That's it. Good girl, Briar. Keep moving like that," he praises, cupping my face and using the hold to bring me close.

Our lips touch as my tongue slips into his mouth, searching for more. For anything to soothe this undying need for him.

I'm on a hair trigger, and when he shifts his hips, jerking upward, I think I tip over for a second before coming back. I arch my back, letting a hand clutch onto his knee and rolling my hips. He presses against my G-spot, and I quiver, gasping his name. Or maybe it's more like a prayer.

Ronan brings his mouth to my chest and takes my nipple into his mouth. He sucks it hard, his tongue laving at the underside as his eyes flick up to snare mine.

"I'm going to come," I mumble, palming his neck.

"Good girl. Give me that first one."

A few more thrusts. That's all it will take. I chase it wildly, the promise of relief finally close enough that I can taste it.

"Fill me up," I whine, squeezing him inside of me, desperate to keep him buried as deep as possible.

"Fuck. Fuck, I will. You'll sit on my bike with your bare pussy leaking on the seat the entire drive home."

The fuel ignites.

With the salty spray of the ocean on my face and the burn of sand on my knees, I shatter. Ronan's cock throbs before the hot spray of him fills me, and I whine, burying my face in his neck, tonguing his scent gland.

"Perfection. You're perfection," he says on an exhale.

I hold on to him, the emotional high bringing tears to my eyes. "So are you."

"Don't sleep alone tonight."

"Sleep in the nest with me," I whisper, kissing his hot skin. "I want all of you to."

"There's nowhere else we'd rather be."

47

Landon

I'm pacing in the living room when Ronan's bike roars through the neighbourhood.

Jasper sighs, having been watching me for the last half an hour from his spot on the couch. I continue to ignore him like I did while I was reading on my phone earlier.

"Pacing isn't going to make them get inside any faster. This is Ronan, Lan. He wouldn't have let anything happen to her."

I wave him off.

The garage door opens, its low hum making my blood pound in my veins. Jasper's wrong about why I'm pacing and struggling to keep myself busy for the last hour.

I trust Ronan with my life and Briar's.

I'm antsy because I miss her. My omega has me so out of my head that when she's gone for even a few minutes in the day, I'm a pacing, anxious mess. I want nothing more than to avoid everything I've ever loved doing just so we can stay together all the time.

It's dangerous.

"Don't overwhelm her when she gets inside, Lan. Let her take a breath," Jasper adds.

I whip around and stare at him in disbelief. "How do you handle it?"

"Handle what?"

"I'm all fucked up. There's this emptiness inside of me when Briar's gone, and I don't know how to fill it. It's almost worse now than it was before. That's why I'm being like this. Not because I think Ronan's going to let her get hurt. I just need to keep busy so I don't get stuck in the gym working myself to death because I'm struggling being without her."

I've been there too many times. It's not a healthy outlet for me when I bring myself to the brink of passing out every time. I can't do that shit anymore. As if Briar would allow me to.

Jasper leans forward, his elbows digging into his thighs. "I get it, Landon. It's like that for all of us, but with you being pack leader, I'm assuming the intensity with which you feel that yearning is stronger. At least until we're all bonded with her. How has the rejection sickness been? Have you been sleeping? You look more rested than you did before. Regardless, I think we should get a doctor's opinion to make sure you're okay."

I stop moving and blow out a fast exhale. "I've been fine. Better. I sleep the longest after I've seen her."

"And the doctor? Can we make an appointment?"

"I don't need a doctor to tell me that I fucked my body up when I turned away my omega, Jasper. That's the last thing I need or want."

"They wouldn't say it like that. It would just be helpful to get confirmation that nothing's wrong on a biological level," he reasons.

I shake my head. "I've already spoken to the team doc. He says I'm fine. Every one of my symptoms were textbook, and they're gone now."

It's not a total lie. He did say that I'd be fine, but no, they're not all gone yet. My energy is back up, and my knee is finally starting to heal properly. It's my restless nights and stubborn knot that's more of a concern. Both of which I didn't bring up to him.

My perpetually swollen knot has made everyday tasks harder than they need to be. I know I'm risking a rut every day I don't give in to the instincts screaming at me, but I'd rather suffer than push Briar into a situation we're not ready for yet.

"Other than the irritability," Jasper mutters.

"You're making me irritable. It's not the rejection sickness," I snap.

"I'm not your enemy here, Landon. I'm your packmate, and I just want to make sure you're taking care of yourself."

"I'll be fine once she's here with us."

Jasper rolls his lips and nods, sinking back into the couch. "Alright."

"I'm inviting her to our game tomorrow," I say, changing the subject.

"We better play well, then."

"That won't be a problem."

Not with the reminder that she's there watching. And this time, I won't be focusing on pretending she's not there. I want her there, watching me play alongside my packmates while wearing our colours and last name.

Jasper doesn't have a chance to add anything before Briar's voice floats through the house. I move in the direction of the back door, barely managing to keep my head on straight.

"I need to get ready for bed."

"Or you could let me take you to the nest just like that," Ronan rasps.

Briar giggles, sending sparks up my spine. "I don't know if the others would appreciate that."

"Appreciate what?" I ask the moment they step into view.

The question is pointless once I smell them. My vision goes dark around the edges as I palm the wall beside me, a groan trapped deep in my chest. The teeth-achingly sweet lemon scent has been swirled around in caramel. Their combined scent tells me everything I needed to know.

"Are they home?" Dash asks, his footsteps pounding down the stairs behind us.

I stare at the torn fabric of her shirt as it peeks out from beneath her leather jacket before focusing on the swells of her naked breasts. The lace tights covering her legs have been twisted, and her skirt . . . fuck. It's shifted higher than it was when she left. The flared hem hardly reaches her upper thighs.

"They're home," Jasper confirms, his voice scraped raw.

I curl my fingers into a fist and push it so hard against the wall I'm surprised it doesn't go straight through it.

"What happened to you?" Dash asks them.

Ronan looks at Briar, his eyes dark and brimming with secrets he'll never share. "We went to the beach."

Our beta cocks his head as he inspects Briar and smirks. "Did you get into a fight with a shark, Bright Eyes?"

"A lady never tells."

"He ravaged you." My voice shakes with restraint.

She meets my gaze, her cheeks pink. "I returned the favour. And now . . . I'd really like for all of us to go up to bed."

"Together?" Jasper's surprise is a shared reaction.

I hate the moment she looks away from me and to him, but it's hard to be upset after being offered a place in her bed.

"If that's something you're all comfortable doing?"

"I'm surprised they haven't run up already," Dash jokes, dragging a knife through the tension that's built.

Ronan scoffs and starts leading Briar out of the back entrance and toward the staircase. The rest of us follow easily.

Dash has gotten more comfortable around Briar, and I know that more now than ever when he continues to joke with everyone, looking like his old self.

His happiness shines through even further when he asks, "So, do you have sand up your ass, Ro?"

"LANDON!"

I zone back into the game when Coach shouts at me and shakes my shoulder. The sweat dripping from my brows and down the back of my neck is a reminder of where I am.

Just like I do every time I'm on the bench, I breathe through my mouth to avoid the overwhelming scents of the other players around me before shoving my mouthguard back in.

The second line plows through the Chicago zone and spreads out. I look away and up at Coach.

"What do you need from me?"

"I need your head here on the bench instead of in the stands."

"I'm more zoned in today than I have been in months."

It might seem backward since Briar's only a few rows behind our bench, but it's the truth. Having her here tonight is different than it was the last time. The only thing I'm focused on tonight is impressing her and showing her why I'm the best player in the league.

It wouldn't hurt to play like a team tonight, either. We're her pack, and I want her to be able to trust in our commitment to not only her but each other. That's the sort of stability we all need.

"You're one away from a hat trick," Jasper states from my right side.

Adrenaline scorches my blood. "I want it."

"You'll get it. We'll do whatever you need us to to make it happen," he swears.

"Does she look impressed?"

"With you?"

"With us."

"Fuck, here it comes. Lovesick fools," Coach says with a dramatic whistle before focusing on the tablet that's handed to him.

I ignore him and lean forward to grab the boards, prepared to jump back onto the ice any second.

Jasper does the same but leans close to me. "She's been shaking all the ribbons off the pompom Dash gave her."

"Good." My grin is wide.

"Let's make her even happier, Lan. One more goal and we'll get to take her home."

I look at our net and where Dash is squatting low, the blade of his stick caressing the ice in short, arched movements. His smile is loopy, the light colour of his eyes even brighter than usual as he stares behind the bench.

The shift in him has been incredible to watch. I've felt the bond between the four of us strengthen and grow and at times become so overwhelming that I have to separate myself from them just to catch my breath.

I wouldn't have believed that it was possible three months ago. Instead, I thought we were going to wind up completely shattered.

Nodding at Jasper, I wait for the second line to start filtering in before hopping over the boards and skating onto the ice. The temptation to look at Briar is a constant gnaw in my gut, but I focus on the game and use every inch of my drive to give her a show she'll remember.

Ronan stays on the ice once Jasper and I have skated over and takes his spot guarding Dash as possession changes. Suddenly, our goalie is locked in. He tracks the puck through his custom blue mask and sinks lower into his squat.

I filter through the players clogging our zone and attempt to block the passes that come close. Ronan plays his position with an ease that makes him an incredible addition to the league and successfully steals the puck from a Chicago player.

Anticipating this, I've already shaken two defenders by the time the puck hits my blade, and I take off down the ice. The blue line disappears behind me, and then Jasper's there, carving up the ice beside me.

My breath saws in and out of my lungs. The fans are loud, and I give in, darting my eyes to the seats behind the bench. I tell myself it'll only last a second. One look and I'll be able to focus on the game.

Only once I catch sight of her standing amongst sitting fans, I can't look away. Wearing a Riptides jersey with the C on the shoulder, Briar waves her silvery-blue pompom in the air and screams my name. My heart goes wild, smashing against my rib cage like it's pissed it can't plop onto the ice.

I'm close to where I want to be now. I move the puck to the middle of the tape on my blade and shift my body to block the Chicago player when he attempts to move around me.

Briar's eyes grow wide, and I know what's going to happen before it does. Anticipating the hit, I spin as much as I can and pass the puck off to Jasper. It's a perfect pass. Tape to tape like we've practiced and pulled off a million times.

I shoulder the player and block his path when he tries to go for Jasper, buying my packmate a chance to use his speed to find an opening. He doesn't hesitate, and a heartbeat later, I watch in awe as he flicks the puck off the ice and buries it in the bottom left corner of the net.

The arena screams as the blowhorn blares, and Jasper hits the boards, a gloved hand raised in celebration. I skate toward him and smack the back of his helmet. The rest of the Riptide players on the ice join us before Ronan congratulates Jasper with a smack on the ass.

My chest warms, content with how the game has turned out. There are a few minutes left, but I'm not worried. My confidence is in this team and my pack and the future we're building. A hat trick suddenly means nothing.

I was just a fool to think this wasn't possible for me.

This time when I look into the stands, I don't care how long I stare for. Briar still hasn't sat down, and her enthusiasm is a fucking sight to see. We've made a hockey fan out of her after all.

She blows me a kiss and wiggles her fingers in a dainty wave. I return the kiss but don't bother trying to wiggle my fingers in my gloves. When I point at her, the omegas seated around her turn to stare, but she doesn't give them any attention.

It's all on me instead. And there's no better place for it.

48

Briar

I check my phone and send off another reply to Clover before slipping past the groups of omegas and into a small hall. It's empty and quiet here, and I use the small break in the endless crowd to catch my breath.

The game ended around twenty minutes ago, but I'm all turned around, mixed in with every designation here tonight. Being so close to the ice meant having to climb up tens of rows to the exit, and by the time I got to the top, so had everyone else in the arena.

Clover texts back instantly, her worry intensifying mine.

Clover: She's incredibly uncomfortable. I'm going to do a cervix check and get back to you.

Me: How's baby?

Clover: Both baby and Sadie are okay. Will update in a few.

We've been waiting for Sadie to go into labour for what feels like ages. It's a terrible coincidence that it would happen on a night where I'm not simply curled up in bed watching a movie, wanting something exciting to happen. Clover isn't positive yet, but when she texted halfway through the third period, telling me Sadie'd called her with concerns, I had this gut feeling that the baby was coming tonight.

It's still too early for the guys to be ready to leave, and honestly, I doubt I could find them in this place even if they were. I have no idea where I'm going.

They're probably too busy to check their phones if I called, either.

I try anyway. Jasper's contact name flashes on the screen as I call and wait, the dial tone drowned out with the noise around me. With the volume all the way up, I press it hard against my ear to hear.

Seconds go by before I get his voicemail. My chest deflates as I lean against the wall and try not to freak out.

I'm one more loud laugh away from ducking out of my hideout and booking it out of the arena when my phone starts buzzing. Landon's name pops up on the screen.

"Oh, my god. I was so close to needing to bribe someone to smuggle me out of here," I ramble, not bothering with a normal greeting.

"What's wrong?" Landon asks, his voice like a whip.

"It's just really busy in the walkways. I think I'm lost."

"I'm sorry, Haven. I should have sent someone to your seat before the game ended."

"Don't apologize. I'm a big girl. Just a little confused on how to get out of here and to where you are."

I had Clover with me the last time I was here, and while we did get a little lost, she's always been the one who isn't afraid to stop someone and ask for help. That's just not me.

Speaking to a stranger—let alone asking one for help with something—makes my skin clammy. It's a dramatic and annoying quirk at times, but I've long since accepted it and all my other annoying quirks.

"What's close by? Describe what's around you," Landon demands.

I stick my head out of my hideout and search for an answer to give him. Other than an exuberant number of people still lingering, I can only make out an exit door with a street number above it and a top-to-bottom mural of . . . Dash?

"I'm beside Dash," I say.

"He made it to you?"

Shaking my head, I step back into the hall. "No, I meant that I'm beside a wall with Dash painted on it."

"Alright. You're not too far away, then. If you're staring at the mural, you need to go right and then straight until you see a security entrance. There should be someone guarding it."

"I'm heading that way now. What do I say when I get there? Please let me in?"

Gripping my phone tightly, I slip out of the hall and into the crowd. Luckily, they're all moving the opposite way and have started to cluster on the furthest side of the walkway. I have more room to breathe this time.

"You didn't take your VIP pass off, right?"

"No."

"Just show it and tell them who you're here with."

I take a deep breath. "They'll believe me just like that?"

"Depending which guard is posted at that door, they'll probably recognize our scents on you."

There's a jolt in the centre of my chest. "It's that obvious already? Even though we aren't bonded?"

He pauses, and my cheeks burn. "Aren't we? A bond is more than just a bite mark, Briar."

"You're right," I whisper, tapping a beat on my throat as it grows tight with emotion. "So, I tell the guard I'm with you, and then where do I go?"

"I'm going to send someone up right now to meet you at the door, and they'll lead you to me."

"Are you with the others?"

"Not currently. I need to get my knee looked at before we leave."

I quicken my pace as worry settles. "Why? What happened? Did I miss you getting hurt again?"

"It's nothing like that. I have doctor-ordered check-ins after every game until I'm back to normal. Things are nearly there already."

"Oh."

His chuckle is a deep rasp. "I'll see you in a few minutes."

"You were amazing out there tonight," I blurt before we hang up.

"I had reason to be."

"I'd have been impressed even if you didn't score a single goal."

"Yeah, I don't doubt that. You're too good to us. Too fucking good to me."

There's a slight curve in the walkway before I spot an Authorized Personnel Only door up ahead. The man standing in front of it is leaning against the wall, his ankles and arms crossed.

"It's funny, I was just thinking the same about all of you," I tell Landon.

The guard regards me with a curious lift of his brow before pushing away from the wall. He peers at the VIP badge hanging from the lanyard around my neck, reading the words there.

Landon leaves my statement alone, and I let him, knowing I'll have the time to bring it up again later if I wanted to.

That's maybe one of the biggest changes between me and him. He's so much more open now.

"My guy is on his way up the stairs to you, Briar."

I offer the guard in front of me a sweet smile while whispering into the phone, "See you soon."

The man waits until I've hung up the phone and lowered it to my side before speaking for the first time.

"Family doesn't usually use this door."

"I'm still learning the do's and don'ts. And I absolutely got lost up here after the game."

He blows out a breath. "Yeah, it takes some getting used to. I don't think I've ever seen you before. If you give me your name, I'll call and get approval—"

There's a knock on the door behind him before it opens. The guard takes a quick step forward out of the way and whips his head around to stare at the person who appears.

It's an older man, maybe in his early fifties, with soft grey hair and a relaxed expression. He fixes calm eyes on me and asks, "Briar?"

"That's me."

"You can follow me downstairs. Landon said to bring you to the treatment room."

The guard laughs lowly and nods, waving a hand for me to pass him. "Well, it was nice to meet you, Briar. I'm sure I'll see you around. Say hi to the Montgomery pack for me."

"Yeah, you too," I reply before slipping into the stairwell.

It's well-lit, but I know if I were alone, I'd be freaked out going this way. Next time I'm here, I'll be figuring out an easier way to meet up with my pack. Preferably in a more open space.

The older man with me doesn't speak as we climb down the stairs, and I don't force him to. I'm too busy worrying about Landon's freaking knee to think of anything to chat about with this stranger anyway.

It doesn't take long to get to another door. I wait for him to swipe a card through a locking system and pull it open before following him into a hallway. It's brighter here. The chunky brick walls have been painted white and blue, and there are several people walking this way and that, either dressed in track suits or slacks and ties.

"It's this way," the man says, leading us further down the hall.

We reach a bulky, very clearly alpha man hauling a huge duffle bag over his shoulder. He stares curiously at me, a smirk appearing as he passes.

At least I know the same de-scenter that blows in my old apartment building is in the vents here. It's a reassurance that I'm even more grateful for when another two alphas pass by.

We stop in front of a door left cracked open a few inches that

I assume is the treatment room Landon mentioned and thank the man before he wanders off. I knock once.

"Come in!"

The female voice has me holding the handle a little too hard when I shove the door open. My chest tightens, but I ignore the discomfort and step into the room.

It's bigger than I was expecting. That's about the only good thing about it.

"You must be Briar. I'm Tiara, the physio who's been working on Landon's knee for the last couple of weeks. It's nice to finally meet you."

She's crouched down in front of him. Her hands are on his skin. He's wearing shorts and nothing else.

There's a pile of supplies and a bucket of ice on the floor beside her. Bright green tape is stretched up Landon's calf and over his knee. He's wearing sneakers I've never seen before, and the pink hue to his cheeks . . .

There's a different look to him in here. A vulnerability that I've only ever gotten a glimpse at.

I'm frozen, forced to watch as the woman brings another piece of tape to his leg and presses it to the dark-hair-flecked skin. She rubs the end with her palm before doing the same with the rest of the strip. By the time she's done, something ferocious explodes inside of me. I stare at her helplessly and take in the smile she flashes before rubbing his leg again.

There's a low rumble filling the room, and I immediately look up at Landon, assuming it's coming from him. If he thinks he can growl at me for barging in on him and *Tiara*, he's insane.

A total alpha-hole who's going to get his ass—

"What's wrong?" he asks, quickly hopping off the exam table and starting toward me.

The growling cuts off when I open my mouth to speak. Shock filters through the rage in my mind.

That was me?

"I'll just leave you to finish," I snap.

His brows shoot up. "What?"

"I didn't mean to interrupt. I've got to leave, actually. Work."

Landon rubs a palm along his jaw and keeps walking in my direction. He doesn't stop until I take a step back and shake my head, lip curling viciously.

His vanilla and cinnamon scent pushes past the thick chemicals and attacks my senses. My knees shake when I refuse myself the opportunity to go to him. If I'd just marked him already, there wouldn't be a reason to need to mark my territory here. That woman would already know he's mine.

Spinning on my heel, I clench my fists and swallow another round of venomous words. I haven't been this angry in a long, long time. It's unnatural and unnecessary. Extreme.

The picture of another woman knelt in front of my alpha—touching him—continues to flash in my mind, intensifying the burn of rage until I'm sweating.

Landon's mine. And this woman, a beta if my guess is correct, was far, *far* too close to him. They're comfortable with each other, clearly. This is the person who's been treating his injury. How many times have they been here in this room together? *Alone?*

I take hold of the door and whip it all the way open. It's like my mind isn't completely my own right now. Landon glides in front of me and slides his hand around the back of my neck, holding it in a vise grip as his thumb rubs my scent gland.

It's impossible to leave now. My omega won't allow it. The longer he holds me in this position, the more she craves to roll over and submit to him.

"Talk to me, Haven," he demands, voice deep and demanding but lacking the bark that would no doubt have me telling him everything I'm thinking.

"No."

The knowing smirk that forms on his lips doesn't help calm me down. "Tiara, I'm good here if you want to head out."

That rumbling noise starts up again at the sound of her name on his tongue.

"Alright! I'll see you in a couple days, then. Have a good night," she rambles before rushing past us on her way out.

I keep my eyes on Landon so I don't rip her throat out when she nearly brushes my shoulder. I'm not myself right now. I'm getting hotter, my temperature out of control. There's sweat dripping down my spine and beneath the strong fingers still pressed into my neck.

An ache grows in my belly, but it lacks teeth. It's more like a weak cramp that swells in intensity before disappearing. Pulsing, almost. They don't stay away for long. Another appears, then another.

"Ohhh," I whine, clutching my middle.

Landon releases my neck and covers my hand with his, guiding them to rub in a circular motion. His nostrils flare when he inhales. "You need to tell me what's going on, Briar."

His hand feels cold. But when he pulls mine away from my stomach and brings it up between us, the glistening of my palm tells me that's not the case. I'm just so hot that he feels cold in comparison.

I shake my head, a panicked sense of arousal drifting into my subconscious. "No."

He reaches out to shut the door, and I stand still, refusing to move a muscle. Another cramp grows, this one sharper and lower.

"Christ, you're burning up. Tell me what to do here, baby. I— Is this another spike?"

Oh, he sounds so sexy when he's worried. The low rasp of his voice is even growlier than normal. I lean into him, pressing my breasts against his chest and mewling at the pleasure that sparks from the light pressure on my nipples. It washes some of the pain away.

"Landon," I moan, lifting my hands to rub his bare shoulders. "You're so hot. I want to lick you all over."

"Not here. Not yet. We're at the arena right now."

My hold grows stronger as I expand my exploration and trace his thick abdominal muscles. His hair tickles my fingers while I push up on my toes and bring my nose to his throat.

"I need to call the guys. You smell—"

His words get lost in his throat when I scrape his skin with my teeth and blow a trail of hot air over the mark I leave.

"Yes, call them. I'm going into the early stages of heat, Landon. I need you to knot me right now while we wait for them to get here to take the edge off."

His snarl isn't aimed at me. "You can't go into heat here. It's not safe like home would be."

"Too late. Maybe if you hadn't let another woman touch you in front of me, I wouldn't be," I hiss, the return of my anger slipping through the haze of lust.

Landon's breath hitches, and I realize a beat later that I've bitten down on his throat, keeping the pressure light but threatening as I don't break skin. A stuttered purr breaks out, vibrating in his chest.

"Mark me right now and you won't be leaving this room until your heat is over and that tight pussy can't take another knot, Briar. Your first heat will take place in your nest. But that doesn't mean I won't help you enough that we can leave here without you being in too much pain."

I release his throat with a whimper. The cramps are no longer teeth-free. My entire body jerks when another appears, and I clench around nothing, too empty.

"Just do something to help before I can't make it home at all," I beg.

Landon's attention leaves me when he twists us and moves me further into the room. The door shuts again, and I cling onto him.

"It's Jasper," he murmurs, stroking my hair.

I moan, needing nothing more than his name to grow hotter, my mouth bone-dry. "Jas."

"I'm here, love. We're going to take the pain away, okay? We'll show you what a heat looks like when you have an entire pack at your beck and call."

49

Jasper

I ONLY MEANT TO SEE WHAT WAS TAKING THEM SO long.

Landon let us know she was on her way to see him, and I made quick work of getting changed so I could take our omega home. We played amazing tonight, and the entire team was on a high when I left the locker room. Ronan and Dash were held up with post-game interviews, but I had no such obligation to stick around.

I got a few feet from the treatment room door when I caught the first whiff of lemon. It sent a zap directly up my spine before I stumbled over my feet and had to steady myself on the wall.

Fuck, so sweet.

My head clouds as I blink back to the present and dig my back into the door to keep from pouncing. The pressure in my groin is otherworldly as Briar's scent perfumes around us, sticking to my skin and the back of my throat. I taste it, and I want more. *Need it.*

"Jasper," she whimpers.

Her fingers curl around Landon's arms, the nails digging into his skin but not breaking through despite the strength she's using. I lock the door and move toward them, drawn close by the bond that connects us. It's pulled taut as my desperation spikes, my knot pulsing.

"Help her to the bed, Landon," I instruct, borderline barking at my pack leader.

He carries her like she weighs nothing before setting her on the bed, the leather squeaking. Before Briar has a chance to tell us what she needs, I tug my shirt over my head. She stares at me with half-lidded, pupil-blown eyes and moans, legs parting.

"Let's get you out of your clothes," I murmur.

Her head sags forward in a nod. "Please."

Together, Landon and I strip her of her jeans and soiled panties. My nostrils flare once she's exposed, her swollen pussy leaking a constant drip of slick that drives me to my knees.

Landon hovers, watching as I part her thighs and nuzzle my cheek against the inside of her knee. Her scent ripens, somehow growing in intensity.

"Don't tease her," Landon says.

Flicking my eyes upward, I watch Briar's chest rapidly rise and fall, every breath sawing in and out of her. The Montgomery jersey is still covering her from the waist up. Neither Landon nor I make a move to get rid of it.

Not unless she demands we do.

"Do you want me to eat your gorgeous pussy, love?" I ask, whiskey smooth.

She nods frantically and snaps a hand out to hold the back of my head. "Yes! Yes, Jasper. I want you to take the pain away."

I trail my mouth up her inner thigh, slowly making my way up to her pink centre. My cock throbs, and I grip the edge of the leather bed when my tongue laps up the first drip of her slick.

It's a drug. One taste of her and I'm falling back into the lust gnawing at me and sucking up the rest. The entire length up her thigh and the other, greedy for more. Only once I've cleaned her skin do I set my sights on the source of my new favourite taste.

"Look at him, Haven," Landon murmurs. "Jasper's starving for you. How about you give him some more slick, mm?"

"Lan," she mumbles, her eyes closing completely.

I want her looking at me while I'm between her legs. Gripping her thighs, I push them up until her heels meet the bed and lick a hot line up her pussy. She responds instantly with a cry that Landon silences with his mouth.

His hand cups her breast through the jersey. I find her clit with the tip of my tongue and move it softly, teasing. Her eyes open and fall to me, watching while I play with her and Landon commands her mouth into a fierce kiss.

I pull her clit into my mouth and suck on it while sinking a finger into her. The wet noise of slick gushing down to coat my knuckle makes Landon groan into their kiss before pulling away to stare down between us.

"Let me taste her," he rasps.

Without thinking twice about it, I pull my finger free and lift it toward him. While we've never shared a woman before, there's no awkwardness when he bends to suck it clean. I'm far too concerned with Briar to focus on that even if there were.

"Perfection," I muse when he swallows.

Briar jerks against my mouth, panting. "More."

I follow her command. Two fingers fill her this time, and she's just as messy this full. I'm licking up the slick as quickly as it's appearing while thrusting my fingers inside and curling them until I brush the place that has her gripping me tighter.

"That's it, Briar. Grind that pussy against his tongue and make him earn your orgasm," Landon coos.

A growl builds in my throat as I suck hard on her clit. My omega uses my hair as reins, yanking on it to bring me closer as she rubs against my mouth and cries out.

"I need more!"

Landon glances at the door before focusing on her again. Then, he pulls her jersey up, showing off her pink lace bra. He ignores the fabric and tugs the cups down to free her tits. Her nipples are already hard and a deep, aching shade of red.

"Fuck her, Jasper," he bites out before lowering his head and sucking a fat nipple into his mouth.

I freeze, making Briar huff in annoyance. "What?"

"He said fuck me," she answers for our packmate, her grip on my hair turning punishing. "Fill me with your cock, Jasper."

Landon lets her nipple pop free of his lips long enough to snarl at me, "Give her what she wants. You don't need my permission."

"We should wait until we're home," I argue despite the ferocious need I feel to sink deep inside of her.

"It needs to be you. I don't trust myself not to bite her here. She needs a knot to settle her long enough for us to leave."

"Yes, a knot," Briar slurs, wiggling on the table to try and break away from both of us. "Jasper's knot."

I follow her cues and force myself back while Landon does the same. She climbs off the bed, and I use the break to palm my cock, squeezing hard at the base without so much as brushing a finger against my knot. It's so fucking swollen and rock hard already. Getting inside of her like this is going to be damn near impossible.

Briar spins around and bends over the bed, wiggling her bare, peachy ass in front of my face while reaching for Landon's crotch. His shorts are easily discarded when she gives them a strong shove and frees his dick.

He tosses his head back and groans when she takes him into her hand and gives the full length a long stroke. I use her distracted state to shuck my slacks down to my knees and run my fingers through her pussy.

The sight of her bent over like this, her thighs parted and tits pressed into the bed while she works my packmates cock into her mouth, threatens to send me into a tailspin. Heat pierces my groin when she bucks back against my fingers and moans around Landon.

"Do it," he says, his voice low and deep.

"You're sure about this?"

Our eyes meet when he nods and thrusts further into Briar's

mouth, fitting himself down her throat. She gags for a moment before pushing herself further, working like she wants to taste his knot.

"Take her, Jas."

I steady myself behind her and line us up. My knees wobble as I restrain myself from sliding all the way in at once and slowly press just the tip inside. She gasps, her ass pressing back against my hips as she tries to take more.

With my tongue clamped between my teeth, I grip her hips and hold her still. Her lemon cookie scent is so thick in the air it's stuck to my lungs as I breathe in through my nose and push another few inches into her pussy.

"How does it feel, Haven?" Landon asks, sounding so close to the edge I'm shocked he hasn't fallen over it yet.

She moans around his cock and swallows, drawing a grunt up his throat.

"She's so fucking tight, Landon. I . . . Fuck, I won't last long," I warn on a strained exhale.

She flutters around me in response. I push in further and follow the curve of her spine with my palm while applying enough pressure to keep her firmly down on the bed.

"You've almost got it all," I praise her.

Suddenly, she's jerking backward, stealing the rest. I'm buried all the way inside of her before I have a chance to prepare myself. There's slick dripping down my groin and onto the floor beneath us as she moves her hips side to side.

Landon watches her move with amazement glimmering in his eyes. "Yeah, that's our girl. Make him give you his knot and then fill you up nice and full. That's what you love, isn't it? A pussy full of your alpha's cum?"

The reminder of catching her leaking Ronan's the other night as she climbed the stairs to bed encourages me to start moving. Out, then back in, I give her a chance to stretch around me before picking up speed. My thrusts turn fevered quickly, and I can't seem to get a full breath in anymore.

Her whine is muffled with her mouth full, but we all hear it. Landon fucks her mouth with a steady, quick tempo, his knot bumping her nose every forward thrust. She can hardly keep her eyes open, yet she's more awake than I've ever seen her. I fuck into her hard, matching his pace on purpose. Each snap of my hips brings her closer to my knot until finally, it starts pressing against her.

"Are you ready?" I ask, digging my hips into her ass and holding myself fully buried.

Landon pulls free of her mouth and cups her cheek while she nuzzles into it. Her makeup is streaked, her lips swollen and eyes distant when she looks at me and flutters her lashes.

"Give it to me. I can take it."

I stroke the underside of her ass cheek tenderly. "Of course you can. This knot was made just for you."

Landon's ready for her moans and cries. When I press forward and start working the first quarter of my knot inside of her, he slides back inside of her mouth and curses.

The tight skin stretches and *stretches* until finally, it gives way, and my knot pops inside. I see a bright fucking light as just like that, my cum erupts against her walls.

"*Fuuuuuck*," I husk out as my knot swells and expands, keeping us locked together.

There's no inch of her that I haven't felt now. I grind my hips, pushing up against the hidden places inside of her when she comes with a muffled scream. The pressure on my knot increases, drawing more cum from my balls as I start to shake.

"Shit, it's like having a vibrator pressed against my cock," Landon groans, trying to watch her but failing every time his eyes close in pleasure. "Squeeze my knot, Briar. Work it with your hand like your pussy's working Jasper's."

Tears leak down her face as she takes his knot into her hand and squeezes it. *Hard*. Landon responds with a soul-deep grunt and buries his cock in her mouth before coming.

"Swallow it, Haven."

I shift my hips again and hiss when she tightens further. Landon pulls out of her mouth a second later and immediately drops to his haunches in front of her. She struggles to keep her eyes open long enough to look at him when he speaks.

"Our perfect omega. You did so well. I'm proud of you."

My heart lurches. "You were incredible."

"I can't really move," she mumbles mindlessly.

Landon strokes her cheeks and runs his thumb over the lipstick smears. "Don't. We've got you. Once Jasper's knot goes down, we'll clean you up and get you out of here before the next wave comes. This should help, though."

"My phone. I need to check my phone," she says, trying to stay alert but failing.

"Where is it?" Landon asks.

"My jeans."

I can't move enough to grab them from the floor like this, so Landon picks them up and pulls her phone out of a back pocket.

"Clover's called a few times," he says.

Briar forces herself onto her forearms and blinks rapidly. Her concern is alarming, especially after what just happened. She's still locked onto my knot and unable to run and hide, at least.

"Did she text? I need to call her back. It's about Sadie."

"Is it Thorne again?" I ask, rubbing her lower back.

She shakes her head and tries to take the phone from Landon. He lifts it out of her grasp and starts thumbing through the notifications.

"You're in heat, Briar. Sadie isn't your concern right now. We need to focus on getting out of the arena before another wave comes. It might not be so easily curable next time," he says.

"That's not your choice to make. Sadie is my patient and friend. I can handle myself long enough to make sure she gets the delivery she wants, heat or not," Briar snaps.

Unease splashes over me. "You aren't talking about going in for a delivery while you're in heat, love."

"That's exactly what I'm talking about." She pushes up onto

her hands and lets loose an angry moan when my knot tugs at her entrance. "I'm going to do my job. Now, tell me if she's in labour."

Landon looks at me, a silent battle waging in his eyes. It goes against our instincts to allow her to do this. To put herself in a potentially dangerous situation when there's an alternative. But isn't that what we said we'd never do? Stopping her from her work right now would be a slap in her face after promising that we wouldn't take her job away.

And *allowing* her to do anything isn't the kind of alpha I want to be.

Landon seems to read every one of those thoughts before I have a chance to speak them aloud. His jaw pulses when he hands her phone over.

Her eyes water as she takes it from him and glances between the two of us. Emotions are running high right now, but I know her gratefulness has nothing to do with the spike of hormones.

"It's our job to protect you always. Heat or not. So, if you're going, so are we. And if it gets to be too much, we're taking you out of there whether you want us to or not," Landon declares.

She nods, sniffing when he wipes her cheeks free of tears. "Thank you."

I just hope that while I know we made the right call for our relationship with her that it won't turn around to bite us later.

50

Briar

I'm melting from the inside out.

That's the only appropriate way to describe the heat that's smothering me the longer I go without a knot locked inside of me and a pair of teeth buried in my throat. The guys have all the windows rolled down in the SUV, but not even the evening air is helping.

I'm positive they knew that going into this drive. Still, they kept it to themselves when I demanded they roll them down the moment we got out of the parking garage.

Jasper's behind the wheel while Landon fiddles anxiously with the directions on the GPS. I can't focus on what they're whispering to one another, and fuck me, I don't care.

Not when Ronan's palm is searing into my thigh, anchored there like the cruellest form of torture. I swallow for the thousandth time to try and bring some moisture back to my mouth and throat before groaning at the strength of the cramp that rocks through me.

They've grown in intensity and are no longer centralized in my stomach. Now, they spear outward and pierce me everywhere, mostly between my legs, before fading. The relief lasts only a few minutes. By the time I've gotten myself under control again, another strikes. Even with Jasper's cum inside of me and pooling in the cheap panties I slipped on before heading to the game.

I never thought to bring a backup pair or thicker ones meant for a heat. Now, I'm left heading into my place of work with soiled panties, perfume that won't disappear, and my pack's last name on my back. If I didn't own half of Harbour of Hope, I'd be fired on the spot.

With a tight exhale, I reach forward and grab the back of Landon's seat. The moisture sticking to my forehead gets wiped away with a soft fabric while I grit my teeth.

"What can we do to help you?" Dash asks, pressing the extra shirt from his duffle bag against the back of my neck.

"Just get me to the clinic. I'm worried out of my mind for Sadie."

Jasper clenches the steering wheel, knuckles blanching. "Are you sure it's safe to take you there like this?"

"Don't turn against me now, Jasper," I hiss.

Dash uses one of his extra shirts to rub my forehead again. "He's not, Bright Eyes. We're just concerned."

"I'll live. Clover said she's already seven centimetres dilated. She has supplies for me there. Some heat panties and ice packs, at least."

My temperature breaks finally, and I accept the abrupt break with a breath of relief. Being sandwiched between Dash and Ronan is great for my omega and her neediness, but not for the unbearable heat. For now, I close my eyes and focus on the wind whipping through my hair and over sweat-slicked skin.

"There's a security team there. An alpha, right?" Ronan growls, hold tightening possessively.

Landon's scent spikes, deeper than usual. Darker. "There's what?"

"Duke and his team are professionals. They're not there to focus on me, and they won't even be anywhere near the delivery room."

"It'll be fine," Dash says, his voice tight enough to betray the calm façade he's going for.

I don't have it in me to get any further into this right now.

"You'll have to get over it. The team is there as another layer of protection for Sadie. With Thorne involved, I'm not going to turn away the help. It's not like I expected you all to be there for this," I snap.

God, I'm a mess. My nipples won't soften, and the constant heave of my breaths forces them to rub against my shirt over and over. Not to mention that my every breath is accompanied by strong scents that make me want nothing more than to climb onto Ronan's lap and ride his cock while Dash helps.

"*Fuck*," Jasper groans.

Ronan grips me tight, that deep rumble I love so much starting up in his chest. "You're perfuming again, Petal."

"I'm sorry," I whine, wiggling into the leather seat.

Dash leans forward and stares at the GPS. "We're only three minutes away."

I nod and bite down on my lip hard enough for it to burn worse than the last spike did. Landon twists in his seat and stares at me, his eyes dark and aroused but focused. And weary. Definitely weary.

"You need to take care of yourself for me, Briar. I mean it. The moment something isn't right or you're in too much pain to be on your own and taking care of someone else, I want to know about it."

Before I have a chance to argue about him trying to make this about me instead of Sadie, he shakes his head, mouth downturned.

"I know how important this is to you. This isn't me doubting you or your capabilities. I'm just looking out for my omega. *My scent match.* That's my job. Your safety is my top priority always, and I'm going to do everything I can to make sure that I don't cross your boundaries, but I also need you to know that I will if it's the only thing I can do to keep you safe.

"This is your first heat after finding us, and from what I've read, it'll be the worst you've ever had. The pain will be stronger, and your temperature will spike higher than it has before on your own because your omega knows we should be there helping you through this."

The backs of my eyes burn as I drop my head to hide the gleam in them. His words crash over me, tearing through the fragile confidence I've built like waves swallowing the shore.

"You've read about heats?" I whisper.

Jasper releases a breathy laugh. "It's what he was doing while you were gone with Ronan to try and keep busy last night."

My heart triples in size and punches against my ribs. It's almost too much to handle just how much Landon has changed in such a short period of time. The Landon I met that night in the restaurant never would have said those things to me, and he certainly wouldn't have been spending his night waiting up for me while reading about heats.

"It felt like the least I could do. None of us have to go through what you do."

"I wanted my first heat with you to be special. So if you wanted to . . ." A sob catches in my throat.

My mind doesn't belong to me right now. It's overrun with hormones and this itch screaming beneath my skin to be scratched with knots and teeth and painted with cum. I want the safety of my nest and not to be stuck in this SUV surrounded by all the men that I can't have yet.

Sadie's delivery will be hell for me. I knew that from the moment I bent myself over the bed in the treatment room and let Jasper knot me for the first time.

"We haven't even talked about whether you'll all bite me!" I cry out, shaking as another cramp grows low in my belly and my core tightens, slick gushing into my thin panties.

"Let's talk about it now, then," Jasper soothes.

I whip my head side to side. "No! Now you're just going to say what you think I want because I'm in pain!"

Ronan's hand grows slack around my thigh, and I stare up at him, another sob jumping for freedom.

"Why don't you want to touch me anymore?" I blubber, a wave of pain stealing my breath. "Is it because I mentioned biting?"

"Ronan!" Landon hisses.

Ronan's hand squeezes, the veins in his tattooed forearms flexing. "Fuck. I'm sorry. That's not—"

"We want to touch you, Briar. You have no idea how much we want to touch you right now and help take all of this away," Dash rushes out.

"So do it! Touch me already. I feel like I'm going to die!"

My legs are already parted. It smells like someone's just zested a lemon in here as I gulp for air and tear at my shirt, desperate to free my nipples. They feel scraped raw from my bra, and I can't take the restriction anymore.

"We're at the clinic, baby," Landon murmurs.

I find his eyes peering into my face and freeze, settling slightly. "You're really going to stay close?"

"We'll be as close as we can be while keeping our distance from Sadie. The moment you need us, you'll have us. I promise."

"Okay," I whisper.

I believe him. Through the thick fog in my mind and the pain in my body, I have no doubt that he means what he's saying.

Jasper pulls the SUV into the parking lot, and I focus on my breathing, zoning in to what's about to come. An omega is in need, and I'm going to help her have the most amazing birth. The one she deserves despite all of the crap she's gone through in her life.

I'll get what I need after we're finished here. My pack isn't going anywhere.

"That's Duke out front," I tell them, already unbuckling my seat belt.

The others do the same and step outside. When I join them, my knees are shaky, but Dash is there with an arm around my shoulders before I collapse. I give him a weak smile and steady myself, leading the way to the entrance.

"Briar," Duke greets me.

He's on full alert, standing before two men who Clover and I approved back when we first hired him. His expression is blank, giving nothing away but a graveness that confirms how seriously he takes his job and position.

The atmosphere is intense already. Every second that we're outside and I'm exposed to this many men that aren't members of my pack makes it worse on me and my omega. Landon's in front of me before I can get myself to walk around the men and into the clinic.

All the men around us except for Duke are betas, but my scent is stronger than ever and clearly having an effect on them regardless. The one directly behind Duke inhales deeply and swallows, taking a voluntary step back before Landon has a chance to shove him away.

Ronan's moving next, shouldering a path through the men. He snarls at the one closest to the door when he opens it for me. The beta shuffles backward, not interested in being Ronan's punching bag tonight.

I clear my throat, drawing everyone's attention. Dash stays exactly where he's been since we got out of the vehicle and hovers at my side.

The weight of their eyes threatens to crush me, but I push past the discomfort.

"Nobody steps foot inside the clinic unless there's an emergency. And even then, only Dash or one of the security team members will be authorized. There will not be any alphas in this clinic tonight, is that clear?"

"Crystal," Duke answers crisply.

With a nod, I start for the door. If I stay out here any longer, I'm going to be the one breaking that rule by begging mine to come in with me.

"Briar," Jasper calls before I can clear the doorway.

There's a sharp tug in my chest, drawing me toward him. I plant my feet firmer to the ground.

His eyes don't waver as he says, "One call."

"One call," I promise.

Then I'm turning and walking away.

51

Briar

"YOU'RE HERE!" ALICIA SHOUTS BEHIND THE FRONT desk.

Similar to me, she's dressed unlike how she normally would at work. In cases like this, that's the only acceptable uniform. In every other case, we're working within normal hours and fully prepared for deliveries. Today is the exception.

"I'm here. Did Clover tell you what I needed?"

She pushes a bag toward the edge of the desk and nods. "It's all in there. Are you sure you can do this, though?"

"Thank you. Is Clover in the delivery room?"

The beta doesn't mention my lack of answer to her question when she responds to mine.

"Room three. I think Sadie's been trying to delay the delivery until you got here."

"Crap. Can you let Clo know I'm just getting changed? I'll be there in a minute."

"You got it."

She scampers off down the hall to the delivery room while I go to the bathroom and strip out of the thick jersey and soiled under-wear. A pair of Clover's pink scrubs are in the bag, and I already know they'll fit like a glove. The extra-thick panties she added have me breathing a sigh of relief.

My reflection in the mirror is scary. It's not often that I'll be up for the task of staring at myself during one of my heats, and maybe that's a good thing.

The woman looking back at me right now isn't who I usually am. This one has red cheeks and ears, dilated pupils, and baby hairs sticking to the sweat on my forehead and throat. I'm a mess. And it's only going to get worse.

I run the tap with ice-cold water and splash it on my face. My chest seizes at the temperature as I gasp and squeeze my eyes shut. The pulse between my legs ramps up. My hands are slippery around the basin of the sink, but I only hold it tighter, rubbing my thighs together. The scrubs Clover grabbed me are a light, soft material. They don't scratch at my sensitive skin yet.

My pack's scents are fading from my nose and hair. I ache so deep in my chest I fear it will always be this way. That's my emotions running rampant, damaging every pillar of confidence I've built with them so far.

Everything will be better when we're together again.

I dry my face with a paper towel before leaving the bathroom. The bonds in my chest tug, attempting to pull me back through to the exit and to where my alphas and beta are waiting, ready to take me home. I can't think of anything better, but it's not time yet.

The moment I knock on the delivery room door and step inside, my heat is the last of my concerns.

Clover looks over at me from her place at the end of the bed, and her expression visibly relaxes a bit. "Finally. She's almost ten centimetres dilated."

"Already?"

I rush to Sadie's side and immediately pull her hair back behind her shoulders. Every boundary and plan we've discussed before today comes barrelling into my mind. I push myself into motion.

She's crying as she snatches my hand and uses a python grip to keep me at her side. There are no chemicals in the air here due to not wanting to block any sort of scent bond between mom and baby after delivery, so it only takes a second of me being here for her to smell the chance in my scent and snap a look up at me.

"What the fuck are you doing here?" she snaps, pain thick in her voice. "Go home, you crazy woman!"

"I'm not going to do that. I'm okay. This is your day, Sadie."

"Briar's right. Focus on you and baby. She can handle herself," Clover says, making sure I see the pride in her expression before she returns her focus to her work.

Tish, one of the two labour and delivery nurses we call on from the local hospital, stands beside Clover, waiting for direction.

Sadie hisses a breath and shifts on the bed, unable to get away with her legs spread so wide. "It hurts."

"I know. Your contractions are about two minutes apart now. If you want to get into your birthing position, I'll work around you," Clover instructs, snapping off her gloves and moving with a calm knowledge that never fails to help calm a patient.

I pull my hand out of Sadie's and help her flip on the bed. "Is this still how you want to push?"

"Yes. Just don't let me collapse. My arms feel like noodles."

"I've got you," I promise, stabilizing her with an arm around her shoulders.

"I'm going to check baby girl's heart rate, and then we're going to start pushing," Clover announces.

She settles at Sadie's other side and uses a handheld Doppler to catch the quick but steady beat of the baby's heart. Sadie sobs when she hears it, and I rub her back, trying to soothe her enough to focus through the emotions.

It's usually not hard for me to keep professional during these situations, but a beat later, I break too. A cramp tears through my belly, and I bury my teeth in my lip to stifle my cries.

My core clamps around nothing, and slick fills my panties, the pulse between my legs strong enough to rock me. Every breath I take burns my throat. I force my fingers to straighten before I can permanently dent Sadie's shoulder with them.

"Alright. Baby is happy and excited to come out and see the world. When your next contraction hits, I need you to push," Clover says, settling on the bed behind Sadie.

She's used to this birthing position by now and falls into habit. With pink gloves on her hands that match the scrubs we're both wearing, she pats Sadie's lower back and guides her into a lower squat.

My tongue bleeds from how hard I bite down on it to keep quiet. There's a shake in my hands while I gather Sadie's hair into a ponytail and use the cold cloth already laid out for me to wipe her forehead.

"Fuck!" Sadie screams while holding on to the bed rail. "I'm pushing now!"

"Listen to your body and do what you need to. We're here for you. You're taken care of," I soothe, speaking to both her and me.

For the next fifteen minutes, that's exactly what she does. With sweat dripping down into her drowsy eyes and weak, shaking legs hardly keeping her upright, she gives birth to a six-pound baby girl with a rock star set of lungs.

The baby's cries are loud enough that I'm sure the men outside can hear while Clover cleans her off and I help Sadie onto her back. The new mom catches her breath between soft, hiccupped sobs and eagerly takes the baby from Clover when she hands her over.

"She's beautiful. You focus on her while I finish up," Clo says before delivering an order to Trish for some more supplies.

Sadie's only paying half attention to her. Most of it stays on her daughter.

I take a step back and watch her kiss the baby girl's forehead and cheeks. She's holding on to her tight, like she's scared somebody is going to come in and try to take her from her arms.

It won't happen. Not ever.

As things settle, so does the adrenaline that was pumping through me. The fall is torture. Second by second, I'm reintroduced to the pain in my stomach and the tightness in my lungs. It's like swimming in battery acid, every inch of my skin burning. I can hardly swallow through the pain.

"Leave, Briar," Clover snaps from between Sadie's legs.

I've learned not to look at what she does after a delivery. Medical school wasn't for me eight years ago, and it still isn't now.

"I can't."

"What else do you need to do right now that I can't? You're in heat and being careless with your body. Go home with your pack."

"This is my job. I'm going to be here until the end," I argue.

Shit, I'm lightheaded now. The lack of full breaths is sending my lungs into an outrage.

"I'm calling Duke. Sadie, I need you to keep your focus on baby, alright? Briar's in heat, and I need to get her out of here before she passes out on me."

I shake my head furiously. "Dash. Send Dash in."

A wall meets my back before I slump forward over my knees. The pain isn't just a warning anymore. It's punishment for not listening to its demands earlier.

I slide down the wall, hitting the floor hard and slipping in and out of consciousness as the pain throttles me. The moment is still so beautiful. So monumental to the people here in this room, and I can't make myself regret being a part of it.

DUKE WOULD HAVE KNOCKED Landon out by now if he could get away with it. He knows just as well as we do that it wouldn't be one of us currently out here or Clover that would have his ass. It would be Briar.

That doesn't stop him from continuing to snap orders at him, though. Our pack leader is struggling right now, and he's taking it out on Duke and the team, who were the ones hired to be here today.

"I'm just asking if you've got someone on the back door," Landon barks.

Duke tightens his jaw. "It's not your business if I do."

"My omega's inside this clinic, so yeah, it's my business."

"Do you think I'm a fool? I've had the back door covered longer than we've been at the front."

"That wasn't so hard to tell me, was it?"

"Leave it, Landon," Jasper says, trying to pull him back to our group.

Landon allows him to, but only so he can get close enough for us to hear his low voice. "She's been in there for too long without us."

"She's our omega. She's got this," Ronan declares.

"She's also in heat. And has been for hours now. Any longer without us and she's going to be in too much pain."

My stomach turns. I know what he's saying, and I'm struggling to keep myself composed for much longer. One look at Jasper and I know he's in the same boat.

Ronan's beyond pretending to be okay. He might be speaking words of confidence, but it's obvious that's for Landon's benefit.

"You can't go inside," Duke says, only adding fuel to the fire.

Landon snarls, charging in his direction. "Tell me what I can and can't do with my omega again."

Jasper steps between them and shoves at Landon's chest. "Don't. This isn't what Briar wants from us right now. You heard her earlier. Only Dash."

"So go inside!" The command is close to tipping over into a bark.

It would have been the first time Landon's ever used his true bark on me.

Wide-eyed, Jasper shakes his head. "No. Not unless he's asked to."

"You might have gotten lucky," Duke mutters.

The four of us spin in his direction. Ronan speaks first.

"What does that mean?"

Duke pockets his phone. "Clover told me to send Dash inside. Briar needs him."

"What's wrong?" Landon asks, rubbing at the centre of his chest.

I stare at him. "I'll find out."

His expression shudders as he forces himself to nod. "Quickly."

"I'm good to go in, then?" I ask Duke.

"Don't go inside the room unless Clover explicitly tells you to. Knock on the door first. The receptionist will take you back," he explains, clearly unimpressed with this decision.

"Got it." *I'm coming, Bright Eyes.*

52

Dash

The receptionist is cautious around me as I rap my knuckles against the delivery room door and wait. She's nice in an awkward way. Like she doesn't necessarily want to be escorting me here but at the same time knows she doesn't have a choice but to smile and pretend otherwise.

I couldn't care less about whether she likes me or hates me.

The door pops opens, and I smell Briar before I have a chance to enter the room. Her perfume is . . . *intense*. It's everywhere, yet not where I need it. I want it rubbed so deep into my skin that it will linger there for the rest of my life.

My cock hardens, pulsing as I gulp and focus on Clover. "Where is she?"

"Under normal circumstances, I wouldn't allow you in here. Sadie has given me approval to let you in long enough to grab Briar, so do that quickly and then leave. Take her home and care for her. Please. She needs all of you right now," she says, her stress obvious.

"All I want is Briar. Sadie's safe with me."

"I know. I wouldn't have asked you to come in—alone or with an escort—if I thought differently. But I'm pissed off at all of you. If I knew she was in heat, I wouldn't have told her about this. Briar shouldn't have been here tonight."

I take the hit. "I know. We all knew that. This clinic is Briar's life, though. This is everything she loves, and we weren't going to take that from her."

"Harbour of Hope used to be everything she loves. It's not anymore. Now, she has all of you to fill the hole she got used to stuffing full of this place. She deserves more in her life than work and a dream of pack life. Just give her that, alright?"

"We will."

Slowly, Clover takes a sidestep and leaves an opening for me to come inside. I chase Briar's scent and find her sitting on the floor. The wet spot in the centre of her chest is almost as bad as the gleam on her forehead. No doubt, she's sweated through the back of her top as well.

Her hair is frizzed and stuck to her throat as she moans and rolls her head to the side. I struggle not to choke on the intense mix of scents in the room and, for once, am more than happy to be a beta instead of an alpha.

"Dash?" Briar croaks, straining to open her eyes.

The dullness in them is alarming. I drop to a squat immediately, cupping her face in my hands and tilting it upright. She rubs into my touch and moans, a shiver moving down the entire length of her body.

"It's me, sweetheart. Time to go home."

"Home," she repeats softly.

She weighs nothing in my arms when I lift her and look at the hospital bed for the first time. The omega lying on it is gazing lovingly at the baby in her arms, so exhausted she can hardly keep her eyes open. The soft words she murmurs are inaudible, but I can guess they're declarations of love.

Sadie pulls her attention from the baby just long enough to give Briar a worried once-over. Then, she's looking at me and pushing forward a silent plea.

Take care of her.

I nod. *Of course.*

"Call me when the heat breaks," Clover says, hovering.

"We will. Thank you for watching over her."

"I didn't do much. She was the one who held herself together."

I lower my lips to Briar's forehead, meeting skin hot enough it burns. "That's my girl."

"Leave before you lose your chance. And don't forget to keep her hydrated. She's going to need a lot of liquids before you even think about getting her into a nest."

"Water, got it."

Briar curls against my chest, her body shaking like she's cold but having the opposite effect. She perfumes again while bringing her face to my throat and inhaling. I'm already out the door by the time she starts squirming, legs rubbing tightly together.

"Have the time of your life, Bee!" Clover calls before we get too far.

Briar doesn't reply. Her mouth is too busy sucking on my throat.

I tighten my hold on her and ignore the ruthless tug in my chest. It's unlike anything I've felt before. Like someone's reached into my chest and started pulling my ribs out one by one. But the only person who could pull that off is in my arms.

The receptionist tells us goodbye, and then I'm rushing us out the front door.

"The police are already on their way. You're out of chances."

There's a deep snarl that I've never heard before. I freeze, stretching my arms further around Briar until she's as covered as possible.

Her scent burns, the thick perfume being snuffed out by her instant fear. She's in too vulnerable of a place to be here in the middle of a fight right now. And fuck me, I'm vibrating with the need to protect her from whatever this is.

I recognize the alpha pushing against Duke's chest, trying to break past him and to where I'm standing. Thorne's feral, his eyes narrowed and dark when he spots us. The curl of his lip forces me back a step.

"Eyes off our omega," Ronan bites out, a growl rumbling in his chest.

Thorne takes a deep breath instead, making sure to show off the flare of his nostrils as a smirk splits his face. "You sure she's yours? From the way she smells right now, she could very well be mine."

I open my mouth to warn him against continuing but hesitate when Jasper takes a step toward him, already speaking.

"Say that again and the police won't be needed here."

Thorne's eyes flash. "Sadie doesn't want me anymore, which means I have no use for her. All I need is to see my daughter. Sweeten the deal right now by giving me some time with Briar."

Landon moves too quickly for any of us to stop him. One second, he's standing beside Ronan, and the next, he's tearing Thorne from Duke and sending him flying back on his ass.

The weight of his dominance presses down on us like a storm about to break. My knees grow weak, the desire to submit to him a constant pressure in my mind. I glance at Jasper and see him tensing his jaw, fingers shaking out at his side.

Ronan's the only one of us who doesn't seem affected by the display of dominance. It makes perfect sense, considering Ronan's always been equal to Landon.

Briar, on the other hand, whines in my arms and clutches my shirt in a tight grip. Her perfume blows away her fear, leaving the air full of sweet, ripe lemons. My cock aches in response to her change in scent.

Landon bends forward over Thorne and brings his foot to his arm, pressing when he tries to scramble back to his feet. He applies pressure to get Thorne's complete focus.

"I know it was you who broke into her place because you wanted more information on Sadie. Your stink was all over the place; I just couldn't place it until right now." He presses down harder, and Thorne cries out in pain. "Desperation has never smelled more like fear than right now. But you're going to get real familiar with the latter if you ever say her name again."

"What kind of a pack lets their omega out of their sight when she's in heat?" Thorne sneers, tugging his arm but failing to get it out from beneath Landon's foot.

"The kind of pack who loves her enough to want her to keep ownership of her decisions, even when she's in heat. The kind who loves her in a way you'd ever understand," I declare.

Briar touches my face, stroking my chin and lips with gentle fingers. Her breaths are strained when I stare at her and let her see how honest my words were. How overdue they were.

She should have heard them from me weeks ago. Back when I met her for the first time and ignored the instincts that told me exactly who she was to me.

My scent match. The woman I've been fated to be with. My one in a billion.

Her blue eyes shine, a brief break of clarity appearing. "I'm ready, Dash. For all of you. Completely. Take me home."

"Step back, Landon. The team has this. It's our job," Duke says.

It's impossible to look away from Briar.

"I'll bring the car around to the front," Jasper says tightly.

Someone sucks in a loud breath, and I assume it's Thorne.

"I could press charges for my injuries."

"Go for it. My lawyers will eat you for lunch," Landon sneers. "Though, you'll be too busy in prison to do anything to anyone. Once you're arrested for breaking the restraining order multiple times, there won't be a chance in hell of you seeing anyone inside of that clinic ever again."

"I have a right to know my daughter," Thorne argues.

Feet scuff on the pavement, and finally, I look away from Briar to see Duke hauling Thorne to his feet and restraining his hands behind his back with zip ties.

"You have a right to nothing anymore," the security lead says while pulling the zip ties tighter than he probably needs to.

Briar's whine shoots from us to the rest of the pack. "Landon."

"Haven." He abandons everything other than her.

I hand her over to him without hesitation. Once she's in his arms, he relaxes enough to snap back into himself. He carries her away from everyone else, kissing her hair, flushed cheeks, and damp forehead. She sighs contently before tightening in pain.

"We need to go," Jasper shouts from the street.

The SUV is there with all the windows still down and the back door already open for Briar. Landon doesn't keep us here for a moment longer. Ronan and I jog after him when he starts down the sidewalk and helps Briar into the vehicle.

Once she's tucked safely between him and me, Ronan climbs behind the wheel. Jasper takes shotgun and cranks the A/C.

Landon struggles to buckle her seat belt when she starts trying to climb into my lap. A high-pitched noise rips out of her when she palms my crotch, the full length of me hard and sensitive. Our pack leader huffs before releasing the seat belt and instead holds her waist and guides her onto my thighs.

"Drive carefully, Ronan," he warns, voice low and tight with arousal.

Dark brown eyes watch us in the rear-view mirror. "I've got it."

"What do you need, Briar?" I ask, flattening my palm to the middle of her back.

The fabric is scorching hot and wet, a reminder that we need to get her home as soon as possible.

"You, Dash. I need your cock."

I shake my head, a heavy sense of dread toppling over me. "I don't have a knot."

"You won't need one. I'll help," Landon puts in from beside us.

His massive shoulders press into mine from his new position on the seat Briar's abandoned. Lemon drowns me, and I take more of it into my lungs with greedy inhales.

"Let her ride you, Dash. Trust me," he adds.

Briar presses forward on her knees before grinding hard against my cock, using it to get herself off. "Yes. Trust him."

"Lean back, Briar," Landon rasps.

She listens without hesitation. Arching back, she grips my knees and lets her head hang between her shoulders. Landon starts guiding the scrub pants down her hips and to her knees before going back for her panties.

The thick black material is typical for heat underwear. They're almost clinical. Yet, they look unbelievably sexy on her.

With a bit of struggle, Landon gets her out of her pants, leaving her bare from the waist down. A low, painful noise trickles into the back seat. Jasper's twisted in his seat to watch.

"Help him get his cock out, Briar," Landon says, pulling her hair behind her shoulder.

When his lips meet her throat, she shakes and moans. Thick lashes flutter over bright blue eyes as her fingers fumble with my slacks. They're already wet with precum and the slick sliding steadily down the inside of her thighs.

"I need to taste her, Landon," Ronan says, panting.

Briar tugs harder at my pants in response to his voice and the desperation thick in it.

Landon curls a finger beneath Briar's chin and guides her face toward his. Her eyes open as she attempts to focus on him.

"Hear that? Ronan wants to taste your pussy, baby. Should I help him out?"

I help her with my pants, needing them off just as badly. Landon's feeding into the desire throbbing inside the SUV, and fuck if it isn't making everything ten times hotter. I'm going to paint the outside of her pussy with cum before I get so much as a touch of the inside.

My pants get bunched mid-thigh, and then she's taking me into her hand, nodding at Landon, giving him all the approval he needs.

"Please. Let him taste."

53

Briar

The pain is so deep inside of me that it's glued itself to my bones. Dash's dick is hard and hot in my hand, but that doesn't help. The first time I get relief from the constant bite is when Landon sweeps his fingers through my pussy and gathers my slick.

My body bows in response, muscles twitching as I gasp for air. "Again."

"Okay, Haven. I'll do it again."

The firm pressure on my clit is enough to make me come. The pain breaks suddenly. I scream and scream until my throat is raw. Someone curses. My ears are blown. I can't do anything but ride the high and the fingers still sliding through my swollen flesh and wait for the next round of cramps.

"Quickly, Ronan."

Landon's fingers disappear, and I whine at the lack of them. In a flash, the pain returns, and my stomach muscles quiver in preparation for the strength of it.

"Fucking delicious, Petal. I'll be eating that perfect pussy the moment we get you in the nest," Ronan promises from the driver's seat.

Dash's eyes haven't moved from where they've settled on my

face. My ability to speak gets swallowed by the intensity of the cramp that rocks through my middle, but I force myself to look at him.

The cock in my hold is thick and arched. It pulses while I stare into the crystal blue eyes in front of me and angle it upward. My omega screams at me to sink down onto it already. There are words I need to hear first.

"Take it, Bright Eyes. There's nowhere I'd rather be than right here with you. My scent match," he murmurs.

My chest caves in from the blow of his words, and I cover that sensation with another. Landon helps me move up Dash's lap and takes my thigh, opening my hips. I moan at the press of the round, wet head against my opening.

Dash nods once, strained, while Landon strokes his hand up my back reassuringly. Slowly, I lower myself and take the first inch. The stretch is delicious, discomfort a thing of the past as I stretch around him and continue my downward glide.

"That's it, Briar. Take every inch of that cock and get stretched for the rest of us. You want to take a thick knot, don't you?" Landon asks, goading me.

Determination flows through me. I drop all the way down, hissing when I bottom out and have to grab Dash's shoulders for balance. My clit grinds against his pubic bone when I rock forward, making stars explode in my vision.

My slick makes it easy to move, the lack of resistance helping create an easy glide. Dash is more than thick enough to fill me exactly how I need, and the curve—

"Yes!" I shout, sitting back and circling my hips.

The position has him pressing against my G-spot. Warm, calloused fingers pull my shirt up over my bra. They pluck at my nipples through the lace, and I move my hips faster, driven by the sparks of pleasure.

"So good," I slur mindlessly, the world around me starting to get foggy.

Dash takes over for me when my strength fades and I can't

ride him anymore. With sharp, staccato thrusts of his hips, he drives his cock into the same spot and palms my neck, keeping my head upright.

"Give me another one," he huffs, breathless.

I can't speak. My body answers for me.

Tightening around his cock, I get lost in a storm of pleasure. Lightning zaps at my limbs while clouds fill my head, keeping me lost in them for what feels like hours.

It's the stretching sensation between my legs that brings me back.

I drop my head forward to find the cause of the stretch and sigh softly, my omega preening at the attention I'm receiving. I'm being taken care of. Landon meant what he said about helping.

"Fuck, Lan," Dash blurts out before sucking in a sharp breath.

Landon's knuckles are pressed alongside the top of my beta's shaft as he pushes his fingers inside the already stretched opening. He widens the intrusion, bringing with it a burn that helps distract me from my never-ending pool of desire.

I press down onto his fingers and whimper at the burn that follows. It's similar to when I had Jasper's knot inside of me, but not quite the same. My body knows this isn't what I had earlier, yet it's willing to give it a try regardless.

"How does that feel, Briar?" Landon asks, spreading his fingers.

I press down on the intrusion and jerk my chin in a haphazard nod. "More."

Without another word, Landon works in a third finger. I choke on the instant relief as he stretches me just as wide as I was earlier. My chest rattles with a purr before I bury my fingers in Dash's hair and force his face into my chest.

"Yes, yes," I breathe out while grinding down.

Landon turns my head with a firm touch and swoops in to lay a searing kiss on my lips. I slip my tongue into his mouth, craving his taste, while he curls his fingers and pulses them against my sensitive walls. Dash jerks his hips, his rhythm broken before heat floods me.

It's all enough to trick my body that I've found a knot after all.

I tumble into another orgasm.

My heart slows with the force of this one, unable to keep up. I float in the darkness as my vision fades.

This time, there's no finding the light.

MONTGOMERY
PACK

I WAKE up in the nest soaked in sweat with slick sticking to my inner thighs.

My mouth is so dry that every breath feels like I'm inhaling sawdust. I let loose a pained noise and flip from my stomach to my side. It's dark in here, and the scents are strong, like I haven't been alone for very long. The fact I'm alone at all makes my stomach tighten, emotion stinging my eyes before I can stop it.

The whimper that escapes me is cruel. It isn't from the returning pain in my muscles and bones. It's pure neediness. Rejection.

I feel the mattress in front of me, searching for a sign of even just one member of my pack but only find cold sheets. My whimper turns into a whine.

My belly spasms with a cramp, and I suck in a breath. Heat blasts through my veins, scorching me inch by inch until it feels like my skin is melting off my bones.

"Petal?"

I jump, ripping the sheets from the corner of the mattress. The voice is familiar. I'm safe, but I can't seem to swim up through the water I'm drowning in.

The rich scent of coffee swarms my senses before there's a wide palm taking my hand and curling my fingers into a fist. Lips brush along the length of my knuckles.

"Are you in pain?"

Ronan. My Ronan.

I blink to clear my blurry vision. It's still too dark to make out more than the shape of him, but even a shadow is enough for me.

"I thought I was alone," I whisper.

He climbs onto the bed and guides me onto my back. The weight of his body over mine is bliss. I arch off the bed and bring my lips to his shoulder, happy to find it bare. He tastes good. Really, really good.

"We'd never leave you alone when you need us. I was on the floor so I didn't crowd you while you slept."

I run my tongue along the curves of muscle and moan at his taste. The biceps beside my head keep him held above me as I loop my thighs around his waist and try to pull him down.

"I need you right now."

His chest rumbles, a sound I recognize. "Need me how?"

"I'm already naked."

"You're burning up."

"Take off your clothes and *fuck* me," I demand.

He lets me hang on to him while wiggling around to shuck his underwear off. The moment I hear them hit the floor, I'm dropping my legs and reaching between us to take his cock into my hand.

"The others are gathering supplies. Jas is making you something to eat," he mutters while scaling down my body, forcing my fingers to slip free of him.

I'm gasping by the time he pushes my knees up to my chest and brings his mouth to my pussy. He licks me from top to bottom before swirling my clit with his tongue and cussing.

"I've needed to do this since I tasted you on the road."

I nod, my mouth hanging open. He feasts on me, sucking my slick into his mouth and drinking it down like it's an expensive champagne. I writhe beneath his mouth and tear at his hair, uncaring about how hard I pull on the strands.

"Gonna make you come like this before I take you, Briar.

You're mine until the others get here. That means your eyes stay on me until I'm finished."

"On you," I repeat softly.

He groans in response before doubling down on his efforts. Each flick of his tongue is determined, and once his fingers join in, he's working my pussy expertly. I'm coming faster than I've ever come in my life.

It doesn't change a thing.

I'm still falling back into my body when Ronan kisses my pussy and sets my legs back down. He brings his face to mine and kisses me, letting me taste myself on his tongue.

"Present for me, Omega," he rasps with a nip at my mouth.

The request makes my clit buzz wildly.

Two hands find my hips, and then I'm staring down at the bedding. My ass sways in the air, and my elbows press into the mattress. I drop my cheek to join them and push backward, eager.

"Fuck," Ronan breathes out.

"Please."

He takes my ass cheek into his hand and squeezes. I mewl, my arousal dripping onto the sheets bunched at my knees.

"You don't have to beg me. This cock is yours. Always yours."

I'm ready for him.

All it takes is one thrust forward to take the entire length of him. The stretch is perfect, stealing my breath for a few moments before it's barrelling back, inflating my lungs.

I spread my fingers and clutch the pillow as he works me in long, slow pulses of his hips. From this angle, it feels like he's all the way in my throat.

"Knot," I pant, twisting at the hips to try and get a glimpse of him. "Knot me."

The darkness frustrates me. There's a desperate noise building in my throat that I can't hide.

Ronan's groin meets my ass as he keeps himself buried to the base and folds over my body. His mouth caresses the back of my ear.

"Here it comes, Briar. Take it like my good girl."

I whip my head back, a scream filling the air when he presses forward and starts working it inside. Only a bit of it pops in before he's pulling back and starting the process again.

Little by little, I'm stretched over his knot until I can't take the tease anymore. I'm on the precipice of euphoria. The release I've been needing since my heat arrived hours ago.

The moment he pops all the way in, my arms give out. I slip into a fog thicker than I've had to wade through before. And unlike last time, I see the way out and run toward it.

"That's—Briar. I'm all the way inside you, baby girl. You're on my knot. *Fuck*, I'm gonna come."

I moan, nodding with my face in the pillow. His fingers make homes for themselves in my waist as he fills with me cum. It warms my belly, the effects it has on my body immediate when the lingering ache softens long enough for me to go limp.

We're locked together, and every small movement has my inner muscles tugging at where we connect. He's testing that out too. With a careful tilt of his hips, he works his knot inside of me, experimenting with the pleasure that follows that sensation.

With a gentle touch, he carefully presses his front against my back and curls an arm around my belly. I close my eyes again, my omega demanding I go back to sleep now that I've got one of my alphas wrapped around me.

"I'll wake you when there's food," Ronan whispers, sweeping my hair back to kiss my neck. "You're amazing."

I'm asleep before I can say I love you.

54

Landon

JASPER CARRIES A TRAY OF FOOD UP THE STAIRS WITH me and Dash at his back. It becomes clearer with every step we take that if we closed our eyes, we could still find the nest without struggle. All we'd need is to follow the toothache-inducing sweet lemon scent drifting through the house, guiding us like a lighthouse in a stormy night at sea.

I'm tense, every inch of me coiled tight with the restraint it's taking not to plow my way past Jasper and into the nest. Leaving Ronan and Briar alone while I was pulled out of the room wasn't something I'd ever like to do again. I need to be with her, but I also know what would have happened if I'd been the one to stay.

As much as I want to mark her, I won't do it without everyone else around us. We do it together as a pack or not at all, even if I have to wait months. Years, even.

As fucking cliché as it is, Briar's worth it.

"Okay, so we've never done this," Dash blurts out beside me.

I snort. "Spent a heat with an omega?"

"Yeah. We've never even shared an omega before Briar came into our lives. How is it supposed to work? Do we take turns? Are you going to be shoving your fingers inside of her alongside my dick again? I didn't mind that, but I'd like a heads-up next time, you know?"

"If I think about that, I'll end up smashing through the door to the nest," Jasper admits tightly.

The time in the gym with Ronan was the first time I'd ever been in a situation like that, and I think it made my arousal stronger.

Ronan's naturally possessive, and the fact he allowed me to share her with him then was something unexpected. I wouldn't be surprised if he felt the same way I do.

I focus on Jasper. "So, you're okay with that, then?"

"With us helping each other out? Yeah, I am. I'm sure once we get inside the nest, nothing will matter but Briar and making sure we satiate her. I don't care how that happens as long as it does."

"Think Ronan will think the same?" Dash asks.

I inhale, dragging Briar's sticky scent into my lungs. "I'm sure we're about to find out."

"She should eat before anything else," Jasper pushes, stopping at the top of the stairs. He turns to look at us with a serious expression. "She'll need the nutrients. More than she'll get from our cum."

Dash nods, eyes flashing to the door. "Has anyone told Coach?"

"I called him," I say hoarsely. "Got heat-leave for the four of us."

Being this close to Briar . . . I need inside the nest. I'll lose myself if I don't get there soon.

Jasper must sense my fading patience. He steps aside and gives me room to pass.

My shoulders curve inward when I press a hand to the wall to keep myself anchored in place. "If you think I'll be able to say no to her once we get in there, you're going to be disappointed in me, Jas. I'm already hardly holding back right now, and there's a door between us. I need to know that the both of you are prepared to pull me away from her if necessary."

"She'll be safe, Landon. You won't hurt her," Dash says.

"I'm not scared that I'll hurt her. I'm scared I'll be *too much* for her. That once I start, I won't stop until I've marked her and we're bound together for the rest of our lives. What if she says yes in the thralls of heat and then wakes up afterward to regret wearing my bite? Regret being with me at all?" My voice breaks, revealing the depth of my worry.

Dash clasps a hand over my shoulder, offering a silent type of support while Jasper fidgets with the tray in his hands and frowns at me.

"She's already given us approval for marking her. Now, you have to trust that she meant it. Ask her again before you do, and dig into the bond you've formed with her already to find her answer again. It's there in all of us. We share that with her, and I have no doubt that she's as ready for the next steps as we are."

"I haven't even given her the courting gifts I've been storing," I blurt out.

Dash clears his throat to hide a laugh. "There's still time for that after she's back to herself."

"You'll be the first one, Landon," Jasper says when I take that first step toward the nest door.

"The first what?"

"To mark her. You're pack leader."

I scrunch my face, the idea of taking that first spot feeling wrong. "No. I don't deserve to be the first one."

"Me either," Dash agrees.

"You and Ronan, Jas. It needs to be you two first. You're the ones who've proven yourselves the worthiest of her, fighting for her longer than we have," I tell him, hating how much it burns to make that statement.

The pain doesn't negate the truth of it.

I don't deserve to bite her first. I'll be last, and I won't accept any arguments on that.

"We'll see what Briar thinks about it. It will be her decision who, where, and when any marking happens," Jasper says stubbornly.

Staring forward at the door, I release a strained breath. "I know."

"Are we all good, then? We can go inside now?" Dash asks.

Fuck. We've been waiting for this for what feels like ever, and now that it's here, I'm terrified I'm going to mess it all up.

When was the last time I even had sex? Years ago, probably. I don't remember what it feels like, and even then, if I did, it wouldn't compare. That much is already obvious.

The high-pitched whine that blasts through the door is more than enough for us to encourage us to move. My chest rumbles as I push inside the nest and rock back on my heels, my senses overloaded by the sights and smells around me.

"Shit, Petal. Never gonna get used to this," Ronan groans.

His hips snap furiously, and I watch the blur of slapping flesh, my clothes becoming too constricting on my body. Briar's leg is flung back over Ronan's hip as he fucks her from behind, both of them lying on their sides on the mattress. She's naked, the sheets draped from the bed onto the floor.

Her chest shakes, nipples hard bullets pointed at us as we watch in awe. The slick glistening on her thighs and dripping down the length of Ronan's cock as he thrusts into her is fucking intense. The mix of lemon and caramel in this room is sweet enough to make my teeth hurt. The pain only turns me on more, my cock a steel bar in my shorts.

"Don't stop," Briar mumbles, her lips swollen and a deep pink.

I stand completely still and watch. Every tiny noise of pleasure that escapes her makes it harder not to immediately join, but I want permission first. There's a part of me that *needs* to hear her say that she wants me included in this. As a member of her pack when there's no risk of her saying yes only because she's busy thinking of me and my feelings.

Right now, there's only one thing on her mind.

Pleasure and a satisfaction strong enough to ease her pain.

Ronan notices us first. His pupils are so large it's impossible to make out any remaining brown in his eyes. The subtle curl of his lip is followed by a low snarl, a warning from the animal part of his brain that's registering that they're not alone anymore.

It's gone in a flash, replaced with a heat that smothers me from across the room. His walls are down, allowing us an inside look at the insatiable craving he has for our omega.

A hand flexes against her stomach when he says, "The rest of your pack is here, baby girl. Look at them. They even brought the food I told you about."

She forces her eyes open. They find me first, locking on and holding me captive. My exhale is shaky when I drop a hand to my crotch and twist the fabric of my shorts in my fingers. I want to touch myself, to shove down the material keeping my cock locked away and give it a stroke, but I don't. Not yet.

"Superman," she breathes out, rolling her hips back to meet Ronan's thrusts.

I gulp. "Haven."

Fingers spreading wide on the sheets, she extends her hand to the side of the bed. "Come here."

"Tried to get her to sleep. Our omega's too fucking needy to keep her eyes closed long," Ronan spears out, taking the tip of her ear between his teeth.

She gasps, throat fluttering with a wild pulse. "Yes. I'm so warm. This is the only thing that helps."

"One of you needs to take my place. If I knot her again, I'll mark her."

Again. I hear it, and the yearning inside of me triples in size.

Briar doesn't share his hesitation. "Mark me, Ronan!"

"You need to know what you're asking me," he grunts, his movements intensifying, growing louder as she grows slicker.

"Do it. Do it, and then let Jasper," I direct gruffly.

As if suddenly remembering that he can speak, Jasper says, "I have food for you, Briar."

She doesn't respond to that. Instead, she reaches behind her head to grip Ronan's hair. Her hips undulate wildly as she chases her pleasure, cheeks and chest pink.

Ronan sucks in a long breath. "Leave it on the dresser."

The tray clatters on the surface before Jasper's cutting through the room, his clothes dropping to the floor as he goes. By the time he reaches them, he's naked, cock hard and gripped in his hand.

Briar pounces forward. Ronan moves with her, turning her onto her hands and knees while continuing to drive hard and deep into her pussy. The effort pays off when she reaches for Jasper's cock but suddenly stops, her arm falling before she falls to her elbows and moans. The entire length of her body shakes with the strength of her orgasm.

"That's it, baby. Show them how good it feels with this fat cock in your pussy. You're so tight I'll have to work my knot back inside."

"Please. Give it to me," she cries out, craning her head back to try and look at him.

Instead, her eyes fall on me. I wet my lips and keep still, watching her like prey would a predator stalking the ground in front of them. It's the opposite of any situation I've ever been in before.

I'm not the top of the food chain here. Briar is.

Jasper stands at the side of the bed with his thighs pressed hard to the mattress and reaches down to stroke her cheeks. It's enough to redirect her attention. He gazes down at her, eyes sizzling.

"Can we come into your nest, love?"

She pauses, surprise knitting her brows before Ronan grinds his hips into her ass, and she moans.

"Yes."

Ronan stays planted deep and stares at Jasper. Something passes between them, a recognition, maybe. Two alphas readying themselves to share their scent-matched omega for the second time. Only this time around, they'll be connecting their lives deeper than sharing one roof. Their souls will be intertwined around hers, their minds and emotions always open to one another until they learn how to build thin walls to keep each other out.

Jasper smooths a hand down Briar's head before cupping the back of it and using the hold to guide it forward. She balances on one arm and uses the other to successfully grab his cock without collapsing. Jasper's breathing stutters while she slowly works him into her mouth, taking him deep enough that her nose presses into his knot.

As the sound of her choking around his length fills the room, Dash settles at my side. He has one foot extended in front of the other like he's actively trying not to join them.

"Go," I tell him.

"Only if you do."

"I said I wanted to be last."

"Last to bite her, not join them in the lead-up. Don't you want to touch her? She smells delicious, Landon. Tastes even better, or have you forgotten?"

A dark noise shakes its way up my throat. "I haven't forgotten."

"Trust your instincts. We didn't before, and it nearly cost us everything. Don't let the doubts or the fear win."

Briar coughs on a sharp breath when Jasper pulls out of her mouth and gives her a break. Ronan's hand has slipped between her legs, plucking furiously at her clit like his release won't come until she gets hers again.

She whines in response and pushes back into Ronan, her eyes rolling back. I fall forward a step. Then another. That bond in my chest screams, yanking ruthlessly. I can't hold myself back any longer.

"Take Jasper back into your mouth, Briar. Show him how badly you want his mark," I murmur, setting one knee on the bed and leaning over her body.

Her eyes flash up at me, and before she can speak, I take her chin between my fingers and tilt it forward. Jasper's there waiting.

"Tongue out for him."

She listens to my command, and he pushes inside her mouth again, dragging the shaft along the length of her flat tongue. When her lips seal around the base, he groans lowly and takes her hair between his fingers.

Dash stands beside me, staring at Briar like a man struck stupid with his first look at an angel. He shrugs his pants off and discards his shirt without being prompted. Briar's perfume flares out again, drawing pleasured noises from all four of us when she notices that Dash has begun stroking himself.

"Put her on her back," I tell no one in particular. "If we're going to do this, we're going to do it properly. All of us together."

And that starts in a position that will allow her unrestricted access to all four of us.

Dash

With our help, Briar splays out on her back and sighs, content for the time being with the attention we're giving her. Ronan's tense as he takes hold of Briar's legs and spreads them as far as they'll go, revealing her swollen, wet pussy.

"I won't last much longer," he warns us. Or her. I'm not sure.

It won't matter either way. We don't need him to last longer than it takes for him to mark her. The rest of us are eager to swap him out. Desperate, more like. Goddamn feral.

"You'll mark me now?" Briar asks, blinking quickly as if trying to clear her mind enough to pay attention to this moment.

Landon crouches beside the bed. He uses the very tips of his fingers to comb her hair back out of her face.

"Do you still want us to mark you?"

Her throat jumps with a thick swallow. "Yes. I want that more than anything."

The confirmation is what we all needed.

Ronan paws at her thigh and guides it around his waist before he slides inside of her again. I watch with wide eyes, still growing used to this situation. It's not taboo, exactly.

We're pack, and this is what pack does with their omega. It's just new. I know every side of these men besides the one they're showing right now.

His rough exhale is followed by her moan. Briar takes the entire thick length of him without struggle. Even the piercings go in easy, and my cock responds to that. I give it a tight stroke and release a puff of air that sears my throat.

"Ronan will go first. Then Jasper. Is that okay with you?" Landon asks, continuing to pet her hair as her body rocks with Ronan's slow thrusts.

A small, needy noise is her only reply.

Ronan tugs her closer, her ass sliding down the mattress. The new position allows for her head to hang slightly off the bed, her throat bared. Jasper settles back at the edge of the bed and pushes his dick into her open mouth.

Lashes fluttering, Briar closes her eyes and moans around him, her throat bulging when he pushes past too far, and she gags.

Landon swallows loud enough to be heard over the fierce smack of skin and Briar's sucking while bringing his hand to her breasts and giving each one a soft squeeze. He's the only one of us with clothes on, and I know he's keeping that boundary on purpose.

"Fuck," Ronan rasps, palming Briar's stomach. "I need to knot her soon."

She moans around Jasper while Landon pulls her nipple between his fingers and twists softly. I tighten my hold on my shaft and slow my strokes, not having realized how fast they'd gotten.

"She's close," Landon says, eyes stuck on Briar.

I move closer, nearly leaning over onto the mattress. "Are you close, Bright Eyes? Are you going to soak Ronan's knot again?"

Jasper falls forward over Briar, barely managing to catch himself with a hand on the bed when she whimpers.

"Stop," he begs us, expression tight. "I don't want to come down her throat."

A dainty, hot hand folds over the one I have around my cock.

I drop my head to stare as Briar takes me into her hand and tries to use her other hand to swat mine away.

Releasing my shaft, I press forward into her hold and bury my teeth in my lip to silence the grunt that's trying to escape.

Landon's chest vibrates, low groans building inside of it but barely escaping through his clenched teeth. I look at Ronan and wait for him to notice me before nodding.

Thank fuck he seems to understand why I'm nodding in the first place.

"Are you ready, Briar?" he asks tightly.

She pops off Jasper's cock and cries out while trying to push herself up and closer to him. It's impossible in this position, and before she can get too upset by that, Jasper's there, coaxing her back down with a hand on her shoulder.

"Mark me, Ro. Please!"

The primal part of his brain seems to take over in response to her demand. He snarls low, a warning for the rest of us to stay back while he bundles her up in his arms. They fall backward together, Ronan holding her in his lap. Briar bears down on him, her head thrown back as the rest of us watch her pussy stretch around the entirety of his knot and tuck it inside her walls.

Ronan roars in pleasure before grabbing her face in his huge hand and looking into her eyes, seeking final approval. Tears stream down her cheeks as she nods and clutches him just as tight.

Then, he's bringing his mouth to the side of her throat and sinking his teeth into the smooth flesh.

MONTGOMERY
PACK

Briar

IT ONLY HURTS FOR A SECOND.

For one frantic heartbeat, I feel the sting of his teeth breaking skin. And then . . . peace. *Love.* Adoration and yearning.

I can almost see the glowing chord between us, calling me closer to the big, intimidating alpha with the buzzed head and loud motorbike. The same one who bought me a custom leather jacket, shimmering helmet, and calls me Petal, something delicate and, to some, even treasured. A symbol of the unrestricted care he offers me, even back when we first met.

It's a moment of clarity in the hours that I've been underwater, my ears muted and senses overrun by the omega living in my soul. I can see the men around me, hear their voices, and feel their hands on my warm skin when Ronan releases my throat.

Jasper, guarding my back and stroking my damp neck. Dash, hovering and watching, learning while whispering reassuring words. And Landon, my damaged pack leader, standing off to the side, still dressed and watching me with such a startling certainty that I whine, signalling that I want him close, even now.

"I love you. I love you. I love you," Ronan murmurs, dragging his tongue up my cheek, collecting my tears.

I don't hesitate to repeat the words to him. "I love you."

"You feel . . ."

"So do you."

There's nothing else to say. Not until I drop my head to the curve of his neck and skim my teeth along it, waiting.

"Do it, Petal. I want everyone to know who I am and who I belong to," he bites out, tensing in anticipation.

In a blink, I dig my teeth in, piercing the skin just enough for my mark to stay forever. His knot swells, locking us together as I sob into his throat, pleasure racking through me as I come.

I swipe my tongue along the bite mark before kissing it gently and pulling back enough for our eyes to meet. He's not only here across from me but inside my chest, our souls connected in a way that didn't seem possible months ago.

The swell of disbelief that tingles in the back of my mind isn't mine. It's his, and I search for it, watching it grow when I smile and reach up to touch the mark on my neck.

Ronan presses forward with his hips. His knot tugs at where we connect, and I coo at the sensation, the threat of falling back into a haze hanging above me on a fraying rope.

"Do you want to take a break?" Landon asks.

"No!" It comes out more alarmed than I meant it to.

My walls clamp around Ronan in agreement. I start to lean back, wanting to be on my back. Jasper's hands move along my naked skin to help me fall backward until I'm splayed out in the same position as before Ronan knotted me.

Landon's at my side instantly, his hand sweeping up and down my middle before returning to its place on my breast. "As soon as Ronan's knot can slip free, it's Jasper's turn, Haven. He's going to fill you up and mark your skin as soon as possible, okay?"

"All of you," I argue without thinking.

The cramps are back, beginning low in my belly before spidering outward to my chest and between my legs where Ronan's still locked with me.

Fingers brush through my hair as the room dims around me, my mind beginning to lull. "Yes, all of us. Once we're finished, you'll get Dash and Landon. Is that okay with you?"

I arch my torso in response, both hands reaching out in search of my packmates. My alphas and beta.

The burn of expensive whiskey hits my nose when I touch skin. Hard, rippling skin that makes me moan the second my fingers make contact.

"Jasper," I whisper, my fingers curling into his abdomen like I'm trying to find a way to pull him closer. "I want you."

I relax my touch when he moves onto the bed, kneeling beside Ronan. He's so gentle with me, every brush of his fingers through my hair and over my body done with such care that it makes my chest ache with a yearning for more.

"You need to come again," he says lowly, voice raw.

"Show Jasper you're ready for him, Petal. Soak this cock again, and we can make him lick you clean before he gets inside this perfect pussy."

My eyes roll back into my skull, the idea of that doing too many things to my body. I buzz beneath my skin with a ferocity that makes it hard to beneath they can't feel it when they touch me.

"I think you like that idea," Dash quips, stepping in to take Jasper's place behind my head.

I want him in my mouth, but he's too far away.

Ronan grunts, his knot pressing and pulling in a smooth rhythm now. "Fuck yeah, you do. You're squeezing me so tight it's like you want me to do the impossible and come inside you a third time."

"Do that. I can take it," I press, pressing down onto him every time he pushes forward.

Landon bends over the bed and kisses my nipple, teasing it with the tip of his tongue. "We know you can, but can Jasper? When he's got his tongue inside you, do you want him to taste that sweet lemon sugar or Ronan's caramel?"

Oh, god.

I'm going to come again from words alone.

Jasper's eyes are dark as they watch me, examining my every reaction to what I'm being told. It's thrilling to know he's paying this much attention.

And when he's made his assessment . . . his confident words shove me into another orgasm.

"I'd do anything for a taste of you, Briar."

56

Jasper

"My knot's going down," Ronan announces, swiftly pulling out and stepping off the bed.

I take his place, dropping to my stomach between her legs. Briar's gaze is fire when it slips down the length of her body and fixes on my face. I burn and burn beneath it.

Her pussy's a deep pink now, and I keep my touch gentle as I spread her open and watch in awe as she leaks both her and Ronan. My throat constricts around a loose groan as I lick my way up her inner thighs, taking my time even while knowing I should be moving fast.

Her energy is low. We're pushing the limits of her exhaustion due to the sear of pain she's had to withstand and the orgasms that have sucked what was left from her.

I can't stop myself from dipping my tongue into her pussy and tasting her, though. Can't stop from grinding my cock into the mattress and pulling her clit between my lips.

Her whimpers shoot straight to the rigid length between my legs before they're gone, stifled. I flash my eyes up her body to find Dash fucking into her mouth. Briar works him with quick, enthusiastic bobbing movements that betray how badly she wants him despite her dwindling energy.

I'm working against the clock here, and I remind myself of that while lapping at the fresh slick dripping from her entrance. Her thighs quiver beneath the hands Landon sets atop them, keeping them splayed wide while she bucks against my mouth.

"Do it now, Jasper," he orders, flashing a heated look between me and her.

The order drifts like a promise in the air.

Briar opens her eyes, focusing on me as I move onto my knees and hike her up by the hips. She doesn't let go of Dash, keeping her mouth around him while I run the tip of my cock through her pussy.

"This is the last time I'll ask, love. But is this what you want? My mark on your skin for the rest of your life?"

She tips her chin as best she can, her beautiful, bright blue eyes glimmering. I don't make either of us wait any longer.

The heat is immediate. I split her open with the first few inches of my shaft before having to stop, breathing through my teeth to calm down. She clenches right around me and mewls into Dash's groin while her fingers search for me. I take her hand and thread our fingers before hovering over her body and sinking the rest of the way inside.

My knot presses against a wet, searing heat as I bottom out and bring my lips to the breast unoccupied by Landon's fingers. I'm too aware of the placement of Ronan's bite and the other two men around us, who no doubt haven't forgotten it, either. It's right there in front of us, both a tease and a promise.

I've known where I've wanted mine since the moment I met her. And I'm selfish tonight because I'm grateful I get to claim it before the other two can.

"Briar," Dash blurts out, his hips stuttering as she sucks his cock so hard her cheeks hollow. "That's enough. I'm—I don't want to come like this."

Her brows furrow as she releases a low, muffled noise.

Dash strokes her cheek as I pull out and thrust back in so hard she loses focus. He steals the chance to pull out, replacing his dick with his lips as he kisses her reassuringly.

My balls are tight, my knot growing harder with every press against her skin. I'm growing frantic.

"Look at me, Briar."

She pulls away from Dash. The full weight of her stare drives me wild as I pick up the pace, pressing forward to rub my knot against her clit with every inward thrust. She flutters around me, her slick dripping down my thighs and onto the mattress.

Her lips are parted, every breath sawing in and out of her chest. She's not anticipating the sting of my teeth in her shoulder or the sudden fullness of my knot popping into place. A blissful scream follows, ringing in my ears and burying itself in my memory.

She says my name like a prayer or a curse. Maybe both. But I hear it. Both in my ears and my mind like an echo of a fleeting thought, here and gone in a flash.

I stumble through my head like a stranger. I'm fuller now, the overwhelming sensation of feelings that don't belong to me searing through my skin and bones. Briar and Ronan. Both of them are here now, but not completely.

After releasing her shoulder, I soothe the mark with my tongue and whisper, "There you are."

Briar nuzzles into my neck, warm breath scorching my skin on the way down to the dip of my shoulder. She finds the same spot I did and gives me her mark.

I flinch before relaxing again, my heartbeat slowing. The contentment I'm feeling doesn't just belong to me. My omega lets her eyes shut the moment she removes her teeth and lies back on the bed.

"You need to eat," I murmur, running a knuckle along her cheekbone.

She frowns, head shaking. "Later. Please. I'm tired."

Landon sets a hand on my unbitten shoulder. "We'll wake

you up to eat in a couple of hours. Sleep while you're not in pain, baby."

"Don't leave."

"We won't." Ronan kisses her temple, then the centre of her forehead.

"We'll be here beside you all night," I promise.

We're still connected as I shift us until we're lying on our sides. Her head finds a place atop my biceps, and then the others are joining us, finding spots on the bed.

It's the first time we've ever slept together like this, but I think I could get used to it. After all, we're pack.

MONTGOMERY PACK

Landon

I WOKE before anyone else had.

The bedroom is so full of pheromones that it's hard to pick up the scent of french toast and eggs, but I know it's there. I risked burning the kitchen down to make her breakfast at the crack of dawn and only got back in bed a few minutes ago. She's been sleeping so peacefully that I haven't had it in me to wake her.

The curtains Briar chose at the nesting store succeed in keeping the light out, blocking out all but a tiny glimmer of early morning sunlight. She doesn't need anything to keep her up. Not until her heat has passed.

My arm is numb from where Briar's rolled onto it. Jasper's still at her back with Dash on his other side. Ronan rolled onto his back after I snuck out of the room, leaving an opening for me to take once I got back. The soft fan of her breath on my face tickles as I tuck her hair behind her ear and just . . . stare.

She's so beautiful. Dainty in a physical way but never spiritually, even when she doubts that herself. There is no other omega that would have stood up to me the way she did while simultaneously leaving a door open between us.

It took me too long to walk through it, but now that I'm here, we can close it forever.

A light moan slips past her parted lips. Her perfume explodes in the air, making my cock stiffen against my stomach. I've kept my shorts on, needing that boundary, but the longer I refuse my instincts to take her, the wilder they're growing.

The signs of rejection sickness that I've fought off to near extinction are starting to return, goading me into giving in. I will. Oh, *fuck*, I will. But it wasn't my turn to have her yet, and after all the shit I've put my pack through over the past couple of years, standing back to watch them have the moments they deserve with her was the right choice.

Briar makes another low, breathy sound. It draws me closer, my fingers travelling from her ear to the bottom of her still-puffy bottom lip. She whines, body rolling closer to mine.

I swallow. Hard.

"You smell so good," she mumbles sleepily, bringing her face to the space beneath my chin.

Her tongue peeks out, swiping along the curve of my Adam's apple before repeating the action.

I clench my jaw so hard it might crack. Precum leaks from the tip of my cock, soaking into my shorts as I thrust forward before I can stop myself.

Briar tips her head back and opens her eyes, blinking heavily at me. The bright blue has dulled, now tired and warped by the effects of her heat.

"You stayed."

"I did for a while. Then, I made you food. The kind you have to eat this time."

Her cheeks pinken as she rolls her lip between her teeth and nods loosely. She shakes on the mattress, her stare wavering as she struggles to keep her eyes from rolling back.

"I don't know if I can," she admits weakly.

Suddenly, there's pressure on my cock. I hold my breath, refusing to look down at where she's touching me.

"I'm empty, Alpha. And wet. *So wet.*"

Fucking fuck.

My knot throbs, hardening to stone. I say nothing as she pushes me onto my back and reaches slim fingers beneath the band of my shorts to tug them down. My brain has gone blank, every argument lost in the wave of lust that plows into me.

"Please. I need your cock. Need you to knot me. It hurts being empty like this."

"Briar," I warn through clenched teeth.

"Call me Haven."

"I'm going to fuck everything up if you don't wait, *Haven*," I growl, fitting her hips in my hands.

She moans in approval and climbs onto my lap once my shorts reach my knees. "I'm not hungry for food. Only you."

The hot press of her cunt to my shaft turns my vision white. She blows out a long breath, attention glued to the space between us. Dropping her hands to my chest, she rolls her body forward, my cock soaked in slick.

"Your knot is so big," she gasps, bucking against it when she glides backward. "I want it inside of me."

With my hands on her body, I struggle not to take complete control of her movements. She feels too fucking good.

I've dreamed of feeling her split apart around my cock and, even more so, taking my knot. In my fantasies, she can barely make it fit. We try for minutes, her begging louder and louder until finally, it pops inside, stretching her wider than any of the others have.

"Can you take it? Will you make it fit?" I bite out, guiding her hips to snap harder, quicker.

She rolls her head to the side, jerking when her clit rubs against my pubic bone. "Make me take it. Don't stop until we're locked together. I'm a good girl, Alpha."

"No, you're not. A good girl would have listened when I said you had to eat first. Instead, you took my shorts off and planted your bad girl pussy on my cock, slicking it up so I have no choice but to slip it inside."

It hurts to breathe. My lungs are too constricted, seizing with the desire to fuck her deep and hard, leaving no option but to fill her with my cum and keep it locked up tight.

Briar bends forward over my chest. Her ass lifts up, waving at the ceiling as she kisses my skin, not leaving an inch of it untouched. Fingers rub over my abs and down the path of my V line before clamping around my knot and squeezing.

I buck into her touch, grunting. "Jesus Christ. Shit, Briar. You're pushing me."

She starts massaging it in her palm while nipping and sucking my pecs, leaving small purple bites on her way up to my throat.

My blood boils. She's so confident right now, working my body within an inch of my life, like if she doesn't get my cock, she'll lose her only chance at pleasure.

"Fuck her, Landon. Stop delaying the inevitable," Ronan speaks up from my side.

I can't take my eyes off Briar long enough to see what he's doing now that he's awake. My attention is so narrowed I can't split it.

"Dash first," I snap.

"Not me first. You, Lan." The voice comes from our beta.

Briar whines, loud and needy, before scraping her teeth across my throat. She's teasing a bite, and I'm—I'm fraying. I won't be able to deny her much longer without risking causing myself physical pain.

I shake my head angrily, my knot throbbing in Briar's hand. There's a pool of precum on my stomach, so close to her pussy.

"I don't deserve it."

Briar hovers above me, her face an inch from mine. The fire in her eyes has returned, not from her blazing body temperature but from determination. She's still inside of herself, even now.

Her lip curls as she snarls, "*You're mine.* Mine, Landon. We deserve each other."

There's no more fighting it.

I lift my hands and fill both with her cheeks before bringing her mouth to mine. She relaxes in my hold, our lips parting and tongues swirling. Then, she's moaning into my mouth. I give her one back when long, rough fingers grip my shaft and line it up with her pussy.

Whichever of my packmates it is touching me makes sure I'm slicked up completely before helping Briar lower herself onto me. She slips down slowly, panting against my lips as she's stretched again.

"Ohhh."

"Feel good, baby?" I ask, chasing her mouth in search of another kiss.

We're running on limited time here. I can't do everything I've wanted to with her this time because I simply won't last. Neither of us will.

There will be time, I remind myself. Decades worth of it.

"So good," she slurs, bucking her hips wildly. "Oh, god!"

Dash's scent is duller than the others, yet right now, it's as obvious as theirs are. I let Briar pull her mouth away as she pushes up on her hands and looks over her shoulder.

The pressure against my cock is different now, and I find out why when Dash appears behind her. He cups her breast in his hand and presses his chest to her back.

"Is this okay?" he asks her.

Her eyes cross from the pleasure of what he's doing to her. She grows tighter, and the realization hits me hard.

She lets her head fall back to his shoulder, eyes on me again. "*So* okay."

"Are his fingers in your ass, Briar?"

Her lip disappears into her mouth while she nods. Dash's knuckles brush my shaft while retreating from her, and then he's encouraging her to lean forward, creating more space between her legs. That's when I feel him stealing the slick from my cock to wet his.

"Will you both bite me? Together?" she blurts out, gaze cloudy.

I find Dash watching me from over her shoulder, a soft, easy expression on his face. He brings his fingers back to her asshole, stretching his fingers out to the point I can feel them prodding the thin skin dividing us.

"If that's what you want, we'll give it to you," I declare.

Dash kisses her jaw. "As long as you still take your alpha's knot, I'll bite you when he does. We'll do it together."

Together.

57

Briar

"Fuck me, Dash. I'm tired of waiting. I can't last any longer."

The two men sandwich me, one alpha and one beta. I'm floating with two anchors keeping me from disappearing completely. Ronan and Jasper are not only in the bed but in my heart and soul. I feel their emotions like they're my own, and it intensifies my arousal knowing that they're turned on too.

While keeping their distance, they're both awake and watching. It's hard to allow them that space, but right now, my focus is on Landon and Dash. The lack of their bonds is a sharp pain in my chest that I need to soothe.

Dash continues to work my ass with his fingers, exploring me in a way I've never been explored before. *I'm so full.* The addition of his fingers makes Landon's cock feel impossibly bigger as I ride it, struggling not to drop down hard enough to take his knot already.

My pack leader coils an arm around my back, keeping me anchored to his chest while Dash adjusts his position behind me. I nuzzle against the warmth of his skin and squeeze my walls, drawing a grunt from his throat as he struggles to hold still.

Dash presses into my ass just enough for me to register the

initial burn. I'm well lubed, but I'm still a virgin back there. Being in heat helps, making me more pliable and able to accept Dash. He retreats and then tries again, gaining an inch or two before repeating the same motions.

"Relax for Dash, baby girl," Ronan says, lying on his back watching me take two cocks. The pierced, thick shaft in his fist glistens at the tip, making my mouth water.

He presses his thumb into the mark I left on his throat, and my eyes flare wide as invisible fingers flick my clit. His desire is fire in my veins.

Landon snaps his head in Ronan's direction, a low, warning noise escaping him. "*Don't.*"

"Dash," I croak, gasping for breath when I never seem to run out of inches to take. "Please."

"I'm trying, sweet girl. You're just so tight," he says tightly.

I frown, tears of frustration burning my eyes. "Please!"

"Move, Landon. Slowly. Move inside of her slowly," Jasper instructs, his deep voice sending a shiver down my spine.

"Shit, yeah, I'm pushing in," Dash grits out.

I lose the ability to think. One second, I'm in the nest, and the next, somewhere else. A place where the only things I can feel are the slow, controlled movements of two cocks sliding inside of me.

My omega purrs, satisfied with the fullness, while her pack's grunts and groans fill the room. I stop trying to hold myself up and let go of control, letting my pack take care of me.

Hands touch my arms and back while lips run over my throat, teeth teasing. The thick bulge beneath me is hard and prodding at my entrance. I rub myself against the firmness and cry out when the alpha beneath me thrusts up at the same time.

"Briar—*take it.* I need to bite you." It's a fierce warning that draws a content noise from my chest.

A fat knot slips inside of me as I push my way up the body beneath me as far as I can and inhale, registering the cinnamon-spiced vanilla before Landon's biting my throat, opposite of where Ronan did. The thread in my chest gets pulled on hard enough to bring me back down to earth, and I know it was Landon who gave it that tug.

I come with a fury. Landon's knot swells, connecting us, while heat splashes my inner walls. Dash tenses behind me, and then there's another set of teeth digging into my skin, right above my shoulder blade.

This time is different. There's less of another voice joining the others and move of a connection being welded together. I feel Dash in my head but, more than that, in my heart.

Our bond is finally complete.

The pleasure of four males lives beneath my skin, and it's the reason I come again, this time followed by Dash. My vision grows spotty, but I don't let that stop me from tilting my head enough to lay my own bite on Landon's throat.

The huge alpha beneath me jerks, his chest rumbling loudly before I release him and throw myself back against another chest. It's not as wide as Landon's but just as firm.

"What's—oh, Bright Eyes," Dash gasps, his name for me rolling off his tongue sloppily.

I can't reply with a mouth full of his throat.

He slips free of my ass and readjusts me in his lap, keeping me as close as he can without tucking me inside of his body. It's wet and sloppy, and Landon has to lean forward with us locked together. His knot tugs in my pussy, and pleasure spikes before dulling, a bone-deep satisfaction keeping my mind at ease while we hold each other.

I release Dash and smooth his mark with a gentle kiss before leaning my forehead to his shoulder and catching my breath.

Landon kisses my arm, then the back of my head. "I love you, Briar."

"I love you, Landon. And I love you, Dash. I love all of you so much it feels like I'm in a dream. Some figment of my imagination that I came up with when I was a little girl."

Ronan's caramel scent floods my senses. "If anyone's living a dream, it's us. You get to be our omega."

Gentle fingers sweep over the mark on my throat before moving to my collarbone. I suck in a wobbled breath.

"Let us feed you now, Briar Montgomery," Jasper coos.

My stomach rumbles as I flash a sleepy smile. "Only if you do it by hand."

**MONTGOMERY
PACK**

"Fuck. You're so fucking tight with Jasper in your pussy and me in your ass. Are you going to come again?" Ronan grunts, his hips snapping at a furious pace.

He's so deep I could have tasted him if Landon wasn't so far down my throat I'm teetering on choking. Cum dips down my throat, soothing the most recent round of cramps in my belly.

Dash waits patiently for his turn, jacking himself while tapping the shiny tip of his cock against my cheek as if to remind me that he's still there. I flutter my lashes at him and moan around the shaft in my mouth.

"Careful, Briar, or I'll knot your mouth," Landon threatens, his voice teetering on feral.

Could he do that? Would it hurt if he did?

His throat strains with a swallow. "Shit, don't look at me like that."

Jasper picks up speed, drilling into me from beneath, his lips sealed around my swaying breast. Ronan's just as wild. I feel their desperation like it's my own. Our mental walls are open, and I accept everything they're showing me right now because I know that once my heat is over, we'll have to learn how to close them.

Landon pulls out of my mouth, and Dash takes his place. I swallow around the thickness, tasting peanut butter and chocolate so sharply my stomach clenches. He threads his fingers in my hair, taking control as he fucks my face.

Teeth pinch my nipple and pull before Jasper's yanking me

down onto his knot and filling me full enough that with the addition of Ronan in my ass—

Landon lifts my chin, staring down at me while I struggle to take the last inch of Dash's shaft. "That's it, pretty girl. Let your alphas make a mess of you. We'll spend hours between your legs cleaning you up when we're done."

I nod, tears wetting my cheeks and clumping my lashes together. Dash curses before panting, jaw hanging open.

"Where do you want my cum? In your mouth or on these pink lips?" he asks gruffly.

Landon's sliding between my lips before I can answer. The one he gives Dash on my behalf is perfect.

"Her lips."

"Press them together," Dash orders.

I roll them and wait, unable to keep still when Ronan comes, thrusting hard enough to rock me so far forward Jasper spits a warning, and I gasp at the stretch. He comes in my ass at the same time Dash holds his cock an inch from my mouth and sprays thick, white ropes across it.

"Keep them closed," Landon rasps, lurching forward.

I moan, parting my sticky lips and licking them clean despite his order.

His smirk is sinful, and my core clenches, anticipating the next wave of arousal that's no doubt going to sweep me beneath its tide.

Instead, there's a moment of peace where I get to catch my breath.

"You're perfect," Jasper breathes out.

"I'm tired."

"Perfectly tired," Dash corrects with a wink.

The nest smells like sex, and the sheets are soiled. I should have let someone change them out hours ago, maybe days ago, I'm not sure. Yet here they are.

My first meal since returning home from the clinic was a cold, blackened grilled cheese that Landon hand fed me, and I'm hungry again. Still, I stay collapsed over Jasper's chest and wait for his knot to deflate before bringing any of that up.

"Can one of you ask Clover how Sadie's doing?" I whisper, letting my eyes close for just a moment.

"Of course," Landon says.

Dash presses a kiss to my forehead. "We'll get you some more electrolytes and something to eat too."

"A shower might be a good idea," Ronan adds.

I simply hum, snuggling closer to Jasper. He husks a laugh and flattens a hand to my back.

"How about you just sleep, love? We'll take care of everything else."

"I like that."

I like it a lot.

MONTGOMERY PACK

RONAN KEEPS the shower cooler than I'd normally like as he washes my hair. Right now, I would have burst into flames if the water was hot.

Now that I'm hydrated, full of protein bars and a bite of homemade oatmeal, I'm being scrubbed clean, my heat having returned with a vengeance.

I grit my teeth and focus on the room-temperature water instead of the constant press of Ronan's chest against my back or the gentle pressure of his fingers on my scalp. He's been hard since we got in the shower yet hasn't touched me sexually. I can feel each individual black piercing curving up the shaft between my ass cheeks, and it's torture not presenting for him right here, right now.

The pain is easier to handle than when my heat began. It's the only sign I have that this will be coming to an end sooner rather than later.

"Are you happy, Petal?"

I frown, twisting to peer up at him. The water runs down my spine now, making me shiver.

"Can't you feel how happy I am?" With a soapy hand, I take his fingers and press them into my chest, between my ribs. "I can feel everything you are right here. Cautious and optimistic, possessive. And your love for me."

His expression softens, eyes glowing in awe. "I don't know how to trust what are your emotions and what are mine. The others are here too. Our bond is stronger than it's ever been."

"We'll figure it out. It can't be that hard, can it?"

"Feels pretty fucking hard."

I pull my lip into my mouth and slowly lower my eyes until I'm staring at something else really hard. Ronan huffs a rugged laugh and steps forward, slipping his wet cock between my thighs.

"I'm supposed to be cleaning you, not dirtying you up," he says.

My heart lurches, every beat quicker than the last. "Good thing we don't want to worry about running out of hot water then."

"The others will come looking for us."

We back up through the water, and I cough in shock when it runs down my face. He drops his head and kisses me, both of us struggling to breathe beneath the heavy pour, but we don't break apart.

I clutch onto him tighter instead.

58

Dash

Briar's heat broke yesterday, four days after it started.

We tried telling her to take another day to rest and regain all the energy she—*we all*—spent, but once she called Clover and was updated on Sadie, the baby, and the scene that took place outside of the clinic, it was obvious that wasn't going to happen.

Instead, Landon's turned to rushing around like a madman, trying to throw his courting gifts into the basket Jasper had delivered overnight in an aesthetic way while Briar takes a shower. *Alone* because, in her words, she's still recovering from the last week and is off limits for the foreseeable future.

Ronan questioned how long that would be and earned us another few days' delay before the bathroom door shut in his face. *Asshole.*

"You know that she doesn't need you to do all of this. I've never seen you tie a ribbon in all the years I've known you," Jasper notes from his seat on the couch.

Landon continues struggling with the two ends of soft pink ribbon. The brown basket on the coffee table is tall and bulging with the presents he's gotten her. There's even shredded paper in the bottom that matches the ribbon colour.

For a guy whose idea of wrapping Christmas presents is rolling something up in plain brown paper and using half a roll of tape to seal it shut, this is a monumental moment.

"She deserves more than a pile of gifts in a reusable bag, Jas," he replies.

"I know that. I'm just saying that she doesn't expect anything grand. Even if we do have a habit of going there for her."

Landon lets go of a breath. "This isn't grand enough. Not even close."

"She's going to love what you got her," I reassure him, picking up on the dull sensation of anxiety that doesn't belong to me.

Ever since we marked Briar, sharing emotions with each other has been . . . interesting. We're five days in now, and I'm still not any better at keeping my boundaries up than I was then. This morning is the first one in a week where I haven't woken up suffering from my own arousal. Instead, it was Jasper's that had me throbbing in my boxers before dawn.

When I rolled over in bed and saw him fucking Briar from behind, it made sense. Obviously, I joined in. But that isn't the point.

Landon looks up from the basket and drags a hand down his face. "I was hoping it would be easier to do these things after her heat. But I almost think it's worse now."

"That's because you want to make sure you continue to be worthy of her," Jasper murmurs.

"We're all bonded now. If I fail with her, I fail all of you. I won't be able to handle losing her and all of you at the same time."

Ronan kicks his feet out in front of him, resting them beside the basket. "Nobody is going to fail her. There's four of us to keep each other in line. We're together for life."

"And we have an advantage now with feeling her emotions. If we still can't stop messing up with the help of that, we just simply don't deserve her," I say.

Jasper nods. "How is everyone doing with that?"

"With the lack of mental privacy?" Ronan asks.

I tuck a piece of paper further into the basket. "It's not a lack of privacy as it is just a bit overwhelming for everything to be so open between us. Now, when you get pissed and run off, we'll be able to have an idea of what's wrong with you, Lan."

"Great," he deadpans, but it's a mask.

Finally, he gets a decent enough bow with the ribbon and leans back on his knees, staring at his work. Ronan gives the basket a nudge with his sock-covered toes, earning a sharp glare from Landon.

"It will just take practice to block out each other's emotions when we don't want to feel them. But I think it could be a handy tool for the time being. At least while we transition into a more stable pack again," Jasper says.

Ronan cocks a brow. "We weren't stable before?"

"Is that a rhetorical question?" I ask while Landon huffs a laugh.

Jasper opens his mouth to answer but freezes before any words come out. One by one, the others snap their heads toward the stairs. I'm the last to catch the whiff of lemon cookie and follow their eyes.

Our omega hops down the stairs, appearing as clear-minded as she's ever been. There's a healthy glow to her skin in addition to the natural brightness of her eyes that's returned since yesterday.

Three foreign jolts of desire and pure obsession shoot through me before they're followed by a fourth, this one the strongest. I swallow when my gaze is drawn to the three healing marks showing on her skin.

Briar's chosen to wear a pastel pink tube top that shows off her throat and shoulders and the three marks spread across them. I lean forward, gripping my knees in anticipation when she jumps off the last step.

She winks at me before spinning, her hair already held up in a clip so I can see every curve of the bite I laid on the back of her shoulder. The only one on that side of her body.

"Well? Do you think they look good?" she asks in a sing-song voice.

Ronan, Jasper, and I throw ourselves off the couch while Landon jerks to his feet, guarding the basket.

"I've never seen anything I've loved more than our marks on your body, love," Jasper declares.

She quirks her lips. "Nothing? Are you sure?"

"Got something you want to show us to try and change our mind?" Ronan asks, his tone deep and rumbly.

"Nope. You can use your imaginations for that one, Ro." She shifts her attention to Landon, cocking her head with a sharp curiosity while lifting a hand to press against his mark. "Why do you look so weird right now?"

Landon's eyes flare wide at the same time we all feel her nerves.

"I could stare at my mark on your neck for the rest of my life, Haven," he rambles.

She releases some of her worry. "So, what's going on?"

When her eyes land on Jasper, he abruptly looks away. He's such a shitty liar, and it's almost comical that he hasn't tried to get better at it by now.

I chuckle, and Briar snaps a look at me. Smirking, I offer my hand for her to take. Once her fingers are in mine, I'm linking them.

"You've got the pack leader still stumbling all over himself, Bright Eyes. Coming down here looking like a goddess certainly isn't helping. You'll have to excuse him."

"I'll excuse him once I know what he's hiding," she sasses while I spin her into my arms.

Her skirt flares out, exposing a flash of the pale skin of her thighs not hidden beneath fishnets this time. The high-top sneakers on her feet are ones I chose to slip into her closet when we set out to fill it.

I bring my mouth to her ear, keeping my voice low. "He's hiding something for you. Go easy on him."

"For me?"

"Act surprised."

When I release her, she goes right for Landon. The sassy sway of her hips puts me under a spell. I dig my heels into the ground to keep from following her.

"So, do I get a kiss? You were already up and out of the nest when I woke up, so I got one from everyone but you," she says, lip jutting out in a pout.

Landon reaches for her with ease despite his lingering anxiety. She cuddles into his chest and wraps her arms around him, squeezing tight. When she tips her head back, Landon's already bending down to kiss her.

"We're going to be late to see Sadie if you don't hurry up, Landon," Ronan says, purposefully cutting them off.

The sooner Landon gives her his courting gifts, the faster he can be proven wrong and see that there was nothing for him to worry about in the first place.

Landon pulls back from Briar and eyes Ronan with annoyance. "You won't be able to go with us with two broken legs."

"What's with all the threats recently? First Thorne, now me?" Ronan palms his chest and sighs, laying it on *real* thick.

Briar rolls her eyes at the two of them. "I actually think it's kind of sexy."

"In that case, I've got a few threats to make myself," Ronan says, straightening.

I snort. "You're shameless."

He shrugs while Briar peers up at our pack leader. She cups his cheek, and he nuzzles into her hand.

"He wasn't completely wrong. I told Sadie we'd be there in thirty minutes at least twenty minutes ago."

Landon stands there for another moment before slowly stepping aside, revealing the gift he's been fussing with. The rest of us watch while Briar blinks at the overflowing basket.

"Are all of these . . . paint-by-number sets?"

"Yeah. Sort of."

There are at least thirty of them. Split between colouring books and thin packs of individual themed sheets, I doubt she'd run out of them for years. Maybe even a decade.

Landon's even gone all out on the paints and brushes. The tiny containers of paint, from white to black, pastel to neon, and every colour in between, take up the majority of the basket. I'd say there's a healthy number of options there for her.

Despite all of that, I think what steals the show is the custom brush case he got her.

Not only is it her favourite colour, but he's had it mono-grammed with her name and bedazzled with real diamonds. The lemon and cookie designs that were added to the inside of the case stole my breath for a second when he first showed it off to us.

The entire thing is really fucking thoughtful. He should be proud that he pulled something like this together for her. If I wasn't so confident in what I've done for her, I'd be feeling nervous.

"And they're for me?" Briar asks softly, dropping to a crouch in front of the basket.

Timidly, she reaches a hand into the basket and runs a finger along the front cover of the first book.

"You mentioned that paint by numbers was your favourite hobby, so . . ." He trails off.

"So, you decided to buy me hundreds, if not thousands, of dollars' worth of them? And this case—oh, my god. It's gorgeous."

Landon's expression is loose, open. His eyes are fixed on Briar, watching her pull the brush case out of the basket. She drops to her knees and sets it over her lap before tracing her name.

"You deserve to have an endless supply of the things you love, Briar. We want to spoil you. It makes us happy to do that," he says.

She sniffles, making me stiffen. "I did my makeup today and everything."

"And you look beautiful, with or without it," Jasper murmurs.

"Thank you. I just wasn't expecting to cry it all away, let alone already. This is incredible."

Briar cranes her head back to peer up at Landon. The grip she has on the case is enough to explain how much she loves his gift. But when she pulls it into her chest, that sends him toppling.

"I'm never going to stop courting you. None of us are," he declares.

She shakes her head, disbelief filtering through the blue in her eyes. "I only need you to love me."

"That's the bare minimum. We're always going to go beyond and above for you. That's the deal, take it or leave it," Ronan says.

"Oh, is that so?" She sets the case back into the basket almost reluctantly before rising off the floor. "I guess it would be silly to keep fighting you on it, then."

Ronan smirks. "You still could, if it would make you happy."

"I think it would make you happier," I poke.

Briar's cheeks pinch with a smile. "You're all ridiculous."

"Yet here you are." Jasper twirls a piece of her hair around his finger. "Standing here continuing to give us all a hard time after we just spent the last five days in bed together."

"Oh, it was such a hassle, was it?"

"I've never been hassled with something I can't wait to do over a thousand more times," Landon chimes in.

She strokes the back of his hand. "A thousand? That's it?"

"If we had it our way, there would be no number high enough," Jasper says.

Briar looks at each of us, her happiness a lightning bolt travelling through my chest. I clutch onto it, holding it in place for as long as possible.

"We'll go with that number, then."

EPILOGUE

Briar

"We're going to Sadie's place, right?"

If we are, we've gone the wrong way. I didn't say anything when Dash took the wrong turn a few minutes ago because I assumed he'd made a mistake, but we're so far away now there's no way he's getting back on track without pulling a U-turn.

"We're taking a detour first," he says, winking at me in the rear-view mirror.

Jasper continues the soft stroking of his thumb over my knee while Landon sends off a text to the Riptides' coach, confirming that they'll be back at practice tonight.

I almost forgot that they have actual jobs they need to go back to now that my heat's over and life can return to normal.

A new normal for the next chapter of our story.

"A detour where? We're close to the clinic now," I say.

Ronan rolls down his window and drops his arm out of it. "I told you we should have blindfolded her."

"Uh, no. Let's not blindfold Briar," I argue.

Dash jabs a finger into Ronan's bicep. "See? Told you she wouldn't have appreciated that."

"Why would you have blindfolded me, anyway? You're

allowed to go to the clinic. Did Clover ask one of you to grab something before we go to Sadie's?"

"No. And I'm not telling you anything yet," Dash says.

Jasper chuckles softly. "Are you getting nervous, Dash?"

"Stop trying to spoil my surprise!"

"What surprise?" I ask, leaning forward toward the break between the front seats. "Is it at the clinic?"

Dash huffs and flicks on his turn signal. "You're all on my shit list."

We turn into the clinic parking lot, and Dash parks in the first stall. It's empty besides us. Not even Duke is here doing his usual creepy walk around the building on the days we're closed.

"So, nobody is going to give me a hint as to why we're here, then?" I ask, already unbuckling my seat belt.

Dash turns in his seat and points his fingers at the guys. "No. And if anyone says anything else, I'm going to start punching balls."

Jasper flinches. "Sounds good."

Landon gets out first, so I dive after him, excitement buzzing beneath my skin once my feet hit the pavement.

I haven't been here in a week, which only ever happens during my heats. My return today is different.

It's the first time I've come back without lingering muscle aches and a cramp in my chest reminding me that I spent another one alone.

As I walk up to the front doors today, I've got my four pack-mates beside me and flesh decorated with mating marks. I'm happy, my heart full.

Dash jogs ahead of us with a set of keys jiggling in his hand. He uses the one I know opens the clinic doors to do just that.

"Did Clover give you her keys?" I ask.

Dash pulls over the door and holds it open. His eyes crinkle at the corners. "No, I stole them."

I dig my elbow into his side before passing him, stepping into the clinic. It's dim with the lights off, and I immediately go to the light switch. Ronan blocks my way.

"No can do, Petal."

"Why not? You want to stand in the dark?"

"You don't make it easy to surprise you," Dash teases.

I laugh, turning my back to Ronan. "It's looking more like you wanted to take me somewhere to kill me off than it does you surprising me."

"Ouch! Do you really think I'd be capable of killing you off? Don't you know how much I love you?"

Dash is in front of me in a blink, his scent invading my senses. I breathe him in greedily, bliss rolling through me. He dips his head until our noses touch.

"Have you not ever heard of a crime of passion?" I murmur.

"The only crime of passion I want to commit is one that I probably shouldn't talk about in your place of work."

I flick my eyes side to side before focusing back on him. "I don't see any of my colleagues or patients."

"Now, this is just cruel. Maybe instead of Bright Eyes, I should have called you Wicked."

"You're a flirt," I say with a nip to his nose.

He runs his fingers along the back of my ear. "And you're mine."

A smooth talker too.

"Do you remember the conversation we had in the parking lot before we went nest shopping?" he asks.

"About the clinic?"

"Mm, and how hard you've tried to make the rooms warm and inviting instead of cold like at a hospital."

"I didn't think you'd remember that."

"I remember everything you've ever said to me."

My pulse skips. "So, you took me here to remind me of that?"

"Almost. I took you here to show you something."

Feet scuff the floor behind me, and then Dash is turning me

around. It's the second time today I've had the breath knocked out of me.

"What is all of that?" I whisper.

"It's stuff that I hope you can use here. Not just in the rooms but here in the reception and to stock up wherever you keep your feminine products," Dash explains, rubbing his hands up and down my arms.

I blink and blink and blink, not believing what I'm seeing. "Did you buy all of this?"

"And give you a chance to make me return it all? No chance. Everything here was donated."

"What?"

There's so much stuff here that I can't even begin to categorize it all, from blankets, towels, slippers, and boxes of brand-new pads and bottles of water.

"I put a call out to a few of the businesses that the Riptides have active sponsorships with and reached out to a few via email since our conversation. They were all more than happy to help donate to Harbour of Hope. Everything here was gifted."

A burn sears my eyes as I bring a hand to my throat, pressing it against the thump of my heartbeat. My inhales are quick, uneven.

"What you do here matters to Rayton, Briar. Your career is a pivotal piece of who you are as a person, and I want to make sure you know that we'd never consider taking that from you for even a second. Instead, we want to see you thrive here. And if a few dozen donations from companies helps with that, then I'm more than happy to do that for you," he says, gently guiding me back to look at him.

"I wasn't sure whether betas felt the same about courting as alphas did. So, all of this? It's beyond my expectations," I admit, almost shyly.

"I might not be an alpha, but that isn't going to stop me from courting you, Bright Eyes," he teases.

Landon's looking at me already when I bring my eyes to his. "I've never felt luckier than I do with all of you."

Landon offers me a smile that's not so rare anymore. "We're pack."

Yeah, we are.

MONTGOMERY
PACK

SADIE SITS in a big yellow chair, rocking the baby bundled in her arms. I tuck my leg beneath me on the couch across from her and watch the two of them.

The soft grunting noises her daughter makes as she sleeps are one of my favourite things about newborns.

"You're a natural, Sadie," I say, keeping my voice soft.

She looks up from her daughter, the exhaustion she's feeling written over every inch of her face. Still, she doesn't let that dull her smile.

"Yeah? I feel like I've already done a million things wrong, and I've only been home with her for three days."

"I'd love to meet one new mom who hasn't felt that way. The day I have kids, I'm positive I'll forget everything I've learned."

"Do you see that day happening sometime soon?" she asks.

I blush, my chest lurching. There's a sliver of doubt there, but it's immediately wiped away when I feel Jasper's answering reassurance. He doesn't even know why I'm doubting, but there he is, putting an end to it before it can fester.

"Maybe not soon. But someday. I'd love a big family."

Sadie lowers her eyes back to her daughter. "You'd fit a big family. You've got the heart for it."

I blush, nodding in thanks. "Let's focus on you, though. I want to make sure you know that you have a support system here for you to use anytime you need to. Whether that's a question about something, even something you think isn't important, or need a break, all you have to do is call either me or Clover. Our care doesn't suddenly stop the moment you leave with your baby."

She presses her lips together, emotion rolling through her stare. "That's what Duke said too."

"Duke?" I hide my surprise behind curiosity.

"Yeah. He's stopped by the last few days. Checking in on things with Thorne and Calla. I think he was actually scared to meet her, but she seems to actually like him more than me sometimes."

My stomach tightens. "How have things been with Thorne? Do you have any updates?"

She wets her lips, anger flashing. "He was arrested the day I gave birth and is being held without bail. I don't think we'll have any other updates until a court date is set, whenever that is."

"That's good news, right? At least he won't be able to try anything else again."

And with Duke hanging around, it would be incredibly stupid for him to come close to her again. As long as Duke knows what he's doing being here to begin with. I've never known him to make reckless decisions, so he has to. Right?

"I think so. Maybe. It's going to take me some time to stop wondering when he'll start showing up again. Even if he does end up in prison, I'm not sure I'll ever stop looking over my shoulder, waiting for him to pop up."

"I can't begin to understand what that feels like."

She continues her steady rocking, but her eyes lift from Calla, focusing on me. "I never apologized for Thorne breaking into your apartment. And for getting you involved in the first place the night he showed up at my place."

"Don't apologize for that. Don't carry his actions on your back, Sadie. You need to focus on your life and the gorgeous baby girl in your arms right now. Nothing else matters."

She nods, but I can see the war raging in her eyes. The inner battle of whether she should agree with me or keep pushing because the guilt hasn't just vanished like we wish it would.

It's going to be there for a while. That's just how guilt works, even the kind that we shouldn't have at all.

"I'm working on that," she says.

"And if there's anything you need while you are—"

She finishes my statement with a quirk of her lips. "Call you."

"Exactly."

"Do you want to hold her?"

My excitement is instant. "Can I?"

"You and Clover are currently two of the three people in the world I trust to."

"Then, I'd be honoured."

She nods once before trying to stand. Her wince has me hopping off the couch and rushing toward her.

"Stay seated, Sadie. You have stitches in places no woman should ever have stitches. Let me do the lifting right now."

"I have been moving around on my own for a few days now," she pokes but doesn't argue further when I sweep Calla out of her arms and into mine.

"And I wish you didn't have to. Just let me help while I'm here. Then you can go back to being supermom again."

"Supermom," she echoes, laughing lightly. "You flatter me."

Calla coos, her tiny face scrunched in sleep. The soft yellow blanket she's bundled up in is the same one we wrapped her in at the clinic. Her name is stitched on the upper-right corner, done by the same older woman who's been doing all of our Harbour of Hope babies blankets since we opened.

Her hair is a blonde so light it's almost white and so thin she could pass as bald. It's adorable, and with her brown eyes, she looks just like her mom.

I rock her gently, rubbing the palm of my hand up and down the small length of her back. There's a yearning sensation in my chest. A pull as I inhale the soft scent of her skin and get bursts of the future.

A heartbeat later, there's a knock on the wall behind us.

"We finished the lawn. It shouldn't need to be mowed again

in a couple of weeks, but once it's too long, you can just give us a call. Fall's coming soon, so it could very well stay short until the spring," Jasper says.

I spin to face the small archway leading to the front door and smile at him. "Did you get the weeds pulled in the flower beds?"

"Is that what's kept you all outside for so long? Doing my outdoor chores?" Sadie asks, halfway between laughing and crying.

Jasper offers her a tip of his chin before his stare falls on me, growing heavier the longer he watches me rock the newborn. There's a tug on the longing I feel, like someone's there plucking at the end of the thread.

When he answers Sadie, he's still looking at me.

"You shouldn't need to worry about chores at all right now."

"Well, I appreciate the help," she replies.

"Any friend of Briar's is a friend of ours."

"Stop bothering them, Jas. There's an entire section of the yard that's covered in ant hills. That's not good for a baby, is it? What if one crawls into her shoes and up her legs?"

Dash's questions ripple through the living room, sending me into a giggle fit. Jasper rolls his eyes, lifting his stare long enough that I can slip mine to our worrisome beta.

He's half-naked and gleaming with sweat when he steps into view. My eyes widen, heat sweltering in my belly as I focus on keeping them from crossing.

Sweaty abs are cruel, wicked things.

Brows lifting, he gawks at me. "Oh, we're so getting you pregnant."

"Dash!" Landon blurts out.

I strain with a laugh, trying my best not to let it out and risk waking Calla. Landon and Ronan follow Dash, stumbling into the living room, equally as sweaty as the other two. They're careful not to go too far in, and I appreciate it more than they know.

"What's going on in here?" Landon asks Dash.

Dash nudges his head in my direction. "Look at Briar."

The only sound in the place comes from Calla as she snores. Then, a thick swallow.

Landon grips his waist in a hold so tight I'll be checking for bruises in the shapes of his fingertips later. "You're holding a baby."

"I am," I reply, mouth twitching with the need to smile.

Sadie clears her throat quietly, no doubt hiding a laugh. "She'll make a great mother of her own one day."

Ronan's eyes are dark, more black than brown as he rasps, "You're right."

"How about let's focus on making sure we can help out the only actual mother first," I say, cheeks pulsing with a blush.

The last thing I want to do here is perfume in the middle of Sadie's living room, and we'll be on a quick trip to Fucking Land if they don't stop looking at me like they want to get me pregnant right here, right now.

Even if the idea of that doesn't sound so far away anymore.

Landon's the last to look away. His lingering stare betrays everything he's thinking.

Someday, Briar. I promise.

EXTENDED EPILOGUE

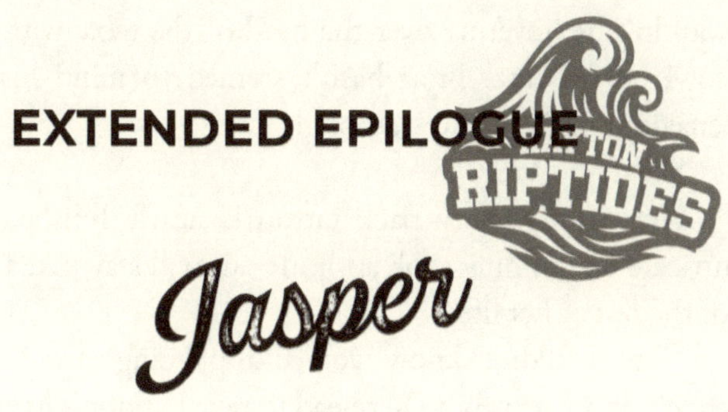

Jasper

TWO MONTHS LATER

"I always thought this was supposed to hurt," Briar says.

Ronan rolls so close to her that his knees bang the leg of the tattoo table. "It depends on the area. Some are more sensitive than others."

"Which one of yours hurt the most?"

"That's easy," Dash butts in, prodding the back of Briar's calf through her black lace tights. "The one he has right here. It's the closest I've ever come to seeing Ronan cry."

"Really? I thought that would have been when he got the . . . you know," she mutters, meeting Ronan's dark eyes.

"The ladder?" he asks.

The tattoo artist starts shaking with a silent laugh before Landon clears his throat, glaring at him. Our poor pack leader has had one hell of a time trying not to be an intimidating asshole during Briar's first tattoo appointment.

"I was the one who gave him those piercings, Briar. You don't have to worry about what you say in this shop. I've just about heard and seen it all," the artist, a guy who goes by John-Boy, tells her.

I'm positive if it were a woman tattooing Briar, Landon wouldn't be hovering over the head of the table with a constant scowl on his face. Briar hasn't seemed to mind his protective behaviour in the slightest, though.

She never does.

Her Montgomery pack tattoo is nearly finished now. The intricate design only took an hour but will stay inked on her hip for the rest of her life.

"Oh! I didn't know you did piercings too," Briar says, stretching an arm above her head to take Landon's hand.

Ronan's already got one locked in his grip, his thumbs stroking her knuckles. He gives Landon a run for his title of Most Protective but hasn't quite stolen it yet.

Dash has busied himself with distracting her from the bite of the tattoo gun by showing her the clips of him on the team's most recent highlight reel. Now that we're heading into the Stanley Cup playoffs, he's been more focused than ever.

"Are you wanting something while you're here?" John-Boy asks while wiping the runny ink from her hip.

I stare at the tattoo, warmth flooding me. The lack of simultaneous emotion coming down the pack band is proof of how good we've all gotten at opening and closing our mental walls. I lift mine, welcoming their varying reactions.

"I'm not sure. I always wanted my belly button pierced," she replies.

Landon's answering arousal shoots to my groin before I shove that invisible wall right back up. There's not a chance that I'm getting hard in here.

"If you want one, do it, Bright Eyes. Being here today is our only plan," Dash says.

She shakes her head, slowly pushing up on her elbow to glance down her front. The widening of her eyes as she stares at the tattoo John-Boy's now wiping cream onto is exactly what I was waiting for.

"I want today to be about this tattoo, nothing else," she tells us.

"Do you like it?" I ask.

Her pretty blue eyes blink up at me as I move to her side. "I loved it before I had it on my skin, and I love it even more now."

"Alright. Let me wrap this for you, and then you'll be good to go," John-Boy says before wheeling back on his stool and leaving us.

I slip into the space he's abandoned and bend to brush a kiss across Briar's cheek. "It looks incredible on you."

"I'm a bit bitter it'll be hidden most of the time, though," Dash adds.

Briar flashes him a teasing grin. "Would you have preferred it on my forehead?"

"Yes," he deadpans.

Landon rolls his eyes and runs his fingers through Briar's hair almost subconsciously while staring through the shop to where John-Boy is.

"We'll live. Knowing that you wear not only our marks but our pack name as well is incredible."

Briar tips her head back against the tattoo table and runs a finger along his side. "I love you too, Landon."

He drops his stare, focusing only on her. "I love you, Haven."

"We all love you," Ronan grunts, squeezing her hand.

Dash flicks him in the thigh. "Don't be jealous, Ronan. You're grumpy enough as is."

I smile to myself, watching the four of them together.

There's a calm to the chaos that seems to be our every day, and right now, this is the perfect mix of that. While we've taken the last two months to strengthen our bonds and learn more about Briar and her us, we're still the people we were before.

Briar has brought out the best qualities of each of us, and I, for one, will never stop thanking her for what she's done. The failing pack we were before she came along is gone, a strong, balanced one in its place. And we owe that to her.

Feeling the weight of my stare, Briar looks at me. I let my walls down just for her and feel as she does the same.

The sear of her silent words leaves me scorched right down to the bone.

And I love you, Jasper.

I leave myself unguarded, bared completely for her. My reply is obvious as she takes a stroll through the hallways of my mind.

You're mine from now 'til forever, Briar Montgomery.

Briar

They're not going to do it.

It feels wrong to admit it, even to myself. The Rayton Riptides are going to be swept through the first round of the play-offs. And to make matters worse?

Landon's father is here to watch it in real time.

Dean Montgomery stands in front of the glass in the sky box, one hand clenched while the other taps anxiously at his hip. His wife, Landon's mother in every way but blood, hovers beside me, just as nervous but doing a much better job of hiding it.

"Oh, I can't even watch this," she murmurs, half-hiding her eyes behind her palm.

"I want to look away but don't want to miss anything, either."

"Landon's going to be devastated."

My chest tightens. I know just how devastated he is because I could feel it for the first two periods. Landon was so focused on the game that he let his walls fall, opening the floodgates. I could have cried from what I felt from him.

I expected the disappointment and frustration, but it was the shame that hurt most. Not because he thought I would ever be ashamed of him but because he expected that from his father.

I've kept my distance from Dean ever since, letting him swear at the glass alone. My omega hasn't stopped pacing and snapping her teeth the entire time we've been up here with him, wanting retribution for the way he's made our alpha feel.

"I hate that I'm so far from them," I whisper.

Daph rubs a hand up my back and leans close. "You're better off up here. Safer too. The crowds by the ice aren't safe."

I cup my throat, nodding stiffly. She's right, but that doesn't mean it doesn't feel wrong.

"Move your feet, Landon! Christ!" Dean shouts before throwing himself around in a circle, gripping the back of his head. "There's no urgency from any of them tonight!"

It's hard to keep from snapping when I say, "They're tired. Landon's played longer shifts tonight than he has all season."

The older alpha glances at me briefly—almost dismissively— before staring back down at the ice.

"This is the NHL. He'll stay on the ice for as long as he has to. It's not an excuse."

Daph sighs, letting her hand fall. "Don't, Dean. He's trying his best, and you're being an ass."

The muscles in his back tense, Landon's number stretching slightly on his jersey.

"The pressure he feels with you here tonight isn't helping, either. He already worries enough about disappointing you. The last thing he needs once they come up later is to hear you say those things to him after a game like this," I bite out, wrangling an omega bark from running free. "Just be supportive. He needs that from us. They all do."

My sweet Dash is torn up inside. The ache of his guilt radiates through me while Ronan's anger bites. Jasper's keeping his emotions hidden, but I don't need to feel them to know that he's carrying the weight of this loss on his shoulders the way he always does.

They're mine to take care of once we're away from this place, but until then, I have to set boundaries for everyone else.

"She's right, Dean," Landon's mother says. "You've only just started speaking more. Don't ruin it now."

Mr. Montgomery regards us with a fleeting look before glancing back, holding our stares longer this time. "Old habits die hard."

"That's why I'm here. I'll remind you of how things are going to be from now on," I say.

After I was introduced to Landon's parent's, he did open up to his father about how he felt about his mother and his childhood because of what she'd done. It was hard, but he's reassured me that they've been closer since then. More open, although it's hard to believe that with how little they still speak today.

Maybe that's just how things will always be. Tense but not completely broken. The speck of hope glows on the horizon, slowly spreading every day.

Well, it will as long as they both watch what they say to one another today.

Mr. Montgomery nods stiffly before returning his gaze to the game. His wife releases a soft sigh and takes my hand in hers, squeezing.

"Thank you."

"It's nothing."

"We both know that isn't true."

I bring my gaze to the window and immediately spot Jasper skating beside Landon. Dash is spread out in his net, focused but calm as he watches everyone move on the other end. Ronan tosses himself into another player and then skates off as he collapses. I smirk at that.

Even nearly an hour later, when I finally get to see them face to face without glass between us, I still smile. I take my spot beneath the weight of their loss and help them carry it.

Dash sweeps me into his arms before the others can and holds me tight, like he's afraid I'll disappear.

"Needed this right now, Bright Eyes."

"Take as much as you need," I whisper.

Jasper comes up beside me and brings his nose to my hair, inhaling deeply. "Thank you for being here."

"There isn't anywhere I'd rather be."

Ronan joins us, and I'm shifted into another set of arms. I glance around the skybox, in search of the last member of our pack when I find him.

Dean has stopped him before he could reach us. My gut sours before I grow frozen. The words that escape his father startle me more than I would have expected.

"I'm sorry, Son. This loss doesn't define you."

Landon stands frozen. I let go of the breath I was holding when he claps a hand against his father's back and lets him pull him in for a hug.

"Thanks, Dad."

I blink away the burn in my eyes and press my forehead against Ronan's chest, caramel coffee swarming me. Peace settles in the room at the same time Landon joins us, stealing me from Ronan.

The skin beneath my pack tattoo stretches as I push up on my tiptoes and kiss him, tasting forever on his lips.

Thank you for reading **Power Shift**! If you enjoyed it, please leave a review on Amazon and Goodreads.

This is only the first in the Harbour of Hope series, with Clover's story **coming in 2026.**

To make sure you don't miss any news, sign up for my newsletter or join my Facebook group—Hannah's Hotties—today!

Until, dive into my backlist on Amazon to find more hockey, and another small town!

Also By Hannah

Swift Hat Trick trilogy

Lucky Hit

Between Periods

Blissful Hook

Overtime

Vital Blindside

Greatest Love series

Her Greatest Mistake

Her Greatest Adventure

His Greatest Muse

His Greatest Treasure

Their Greatest Strength

Cherry Peak series

Strung Along

Catching Sparks

Chasing Home

Stealing Sunshine

Amateurs In Love duet

Craving The Player

Taming The Player

Snowbell Ridge

Snow Harm, No Foul
Till cupid do us part

Harbour Of Hope

Power Shift

Acknowledgements

Writing the *fucking* end has never felt as good as it did with this book. First of all, I'm so proud of myself for writing this book. Not only did I write this one for ME, but I did without backing out when it got really, really hard.

This is a genre that I truly love SO much, and after writing this book, I have the most respect for the authors who do this all the time and have created some of my favourite books of all time. Briar and her men pushed me so far out of my comfort zone that I nearly gave up too many times than I'm going to admit. But I got there. 140k words of story, and I am so beyond proud of each one.

I honestly owe this one to my best friend. Nicole, you HELD ME IN HERE. I'm so sorry for the 10+ minute voice memos during the course of the weeks this book took me to write, but just know that I'm so grateful for all of your ideas and support. I love you so much.

Thank you to LB, my amazing PA and close friend, who I cherish so deeply. I feel honoured to have you in my life.

Thank you to the phenomenal team of creative masterminds who have been here with me for such a giant chunk of my career. Mary + Julie at Books and Moods, Sandra with One Love Editing, Cassie at Cassie's Creative, thank you for helping me turn my words into something beautiful.

Thank you to my incredible influencer team, who still continue to show up for me with every book I write. You make this possible for me with all of your posts, comments, and support. I am endlessly grateful.

To my alpha reader group for this book: Nicole, Sierra, Melissa, and Morgan, thank you for always being here with me.

Your comments and feedback truly do make the world of a difference. ILY.

And thank YOU. If you've picked up any of my books, please know that you're appreciated.

Here's to many more stories to come that continue to push me to insanity.

About The Author

Hannah is an Amazon top 50 best-selling author from Canada. Obsessed with swoon-worthy romance, she decided to take a leap and try her hand at creating stories that will have you fanning your face and giggling in the most embarrassing way possible. Hopefully, that's exactly what her stories have done!

Hannah loves to hear from her readers and can be reached on any of her social media accounts.

Instagram : Hannahcowanauthor
Facebook : Hannah Cowan Author
Facebook Group : Hannah's Hotties
Youtube : Hannah Cowan Author
Website : www.hannahcowanauthor.com